DEMON OF
DESIRE

For men the royal court of King Henry VIII of
England was a dream of pomp and power come
true. But for women it was a nightmare from
which there was no escape.

The reason lay in the King. Henry was more than
a mighty monarch, master statesman, superb sol-
dier. He was a vibrantly virile man driven by an
obsessive need for sexual conquest and a desperate
hunger for the son whom fate had so far denied
him.

*It was in this court that Corianne Trigg,
a beautiful innocent young girl, came to
the attention of Henry—and learned to be
a woman in the dangerous arms of desire....*

MADAM
TUDOR

Big Bestsellers from SIGNET

MADAM TUDOR

Constance Gluyas

A SIGNET BOOK
NEW AMERICAN LIBRARY
TIMES MIRROR

SIGNET TRADEMARK REG. U.S. PAT. OFF. AND FOREIGN COUNTRIES
REGISTERED TRADEMARK—MARCA REGISTRADA
HECHO EN CHICAGO, U.S.A.

SIGNET, SIGNET CLASSICS, MENTOR, PLUME AND MERIDIAN BOOKS
are published by The New American Library, Inc.,
1301 Avenue of the Americas, New York, New York 10019

First Printing, December, 1979

1 2 3 4 5 6 7 8 9

For my husband, Don,
and
my daughter, Diane.
With love.

MADAM
TUDOR

1

The king shivered in the brisk September wind that came swooping into the antechamber, bringing with it a drift of dead leaves, dust, and the smell of decaying vegetation. It rattled the half-opened windows violently and caused the heavy red velvet drapes to belly out into the room. This did not improve the king's temper, which, owing to the severe pains in his stomach from a surfeit of eating, was already foul. Hunching his shoulders against the chill and swearing beneath his breath, he slammed the window shut. Turning abruptly on his jeweled heels, he regarded his wife with eyes that were narrowed to glittering blue slits.

The queen did not glance his way, though she had started at the slamming of the window. Her smooth, dark head was bent over the child in her arms, and a little smile curled her lips. It was as though she had retreated from the king and her surroundings, and only the child was real to her.

How dare she! the king thought, furious color staining his cheeks. How did she dare to sit there with that fatuous smile on her lips, when, in place of the son for whom he longed, all she had to offer to him was a miserable girl child!

Tears of self-pity filled his eyes. She looked almost plain, she who had been so vibrant and lovely. He could scarcely bring himself to believe that it was Anne Boleyn who sat there, so changed was she. He remembered the days when she had gone to his head like a draught of strong wine. When she had laughed with him, even dared to tease him. By Christ, the barren slut must be a witch! She had excited him to such a frenzy of passion that, for her sake, he had cast aside that good and virtuous woman, Catherine, his wife of more than eighteen years.

The king rubbed at his eyes with fat, jeweled fingers. He sighed heavily, pursing his small mouth primly. He was him-

1

self virtuous and he could not understand why the memory of Catherine continued to haunt him. His conscience was clear. He was a good man, a good king, and an admirable husband. Aye, it had not been without pain that he had divorced Catherine and made Anne Boleyn Queen of England.

He glared across at the still smiling queen. He found himself remembering how Anne had constantly goaded him when he had tried to dispense with the marriage ceremony. With her large, dark eyes looking gravely into his, she had repeated as she had done many times before, "You have a wife, sire. Your mistress I cannot and will not be!"

He had told himself that few women could stand firm against the ardent entreaties of Henry VIII of England, and in the end he had been proved right. Anne, after all those fruitless and frustrating years, had suddenly yielded, all her pride and haughtiness dissolving before his delighted eyes. He was still married to Catherine then. But when Anne had told him she was with child, he had hastened the divorce. The child she carried might be a son, and a son he must have! So, with the able help of cunning Thomas Cranmer, he had set aside the authority of the Pope. Catherine's bitter tears, the disapproval of his people, had not moved him. Anne was the woman he longed for, and she was with child. And so it was that he had made Anne Boleyn his queen. The marriage had been right, he thought, blessed. And then Anne's child had been born. Henry gritted his teeth together. It was another girl! It seemed that God had turned his face from Henry of England.

He moved restlessly, pricked as always by his uneasy conscience. How wild had been his daughter Mary's grief and anger when he had tried to explain to her that Catherine of Aragon, her mother, had willfully deceived him. He could hear his words now. "She is no longer my wife," he had told the weeping and distraught girl. "She was the wife of my brother Arthur when first she came from Spain to England. When Arthur died, I married her, believing her marriage to him to have been unconsummated. She lied to me, Mary, she let me believe that she came to my bed a virgin. The marriage was consummated, I have proof. Therefore, such a marriage could only be an offense in the eyes of God."

"A lie! A wicked lie!" Mary shouted passionately.

For a moment his anger had hardened him against her, but

then, after a moment, he relented. "Nay, Mary," he said, trying to gentle his booming voice, "it is no lie. Do you not think that it has been a great heartbreak for me? You know well that I have ever loved your mother with the truest devotion. I am a simple man, child, and, alas, easily deceived. But king though I be, I cannot ignore the fact that I am God's servant. Even kings must make shift to put things right. 'Tis a matter of conscience, do you see?"

Mary's pale, bitten lips spewed out words, and the flame in her eyes was disconcerting. "It is a true marriage, you know it, sire! Mother of God, how can you rest easy when you have cast my mother aside and declared me to be a bastard! My mother is innocent of all wrongdoing, that too you know. I am your lawful daughter. Say what you will, make any excuses you can lay your tongue to, but nothing can alter these facts!"

Then his temper had burst its bounds. "Be silent!" He shook her savagely. "You will hold your tongue, wench, or else will it be the worst for you!"

Gone was the meek daughter he had been accustomed to, in her place was this hysterical virago. "I am your daughter," Mary shrieked, pulling herself from his grasp. "I am, I am! My mother is your wife. And we are so by both God and law. Think you the people will tolerate Anne Boleyn? Nay, they will not. Haven't you heard them shouting in the streets? Anne Boleyn, the goggle-eyed whore, they call her!"

Astounded, outraged, he stared at her. That she could talk so to him! He who had passed through such great sorrow and unbearable tribulations. By God, it was not to be borne! Deceived by Spanish Kate, rebuked now by her bastard daughter. Nay, he'd not stand for it. "Get you gone from my sight!" he roared. "Go, you insolent, whey-faced jade, else will I be forced to punish you!"

The tears had dried on her cheeks. She looked at him with contempt and hatred. Holding her brocaded skirts away from contact with the floor, she curtsied stiffly before him. "Then it only remains for me to wish you joy, sire. For well do I know you will have need of it." She turned away and went quietly from his presence, leaving him to fume impotently.

Thinking over that encounter with his daughter, Henry felt a sudden and surprising pang. Bastard though she had proved to be, one had to admire the chit's courage. His marriage

3

with Catherine had not been legal, but even so the blood of Henry Tudor flowed in Mary's veins. Just as fearlessly would he have conducted himself had he been in her place.

Anne's crooning voice brought him back to the present. "My dear one!" she was saying to the child. "My sweet, pretty little Elizabeth!"

"Bah!" Henry exploded. He turned his glare on the flustered nurse, who was hovering over the queen, waiting to take the child from her. "You there," he barked. "Why are you standing there like a dolt? Take the child from Her Grace. 'Tis time the princess was prepared for her christening."

"Yes, sire." Lady Margaret Fordyce, nurse to the Princess Elizabeth, quailed visibly as she met the king's eyes. Beneath his flat cap of green velvet, his heavy face was purple with fury and his sandy brows drawn together in a straight, intimidating line.

Anne looked at the king. "Just one more moment," she pleaded. "I have spent so little time with her, and she is but four days old."

He took a step forward. "Have done, madam. Have done, I say! You know well that I am a man of infinite patience, but God's beard, your drooling over that child sickens me!"

Anne's dark brows rose in the haughty way he remembered so well. The boor! she thought. How dare he humiliate her so! "That child? She is our daughter, Henry."

"Hold your tongue!"

With his small, glittering eyes fixed so menacingly upon her, Anne was reminded of his terrible anger when Elizabeth had been born. His violence still lingered unpleasantly in her memory. He had raged up and down the bedchamber, caring little for the ordeal through which she had just passed. "A girl!" he had screamed at her. "So you have presented me with a girl, have you, madam. Christ in His eternal mercy, what have I done to deserve this? How have I failed Thee, Lord?"

She had cried out to him, hoping for a return of his tenderness, "Sire, my heart is heavy that I have failed to bring you joy. But ask me not to regret the sex of our child. She is beautiful in my eyes, and I love her well!"

His eyes told her that she was insolent, that he was seeing her once again as the lowly woman he had raised to such a great position. "Is that so, madam? I would remind you that just so did Catherine speak, and she no more capable of whelping sons than yourself!" His face had flushed an ugly red. He came closer to the bed and stared into her flinching face. Words spewed from his twisted mouth, coarse, cruel, ugly, and insulting words that hit her with the impact of jagged stones, wounding her pride and withering her spirit.

"You are Catherine all over again!" Henry roared at her. "Just like her, you are barren of boys!"

Listening, Anne Boleyn had known then that she was no safer than the tragic Catherine. Then, like a hot lance, anger pierced through her terror. She cried out passionately, "Are you then so unfair, Henry Tudor, that you must compare me with Catherine, a woman a full six years older than yourself? Seven times Catherine conceived, and seven times did she fail to give you your desire." Her head lifted arrogantly, her eyes daring him. "But I am young, and my body is strong and capable. You shall have your sons. I make you this vow!"

Her sudden defiance had given him pause. That she should actually dare to talk to him so, the strumpet! His hands gripped the bed rail as he continued to stare at her with malignant eyes. But Henry was a man of many and bewildering moods. He felt something softer and gentler stirring inside him. Against his will, he found himself touched by her wan face and by the dark, almond-shaped eyes that, despite her burst of courage, were not quite able to hide her fear of him. As was characteristic of him, he changed immediately. He now seemed to be genuinely bewildered. "Why, Anne," he cried out, "what ails you, my sweetheart?" Releasing his grip on the rail, he sat down carefully on the edge of the bed and gathered her into his huge arms. "Come, come, my love, surely you did not take me seriously?" Rocking her, he went on in a voice that quivered with sentiment, "If you did, then you do not know me. Do not cry, Anne. Do not destroy me with your tears! You must know that I will never forsake you!"

Anne shivered. But she was not convinced by his loving words. For the moment she was safe. But the thought of forsaking her had certainly entered his head. She knew him so well by now that he was no longer capable of deceiving her.

Anne glanced at the nurse who still waited patiently, her arms half-extended. "You may take the princess now, Lady

Margaret," she said in a sharp, clear voice. "See to it that the room is well warmed before you disrobe her. I would not wish her to take a chill."

"Yes, your grace." Lady Margaret's fair, freckled face was flushed. Avoiding the king's eyes, she curtsied with clumsy haste. Then, gathering the child very carefully into her arms, she almost ran from the room.

Anne broke the silence that had fallen. "Is it necessary to speak so to me in front of others, Henry? I am your wife. I'll not endure such humiliation!"

"I see." Henry's face darkened. Planting his hands on his hips, his legs wide apart in his customary attitude, he glared down at her. "So I have need of lessons in courtesy, eh? You forget yourself, madam. I would remind you that I am the king!"

"I need no reminder, Henry. Though you, it would seem, have forgotten that you address your wife."

There was malice in his blue eyes. A sneer touched his lips as he looked down at her slight figure reclining on the silver-draped pallet. "Nay, I have not forgotten. You are indeed my wife, to my everlasting regret."

Anne's face whitened. "How have I offended you, my lord king?"

For a moment Henry seemed at a loss for words. Then, recovering, he burst out, "I'll tell you how! Did I not give up my wife for you, you cursed saucy strumpet? Was I not a contented and faithful husband until you entered my life and beguiled me with your witch's ways?"

Anne stared at him with horror. Was he mad? He himself had declared his marriage to Catherine to be a sin in God's eyes. She could still hear his voice quoting from the Bible the curse of Leviticus—"If a man shall take his brother's wife, it is impurity, he hath uncovered his brother's nakedness; they shall be childless." With the ready tears filling his eyes, he had added, "Spanish Kate need not think to cozen me. She was my brother Arthur's wife before she was mine. What did I know of the woman's deceit and ambition? I was a mere lad of eighteen when I wed her."

Thinking of his words, Anne put a hand to her long, white throat and began to stroke it nervously. This man she had married was an enigma. He could be so cruel, and yet other times he seemed like a young boy in love for the first time.

6

He would be gentle, loving, sentimental, but then, without warning, would come the terrible change. At those times she could see the merciless tyrant looking from his slitted blue eyes. It frightened her, as she was frightened now. "I—I do not understand you, sire," she faltered. "Can it be that you now consider your marriage to Catherine to have been true and valid?"

Henry did not answer at once. He thought of Catherine, once so fair. When last he had seen her, it was as though he was really seeing her for the first time. The taut lines of her face sagged, there was a hint of a double chin, and her figure had thickened. Her hair that he had once so loved for its bright thickness, was dull and lusterless. He shuddered. Realizing that Anne was waiting for him to answer, he said quickly, "What mean you by this strange talk, sweet Anne?" He hesitated, then added lamely, "Ah, but I was forgetting. You have not long risen from childbed and women, I know well, are subject to odd humors at this time."

"But you spoke of regrets, sire," Anne pursued. "You meant, or so I believe, that you regretted our marriage."

He laughed, his great stomach heaving. "Nay, nay. You have sadly misjudged me, sweetheart. It was the happiest day of my life when, four days ago, you presented me with our little Elizabeth. It does not matter that she is a girl. After all, we have plenty of time to produce sons, do we not?"

With his great, booming laugh sounding in her ears, Anne felt a sudden icy chill of premonition. Sons, sons! Ever does he prate of them! Was it so that he might beget sons that he had cast Catherine aside, and not for love of herself? And what would her fate be if she, too, failed him? Very soon the lords and ladies would be congregating here, at the Palace of Greenwich. They came to honor the birth of the Princess Elizabeth, but what would be their true feelings when they looked upon the child? Mary had been made a bastard. Would they see in Elizabeth another in the making? It might be that they would feel pity for Anne Boleyn, or perhaps, more likely, a certain pleasure in knowing that she was like to suffer the same fate as Catherine of Aragon.

His little eyes shrewd, Henry smiled at her. "Come, come, Anne, why are you looking so wan?"

Her lids drooped wearily. Sometimes she grew so tired of fencing with him. "I'm quite well, thank you, sire."

" 'Tis well," he rallied her in a hearty voice. "When our guests come to preside at the christening of Elizabeth, 'twould not do to turn such a gaunt, white face upon them." His fingers pinched her cheek painfully. "They must not say that Henry Tudor has taken another such as Catherine for wife, eh?"

She shook her head. "They will not say it, my lord king, I promise you."

"Good, good." Straightening up, he squared his shoulders. "I have been called the most handsome of princes, therefore must you be my equal in beauty." The tone of his voice told her that he considered this to be an impossibility.

From beneath her long, thick lashes, Anne studied him closely. Were it not so frightening, his intolerable vanity might be amusing. Once he had been handsome, but one could scarcely call him so now. His face was florid and heavily jowled with good living. Lines of dissipation were grooved deeply beneath his eyes, and his tall, once muscular figure was blurred with the fat of excess eating. Yet, Anne conceded, he was still striking in his diamond-sewn jerkin of green velvet. His surcoat of orange velvet was lined with light green satin, and the great flaring sleeves were slashed boldly with green and purple satin, lavishly embroidered with circular patterns of pearls. A thick gold, diamond-encrusted chain was fastened at both shoulders, and his short neck was encircled with a wide collar of gold set with darkly glowing rubies and huge square-cut diamonds. His flat cap of green velvet, perched rakishly upon his sandy head, was embellished with a jaunty orange feather and edged with a border of shimmering pearls. Anne glanced at his hands. His pudgy fingers were weighted with rings which flashed the multicolored fires of emeralds, rubies, diamonds, and sapphires.

Henry moved uneasily, eying her narrowly. He was uncertain whether to be pleased or angry. Was she admiring him? he wondered. With Anne it was difficult to tell. Her moods were as variable as an English springtime. Where once this trait in Anne had enchanted him, he now found that it irritated him almost beyond endurance. He did not like mystery, he told himself. He liked people to be straight, open, and honest, as he was himself. "Well, Anne," he said, forcing a note of joviality into his voice. "You have been staring at me overlong. What think you of your husband?"

"I think as I have always thought, sire."

He frowned. Curse her! Why did he always have the uncomfortable feeling that she was laughing at him? If she did not appreciate him, though he did not believe this could really be so, there were many other feminine eyes to tell Henry Tudor that he was handsome and desirable. Aye, he knew well that they waited with eager anticipation in the hope of taking Anne's place in his affections. Because he still suspected her of secret laughter, he said sharply, "Are you sulking, madam? I do not like sullen faces about me."

"No, sire, not sulking. Let us say rather that I am a little hurt."

"Hurt? What's this?"

Anne held out entreating hands to him, and her face, tinged now with a soft flush of color, was suddenly very lovely. "I know well that you are disappointed in our child, sire." There was an unconscious note of pleading in her voice. "But only think, Henry. Does she not have the beauty of your features? Does she not have your same rich coloring?"

It was the right thing to say. He softened at once. "So she does, sweetheart." He took her hands in his and held them tightly. He felt the nervous jump of her fingers and he was consumed with an almost overpowering tenderness. The ready sentimental tears welled into his eyes as he recalled the first time he had seen his beautiful Anne Boleyn! His little sweetheart! He had been seated in the rose garden of her father's home, his eyes idly contemplating the scenery, and thinking to himself that he was becoming more than a little bored, and then suddenly she was there. Anne Boleyn, her hands clasping a bouquet of blossoms, was standing there before him. So suddenly had she appeared, and so incredibly beautiful did she seem to him that he had looked at her with dazzled eyes, thinking for a moment that he must be dreaming. She stood very still, framed within an archway of climbing roses. Her long, black hair was tumbled in rich, gleaming blackness about her slender shoulders, and her large, dark, exotic eyes were smiling.

Henry continued to stare at her like a bemused boy. It was from that moment that he had known she was the answer to all his dreams. She was beauty, she was romance, she was poetry. He looked deeply into her eyes, and fell in love with her with all the romantic ardor of a callow boy. Time had taught him that she could be difficult and arrogant and imperious. Also, she was too often inclined to make jealous scenes over what were after all the merest trifles. Why could she not understand that he was a healthy man, that it was natural to him to respond to the invitation in a pair of lovely eyes. It was not his fault if women found him irresistible. Nevertheless, in spite of the many lures cast his way, it was Anne he loved, and would love to the end of his days. His Anne with her lithe, strong body. He would have many sons from her. There was time a-plenty. Anne was young, and he only in his forties.

Still gripped by his strong emotion, he knelt down before her, wincing a little at the pain this sudden movement brought to his ulcerated leg. "My queen, my little love!" he said huskily. "Our daughter is indeed beautiful. But never, though she live a thousand springtimes, could she be as beautiful as her mother."

Anne shrank a little from the heat of his body and his faintly rank odor, then she forced herself to relax. Resting her head against his shoulder, she said in a soft voice, "I thank you for the compliment, Henry. When your son is born the people will say that he is a likely lad, but certainly no match for Henry Tudor."

Henry laughed with delight. This was the way he liked her to talk. It showed appreciation of himself, by God it did! And after all, the compliment was not unmerited. "Saucy wench!" he murmured, hugging her closer. "So you think me handsome, do you, madam?"

"Aye. What woman would not?"

Fortunately for her, he did not hear the faint, resigned sigh that followed her words. "Ah, Anne, my Anne, there is no one like you. You are supreme in my heart!" Beaming, he bestowed two smacking kisses upon her cheek. "However, madam," he went on, laughing, "I would have you know that 'tis unseemly to flirt with your own husband."

Anne gritted her teeth together. He actually thought that she was attempting to flirt with him! If he only knew how distasteful he was to her at times! Conquering the hot retort that rose to her lips, she lifted her head and smiled at him brightly. "And with whom else would I flirt, dear Henry?" Her small, straight nose wrinkled mischievously. "Were I to cast my eyes in another direction, I feel sure that my lord king would not only have me imprisoned in the Tower, but would doubtless order my head to be struck from my body."

The good humor drained from Henry's face, and his eyes looked spiteful. "Aye, I would. Make no mistake about that, madam. I like it not when you speak so. Of whom were you thinking? At whom else would you look? Would it perhaps be at Wyatt, mayhap Norris, or even Henry Percy? Aye, were Henry Percy allowed to return to Court, he would be the one, eh, Anne?"

At the mention of Henry Percy, Anne felt the old surge of choking bitterness against her one time enemy, Cardinal Wolsey. He it was who had ruined her life. She had loved Henry Percy deeply, truly, and he had loved her. Or he had until Cardinal Wolsey's constant sneering at Anne Boleyn's lowly connections had changed his mind for him. Percy's love, it seemed, had not been strong enough to withstand the cardinal's determined onslaught. He had been a weak fool. She no longer loved him. She had vowed then that Wolsey would be made to pay for his interference. Wolsey! How she had hated him! She had thought she would never rest until she saw the old man humbled and degraded. And so it had turned out to be. Wolsey had died a poor man, in disgrace with the king, the master he had served so well. But she, the Queen of England, was not content with this. She would never forgive him!

"Why do you not speak?" Henry's voice rumbled. "Your silence pleases me not. Could it be that you have trouble deciding from among your many suitors?"

"Henry! What a thing to say!" She wound her slim arms about his neck. "It is sheer astonishment that has rendered me silent. I am the beloved of Henry Tudor. Think you I would have the wish or desire to look at another man?"

His eyes searched her face, hard, suspicious. "Play not your tricks on me, Anne. Rather than you should look with love upon another, I would gladly see you dead!"

Sick with fear, she shuddered. "Don't, Henry!" she cried.

"I mean it, madam. Though to order your death would kill the faithful heart within me, you would die!"

She stared at him, her jaw slackening. The laughing, loving man was gone. The tyrant was uppermost now. He had no need to assure her that he meant it, she knew that he did. In ordering her death, he would have no compunction. "Henry, please! You must know that I spoke only in jest."

He hesitated for a moment, then, his vanity convincing him that she spoke truth, he lowered his head and ground his lips to hers. "You are mine, mine alone, Anne Boleyn," he mumbled between kisses. "God help the man who looks upon you with desire. And God help you, madam. He might do so, if it pleased Him, but of a certainty I myself would show you no mercy."

Submitting to his hard, fierce kisses, she was seized with bitterness. She must never look upon another man with longing. But Henry of England could and did bestow his favors liberally upon the ladies of her household. Always her eyes must be conveniently blind to his ardent pursuits. She must be a patient and submissive wife if she were not to incur his grave displeasure. To rail and storm at him, as once she had been wont to do, would bring about one of those painful scenes in which he never failed to remind her that he, having lifted her from obscurity to become his queen, could, if he so desired, cast her down again.

Thinking of those scenes, so often repeated, she was shaken with rebellion. She was not by nature patient or submissive. In those times when she had allowed heated words of denunciation to leave her lips, she had seen the real Henry Tudor. Egotistical, ruthlessly cruel, and stripped of all pretense, he would glare at her with pure hatred in his small, bright blue eyes. Afterward, when his anger had died, he would hold her in his arms and murmur endearments. But his words of love meant nothing, for she knew well that he was tiring of her. She was not a foolish woman, and the evidence of his tiring was plain in his every action. To Henry she had once been the unobtainable. Now the long chase was over and his eyes were already beginning to look elsewhere. But for the sake of her daughter she must and would endure. She must somehow hold Henry to her. Elizabeth, if she could not produce sons, would one day be Queen of England. As it often did these days, the thought of Catherine came to Anne. Poor, deserted Catherine with melancholy looking from her eyes. Mary, the daughter of Catherine and Henry, who regarded Anne Boleyn with such hatred and scorn. For perhaps the first time Anne felt her heart moved to pity for the forsaken woman and the deposed queen. But Catherine's fate must not become hers. Henry must not be allowed to cast her aside. He must not, as he had done with Mary, make her little Elizabeth a bastard.

Annoyed by her silence and her slight frown, Henry clicked his tongue impatiently. "Well, sweetheart, what ails you now?" A complacent smile robbed the words of any suggestion of rebuke. "You are trembling." His smile broadened. "Perhaps it is because you are overcome by your husband's embrace. Is that it, eh?"

She forced a smile to her lips. "What else could be the reason?" She was uneasily aware of the note of near hysteria in her voice and she fought to quell it. Succeeding, she went on, "I am overcome by your charm as I have ever been and shall ever be, dear sire."

He stroked her hair gently. "Were it not for the fact that our Elizabeth is but four days old and you still bleeding from the aftermath, I would believe that you are actually trying to tempt me to mount you. Can that be so, my Anne?"

She looked at him. "The temptation is great," she lied smoothly. "And were it not for the weakness of my wretched body and the imminent arrival of our guests, I would be tempted to cast all discretion aside."

He placed his large hand upon her knee, squeezing it painfully. "Very well then, minx, you'll get no more of Henry Tudor's loving attention until the ceremony of the christening is over." With a sudden desire to please her, he added, "This christening will stand out in memory. For 'tis the christening of the most beauteous princess ever to draw breath."

Her answering smile was so radiant that he blinked. "Why, Anne," he said, touched, "do you love the little creature so much, then?"

"Aye, Henry, I do. Very, very much."

"More than your husband, perhaps?"

She saw the slight frown between his eyes, and she drew back quickly from the edge of threatening danger. How best to please this vain man-child? she wondered. Surely it was a task beyond any woman, no matter how tactful or clever she might be. "Nay, Henry," she answered. "I do not love her more. But I do love her as much, though, of course, in a different way. How could I fail to do so when she is part of you, my dearest?"

"I am glad to hear you say so." His hand stole forward to

caress her breasts. He was smiling, but once more there was that sly gleam in his eyes. "She is like me, our Elizabeth. It is as well. It would indeed be unfortunate for all concerned were she to resemble Wyatt. Do you not agree, Anne?"

She sucked in her breath sharply. Her anger brought bold and defiant words to her lips. "And do you accuse me of adultery, sire?"

He drew back, startled. " 'Tis not like you to take a simple jest seriously."

"Was it a jest? If so, then I apologize. But I like not such humor."

"I feel that a serene conscience would take but little heed of it, madam."

"Indeed. My conscience is clear, Henry, I assure you."

"See that it remains so, Anne," he growled. "Else would it go ill with you."

She hastened to change the subject. "What news of Adam, sire?"

He was instantly diverted, as he always was at the mention of Adam Templeton. "Good news, Anne. The young scoundrel will be here for the christening. He planned to stay much longer with his sister. But I could not have that, so I commanded his return. 'Twill be good to see him again. I have missed him sorely, and I have ever looked upon him as a son."

"I know it," Anne said, ignoring the hint of reproach in his voice. "I will be pleased indeed to welcome him back."

Henry would be happy now, Anne thought, relieved. He was always content and relaxed in the company of Adam Templeton. She herself had a genuine affection for Adam, the dark and handsome earl of Somercombe. He was a great favorite, too, with the ladies of the Court, though she knew they were sometimes angered by his aloof air and his apparent indifference to the lures thrown his way. There was at times, Anne thought, something cold about Adam, yet it was not a repellent coldness. She had reason to know that a great deal of warmth lurked beneath the outer surface. To herself he had never failed to show a proper respect. She, who had grown used to sly comments and to the scandal attached to her name, would have warmed to him for this alone. But there was more to it. To Adam she was the queen, not the king's concubine, as she was generally called. He treated her with all the courtesy due to her rank. If he entertained any sympathy for Queen Catherine, whom many continued to call the rightful queen, no trace of it showed in his manner. He was, rumor had it, a remote connection of the king's. But far too remote to make any claim to the throne. It might be that there was truth in the rumor, but if so, Adam had never attempted either to confirm or deny it. Because of this, he was beyond Henry's ever-present jealousy. On his seventeenth birthday, he had been granted a place at Court. He was now in his twenty-seventh year, and he continued to retain the king's usually fickle affection.

"There is news too of Tudor Trigg," Henry said. "Dost remember him, Anne?"

"He whom you recently created the earl of Marchmont. Nay, Henry, I cannot remember that we ever met. But I feel as though I know him, for, through you, I have heard much of him. 'Tis a pity he is more absent than present at Court, isn't it?"

Henry scowled. "Aye, Anne, you speak truth. He and his two children spend little time in this country. One would think him a foreigner rather than an Englishman." He pulled thoughtfully at his lower lip. "But for all that, I have a fondness for the man."

"His wife died in childbirth some fifteen years ago, did she not, Henry? I have heard that the poor man mourns her yet."

The king nodded. "Aye. Ofttimes his constant journeyings have displeased me. But I cannot find it in my heart to begrudge him some measure of forgetfulness."

Anne hid her surprise. It was rare indeed for Henry to show such consideration for others. She found herself softening toward him. "I pity him, Henry, as all must. 'Tis a rare and beautiful thing to find such enduring constancy. Tell me more of this elusive Tudor Trigg."

"I have told you before, Anne." He smiled at her indulgently, not displeased by her eager look that bade him speak. "My son, as you know, was born the day before Tudor's son. Mine was stillborn, as were all Catherine's sons, save one. And that one lived but a scant four months." Tears glistened in his eyes. "He would have been a fine boy, Anne. 'Tis cruel that I should be denied sons!"

"Nay, sire, do not grieve for the sons that were. Rejoice instead in the sons that are to be."

He looked at her with brooding eyes. "The sons to be? Think you so, Anne?"

She pitied him then. His wish for a strong and healthy boy was a constant ache inside him. She said gently, "Aye, Henry, I know it will be so. But pray tell me more of Tudor Trigg."

Bitterness clouded his face for a moment. "His son lived, of course, 'tis only mine who die. I did not consider my own overwhelming grief over my dead son. I thought instead to send the royal physician and the midwife to aid his wife's distressful labor. You might say that Tudor Trigg owes his son to the thoughtfulness of his king."

Anne heard the sharp, bitter note of envy in his voice. " 'Tis like you, Henry, to think first of your friend and lastly of yourself. You have a tender heart toward all your subjects."

"Aye," he agreed complacently, "that is true." He basked for a moment in the warmth and softness he saw in Anne's eyes. "I was much distressed that the physician could not save his good lady."

"But that was in God's hands, Henry, and certainly no fault of yours. Tell me, is Tudor Trigg's son in good health?"

Henry gave her a loving look. He liked Anne in this quiet and tender mood. It was a thousand pities that she was not always this way. He disliked arrogance, and hers was so often to the fore. Nor did he like the sharply accusing tone she sometimes used toward him. Hastily he thrust thoughts of that other and shrewish Anne from him. He must not brood upon her many imperfections. He must strive always to remember that she was his one true love. "The boy is strong enough, I believe," he answered. "Yet it does seem strange to me when I consider the fact that I have never seen him. I think it is high time I did. I have spoken many times of the boy to his father, but each time I do so it seems to me that the subject is swiftly and adroitly changed." He frowned. "I like not this evasion in one whom I have created earl."

Anne's winged, dark brows drew together in a puzzled frown. "But why should the earl be evasive about his son?"

"You may well ask, sweetheart." Henry turned to look at her fully and her heart gave a great leap of fright when she saw the strange glitter in his eyes. "Perhaps," he went on in a significant voice, "he has a very good reason."

"But what reason?"

Henry felt that dark worm of suspicion stir in his brain again. His puffy, jeweled hands clenched tightly. "I only know that Tudor Trigg's desire for a son was as great as mine."

"And so?"

"And so I have sometimes wondered if the lad he calls son might not be my own. It is not such an unusual thing for babies to be switched, you know, especially in royal households. I have proof that it has happened many times before." He paused. "Do not forget that his son was born on the day that mine supposedly died."

"Henry!"

Anne was looking at him with such horror that Henry flushed angrily. "Why do you look at me like that, you impertinent jade?" he shouted.

"Henry, you surely cannot believe such a thing? The earl is your friend. It is insanity to harbor such a thought."

"Are you calling me insane, madam?"

Anne swallowed hard. "Nay, sire, you mistake me. 'Tis not insanity but your ceaseless longing for a son that prompts your words." She put a pleading hand on his arm. " 'Tis only that, Henry, is it not?"

"I tell you that boy could be mine," he thundered. "Let me but get one look at him and I shall know."

"I believe that treachery has been worked against me," Henry said in a decided voice, "and I mean to find out one way or the other."

Anne's lips tightened as she studied Henry. "Your longing for a son has grown too much for you. But surely even you would not attempt to claim another man's son?" She gave him a quick, sidelong look and she saw that his face had hardened into a mask of implacability. "Oh God!" she prayed inwardly. "Let him not get this idea fixed into his head. Henry believes himself to be omnipotent, having powers even above Your own. He does not recognize this in himself, but I know it is there. What he cannot have, he will take. In my own heart I feel sure that he does not really believe in this fantasy of a change in babies. But that will not stop Henry if he wishes to convince himself that it is true. If he attempts to take that boy, I know that tragedy must inevitably follow. Let me conceive again quickly, Gracious Lord. Let me give him a son. But he must not be allowed to steal another man's son!"

Henry was watching her intently. "What are you thinking about?"

"Nothing of importance, sire."

Henry grunted. "Don't lie to me, madam. I know what that sour expression on your face means.'" He stabbed a fat finger forward, causing her to start back. "There is a reason for my suspicion about that lad, and I'll question the earl upon the matter. I have repeatedly requested that he bring the lad to Court, and always I have been fobbed off with various excuses. But now, patient though I normally am, it has come to an end. I will no longer be put off."

The earl had known the king for a very long time, Anne thought. He knew the way his mind worked. Perhaps he had even guessed at the plan forming in Henry's mind. Anne, seeing that Henry was fast working himself into a rage, said quickly, "Mayhap the boy is still sickly, Henry. You told me that it was not at first thought that he would live. Remember?"

"True," Henry agreed. "It was not thought that the boy could survive the birth." He was silent for a moment, then he turned those strangely glittering eyes on her again. "Tudor told me at that time, when he realized that his wife was dying, and very likely his son, too, that he was tempted to steal from somewhere a healthy boy. A boy that he might hold up before his wife's eyes and thus comfort her dying moments."

"What a compassionate and wonderful idea," Anne said softly.

"Compassionate and wonderful, or treachery. Which, Anne, which?"

"Henry, pray do not. The earl is your friend."

"Is he? Did he steal that healthy boy with the aid of my physician and the royal midwife? Was it his son who died and mine who lived?"

"Your physician, while he lived, was loyal to you. I believe that, Henry."

"Do you indeed. Then, madam, you are a bigger fool than I have hitherto thought you. Loyalty is all very well, but it falls down into the dust if a sufficiently large bribe is offered.

"And you think the earl offered a bribe?"

Henry hesitated. He did not believe the earl had offered a bribe. He did not really believe that the young Tudor Trigg was his own son. But he wanted to believe it. He wanted to believe it so badly that he had coddled that dark worm of suspicion in his brain to such an extent that the idea had taken on credibility. He glared at Anne. "Yes," he shouted. "Yes, that is exactly what I believe."

"Henry, you cannot be sure."

"Can I not? I will know today. The earl and both of his children will be at the christening. I have commanded his presence and that of his children. He dare not refuse."

"Henry, if you are wrong about Tudor Trigg's son, do you intend to provide him with a place at Court?"

"Aye, if I am wrong. But I do not believe I am, madam. As for the girl, I have little interest in her, but, if she pleases me, she too may take her place at Court. As for Tudor, 'tis time he gave up his wanderings and settled down."

Anne gave Henry a long, thoughtful look. "The daughter is pretty?"

Henry shrugged. "I have not seen her, either. But I have heard that she is pretty." Henry's lips curled into a faint sneer. "Have you heard the name the earl has bestowed upon his daughter?"

Anne shook her head. "Nay. As you know, Henry, I know little of the family."

"The wench was christened Corianne Tudor Trigg, a name, you will admit, that has a pleasant ring to the ear. But the name apparently did not content him. In the great affection he bears her, he calls her Madam Tudor. Madam Tudor! Anyone hearing her called so would believe her to be royal!"

Anne smiled. "Doubtless it is a pet name. Though I will agree that it is one more fitted to our daughter."

With another sudden reversal of mood, Henry said almost jovially, "Well, we'll not begrudge him the name if it pleases him to call the wench so. No doubt, in time to come, he will be in need of comfort."

"Henry!"

"No more, madam." He held up a commanding hand. "If you think the girl to be a likely lass, then mayhap you can find her a place in your household?"

Anne nodded. "How old would young Tudor be?"

"Fifteen. The very same age of my son."

"And Madam Tudor?" Anne said hastily.

"Seventeen. A delectable age, is it not, Anne?" His hands began to caress her again, and she stiffened, her dark eyes taking on that cold look that could so infuriate the king. Anne's thoughts turned away from the problem of Tudor Trigg and his son. She began to remember the calculating looks Henry often turned upon her. If she could not give him a son, would he eventually abandon her as he had Catherine? She thought of her newest maid-of-honor, little Jane Seymour. It seemed to her now that Henry beamed far too fondly upon Jane.

Henry's booming voice caused her to start nervously. "Madam, I do believe your attention has been a-wandering."

"Aye, I admit it. Pray to forgive me. I have much on my mind."

"Oh?" Henry gave a thin smile. "It would be a matter of greater import than your lord, I vow. But if you are worried about aught, madam, then I would hear of these things."

" 'Tis my concern for you, Henry. You must not kneel before me, else will the pain in your leg be aggravated."

His eyes dwelt on her face, their expression changing. " 'Tis like you, sweetheart to think of the comfort of your king," he said huskily. "But a plague on my leg. Henry Tudor was ever one to kneel to beauty. I shall stay here in reverence before you."

Anne stared at him. Henry had charm when he chose to exert it, and at those times there was something very appealing about him. "My lord king," Anne said softly, "our daughter is indeed fortunate in her father. With you to guide her, harm would never dare venture near to Elizabeth of England."

"Elizabeth will ever be my most precious jewel," Henry answered heartily. "Doubt it not, Anne."

Anne heard the bastardized Mary Tudor's mocking voice in her mind. "Your turn will come, Anne Boleyn. He will cast you from him, even as he cast my mother, his lawful wife. Should you fail to bear him sons, I could almost find it in my heart to pity you." Anne closed her mind quickly, shutting out the voice. "I—I am happy to hear that you are well pleased with Elizabeth, Henry." She stroked his cheek. "Will you not rise, to please me?"

Grunting, the king got to his feet. Rubbing at his ulcerated leg, he sat down heavily beside her. "What of the earl of Somercombe, Anne?" he said, placing his heavy arm about her shoulders. "Is it not time we found him a bride?"

Anne laughed. "But you know well, sire, that there is no pleasing Adam. He views the Court beauties with cold indifference. Have you not noticed?"

"I have." Now the king's face took on a look of stern virtue. "His single state pleases me not. I would wish for him the same happiness I find with you, sweetheart."

"You have someone in mind, Henry?"

"Nay. But I think——" he broke off as a tap sounded on the door. "Come in, come in," he cried.

The door opened and Jane Seymour entered. She looked startled when she saw the king. "Sire!" Blushing, she sank to her knees in a welter of satin skirts. "Forgive the intrusion, I pray you." She looked at the queen. "Madam, 'tis time you were robed for the ceremony."

Henry was looking at the shy, blonde girl with beaming approval. "Rise, girl. I had far rather look upon your face than the top of your head."

"Your majesty is gracious." Jane rose to her feet with a swift, graceful movement. Standing there, her delicate face suffused with blushes, her shoulders held well back, a maneuver that thrust into prominence her scantily veiled white breasts, it seemed to Anne that she deliberately invited the king's attention.

"You may retire, Mistress Seymour," Anne spoke more sharply than she had intended. "I will call you when I need you."

"Yes, your grace," Jane said, a little catch in her voice. She cast a frightened look at the king, then, curtseying again, she went out the door.

" 'Pon my soul, Anne," Henry rebuked her, "you frightened that poor child. What need was there to speak to her so?"

"I'm sorry." Anne lowered her lids, shuttering her face into that mask of cold reserve that never failed to anger him. "Perhaps I was unfair, but I do not care for Mistress Seymour. I feel that there is something sly and secretive about her."

"Nonsense!" Henry smiled at her, but it was a mere movement of his lips and the smile did not reach his eyes. "I have spoken occasionally to the wench. I tell you, madam, that you have much misjudged her. It seems to me that she is of a shy innocence and purity that is altogether delightful."

"Have I indeed misjudged her, Henry?"

There was such meaning in her voice that it brought him abruptly to his feet. "Aye, madam, you have," he said, glaring down at her. "I know not what festers in your mind, but I advise you to watch your tongue!"

Turning away, he made his way to the door, a tall, glittering, commanding figure with the face of a petulant boy. "I will return shortly, when, I trust, your mood will have improved, madam."

Left alone, Anne slumped wearily. She was remembering the time when she had but to issue a command to Henry of England and he would obey with alacrity. There was nothing he would not do for her then. She had played for high stakes. She had told herself that she would be Queen of England, nothing less, in his eyes or in the eyes of the people. So she continued to refuse the surrender of her virginity without the sanctity of marriage. "Sire," she had answered the king's every plea, "I cannot be your wife. I am come from humble estate, and you, my lord king, are already married. I must repeat as I have ever done, your mistress I cannot and will not be!"

Her mouth twisted bitterly. But in the end, despite her great pride and arrogance, she had been forced to yield, because she sensed that Henry was growing tired of the chase. Later, when she told him she carried his child in her body, he had made her his wife. For her he had set the Church at naught, for her he had rocked the country to its very foundations. Queen of England she was in truth, but without the consolation of her daughter Elizabeth, her hard-won victory would be bitter indeed. "Elizabeth, my child," Anne whispered. "Let him lie with his women, if it pleases him to do so. But somehow I will hold the succession for you, daughter. I swear that none shall oust you!"

It was a brave and bold vow she made, but she could not altogether control her doubts. There had been too many women to enjoy the king's favors, and there would be many more. Now he asked her to add Tudor Trigg's daughter to her household. Another wench to make a noose about the neck of Anne Boleyn.

Wearily, Anne closed her eyes. There had been Mary Wakefield, for instance. Mary, who even as she attended upon her, was secretly boasting of her love affair with the king. When news of the affair came to her ears, she had sent for the girl and coldly given her leave to retire to her parent's estates in Berkshire.

Henry, who had looked upon Mary Wakefield as a pretty diversion, roared like an angry bull when he found the girl had left the Court. Storming into the queen's apartments, he bade her recall the girl at once.

Her heart beating rapidly, Anne had refused. "How dare you, sire! I will not have Mary Wakefield in attendance upon me. She is your mistress, she has admitted as much. I'll not have her. I demand that you close this matter!"

She demanded! She had touched Henry in his most vulnerable spot, and her eyes accused him of lust. He was a man who, however much he might indulge his sexual appetites, was incapable of seeing himself as other than upright, sternly moral, faithful, and much misjudged. When his self-blindness occasionally lifted and his conscience, as it sometimes did, disturbed him, he would tell himself that he was after all a man in sore need of comfort and understanding. He did not get it from Anne, for she had turned cold and unloving. She had deceived him with her sweet smiles and the soft, tender murmurings of her voice. Bah! She was no better than Catherine. Doubtless the child she carried would be born dead. He was the most unfortunate man in the world! Why could not Anne have remained as she had been in those halcyon days when he had first found her? Standing before him in her white, silver-girdled gown, her long, black hair flowing about her shoulders, she was still the loveliest creature he had ever seen. In his rage and his sense of loss, he roared at her, "It is not for you to demand, madam! I am the king, I do as I will!"

Her head held high, she continued to defy him. "I will not have your mistresses about me."

"You lie, madam. The girl was not my mistress. Do you stand there and accuse Henry Tudor of immorality?"

"I do so accuse you. I am not a fool. I see the world about me with clear eyes. When I look at you, my lord king, they are no less clear."

He could not bear to see himself thus revealed. He lunged forward and gripped her shoulders in his big hands. "I'll not suffer your insolence!" Her hair flew about wildly as he shook her violently. "Does the Boleyn bitch now seek to dictate to her king?"

The Boleyn bitch! The name hurled at her by the people of the streets. "Nay, Henry," she cried out to him in a shaking voice. "You shall not call me so. I am—I am your wife."

He flung her from him so that she almost fell. Recovering herself, she stood before him, her head hanging, her hair veiling her face. "How can you treat me so, when, in a matter of a few weeks, I am to bear your child?"

The child! His previous doubts were swept aside. Of course she would bear a living child. It would be a son. It must be a son!

"Anne!" The change in him was almost ludicrous. Fear in his eyes, he stammered out, "Forgive me, sweetheart. 'Tis only that your false charges angered me so. I do not like to be misjudged. I fear that in my anger I had forgotten that my Anne is soon to make me the happiest of men."

The happiest of men! Anne opened her eyes. But he had not been happy when she had presented him with Elizabeth. He would never be happy until he held in his arms a healthy son. "Or," a voice in her mind said, "steals the son of another man." If the earl of Marchmont dared to protest, as of course he would, then Henry was quite capable of having him sent to the Tower on a false charge. But she must not make an issue out of Henry's mad idea. Not yet, at least. It might all come to nothing. She thought of her brother George, whom the king had created Lord Rochford. George, her beloved brother, was forever cautioning her. "You must use wisdom with the king, Anne. Since you cannot change his nature, 'tis not wise to rail at him like a fishwife. The king, as you must appreciate, so deceives himself that it is hard to deal with him as one would with a more normal man."

"But, George, you do not know what I am called upon to endure!"

"I have a very good idea. But the price of a crown comes high, sister."

Anne rose from the pallet. She stood there swaying slightly, very conscious of the weakness of her legs. She knew well that it was far too early to rise from childbed, but she had determined to be different. She would overcome her physical weakness. She would be present at the christening of Elizabeth.

She moved unsteadily toward the door. "Elizabeth, Queen of England," she murmured. "Aye, my dearest daughter, it shall be so. It must and will be so! I will not think of Tudor Trigg. I will not think of your father's new obsession. It is a temporary insanity that has him in its grip, or so we must pray, my little daughter. I could not bear to see you ousted, Elizabeth. I will not see it. Rather than that, I would kill Tudor Trigg with my own hands!"

2

The earl of Marchmont left his room. Closing the door of the chamber, he walked unhurriedly along the white and gold corridor. His manner, as he began to descend the stairs, was calm, but his dark eyes were heavy with anxiety.

He paused at the bottom of the stairs, one thin hand gripping the carved newel post. The summons to Greenwich Palace to honor the birth of the Princess Elizabeth had naturally not been unexpected. But it was the king's manner on the last audience he had had with him that was causing his worry now. The king had spoken in a curt voice and his face had been unsmiling. "You will bring your children to the christening of our daughter Elizabeth, my lord," he had said. "Later you will bring them to Court for a more formal presentation."

"But, sire, I——"

Henry held up a quelling hand. "We will hear no more of your arguments, my lord. Mistress Corianne is seventeen years of age, and 'tis high time she was brought before us. If the queen be so disposed, it may be that she will find the maiden a place in her household. As for your son," he continued, laying heavy emphasis on the last two words, "in a sense, or so I believe, you owe his living presence to our thoughtfulness." He folded his hands together. "And perhaps a little to our stupidity and our blind faith in a friend. Present your son. We will likewise approve him a place in our Court."

Looking into the king's narrowed blue eyes, the earl had felt the fine perspiration dewing his forehead, and, seeing the malicious smile directed at him, he knew that the king had noticed it, too. What had Henry meant when he spoke of stupidity and blind faith in a friend? The vague anxieties that had been gnawing at him of late suddenly rushed together and formed into a monstrous suspicion. Henry was jealous. He wanted a son. It was the one driving motive in his life. A son! But surely he would not take—— The earl's thoughts broke off in confusion. No, he must not think that way. But what had he meant by those remarks? Had he been hinting that——

"You seem nervous, my lord." The king's usually booming voice was a soft, menacing purr. "Why would this be, I wonder?"

Hiding his fear and his dismay, the earl answered calmly, "No, sire, I am not nervous. I have no cause to be."

"Have you not? We will see."

"If you command my children's presence, sire, then of course it must be so."

"We do command it."

"It is simply that I believe my daughter, Madam Tudor, is overyoung to face the rigors of Court life as yet," the earl said desperately. "And Tudor, as you know, is but fifteen years of age."

"We know his age, my lord. We have cause to know it very well indeed." The king's small blue eyes in the plump flushed round of his face narrowed yet further until they became only glittering slits. "My lord earl," he said coldly, "we like not these arguments and evasions on your part. Madam Tudor, as you choose to call her, is of a suitable age, as is my son."

The earl started. "Your son, sire?"

The king's sandy brows drew together in a frown, and for a moment he seemed almost confused. "We meant it not, my lord, it was a mere slip of the tongue." His confusion fell away, and he resumed with icy significance. "You have ever sought to hide your children from us. Why is this? Are they perchance deformed? Or is there something you do not wish these keen eyes of ours to note?"

"Nay, sire, they are not deformed. And I assure you that I have nothing to hide."

"I wonder, my lord. I do wonder."

The earl's hands clenched. "May I ask your majesty to explain your meaning?"

"You may not, my lord. But the time will come when we will be delighted to make all clear to you."

The uneasy scene fled his mind as he raised his head at the

sound of Madam Tudor's voice. His daughter, as was all too usual, was engaged in a heated argument with her brother. The earl's faint frown gave way to a smile. Deformed? His lovely, fiery Madam Tudor, his handsome son? Nay, the king knew well that no deformity cursed his children. Vain and arrogant though he was, Henry was certainly no fool. He sensed a mystery in the persistent refusals to obtain for his children the honors that could be theirs. Henry did not like to be baffled. When he was baffled, he worked himself into a rage that was awesome and terrible to behold. But this time, though he was clearly angry, there was no hot gust of rage. There was, however, a menace about him that the earl found infinitely disturbing. "My lord earl," the king said, "you know that we have ever looked upon you as a good friend. But certain rumors have reached our ears. We have been brought to understand that you like not the work of our good servant Thomas Cromwell. And this despite the fact that you are aware that he, at our express command, does but seek to punish the arrogance of the monks, and to confiscate from their monasteries the riches that are rightfully your king's."

Taken aback by this sudden attack, the earl had stared at him with unbelieving eyes. "I know nothing of this thing of which you speak, sire. I am, as you know, but lately returned from France. Who has dared to accuse me?"

The king ignored the question. "We have heard that you side with the rebels. We have heard that you stir these malcontents to rise against their king."

Again the earl felt the grip of cold dread. "Sire!" he exclaimed. "How could you believe such a thing of me? You know well that I have seen little of England in these past years."

"We do know. And that in itself pleases us not." The king leaned forward in his chair, stabbing the air with a jeweled finger to lend emphasis to his words. "My lord, there are always ways of obtaining information. And, even though it be done from a distant country, ways of stirring unrest and rebellion. We would have you remember, my lord, that we have a very short way with those who engage in treasonable activity against us."

The earl put a bewildered hand to his forehead. His fingers came away wet. The king could not really believe him to be a traitor. No, there was something else behind his words. Some other motive that was far removed from the unbelievable words he had just heard. The king knew him to be loyal. One did not invest a traitor with a title, as he had recently done, nor with a manor house and an imposing estate. The king wanted something from him. But what was it? Suspicion leaped alive again, but he pushed it firmly from him. Nay, it could not concern Tudor, for that would be too insane. Yet he did want something, he was certain of it. It was the king's nature to make up stories that suited himself and gave him a handle by which he might threaten and bully the victim of the moment into giving him his own way. Nevertheless, even knowing this peculiar trait in his character, only a foolish man would ignore the fact that the king, if sufficiently enraged and frustrated, had been known to believe quite firmly in the fruits of his fertile imagination.

Anger stirred. Unable to hide his cold affront, the earl covered it by bowing low before the king. "I must beg Your Majesty to hold me guiltless of such outrageous charges," he said in a carefully controlled voice. "I never forget that I am an Englishman. That being so, even were I to believe my king to be unworthy of his high office, I would never attempt to conspire against him."

"Other Englishmen have done so, my lord."

"Perhaps, sire. But not I."

Reassured, the king now underwent another of his bewildering changes of mood. Beaming, he rose to his feet and placed a heavy arm about the earl's shoulders. "Tudor," he said huskily, "we have ever been the best of friends, have we not?"

"Aye, sire. I have the great honor to call you friend."

Henry heaved a sentimental sigh, and there was a sheen of tears in his eyes. "We were lads together, you and I, Tudor. Such a long close friendship is not a thing that a man may easily forget, is it?"

"No, sire."

The king wiped the back of his hand across his moist eyes. "I have not so many friends that I can afford to lose one such as you.'"

"Rest assured, sire, that my friendship will never falter."

The king's arm fell away from the earl's shoulders. "You know, do you not, my friend, that I would be ready to forgive any wrong you had done me in the past?" The little eyes studied the earl's face keenly. "Now, had you done me a wrong, of course, would be a good time to confess. And were you ready to right that wrong, you would not suffer."

"I do not understand, your majesty. To my knowledge I have done you no wrong. But perhaps, unwittingly, I have offended in some way of which I am not aware?"

"You are sure you have no confession to make, my lord? It might be, if you allowed too much time to pass, that I would not be so lenient."

The earl stared at him with bewildered eyes. "Does your majesty refer to the charges of treachery which I have already denied?"

"You know that I do not."

"Then I can only repeat, sire, that I do not understand."

"You understand me well,'" the king snapped, his mood veering again. "Let the consequences of your obstinate silence be on your own head then!"

"If your majesty would but deign to explain."

"Search your conscience, my lord. You will find there an explanation."

"But, sire——"

"Enough!" the king cut him off impatiently. "See that your children are presented to me, or else will I be seriously displeased."

"Sire, I——"

"You may go, my lord."

Thinking over that conversation as he walked toward the half-opened door of the room in which his children awaited him, the earl felt worry weighing heavily upon him. He was accused of some mysterious charge of wronging the king. And the king believed there was a mystery also concerned with his children. There was a mystery, but it was not one the king could possibly envision. The mystery about Madam Tudor was that she was much too beautiful to be exposed to the king's lascivious eyes. She would be unlikely, if Henry had his way, to remain a virgin. With young Tudor it was another matter. Oddly enough, it was pity that had caused him to keep Tudor from the king's sight. Tudor had his mother's coloring, and, with his great height, his broad shoulders, his thick crest of red-gold hair, his fresh complexion, and his vivid blue eyes, he was almost certain to arouse the king's bitter envy and jealous anger. Tudor, in looks, was a combination of his mother and of himself, and yet, because of his vivid coloring, so like Henry's, he bore a faint resemblance to the king. Another thing that would arouse his violent emotions. It was a great pity that the son born to the king by his mistress Bessie Blount was not strong. He seemed unlikely to live to any great age. The king, who seemed to dote on the boy, had invested his bastard son with the title of duke of Richmond. It had also been hinted that if the king were not soon blessed with sons, that he planned to disregard the succession and that he would place the duke of Richmond the next in line to the throne. He loved the boy well, and he had shown it in many ways, but there was no doubt that the young duke's delicacy of constitution caused him great uneasiness.

The earl paused by the door. It was doubtless stupid of him, he thought, and he would be well advised to curb his too vivid imagination, but it was the king's very uneasiness over the duke of Richmond which now made him reluctant to present Tudor. There was something about the king's manner that he did not trust. Henry had hinted at times, though always laughingly, that he believed his friend had substituted the babies and that young Tudor might be his own son. To his indignant denials the king had laughed even more heartily. "Come, come," he had cried out in a jovial voice, "can you not take your king's little jest in good part? From your attitude, one could almost believe you to be possessed of an uneasy conscience. You are not uneasy in your conscience, are you, my lord?"

"No, sire."

"Good, good!"

The earl's brows drew together in an uneasy frown. Was that what the king had meant on that last audience? Could he possibly believe that he had substituted the king's living child for his dead one? If he really thought that, it could be very dangerous. Once an idea got into the king's head, it was all but impossible to dislodge it. If he made up his mind that the babies had been substituted, then he would take Tudor. By force, if necessary. A sudden thought came to the earl, and he heaved a great sigh of relief. He could prove Tudor was his own son, for the boy bore the small star-shaped mark on his left shoulder that had been borne by all the Triggs for the past three generations. Even Madam Tudor had the mark. He

31

thought of the king's hard, glittering eyes, and his relief began to fade. The king had ever believed what he wanted to believe, and it might well be that he would disregard any proof that he might attempt to offer. A great weariness swept over him. He was a fool! Doubtless it was all in his imagination. For the moment he would think no more about it. Shrugging, he pushed the door open wider and stepped silently into the room. His children, unconscious of his presence, were still quarreling.

The earl's eyes softened as he looked at his daughter. Hers was a very rare beauty. With her huge, black-lashed, dark-blue eyes, she always reminded him of the Oriental beauties he had seen on his travels. The slight, intriguing tilt at the outer corners of her eyes served to heighten this impression. "Exotic" was perhaps the best word to describe her charms. Her long, black hair had the sheen and richness of thick satin. Her skin was creamy, an asset she had inherited from her mother, and her mouth was full and soft, a red rose of a mouth. She was a tiny creature, but dainty and beautifully formed. Today, dressed for the christening of the Princess Elizabeth, she was looking exceptionally beautiful. Her dark blue satin gown, almost an exact match for her eyes, was banded at neckline, cuffs, and hem with triple rows of small pearls. And her small bonnet, set coquettishly on her head, was made of the same material, but the pearls edging the brim were interspersed with small rubies.

The earl's eyes turned to his son. Tudor liked violent colors and he was dressed in his usual abominable taste. His short velvet robe was of a vivid orange, the puffed sleeves slashed with green, and he wore green hose clocked with orange. Over his arm he held a green cloak. The earl smiled fondly. Despite his bad taste, he was a handsome lad. He was very proud of both of his children. Madam Tudor moved her arms in a savage gesture, and a drift of her perfume teased the earl's nostrils. Worry nagged at him again. She was so lovely, and the king so very susceptible. It had, of course, always been said that the king preferred more buxom charms. But if that were so, why had he chosen Anne Boleyn, whose body was slim and willowy?

The earl started slightly as Corianne Tudor Trigg, her voice rising, said defiantly, "You may laugh all you please, you great lout, but I tell you that I will achieve my ambition.

Eventually I shall go to Court, and I shall become a lady of the queen's bedchamber."

Tudor Trigg grinned at his sister. "Bah! The queen'd not have you, pest that you are. Besides, have you not heard that the poor lady is reputed to be dying of a broken heart?"

"You are deliberately choosing to misunderstand me. I do not refer to Queen Catherine, but to Queen Anne."

"Ah, I see. Then you must forgive me. I had not thought you were speaking of the Boleyn whore."

"Tudor!"

Tudor sat down. "You'll not deny," he said, looking up at her, "that 'tis sloe-eyed Anne who has ruined the queen's life? And what of the Princess Mary? You know as well as I do that unless the king chooses to change partners again, it will be Anne Boleyn's brat who will sit upon the throne of England. What then is to become of the Princess Mary?"

Corianne shook her head. "I know not. Though I pray good fortune may attend her.'"

"And I," Tudor answered soberly. "Poor Queen Catherine and her daughter have been hardly used. If the king can cast the true queen aside, and she a princess of Spain, what think you will be the fate of Anne Boleyn?"

The earl, who had drawn back into the shadow of the doorway, was about to go forward and acquaint them of his presence when Corianne's next words arrested him.

"You know, Tudor," Corianne said in a softer voice, "I cannot understand why Father, who is usually so adamant about keeping us away from all connection with Court life, has suddenly changed his mind." She clasped her hands together. "I am so excited and happy that we are to be allowed to attend the christening of the Princess Elizabeth. Are you not?"

Tudor shrugged. "The Lady Elizabeth," he said in an adamant voice. "I acknowledge only the Princess Mary. As to your question, I daresay Father has his reasons." He grinned at her, a mocking gleam in his eyes. "Did you know that this queen you are so eager to meet is said to be a witch? They say she has the witches' mark upon her neck, which is why she always keeps it covered with a velvet ribbon."

"They say!" Corianne answered him impatiently. "I'll not listen to the ill-natured gossip of fools."

Tudor ignored her outburst. "They also say that she has

the beginning of another finger growing from the little finger of her left hand."

"Enough!" the earl cried, striding forward. "I'll not listen to such unseemly talk."

Corianne swung around, her face dimpling into a smile. "So you were listening to us. For shame, Father! How long have you been standing there?"

"Long enough." Unable to resist her smile, he said lightly, "Well, do you think I am suitably garbed for the great occasion?"

Corianne looked him over carefully and felt her usual pride in his appearance. The slight touches of gray in his dark hair gave him a distinguished look, matching the silver-gray of his short velvet robe. The immense puffed sleeves were slashed in a lozenge pattern of green and scarlet. His hose, gray too, were clocked with scarlet, and his flat gray velvet cap sported a scarlet feather. She looked at the jeweled chain circling his lean waist. She had given him that chain for his birthday. He had many chains, and the jewels in this one were imitation, but it pleased and flattered her that he had chosen to wear it.

"You look very handsome," Corianne said, giving her verdict, "and right well do you know it." She paused to examine the scarlet cloak slung about his shoulders. "But I think it would be better if you were to wear your gray cloak."

Tudor, true to his love of bright colors, said quickly, "Nay, sir, do not heed her. 'Tis perfect." Critically, he eyed Corianne's blue satin gown with its low neckline and the little blue jeweled slippers that peeped from beneath the hem. "I like not her gown," he said at last, " 'tis too dark a blue and, in my opinion, it is quite indecent. You had best abide by my judgment, sir, for 'tis apparent that the wench has little taste. Wear the scarlet cloak, I say."

The earl smiled. "There are times when your sister resembles a gypsy. But at this moment I cannot quarrel with her taste. I think she looks very beautiful." His eyes rested on Tudor's bright orange tunic. "I see that you, my son, have indulged yourself in your usual rainbow of colors."

Tudor put a hand on his velvet sleeve and said almost defensively, "I have ever believed that green and orange go well together."

Still smarting from her brother's criticism, Corianne cried

out indignantly, "He to talk of appearance! He is naught but a great fat lout who is forever bursting the seams of his clothing."

His vanity stung, Tudor shouted in an enraged voice, "I am not fat! I am sturdy and well-muscled. As for you, you are naught but a skinny stick!"

The earl held up a quelling hand. "I am tired of your interminable wrangling. I am ashamed of you both. But perhaps more so of you, Madam Tudor. You are the older. You should know better."

Corianne's lips tightened. "I am sorry. I will try to do better in the future." She hesitated, then added, "Father, thank you for allowing Tudor and me to attend the christening."

"It was not my wish. The king commanded it."

Corianne eyed the grim set of the earl's lips, then ventured another question. "But why have you always been so reluctant to present us at Court?" Her small nose wrinkled mischievously. "One would almost think you were ashamed of us."

"I am not ashamed, Madam Tudor. I am proud of both of you."

"Then why, Father?"

"No more, please," the earl said firmly. "Let it suffice that you are to attend the christening. There is nothing further to discuss."

Angered by what she considered to be his unreasonable attitude, Corianne looked mutinous for a moment. "Very well, Father, if you will have it that way. I cannot make you speak."

"True. You cannot."

"Then I will remain silent, sir," Corianne said. With great dignity she seated herself upon a blue-velvet covered chair. Arranging her skirts carefully about her, she clasped her hands in her lap. It was true that she had achieved one wish, she thought. She was going to the christening. But it was doubtful if her father would allow matters to proceed further. It was so unfair! She was seventeen years old and no longer a child. Lady Anne Renshaw, who was a full year younger than herself, was already well established at Court.

"Madam Tudor," the earl's severe voice startled her. "I will have none of your sulking."

"I was not sulking. I was thinking of Anne Renshaw."

The earl nodded. "And Anne is at Court," he said understandingly. "Your time will come, Madam Tudor. I promise you. But I believe you are as yet too young to face the temptations of such a life."

She opened her mouth to make an indignant reply, but the earl, evidently anticipating it, turned away and walked over to the door. "Get your cloak. 'Tis time to go now." He turned his head to look at them. "I have heard that Adam Templeton returns to Court today. Mayhap we will meet him on the road."

"Adam Templeton?" Corianne's lips curled scornfully. "He who is now the earl of Somercombe?"

"The same. I see from your expression that you have heard of him."

"I have. And nothing to his good. I have heard that he is the king's toady, and that none of the Court ladies are good enough for his high and mightiness."

"That is not true," Tudor said hotly. "I have heard quite differently. Tell her, Father."

"I have known Adam since he was a lad," the earl answered, smiling. "And I assure you that he certainly does not deserve the name of the king's toady. Could it be, Madam Tudor, that your dislike of him is because he shows so little interest in your sex?"

"Certainly not. Why should it concern me?"

Tudor grinned. "Why should he like the ladies? I don't care for 'em myself. Silly, sniveling creatures, that's what I think they are."

The earl's eyes twinkled. "I think perhaps you are over young to make such a judgment, Tudor. I have not heard that Adam despises the sex. It is merely that he is hard to please." He looked at Corianne. "He is a remarkably handsome and independent young devil, you know."

"I care nothing for his looks," Corianne flashed. "And I like not the stories I have heard of the earl of Somercombe."

"You must be sure to relay to him your strong disapproval, Madam Tudor."

She broke into laughter. " 'Tis like you to have the final word."

Rising, Tudor threw his green cloak about his shoulders. He waited impatiently as Corianne picked up her white velvet cloak and, careful of her gown, draped it about herself.

In the coach, her father and her brother riding before it, Corianne found her thoughts straying back to Anne Renshaw. Lucky Anne! She had told her some strange stories about Queen Anne Boleyn.

"The queen is a very beautiful lady," Anne had said, "but decidedly odd. There are times when she seems not to see those about her. She has such large, dark eyes, and they seem to stare right through you. She has terrible nightmares, too."

"Bah!" Corianne had scoffed. "What could you know of the queen's nightmares? Next you will be telling me that she confides in you."

"Not in me, no. But she does confide in Lady Margaret Sampson, who is one of her most intimate friends. I overheard her telling Lady Margaret of her nightmares. It seemed that they had forgotten my presence, so I kept very still and listened."

"How like you, Anne. Well, what did the queen say?"

"She said that night after night she dreams that her head is stricken from her body. She sees it roll into the straw like a bloodied ball."

"You are making that up," Corianne accused. "You are exaggerating."

"Nay," Anne protested, "I swear that I am not. She told Lady Margaret that she sees the executioner standing there. His masked face is turned to the people, and there is blood on his sword. He stoops to pick up the queen's head from the straw. Grasping it by the hair, he holds it aloft."

Corianne stared at her. "Nay. I do not believe you."

"It is what she told Lady Margaret. Unless the queen herself is lying, she has this same dream night after night."

Convinced against her will, Corianne was moved to pity. "Poor lady," she said softly. "I should not like to have such troubled dreams."

"Save your sympathy." Anne shrugged indifferent shoulders. " 'Tis foolish to make such a pother over a mere dream. In any case, it would be more fitting were you to reserve your sympathy for the true queen."

Corianne looked closely at the girl. Because of their frequent absences from England, Anne Renshaw was the only one she could call friend, but it seemed to her that Anne had grown hard. "I have sympathy for both," she finally answered.

"I will tell you something else," Anne said, dropping her voice to a whisper. "I often have conversation with Jane Seymour, one of the queen's ladies. She told me that she believes Anne Boleyn is touched by the devil. She said that it might be because of the wicked injury done to Queen Catherine that her dreams are so troubled."

"Nonsense!" Corianne exclaimed. "I have met Jane Seymour once or twice," she added dryly. "I did not care for her at all. She seemed to me to be very sly."

Anne giggled. "Ah, but she has a brother. And such a brother! Have you met him, Corianne?"

"She has brothers," Corianne corrected. "But no doubt you are referring to Thomas Seymour?"

"Who else? The older brother is a dry stick and scarcely worth a thought. Well, have you met Thomas?"

"Once."

"What did you think of him?"

"I thought him handsome and quite charming. But that does not make me like his sister."

"Jane is well enough," Anne said lightly. "At least she is meek, and is not unwilling to leave me alone with the fascinating Thomas."

"What of the king?" Corianne said, changing the subject. "What manner of man is he?"

"Oh, Corri!" Anne's eyes took on a bright shine. "There is none like him! To me he is more god than man. I have spoken to him, you know. He has this special way of looking at you. His eyes seem to be telling you how beautiful you are in his sight."

Corianne smiled at her indulgently. "Naturally that would please you, vain creature that you are."

Anne's blonde head drew nearer to Corianne's. "Corri, I have been fondled by his majesty. It happened when I chanced to meet him in one of the upper corridors. He raised me from my curtsey with his own hand. 'Well met, my lady,' he said. He began to caress my shoulders. And then his—his hand slid lower and he pinched my buttocks. He kissed my lips and told me how honey-sweet was my breath." Anne paused for a consciously dramatic moment, then went on in a breathless rush. "And then he put his hand inside my bodice and fondled my breasts."

"I would not have liked that," Corianne said, frowning.

"Why, Corri, I had not thought you to be a prude." Anne giggled again and tossed her blonde curls. "While he fondled my breasts, the king said to me, 'Do you know, sweet lady, that two plump white pigeons have made their nest within this sheath of velvet and lace?' I knew not where to look, Corri, so overcome was I. When I could manage to speak, I whispered to him, 'Aye, your grace, and both of them are your loving subjects.' "

"Anne!" Corianne was genuinely shocked. "How could you say such a thing?"

Disappointed in Corianne's reception of her thrilling news, Anne pouted. "I see that you really are a prude," she said sullenly.

Corianne shook her head. "Nay, Anne, I am no prude. But I would not have allowed him to so lower my dignity. You should have slapped his face."

"Slapped the king's face!" Anne gaped at her in shocked amazement. "You cannot be serious. I would not dare!"

Thinking back, Corianne could not help wondering if she, for all her brave words, would have had the courage to strike the king. Like Anne, it might be that she would not have dared. Nevertheless, she would have rebuked him. King or no king, it was not seemly that a man be permitted to handle a woman's body in such a free and familiar fashion.

Corianne sighed. But for all the licentiousness that apparently went on in the Court, she still envied Anne Renshaw. She would not, as Anne seemed to do, care for the king's hands upon her body, but life must be so much fun at the court of Henry VIII.

Corianne started out of her thoughts as the carriage came to a halt within the courtyard of the palace. She jumped up from her seat and stared at the bustling scene outside. Her face flaming with excitement, she could scarcely wait for the dignified coachman to open the door and assist her down.

3

The king's eyes roved sullenly over the guests who
thronged the antechamber. They looked like gorgeously
plumaged birds in the brilliance of their silks and satins and
velvets and their flashing jewels. But to him, in his present
mood, they resembled more a gathering of irritating, chattering magpies. He shot a sour look at the queen, who was
standing beside him. No doubt, the king thought with a rush
of anger, these people were sniggering among themselves because he had once more been cheated of his son. But he would
show them all! He was Henry of England, and not just any
man. He would do as he pleased. By God! But he would certainly show them!

Those standing near to him, seeing the flush of anger in his
face, the prominent vein throbbing in his right temple, the
slitted blue eyes, moved uneasily. He was a dangerous man,
this king of theirs. There was constant dread in the
knowledge that his venom could be turned on innocent and
guilty alike. It had been so in the past, and could well be so
again.

Anne Boleyn glanced at him from the corner of her eye.
She knew that he was waiting for the appearance of the earl
of Marchmont and his son Tudor, and she dreaded to think
of what he might make of that moment. Furtively, she
crossed herself and prayed once again that it would come to
naught. She knew too what he was thinking at this very moment. She should know, for she was so familiar with this particular mood. But why could he not be consistent? At one
moment he was pleased with their daughter and loudly
trumpeting his pride to all about him. At the next, his pride
would be drowned in a deep sense of grievance that the child
was not a boy.

Anne put a hand to her eyes. She felt lightheaded and weak. She would have given much to seat herself on the silver-draped pallet. But, obstinately ignoring the advice of her ladies, she had insisted upon standing. Though it killed her, she would continue to stand there and greet each guest in turn. Anne Boleyn must be different, she told herself. When her many enemies departed from Greenwich Palace, she hoped that they would say of her, "Not even birth can overset her. She is not as other women. She is indomitable."

Indomitable! Anne pressed her lips firmly together that her bitter laughter might not escape. How she wished that she could be indomitable. But the truth was that she was only a weak and frightened woman. But what was it she feared? she asked herself. She knew that Henry was tiring of her, but surely he would not declare their marriage to be invalid? Impossible to think that he would treat her, who had held his heart for so long, as he had done Catherine. Of course he would not, she tried to assure herself. Nevertheless the terror was still with her. It rode her back like a bird of ill omen.

Anne caught sight of Jane Seymour, and instantly her eyes became hard and watchful. Jane, looking as fragile as a flower in her gown of white and gold velvet, her pale hair shining from beneath a jeweled headdress, was smiling shyly at the king. Thinking of the rumors that the king spent much time in the company of Mistress Seymour, Anne studied the girl closely. Wherein, she wondered, lay Seymour's attraction for the robust and full-blooded Henry? The girl had looks of a sort, but she was too pale of complexion. Her weak, blue eyes were shielded by lashes as pale as her hair, and she seemed to have no humor at all.

Anne bit down hard on her trembling lower lip. Absurd to let thoughts of Mistress Seymour upset her. The king's affections could not possibly be seriously engaged with that pallid and uninteresting girl. Jane was too meek, too easily frightened in his presence, and Henry, for all that he liked his subjects to show awe, liked a dash of spirit, too.

Jane Seymour became aware of the queen's penetrating eyes upon her. Coloring, her small, white hands fluttering like distressed birds, she curtsied hurriedly. Then, stepping back, she lost herself among the press of people.

The king darted another look at his queen. She was looking exceptionally lovely, he thought, some of his ill-humor fading. Her gown of pale pink satin was plain, as were all Anne's gowns. But somehow she always managed to appear more elegant than the other and more fancifully gowned women about her. The billowing skirt of her gown was edged at the hem with a wide band of diamonds, and her long, hanging sleeves trailed almost to the floor. Her small, gabled headdress, fashioned from the same pale pink satin, was banded with pearls and diamonds. She had set it well back on her head so that her glossy black hair showed to its best advantage.

The king felt a sudden stir of desire. All smoldering fire his Anne had been at first, as he had good cause to know. But lately that fire was not so much in evidence. Even her manner was not as it had been during the time of their long and difficult courtship. What thoughts, he wondered, were going on behind the inscrutable mask of her face? But then, had he ever really known what Anne was thinking? Once he had felt that he could not endure life unless he took Anne Boleyn to wife. But somehow the reality of her was tame compared to the dream he had lived with for so long. Many claimed that she was a witch. Was she? Had she trapped Henry Tudor by witchcraft? He only knew at this moment that though he desired her still, he was disappointed with her responses to his love-making. With this thought, the stir of desire faded.

Henry placed his weight unthinkingly upon his ulcerated leg. Tears of self-pity welled into his eyes as pain stabbed savagely through the diseased limb. Like a goaded bull, his thoughts swung to the women in his life. It seemed to him that it was his fate to saddle himself with females who were ill-suited to his particular temperament. First Catherine, older than himself but fair enough when he had wed her. Catherine, who had given him dead sons and one daughter. It was true that one son had drawn breath, but he had lived only a little while. Catherine's charms had faded rapidly. She had grown increasingly long-faced and pious. She had been forever at her prayers, the barren Spanish bitch! He had sometimes wondered why the skin of her knees did not wear out, so often was she upon them. And she had actually dared to rebuke him, who was the most devout of men, because one day he had chosen to miss Mass and go hawking instead!

Anne Boleyn, who more and more was proving herself to be cold and withdrawn. No wonder he could not get a son from her. Doubtless his seed curdled in the cold and unwilling receptacle of her body.

It was too much to bear! Lord, Lord, why hast Thou forsaken Thy good and willing servant Henry Tudor? He was strong and virile, he was a handsome and loving man, so why should the women of his choice always be barren of sons? By Christ, he knew well that the fault did not lie with him. He had proved it. Had he not fathered a living boy on his mistress, Bessie Blount? He had been so wronged and deceived by women, and he who was so guileless, so simple and humble of heart, was all too easily deceived.

He moved again and gave a sigh of relief as the pain in his leg faded slightly. Even now, Catherine still refused to acknowledge the divorce. She still called herself his wife and the true Queen of England. Indeed, she had made so much of her plight that the people tended to champion her cause and to turn sullen faces to their king, who was the wronged one. God's wounds! If only she would die! If she did not soon desist calling herself wife and queen, he would punish her yet more. He would move her to meaner lodgings. He would strip her of her friends and of everything she possessed. Die! Why do you not die, you lying, false-hearted bitch?

God, when I stand at last before Your throne, remember what has been done to Your servant. To gain Anne Boleyn he had defied the Holy Roman Empire and had set a nation aflame. And now she had repaid his long years of love and devotion by presenting him with a miserable daughter. Aye, Anne Boleyn, whose malice had robbed him of his good and trustworthy Thomas Wolsey. Anne, who seemed secretly to laugh at him. And who, by her very manner, made him feel like a lumbering oaf. And now, after all his heartburning and anguish, he found that he loved her not!

This last thought, coming unbidden, so startled him that he took an involuntary step backward. Unconscious of the eyes upon him, his thoughts roved on wildly. He loved her not? Quite suddenly he knew that he did not. His subconscious mind had supplied him with the truth.

Henry wiped a hand across his sweating brow. It was none of his doing, this death of his love, he excused himself. He had tried, Christ knew, he had tried. But Anne had never really let him know her. Always she seemed to hold him at arm's length. Always she wrapped herself in mystery which, try though he might, he could not penetrate. If love were to survive, then surely one must know everything about the loved one. What were her thoughts? What was it that brought that faintly mocking smile so often to her lips? He remembered those times when, after some remark or other of his, she would look at him scornfully. She dared! She dared to scorn Henry Tudor! She whom the people still continued to call the Boleyn whore. Did she not realize that he could break her, humble to the dust all that haughtiness and pride, if such be his will? Aye, she had a lot to answer for, did that base-born bitch. His eyes narrowed as he thought of certain tales he had heard concerning his queen. At that time, he had chosen to disregard those rumors of Anne's too overwhelming love for her brother George. It was hinted that the love between these two was an unnatural love. Was it true? Had he once more been played for a fool? By God, he would look into that little matter one of these days. He would find out the truth!

The king was distracted by a glimpse of Jane Seymour's pointed and jeweled headdress and the blushing face beneath. The hard glare in his eyes faded. Little Jane Seymour. Sweet, sensible, and devoted Jane. Now there was a true woman. She made a man feel like a man, by God she did! Jane would not dream of answering him pertly or boldly, as Anne so often did. No matter what he said, Jane always agreed with him. She thought his every utterance quite wonderful, and she did not scruple to say so. The smile that had come to his lips became a little set. Aye, Jane was a very sweet and demure lass, but there were times when he found her just a trifle dull. It might be, of course, that he was hard to please. Or it might be that the fire and ice of Anne's witchery still lingered on. Anne! No, he did not love her, yet she fascinated him still. Almost he felt like weeping for his dead love. After all, he told himself, a dead love was a very sad thing and, at heart, he was but an idealistic boy. Nevertheless, love her or not, she still belonged to him. What he had said to her was still true. He would kill any man who looked upon her with desire!

The king's brooding face brightened to an expression that might almost be described as joy as he saw Adam Templeton making his way through the crowd. Adam was looking exceptionally well, Henry thought, in his short robe of black velvet adorned by the chain of emeralds and diamonds that circled his lean waist. He knew how to combine somberness and color in his costume, did Adam, for the sleeves of his tunic were slashed with green and silver, and his black hose clocked with green. He himself liked to be all brightness, but Adam, like Anne, managed to look extremely elegant in the plainer styles they favored. The king sighed. Adam was remarkably handsome, and he was genuinely fond of him. He would give much to own him for a son. How would it look to his people, Henry thought with a touch of humor, were he to have a son like Adam with night-black hair and eyes? Yet, just so might Anne's son look, were she capable of producing one. It was true that he would prefer his son to have his own rich, red-gold coloring, but he would not say no to such a one as Adam.

"Rogue!" Henry bellowed as Adam stopped before him and sank to his knees. "I would have you know, my lord, that 'tis treason to your king to make such a tardy appearance."

Adam Templeton, earl of Somercombe, smiled. "I ask your grace's pardon. It was the thought of once more facing your magnificence that caused my footsteps to falter. Especially, you will appreciate, after so long an absence from Court."

The queen stifled a laugh. Only Adam, with that faint edge of mockery in his voice, could say such a thing and still be assured of the king's continuing good humor.

Thomas Cranmer, Archbishop of Canterbury, who was hovering nearby, heard the words. Dismayed for the bold young man, he drew in his breath in a sharp gasp of horror. The fool! Cranmer thought, to speak so to the king. He, who was the king's primate and who listened to the king's most intimate thoughts, had never yet dared to be so bold. Nor would he ever be. What had come over the earl of Somercombe? Surely he must have taken leave of his senses. Glancing sternly at Adam, Cranmer braced himself to soothe the king's anger.

"Damn you, Adam, for an impudent scoundrel!" The king said. Cranmer was amazed to hear the laughter in his voice. "By the holy sword," the king went on, "had I a mind to, I could have your head for that."

Adam rose to his feet, his intensely dark eyes smiling into Henry's small, blue, twinkling ones. "And is your grace of such a mind?"

"Nay, nay, you young cub, stop your nonsense. Make your bow to the queen."

"Your grace," Adam said. Taking the queen's extended hand, he kissed it. "I have seen the princess, madam," he said softly. "She is a very beautiful child."

Anne's eyes glowed at this praise of her beloved child. "Aye, she is the loveliest little creature. Thank you, my lord."

Adam gave the queen's hand a warning pressure as the king's head turned their way. "What's this, eh?" Henry growled. "We like not whispering in our presence."

"But, your grace," Adam said smoothly, "I can but whisper when I stand before such beauty."

It was a compliment to his choice, and Henry beamed his approval. "So," Henry boomed, "you are dangling after the queen, are you? Remember this, my lord. The lady is bespoken by your king."

Anne winced. How crude this mighty Tudor could be at times. She heard Adam's easy laugh and his casual reply. "How could it be otherwise? All that is rare and beautiful must inevitably belong to your grace."

The mockery in Adam's voice was now apparent to all. Henry either did not mind or did not notice, for he broke into noisy laughter. "Worry not, Adam, for I have ever been a generous man." His eyes lingered on Anne for a moment. "Aye, Adam, I'll remember to fling you some scraps now and again. That is, if you'll not mind my leavings."

Anne's pale face flamed scarlet. Did he hold her so cheaply, then? How could he say such a thing, even in jest! If indeed it was a jest.

Adam made no answer to the king's last remark. Smiling, apparently unruffled, he skillfully turned the conversation in another direction. Dear Adam, Anne thought gratefully. Ofttimes people believed him to be cold and hard and too arrogantly proud, but how kind and understanding he could be when he chose. This was the real Adam, which gave the lie to his handsome, arrogant outer appearance.

The king was making absent replies to Adam's remarks, for once again his attention was on Jane Seymour. She was standing quite near, with her brother Thomas Seymour beside her.

With some difficulty, Henry forced his attention back to the conversation. "Anne, sweetheart," he said, "do you hear how this scoundrel speaks to me? Tell me, what punishment shall we mete out to the earl of Somercombe, who is surely the most impudent of our subjects?"

There was a light touch of malice in Anne's voice as she answered. "I know not, sire, unless it be the unrestricted company of Mistress Seymour. I have heard it said that the utter tedium of such a fate would eventually drive a man mad."

Henry was outraged. He had known that Anne Boleyn was low-born, but he had not thought her capable of such spite. He saw the shamed tears filling Jane Seymour's eyes, and he decided that Anne should be shamed in her turn. "Madam!" he thundered, his blue eyes flaming, "It would seem that your tongue curdles too easily to venom. Are you so lost to all charity and decency that you must so outrageously slander an innocent maiden?"

Anne's whole body was trembling. Oh God! What had possessed her to say such a thing? If Henry had cheapened her previously, then she had cheapened herself still more with her jealous and spiteful words. She saw Jane Seymour's triumphant smile, her modestly lowered lids, and the nervous flutter of her light eyelashes, and she hardened herself to resist Henry. He was waiting for her to answer him. Perhaps to make an apology to Mistress Seymour. But she would not. She would retract nothing. Lifting her head high, she said coldly, "An innocent maiden did you say, sire? Do you really think so?" She shrugged indifferent shoulders. "It may, of course, be so."

Henry's face was purple, and his eyes looked dangerous. "We will speak more on this matter at a later date, madam," he said ominously.

"As you will, my lord king." Anne turned her head and smiled upon the three people approaching—a tall, lean man clad in silver-gray, a flame-headed boy, whose orange tunic clashed atrociously with his hair, and a small, slight girl of quite astonishing beauty, clad in a gown of dark blue. Anne's heart began to beat very fast as the man and the young boy made their bow before the king and the beautiful girl sank into a graceful curtsey. She did not need to hear their names. She knew who they were. She heard the king give greeting to the earl of Marchmont. She saw how his eyes flickered first to the girl and then to the boy. Looking into young Tudor Trigg's flushed and excited face, her heart gave a great leap of relief. In coloring and height and in breadth of shoulders, the boy bore a faint resemblance to the king, but he had the earl of Marchmont's features, the narrow nose, the thin, sensitive mouth, and the distinctively arching eyebrows. Henry was wrong. It was the earl of Marchmont's son who stood before him, not his own, as he had tried so hard to convince himself.

The king did not know where to look first, so startled and moved was he by Corianne's beauty. He had felt exactly this way when he had first seen Anne Boleyn. A movement from the tall, red-headed Tudor Trigg drew his fascinated eyes away from Corianne. He turned his head and stared closely at the boy. He felt a sinking sense of disappointment. This was not his lad. Despite his red-gold coloring, coloring so like his own, he had the Trigg features. The boy smiled at him, his teeth white and even against the healthy brown of his face. Returning the smile, Henry felt the slow burn of anger. The boy should have been his, not Marchmont's. He might bear the Trigg features, but with that coloring and that height, the people would accept him as the king's son. He should have been his! He would be his! A pulse in his throat began a rapid beating. He had made his decision. He would claim the boy as his own. He was the king. He was the supreme ruler of this land. Marchmont would not dare to fight him. Henry's hands clenched tightly at his sides. And who would dare to question the king when he told the tragic story of the changed babies? Staring hard at the lad, he no longer saw the Trigg features. Tudor was his, his, and he would have him! His son, not Marchmont's, his!

Anne's relief had faded. That look on Henry's face! She knew it well. He could not, would not accept disappointment. He would take Tudor, she knew it. But she could give him sons, she knew that she could. What need then had Henry of Tudor Trigg? Quite suddenly her question answered itself. Henry would seize Tudor. He would hold on to him. He would use the boy to threaten her. If she did not give him the son he desired, then Tudor Trigg would be the next King of England. And what then would remain for her Elizabeth? She would be in the same unhappy position as Mary Tudor. It must not be! She looked at the earl of Marchmont and she saw that he, too, was watching the king. He turned then, his eyes meeting hers, and she saw her own certain knowledge reflected in them. So he knew, too? He had known Henry a long time. He knew, perhaps better than she, the way Henry's mind worked.

She smiled tremulously as the earl of Marchmont came to bow over her hand. "My lord," she began in an urgent whisper. "I must——"

"Hush!" His fingers tightened about her hand. "All will be well, madam."

"You do know, then?"

"I do. But have no fear, madam." He saw the tears in her eyes, and his sympathy overcame him. Without conscious thought, he pressed her hand. "Remember what I have said, madam. All will be well."

She looked into his stern yet arresting face, and she believed him. "Thank you, my lord."

Gently withdrawing her hand from the earl's, Anne found her thoughts swimming in confusion. Tudor Trigg, who now stood beside the king with that huge arm draped affectionately about his shoulders. Jane Seymour, that little white mouse of a girl to whom Henry's ever light fancy seemed to have turned. The beautiful, exotic girl, Corianne Trigg, who now seemed to be engaging his full attention. They all seemed to be jumbling together. And with the confused pictures there came the echo of Henry's voice, the words he had spoken earlier—"Rather than you should look with love upon another, I would gladly see you dead! . . . You are mine . . . Anne Boleyn!" Anne's lips twisted into a mirthless smile. Fine words! Dramatic, high-sounding, but they meant nothing. She had seen the hatred in his eyes. She knew that he no longer loved her. How could she help knowing it? She shivered, forgetting the man who still stood before her. There was the menace of Tudor Trigg, and now yet another. Would he turn from her to Jane Seymour, or to Corianne Trigg, who, after curtsying, was now moving away. Who would take her place on the throne of England? And what would her fate be? She thought of her constant nightmares and the color fled her face. Not that! Please, God, not that! A hand touched her arm, and she looked dazedly into the earl of Marchmont's anxious face. "Madam," he said gently, "you are not well. Will you not sit down and rest a while?"

Anne smiled upon him brilliantly. She must not show weakness. Not even to this man who seemed so very kind.

"Thank you for your concern, my lord," she said softly, "but I am quite well."

The king must have heard her words, softly though they had been spoken. He turned his head and fixed belligerent eyes on the earl of Marchmont. "Why do you gaze in such a manner upon our queen, my lord?" he demanded in a loud voice. "We do not care to have you stare at our queen as though you thought her to be naught but some tavern slut."

"If I have offended your grace by my admiration of the queen," the earl answered quietly, "then I humbly crave your pardon."

But the king, it seemed, was not to be appeased. Heedless of the startled faces turned in his direction, he went on in the same loud and aggressive voice, "You have looked upon our queen with lewd eyes, and we like it not. What have you to say for yourself, my lord?"

The earl looked into the king's mottled face. So it has started, has it, Henry? he thought. Some way, any way, you are determined to discredit me, you are determined to take from me what is mine. But I have seen into your mind, and it is all clear to me now. You shall not succeed. You will not get your greedy hands on my son. Aloud, he said calmly, "I beg you to believe, sire, that I can only look upon the queen with the greatest respect and admiration."

Beside him, Henry felt Tudor Trigg stiffen. Instantly, he tightened his arm about the boy's shoulders. He must not antagonize the boy as yet. He needed him in his life. He needed him to love him and accept him as his true father. If he did not, it would be the worse for him. He was Henry Tudor, King of England, and he would not be defied. But for the moment, go gently, gently. "It may be so, my lord," he said in a quiet voice. "We like to be fair at all times." He managed a slight smile. "Mayhap we are more at fault than you, my lord, for we often accuse ourself of hastiness where our most precious treasure is concerned." He looked at Anne. "Is that not so, sweetheart?"

"Aye, sire." Anne turned her head away. That look in his eyes! It frightened her!

Corianne had been aware of the king's raised voice, but she was too excited to make out the words being spoken. She knew that the king was displeased about something, but it did not occur to her to connect his displeasure with her father.

She gazed about her, staring with awe and admiration at the scarlet and gold tapestries covering the walls, the softness of the scarlet carpet beneath her feet which must, she thought, have been imported from France. Everywhere was reflected the king's love of color—banks of flowers along the walls, great tinted, hanging chandeliers, each one bearing at least a hundred candles. Gilded baskets were suspended from the ceiling by thin silver chains, holding yet more flowers, and the great windows were draped in rich cloth of gold.

"Do you care for all this color and glitter, mistress?" a voice said from behind Corianne.

Startled, Corianne swung around to face Adam Templeton. It was the dark, handsome man she had seen standing beside the king. Beneath the smiling scrutiny of those dark eyes, Corianne felt the hot color flushing her face, and she was annoyed by the odd flutter of her pulses. "I think it all very beautiful," she answered, smiling at him. "But for myself, I think I would prefer something a little more subdued. I think, too, if one always lived in such a place, the eyes would begin to ache from the glare."

Adam laughed. "Quite right. You do but echo my own sentiments. I fear the king indulges his love of color on too grand a scale." He folded his arms and looked at her intently, his dark brows arching as he opened his sleepy-looking eyes to their fullest extent. "I wonder, little mistress, if you know how very beautiful you are?" As soon as the words left his lips, he felt foolish, and he longed to retract them.

Corianne smiled. "If you find me beautiful, sir, then I am happy to place my faith in your judgment."

"I have not offended you?"

Corianne shook her head. "You are a little outspoken, but no, I am not offended. What woman would be?"

"Woman?" There was a dancing mockery in his eyes now. "You are little more than a child."

"I am not! I am seventeen."

"Seventeen. Ancient indeed."

"You mock me, sir!"

"Only in the very kindest way, I assure you. May I know your name?"

"My name, sir, is Corianne Tudor Trigg."

"You are Marchmont's Madam Tudor?" he said, looking

51

startled. "I would not have believed he had it in him to whelp such a little beauty."

She felt that she should draw herself up and rebuke him for his coarseness of tongue, but he was so handsome, and the way he was looking at her was most exciting. She could not help smiling as she answered him. "My father, I would have you know, is a very handsome man, and my mother was accounted to be a great beauty."

"But not more beautiful than yourself?"

"Much more so."

"Impossible. I cannot believe it."

"Could you but see her portrait, you would believe it. Now, sir, I have told you my name. Pray favor me with your own."

"Forgive me." He made her a slight bow. "Adam Templeton, at your service, Mistress Trigg."

"Adam Templeton?" Her smile faded. "You are the earl of Somercombe?"

"I am, mistress. Does something about the name displease you? From your expression one would think you had bitten into something very sour."

"Perhaps I have, my lord. I have heard of you."

"And what you have heard does not please you?"

"It does not, my lord."

"Ah, I see." A glint of anger showed in his eyes. "Beautiful you are, Mistress Trigg. It is a little sad to know that you are also a holier-than-thou little prig."

"How dare you!" She glared at him. "I may be a prig, if you are pleased to call me so, but at least I am not known as the king's toady, as you are."

"What!" The blaze in his eyes terrified her. She wanted to turn and walk away, but she found she was unable to move. "Do you have the infernal impudence to call me so, Mistress Trigg?"

She lifted her chin defiantly. "I do. I believe you have earned the name, have you not?"

"Never call me that again, do you hear me? By God, I'd like to break your blasted neck!"

She was frightened by his barely suppressed violence, but she would not show fear. "Then why do you not do so, my lord," she said in a voice she strove to keep calm. "I would imagine you to be capable of anything."

His hand grasped her arm, pushing her across a small space to a bank of flowers. Out of sight, he stood there towering above her. "Now then, you will apologize to me at once for your damned insolence."

"I will not!" she blazed. "And may I say, my lord, that your manners are hardly those of a gentleman."

"I fear, Mistress Trigg, that your insolent and unbridled tongue would bring out the savage in any man. Am I to understand that you refuse to apologize?"

"I do refuse."

"In that case, since I am so hateful to you, I will do something that you will dislike very much."

"What?"

His hands grasped her roughly and pulled her close to him. "Just this, Mistress Trigg." His mouth came down on hers, grinding savagely against her soft lips. "There," he said, pushing her from him. "Add that to the account you apparently have against me." Unsmiling, he turned from her abruptly and walked away.

Corianne stood there dazed and trembling, staring down at the little jewel-bordered cap that had fallen from her head. She touched a finger to her bruised mouth, then, mechanically, she stooped down and retrieved the cap. Settling it once more upon her head, she wondered why the kiss of a man she had long disliked from repute should fill her with such a delicious excitement? How angry he had been, how violent, and how those dark eyes of his had blazed. Could it be that he was misjudged? Her father had said the stories about him were all nonsense. He had known Adam for a long time, and he was usually accounted to be a very good judge of character. Adam. Yes, she liked the name. Now that it was too late, she found herself wishing that she could apologize to him. But, of course, she could never do so now. He had insulted her. He had handled her like a tavern slut. All the same, as she walked back into the glitter and color of the room, she had a wistful hope that she might encounter him again, and that when she did he would insult her in the very same way.

As she walked back to join the group about the king, she heard Adam Templeton say, " 'Tis an auspicious occasion, the christening of our princess, sire. Mayhap it is time we formed the procession."

The king's eyes seemed to be searching for someone or

something. "We will say when it is time, my lord," he said curtly. The searching eyes found Corianne, and a smile lit the king's face. "So there you are, Mistress Trigg." The jeweled fingers beckoned her forward. "I had begun to think you had deserted your king."

"I would never do that, sire."

Pleased, the king put his free arm about her shoulders. The other arm was still about Tudor. "You and my—I mean your brother, will walk with me when the procession forms, Mistress Trigg."

"It will be an honor, sire. But the queen——"

He cut her off with an indulgent laugh. "Naturally the queen. I had not thought there was need to mention that."

"No, sire. Forgive me."

He looked down into the dark blue, strangely tilted eyes and his mouth went dry with desire to possess her. "I could forgive you anything, my sweeting."

Corianne was embarrassed; she was unused to such compli-ments. But she found that they were strong and heady wine. How pleased her father must be to see both of his children thus honored. She stole a quick glance at him. He did not look pleased. If anything, he looked unhappy and unwell. The tan of his face seemed to have faded. There was a sheen of perspiration on his forehead, his mouth was tightly compressed, and there was a pinched look to his nostrils. Ever impulsive, Corianne spoke out. "Sire, I fear my father is unwell."

"Unwell?" The king turned his eyes to the earl of March-mont, and Corianne did not see the malice in them. "Are you indeed unwell, my dear friend?"

The earl shook his head. "Nay, sire. I am perfectly well."

"You look troubled, my lord," the king persisted. "I have heard it said that a man will look so when something lies heavily on his conscience. Does something lie on yours?"

The earl looked first at Tudor, then at the king. "Nay, sire," he said clearly. "Not on mine. May I hope that your majesty will ever rejoice in the same happy condition."

Dull red touched the king's cheeks. Marchmont had ever been able to read his mind, and this was the thing about him that he had never cared for. Nevertheless, he would have Tudor. Aye, he would, even if he had to wrench him by force from his false father's home! The people might object to

Richmond, his bastard son, but they could not object to this boy, who, though he had been stolen from him, was flesh of his flesh. Something stirred in Henry's mind. A small voice that whispered, "You know that Tudor is not yours. Would you steal him? Would you proclaim him Prince of Wales and heir to the throne?" Henry drowned out the voice. Yes, he thought, I would. I would proclaim him so a thousand times or more, rather than I should have no male heir to leave behind me. But I will take my own time. I will wait until I am sure that the witch Anne Boleyn is incapable of producing a son. Aloud, he said, "I am a fortunate man, Marchmont, for there has never been a day in my life when my conscience has not been clear. There never will be."

"I am happy in that knowledge, sire."

"So you should be. I am not only your king, but I am also your friend."

Tudor stirred uneasily. He did not like this verbal exchange between his father and the king. Suddenly he felt deeply troubled, stifled by the mingled smells of perfume, flowers, and perspiration. The king's arm about his shoulders seemed overheavy, weighing him down. He had been glad when the king had made this friendly gesture, but now he wished that he would take his arm away. The king and his father spoke as friends, and yet he felt that they were not friends. Something dark and dangerous seemed to emanate from the king. Something that could touch his father's life and his own, perhaps even Madam Tudor's. And how was Madam Tudor feeling at this moment? He craned forward to peer at her. Her eyes were very bright and she was smiling. Yet he knew Madam Tudor, and, despite their many quarrels, he loved her. He sensed that at this moment she was as uneasy as himself. He moved slightly, hoping that the king would take his arm away. Instead, he felt it tighten. He felt trapped. He glanced at his father, and something of the desperation he was feeling must have shown in his face, for the earl of Marchmont's tight lips relaxed into a reassuring smile and he shook his head very slightly. Tudor relaxed. Whatever the dangerous something was that seemed to threaten them, his father would deal with it. His father could deal with anything.

The tension was further broken when a clear, sweet voice demanded, "Make way, please. Make way. I would see the king."

Henry scowled. He had been thinking of a few things he might say to Marchmont, things that might temporarily put him off his guard. Not that it really mattered whether he was off or on guard, for he would have his own way in the end. He was the king. He had always had his way. Nevertheless, he did not like to show all his cards at once. He would take Tudor, but perhaps not at once. For a while he would play with Marchmont, perhaps goad him into saying something indiscreet. He spoke now in an irritable voice, and waved an impatient hand. "Move aside. I would see who speaks."

Through the lane that was quickly cleared, a young girl approached. She stopped as soon as she saw the king, looking at him with awed eyes. She moved then, and, with a fluid movement, she sank to her knees before him. "Your grace!" she said in a breathless voice. "Oh, your grace!"

Releasing Tudor and Corianne, the king extended his hand for her to kiss. Looking at her downbent head and the coppery strands of hair that had escaped the confines of her green velvet hood, the childish softness of her neck, Henry's eyes softened. "Rise, my child," he said gently. "Your king would look upon you."

The girl rose quickly to her feet, her silver and green gown swaying with the movement. The king stared into wide, candid blue eyes. "We would know your name, mistress."

"Sire," the queen spoke out, "the girl is my cousin, Catherine Howard. I had meant to present her to you ere this."

"Catherine Howard, eh?" He nodded to Anne. "Aye, madam, I recall you mentioning her." He beckoned to the girl. "Come closer, Mistress Howard." He saw her hesitation and the frightened glance she cast at the queen, and he added impatiently, "Come, come, we will not hurt you."

Catherine went to him. She stood very still, flushing a little as his eyes scanned her face. The wide forehead, the lovely eyes and the slightly tilted nose, the full soft lips and the deep dimples in her cheeks when she smiled at him nervously, made up a very pretty picture, Henry thought. "We like you, Catherine Howard," the king said after a moment. "Your coloring is different, yet you have a look of our queen. What age have you?"

"I am twelve years old, your grace."

Henry's eyes moistened and he sighed deeply. "Twelve. Would that I were the same age." He drew himself to his full, imposing height. "Well, Catherine, what think you of your king?"

Catherine looked long at the magnificently glittering figure. "I would that I were the queen, sire," she said, clasping her hands together in ecstacy, "so greatly do I envy her."

For the moment, Henry had forgotten Tudor and Cori-anne. His vanity tickled, his voice roared out in delight, "Why, Catherine, would you be saucy to us?"

Catherine gasped. "Oh no, sire, never! I entreat you to be-lieve me."

Henry cupped her chin in his hand. "We believe you, little Catherine." He released her and turned a beaming face to the queen. "Did you hear Mistress Chatterbox, sweetheart? She would take your place as our queen."

Anne managed a slight smile. "I heard her, sire. Her words show the excellence of her taste."

Henry moved closer to Anne and slid his padded and jew-eled arm about her waist. "So the cousins are rivals for my love, eh Anne?" He looked at Catherine, his smile inviting her to speak.

"If I were but older, sire," Catherine said boldly, "then indeed would we be rivals."

Henry's laughter rang out again. "Well said!" he cried. "Now, ladies and gentlemen all, let the procession form. As for you, Mistress Howard, get you to your place. Or else will we take our hand and apply it to your pretty behind."

Her cheeks hot with mingled confusion and delight, Catherine Howard curtsied once more. As she took her place in the procession, her head was held very high. She was con-scious of her dignity and her new importance as cousin to the queen. She did indeed envy the queen. What delight it must be to be married to that huge, glittering man. Anne, so beau-tiful and bright, had surely obtained supreme happiness through her marriage to the King of England. Catherine's lovely, childish mouth pouted. Why must Catherine Howard ever be the poor relation? She did not like to think that she must hang on to the queen's sleeve to obtain even the small-est favor for herself. Her very gown had been presented to her by Anne. I would that I were lucky Anne, she thought wistfully. I would that I could be Queen of England.

Catherine thought of Mary Tudor, the king's daughter. Poor Mary, sullen of manner, already, though still young, failing in looks and health. Because she had been declared a bastard, she must now be known as the Lady Mary rather than as the Princess of Wales, which had been her former title. Her eyes expressionless but her mouth mutinous, Mary Tudor had taken her place in the christening procession. She had been commanded to this by the king. He was her father, but she, like his lowest subject, must still bow to his will. It mattered little to the king, it seemed, that the bitterness in her heart must poison her with hatred toward him and his new queen. "Concubine!" Mary had been heard to call Anne. Well, Catherine thought with a flash of pity, I too would be reluctant were I in her shoes. I do not think I could have endured as well as she the things that have been done to her mother and herself. It must be especially hard for the Lady Mary, for she adores her mother. Poor Queen Catherine. How terrible to be at one moment the queen, the beloved of the king, and the next moment to be nothing, nothing at all!

Catherine resolutely pushed both pity and envy from her. Today she would enjoy herself. She would dance and sing and sip wine. She was but twelve years old, but there were many to tell her that she was mature and exciting for her age. So it might well be that as well as the singing and dancing there would be flirtations, too. She was pretty, very pretty, her mirror told her that. And today the king's admiring eyes had told her so, too. It was true that she did not have the dramatic looks of her cousin Anne, or the breathtaking beauty of the girl in the dark-blue satin gown, who walked now in a place of honor with the king and queen, but she was well satisfied with her own looks. So why not dance and sing and flirt the hours away? She was a child, but she did not feel or look like a child. Neither, were she to be strictly truthful, did she behave like one in her encounters with the men in her grandmother's household. "Strumpet! Shameless bawd!" her grandmother called her. Well, she had lost her maidenhead at the age of ten, so mayhap she was. Her grandmother beat her mercilessly for her lack of morals, but after the smarting pain had eased, she no longer cared what her grandmother thought. Above all other sensations, she liked to feel a man penetrating her body.

Catherine walked on lightheartedly, her eyes sparkling with anticipation, her cheeks prettily flushed. Her mind gave one last thought to the matter that had previously engaged it. "All the same," she murmured beneath her breath, "I would still like to be in Anne's place. I would still like to be Queen of England."

No presentiment came to warn her that she was walking along that same place that nine years later was to echo with her frenzied screaming and her babbling pleas to the king. "Sire! Have mercy on Catherine Howard! Have mercy on your queen!"

The procession wound its majestic way to the lower hall, passing finally through into a tunnel whose walls were hung with magnificent arras of rich crimson and gold. The stone floor was strewn with sweet-scented rushes that gave off a heady and pleasant odor. And so they came at last to the church of the Greyfriars.

As the procession filed slowly through the heavy oaken doors of the church, a chorus of young boys began to sing. Their voices rose up high and sweet. They sang much as angels might have sung, could mortal ears have been permitted to hear them.

The dowager duchess of Norfolk, bearing the tiny princess, all swaddled in a heavy robe of purple velvet, in her arms, moved slowly toward the raised silver font in the center of the church. Archbishop Cranmer, godfather to the four-day-old princess, took the child from the duchess. Beneath a canopy of crimson satin fringed with gold, she was baptized.

"God of His infinite goodness," Garter King of Arms cried out in ringing tones, "send prosperous life and long to the high and mighty Elizabeth, Princess of England!"

A hush fell over the church as heads were craned forward to watch the archbishop begin the sacrament of the confirmation. The child, apparently resenting the ceremony, set up a lusty bawling, the sounds of which were lost in a sudden blare of trumpets. The princess's red and angry face, topped by a light fluff of red-gold hair, was screwed up in rejection of the gifts now being presented in her name. Wine was passed to the guests thronging the church, together with sweetmeats, small cakes, and wafers. The child's bawling stopped as suddenly as it had begun. Her lids drooped. Indifferent to the importance attached to her small person, the Princess Elizabeth slept.

With her father's malignant eyes upon her, Mary Tudor

took one small sip of the wine, but thereafter she made no more pretense. Sitting very still, the silver beaker clutched in her hand, she looked with hatred at Anne Boleyn, who, holding her child, was looking flushed and beautiful. Princess of England, they called the child. But she was not, she was not! She, Mary Tudor, was the true Princess of England. She and she alone was her father's rightful heir. She thought of her mother, heartbroken, old before her time, her health fastfailing, and her bitter tears dripped into the dark-purple wine.

Corianne Trigg, standing to the left of the church, met Adam Templeton's eyes. Unsmiling, he looked calmly back at her. Flushing, she looked hastily away. She had, with her foolish impetuous tongue, made an enemy of him. The thought brought with it a surprising pang.

The ceremony over, the princes of the Church, the foreign dignitaries, the nobles, and the lords and ladies began to issue forth from the church. Corianne, her father on her left and her brother on her right, followed after them.

Adam Templeton, the last to emerge, looked long and thoughtfully after Corianne's slight, graceful figure. The anger she had aroused in him had gone completely now. Instead, he felt a touch of amusement. She had spoken to him as a heedless, foolish, very rude child would speak, and yet she considered herself to be so adult. He had indulged in numerous light affairs, yet he had never truly loved, never truly wanted a woman. But he had a strange feeling about this little beauty, Marchmont's Madam Tudor, a feeling that he could love and want her as no woman had ever been loved and wanted before. He smiled slightly. Woman? Nay, she was as yet a child. But she would grow up. He would see to it. For he wanted her, and, by God, somehow, some way, he would have her!

Much later, taking their leave of the king and queen, Corianne was pleased and flattered at the affection the monarch showed toward herself and her brother. So pleased indeed that she did not notice the crackling discord in the air between her father and the king, when the earl of Marchmont made his own farewell. She did, however, see the expression of terror in Ann Boleyn's eyes.

She was still pondering on this when she settled herself in the coach. Why should Anne Boleyn look terrified on this most happy of days? And why, when she had bade her father farewell, had the expression of terror changed to one of pleading? Unable to resolve it, Corianne shrugged and put it aside. It had been a wonderful experience, but she was nevertheless glad to be going home. She had the beginning of a headache, brought on no doubt by her struggle to keep Adam Templeton from crowding into her mind. He had looked at her so indifferently in the church that it had stung her vanity badly. But even worse, he had made her feel ashamed. Looking into his dark eyes for that brief moment, she had felt petty and spiteful. She put a hand to her lips, and her heart jerked as she remembered the savage kiss he had forced on her.

The door of the coach opened and Corianne looked her surprise as her father and brother entered. Usually, she knew, they preferred riding their horses in the fresh air to being cooped up within the stuffy confinement of the coach.

The earl of Marchmont smiled at her, but he made no explanation, and he did not speak until they were well on their way. When he did speak, it was in his usual fashion, calm, sure of himself. My children," he said, "we go on a journey. Spain this time, I think. Yes, Spain. It has a delightful climate."

Corianne stared into Tudor's puzzled face and she felt a surge of dismay. It would seem, then, that she would have no chance to encounter the arrogant earl of Somercombe again. By the time they returned to England, he would have forgotten all about her. If indeed, after her outburst, he bothered to give her a thought. "But, Father," she said quickly, "I think I would like to stay in England for a little while. Could we not do that?"

The earl shook his head firmly. "I have a desire to go to Spain. We travel tonight."

"Tonight!" Corianne and Tudor stared at him. "But why must we travel tonight?" Corianne asked. "It seems so strange. You are not in trouble, are you, Father?"

The earl hesitated, wondering if he should explain the position to them. He decided against it. Let them be young and carefree as long as they may. He did not want them to be touched by the shadow of his own fear. "Nay, Madam Tudor, I am not in any trouble." He smiled at her and added in a voice that would admit of no argument, "I am anxious to be on my way. It will be an adventure to travel by night."

"This night?" Corianne said dryly. "You must indeed be very anxious, Father."

Tudor was excited. Already he had forgotten the feeling of being somehow menaced. His blue eyes sparkling, he said eagerly, "Never mind Madam Tudor, Father. You know how averse she is to new and original ideas. I like the thought of traveling tonight, and it will be an adventure."

The earl drew the curtain aside and stared out at the gathering darkness. "I thought the idea would appeal to you, my son," he said quietly.

Corianne said nothing. Studying her father's averted face, she knew that he was running away from something. But what? To run was not characteristic of her father. Usually, when trouble came—and he had known much of it in the past—he faced it boldly. Why could he not speak out frankly to them? Surely he must know that she and Tudor would always stand by him. Running away! Running away! The quickly turning wheels of the coach seemed to be beating out the words.

The earl of Marchmont dropped the curtain. Anne Boleyn, he felt sure, would deliver to the king the son he so ardently desired. Then all of Henry's outrage and anger at finding his command ignored and his victims flown would be gone. He prayed it would be that way. It must be that way!

4

In the two years following the birth of the Princess Elizabeth, the menacing shadow of Henry's despotic reign
loomed ever larger over the land. The people were uneasy.
Whenever the king rode among them on his beribboned and
jeweled steed, they were either sullenly silent or their cheering
was at the most half-hearted. Why had the good Queen
Catherine been put aside for the sake of the Boleyn bitch?
they continued to ask themselves. Catherine was Spanish, but
she had made herself loved. No matter what the king might
say to excuse his outrageous conduct, they still believed his
marriage to Queen Catherine to be valid. He had lusted after
Anne Boleyn, and that was the one and only reason for his
cruel treatment of Catherine and her daughter. Cruel? Yes,
their bluff King Hal had proved that he could be mercilessly
cruel, and not just to his discarded queen and daughter.
Good and saintly men had been martyred. Their trials had
been a mockery of justice, for all knew they had been murdered at the behest of the king.

Another rumor came to the people. The king grew tired of
Anne Boleyn. It seemed that he had now turned his little lust-
ful eyes on Jane Seymour. They had been sullen and unwilling to accept Queen Anne. It would be a little too much
to bear if they were asked to accept a Queen Jane. Conjec-
ture was high. Would the king declare his marriage to Anne
Boleyn invalid, as he had done with Catherine? What would
be the outcome of the king's seeming infatuation for that pale
and listless looking lady, Jane Seymour?

On a sunny, flower-scented day in the month of August,
the earl of Marchmont was asking himself these same questions. When he thought of the severed heads hanging from
pikes on the London Bridge, he felt sick. Those heads were a
gruesome reminder to all those who sought to oppose the

king. He had opposed Henry, and he had been brought back to England by a lie! The heads hanging from the pikes were a commonplace sight now, but no less horrible to the sensitive. Men had been thrown into the Tower on the most trivial of charges. What particular charge, he wondered, would Henry's fertile brain invent for himself? Henry's victims, once in the Tower, had found that the trivial charges against them had been woven into a net of lies from which they could not extricate themselves, and so they paid with their lives. The king's spies were everywhere, his shadow was long, his memory equally so. The earl's hands clenched. Did he not have good and bitter cause to know that?

The earl of Marchmont tried to put his uneasiness from him. It was true that he had been brought back to England by the carefully prepared story of Henry's spies that Anne Boleyn had borne to the King of England a healthy, living boy, only to find that Anne, although pregnant, still had no son. Henry had been too clever for him. His spies had tracked him down. And he had believed the story they told him, for of course he had not known them for spies.

The earl rose from his chair and wandered over to the window. But it was also true that Henry as yet had made no move against him. Perhaps he would not until he knew the result of Anne's pregnancy. He looked at Madam Tudor, who was lying full length on the lawn just outside the window. She was looking up at the cloudless sky, her hands clasped behind her head. From the distance, Tudor's raised voice came to him. No doubt, the earl thought, he was arguing with one of the gardeners. Since their return from Spain a few days ago, these harassed and hard-working men had had cause to make many complaints of the boy's continual raids on the young fruit trees.

The earl moved away from the window. Seating himself again, he thought of his son. He continued to see Tudor as a boy, but he was scarcely that. Next month would see him into his seventeenth year, Madam Tudor into her nineteenth. Now they were back in England, and facing certain danger unless he could do something about it. He was still certain that Henry had plans for both his children. And he knew too that if they defied him, he would see them dead for their disobedience to the royal will.

Was it his own yearning for England, the earl wondered,

that had made him believe, after two years of the utmost caution, in the story that the king had his son? It must be. For even had Henry a son, he had failed to remember that he did not like his commands to be ignored. That he would always punish a slight to his kingly authority.

The earl moved restlessly. Having placed himself within the cleverly baited trap, what would be the outcome of his disobedience to the king's will? Four days ago the king had sent for him. Knowing that the king was still sonless, he had gone with dread in his heart. But Henry, surprisingly, had made no reference to the children, or, for the matter of that, of the false story that had brought him back to England. He had ignored it, as though he had no part at all in the earl of Marchmont's return to England. And after all, one could not very well stand there bold-faced and accuse the king of treachery. And he could not delude himself that the king had forgotten about Tudor. Looking into his eyes, he knew that he had not.

The king had begun the audience with an affable smile at him, but the words that left his lips were the reverse of affable. "Rumors are still reaching our unwilling ears, my lord, that your activities against us have become yet more persistent. What say you to that?"

So he was still harping on that old story. "As I have ever said, sire," he replied steadily, "and as I ever will continue to say, I am loyal to my king and country."

Still smiling, the king patted his shoulder. "Think you we believe these rumors, my friend? If you do, then you do us a great injustice. Nay, not for a moment do we believe you capable of that particular treachery against us." The plump, ringed hand continued to pat his shoulder soothingly. "However, there are those who say they can offer indisputable proof of your treason against us."

"Indeed, sire. I would know the names of these people."

The king's eyes were hard, his laugh jovial. "Why are you so cold and formal in your manner, friend? Did we not know better, we would almost be inclined to believe that you offered your king a rebuke. Would you offer your king a rebuke, my lord?"

"I would not so presume, sire. But it is my wish to face my accusers."

"Ah! Do you then have such a clear conscience, friend?"

"I do indeed, sire."

The king's laugh rumbled out. "I will investigate these rumors myself. If I find nothing against you, and I feel sure that I will not, all will be well."

The king had dropped his formal manner of speaking, but the earl was not lulled by this into a false sense of security. Formal or informal, the king was dangerous. Henry was vindictive. If he willed that a charge of treason be brought against him, then it would be so brought, and proven, too.

The earl clutched at the arm of his chair with tense fingers. Henry would have no regard for their long years of friendship. The young and charming Henry he had known was no more. In his place was this cruel and tyrannical man. More monster than man, if all the stories he had heard could be believed.

The earl rose swiftly to his feet. Why wait here tamely for the king to take his revenge. The three of them must depart England again. Somehow they would manage it. They would manage it, even if they had to go disguised.

There was no clear plan in his head as he strode over to the door, but he was suddenly impatient for action. As he put his hand on the latch, he heard the drumming of hooves and the creaking and jingling of harness. "Halt!" the shouted command was like a blow to his heart. So they had come for him? It was already too late! The command was followed by the sound of heavy footsteps and a thunderous rapping on the door. "Open!" the same voice cried harshly. "Open in the name of the king!"

"What do you here?" Madam Tudor's imperious voice. "You, fellow, state your business."

The earl waited for no more. Opening the door, he walked into the hall. Gently putting aside a frightened maidservant who had been sent to summon him, he walked through the open double doors into the blaze of the sunshine. He looked calmly at the company of mounted guards, their faces expressionless beneath their helmets, then he turned to the man who had knocked. "Well?" he said. "Am I to understand that you are come upon the king's business?"

The man looked at him with cold eyes. "You are Tudor Trigg, earl of Marchmont?"

"I am."

The man laid a gauntleted hand upon the earl's shoulder.

"My lord Marchmont, in the name of our most sovereign lord, the king, I hereby arrest you on a charge of High Treason."

The earl glanced at his daughter. Her eyes were wide and very blue in a stark white face. He wanted to say something to reassure her, but he could not seem to find the words.

"Liar!" Corianne awoke from her terror to a sudden blazing life. Rushing forward, she attempted to force the man's hand away. "How dare you touch my father. Liar! Your charge is false!"

The man, temporarily at a loss, looked rather helplessly at his mounted companions. Unmoving, in attitudes of stiff attention, they stared back impassively. Angry because she was attempting to interfere in the king's business, made uncomfortable because he suspected that the men were secretly sniggering over his discomfiture, he forced her tearing hand away. With a hard push, he sent her sprawling.

She was on her feet in an instant and back to the attack. "Let him go! Release him, you fool! You have the wrong man."

"I pray you not to interfere, Madam Tudor," the earl spoke with some difficulty. "The fault does not lie with this man. He does but do his duty."

Corianne did not seem to hear him. She looked distractedly about her. "Tudor!" she screamed. "Hurry! Help me!"

The earl prayed that his son would not hear the cry for help. If his daughter was impulsive and hot-headed, his son was even more so.

"Madam Tudor," he pleaded with her, "do not call upon your brother. If you would please me, go back into the house."

"No! No, I will not let this man take you!"

The guard sought to restrain the girl, but she was everywhere, trying to strike at his face with her nails, kicking out at him. Swearing beneath his breath, he withdrew his hand from the earl's shoulder. Once more he pushed her, and once more she went sprawling.

"Hold!" a stern voice cried. "Hold, I say. You exceed your authority!"

So enraged was he now that the guard forgot the deference due to the man who had called to him to desist. He turned and gave the rider spurring along the path an angry glance.

"Then mayhap you can hold the wench, m'lord Somer-combe," he shouted back defiantly, "for 'tis a certainty that I cannot. She seeks to interfere in the king's business, damned wildcat that she is!"

The earl felt suddenly weak with relief. Adam here? It was like a small miracle, for even now Tudor, having heard his sister's call, was running at full pelt toward them.

Flushed and breathless, Tudor reached them just as the earl of Somercombe dismounted and moved toward his father. He stared at his father's colorless face, at the company of mounted guards, and at Madam Tudor, who was still lying on the grass, her incredulous eyes on the earl of Somer-combe, and he felt a fear such as he had never known before. He stood there as if rooted to the spot, his hands clenched at his sides. He was listening intently, but at the same time dreading what he might hear.

"My lord Marchmont," Adam bowed. "It has been long since we have met."

A tinge of color crept back into the earl's pale face. "I am glad you have come, Adam. I imagine you are here to correct this ridiculous charge?"

"I fear it is not so, my lord." Frowning, Adam's eyes met the earl's. "I wish that were my errand." He held out a tightly scrolled parchment. "I come at the behest of the king. I have here, my lord Marchmont, the formal warrant for your arrest on a charge of High Treason."

"High Treason?"

"Aye. The specific charge against you being that you did take the king's living child for your own. That you did, by devious means, place your own dead child in the royal cradle."

"Nonsense!" The earl looked at him coldly. "I feared something like this. That is why I fled the country. It was a lie that brought me back to England. But I imagine you must know this. It grieves me to see you a party to this treachery, my lord Somercombe. I have ever looked upon you as a friend."

Bending his head, Adam whispered urgently, "My lord, you do not have to tell me it is all nonsense. In his heart, I feel sure, the king knows his claim is false. But the craving for a son has mastered him to such an extent that I fear he knows not what he does."

"He knows. Never doubt it."

"Nonetheless, I beg you to believe that I am your friend. In this dirty matter, I was given no choice but to obey."

"I see." The earl nodded. "It would please the king's rather warped sense of humor to have a friend deliver my death warrant."

"Death warrant? Nay, you are wrong!"

"I am not wrong. I must be got out of the way finally and forever, before the king can begin to convince himself that his conscience is quite clear." He looked at Adam, his eyes penetrating. "Do you speak truth, my lord? Are you really my friend?"

"Always. Never doubt it. I will work in your cause. Upon my honor, I promise you this."

"Thank you, Adam. I believe you."

"And for your faith, I thank you, my lord." Adam turned to look at the girl lying on the grass. "Pray allow me to assist you," he said, extending a gloved hand.

"You!" Hatred flared into her eyes. "You are here to arrest my father, and you actually dare to stand there and ask if you may assist me. I had sooner be helped by a snake than by you!" Because she had thought of this man so much, an overwhelming bitterness colored her next words. "I have remembered you, my lord. But after this I know I will never be able to forget you. You are even more perfidious than I had supposed."

Pitying her suffering, Adam chose to ignore the insult. He smiled at her. "And I have remembered you, Mistress Trigg. It has been two years since last we met, but I found that I could not forget you."

"Bah! I would that it had been two thousand years, so greatly do I loathe you! Pay me no smooth compliments, my lord. Keep them for the ladies of the Court. By his actions a man must be known. So, by yours, I can but repeat what I said to you on that first occasion. You are naught but the king's toady!"

"Be silent!" Pity swept to one side, Adam could not quite restrain his anger.

Corianne looked up into his dangerous eyes. "I will say what I choose. What I have said is true."

With a stifled exclamation, Adam reached down. Grasping

her by both arms, he jerked her roughly to her feet. "Be glad your sex protects you!" he said grimly.

Tudor, who had been able to make out nothing of the whispered conversation between his father and this man save some nonsense about an exchange of babies, started forward angrily. "Take your hands from my sister, my lord," he said menacingly. "If you do not, then I will be obliged to knock you down."

"Certainly, lad," Adam's hands dropped away. "I can assure you that the contact gives me no particular pleasure."

"My lord, if you continue to insult my sister, I——"

"Tudor!" the earl of Marchmont said warningly. "That will be quite enough. Say and do nothing, if you please."

"But he——"

"You heard me, my son. I will not have an unseemly brawl added to the distress of this moment. There are some things you do not quite understand."

Subdued by this, Tudor nodded gloomily. Corianne, however, was in no way subdued. "King's toady!" she jeered at Adam. "You are naught but a toady to a fat, overfed hog who calls himself king."

The guard took a step forward. "My lord! The wench speaks treason."

Adam whirled to face him. "Hold your tongue! It seems to me that you are overzealous in your search for treasonable statements. I willl decide that which is treasonable and that which is not."

Before the blaze in the earl's eyes, the guard stepped back a pace. "But you heard her, m'lord," he said sullenly. "She called the king a fat, overfed hog."

Adam's eyes narrowed. "And now you, too, have called him so. Have a care, fellow."

"I?" The man stared at him, his ruddy color fading. "Not so, m'lord. I did but repeat the wench's statement."

"To repeat it could also be called treasonable."

"W—would you deem it so, m'lord?"

"I might. That, you understand, is up to you."

"I see. Then I will say no more on the matter, m'lord."

"See that you do not. We understand each other, I think?"

The guard's eyes traveled to Corianne. "Aye, m'lord, we do."

Corianne's eyes roved over Adam's tall, elegant figure. She hated him so much that the fiery emotion all but choked her. And yet still, to her shame, she could not help admiring his dark, spectacular looks. He was clad in a sapphire-blue velvet doublet, cut low at the front to reveal a waistcoat heavily embroidered in a design of pearled flowers. The wide sleeves of the shirt ballooning from the sleeveless doublet were embroidered in a like pattern. His coat, which evidently he had donned hastily, was slung about his shoulders and held in place by a silver chain. The coat, lined with ermine and the lapels faced with cloth of silver, was of a fine black material. His legs were encased in sapphire-blue hose, and he wore short, soft riding boots of the same color.

He turned about suddenly and stood very still, his eyes regarding her intently. Corianne flushed crimson. Why did he stare at her so? Did he expect an apology from her? If so, he would wait for a very long time.

As had happened once before, Adam felt his anger dying as he looked at her. Her black hair was tumbled and her creamy skin was brightly flushed, and those strange eyes of hers were glittering and defiant. She wore a gown of blue and white cotton, the bodice of which was cut low to partially reveal her small, firm breasts. Beautiful! he thought. Hers was a beauty that had an exotic, slightly foreign quality.

Unable to bear his scrutiny, Corianne turned her back on him and ran to her father. She flung her arms about him and held him close to her. "What are we to do? I can't let them take you, I can't!"

"There is no choice, my darling." The earl stroked her hair gently. "Be calm. It is all a mistake. You will see. We will be together again very soon." He himself had no such conviction. But what else could he say to the child?

She turned her head to look at Adam. "But that hateful man said you were charged with stealing the king's child. What did he mean?"

The earl sighed. "If the king believes this, then there is nothing I can do about it." He felt her start, and he added hastily. "At least, not yet. I have no need to tell you that the charge is false?"

"No need at all." Corianne's mouth trembled. "Besides, we have proof that——"

"Hush!" the earl cut her off quickly. He was suddenly afraid that if the king saw the birthmark Tudor bore, if he were forced to recognize before witnesses that Tudor was not his son, it might result in the boy's death. The king knew that he lied to himself, but knowing and having to admit it, were two different things in Henry's complex mind. "Listen to me, my darling," he whispered urgently. "Never speak of the birthmark to the king. Promise me!"

"But why not? It would——"

"No! It might result in the death of the three of us. Promise me, Madam Tudor, promise!"

She nodded. "I promise." She glanced once more at Adam. "You have false friends, sir, but never will you be able to say that your daughter played you false."

"No indeed. I have a very loving daughter," the earl said gently. His arms tightened about her. "I believe that Adam did the king's bidding unwillingly," he whispered. "He will aid me, if he can. I know it."

Adam had drawn close enough to hear the whispered words. "You may depend upon it, my lord," he said in a low voice. "My first task shall be to endeavor to persuade the king to release you from the Tower."

The Tower! Corianne jerked herself from her father's arms and stared wildly at the waiting guards. The Tower! That grim place that had seen so much misery and so many deaths. The place where Thomas More, the lord chancellor, had met his death. He had died because he did not believe the king's marriage to Catherine to be void. Corianne had heard it said that More, as he prepared for his execution, had uttered these words, "I die the king's good servant, but God's first." And again, facing his judges at his trial, More was reputed to have said, "I see there is no help for me, my lords. You are determined to condemn me!"

Determined to condemn me! The words were like thunder in Corianne's brain. What if the king were equally determined to condemn her father. Was the king mad? Why did he say that her father had stolen his child? She had thought the king to be her father's good friend. It was because of this friendship, begun so long ago, when the two men were but tiny lads, babes almost, that she had been inclined to discredit the many evil stories she had heard of his tyranny. It had seemed to her that were the king such a tyrant, her gentle father could not possibly love him and hold him in esteem. Now she was not sure of anything.

"Madam Tudor," the earl of Marchmont's quiet voice brought her around to face him. "You must promise me to be of good cheer. I am innocent of wrongdoing, therefore nothing can be proven against me." He nodded to Tudor, who was dumbly looking on. "You, too, my son. Be of good cheer. Adam," he said, glancing at him, "you will not deny me a few moments alone with my children?"

"Of course. Take Madam Tudor and your son and go into the house, where you may have privacy."

"Do not call me Madam Tudor!" Corianne blazed at him. "It is my father's name for me. It is not for strangers to use."

"Your pardon, Mistress Trigg." Adam turned to the guards. "Stay where you are, please. It will not be necessary to follow my lord Marchmont." He nodded to the earl, smiling slightly. Several of the guards, at an order from their commander, had dismounted. And Adam did not see that one guard, stepping quietly back, was already making his way around the side of the house.

Alone once more, the young, troubled eyes upon him, the earl told them the whole story. Beginning with the suspicions he had had of the king's intentions, what he had felt to be his mounting mania, and finally the certainty that had come to him on the day of the christening. "I know the king very well, you see. I do not relish what he has become, but I still know how his mind works. I saw his eyes, and I knew then that he meant to have you, Tudor."

"I will not pose as his son," Tudor cried. "He cannot make me do so!"

"It might mean your life."

"What of that? I had rather die your son, than live as the king's."

"I shall cherish those words, Tudor," the earl said, putting his arm about the boy's stiff shoulders. "But you must live for me, because I love you and I could not bear to know you had gone to your death. Say nothing against the king. It might even be well to pretend to agree with him. Be quiet, be careful. And one day, if you see your chance, it might be that you will manage to escape. There is one other possibility. If Anne Boleyn gives the king a healthy son, he will lose interest in you rapidly. That will be your chance."

"But, Father," Corianne clung to his other arm, "what of you? I—I fear that the king will demand your life."

"Never think it, darling!"

"Are you sure?"

"Very sure," the earl lied calmly. "Henry will not order the death of such an old friend. At the last moment he will relent. You will see." Another thought came to him. "Perhaps, after I am departed with the guards, you could attempt to make your way to your aunt's house. It is a far distance, I know, but if you were careful, it could be done."

The earl saw Corianne's quick glance at Tudor, the stubbornness of their expressions, and he sighed. It had been worth mentioning. But he had had little hope that they would agree. "You will not go, then?"

Tudor shook his head. "As you say, we will not go." He gave a strained smile. "Whatever you may believe, sir, your children are not fools. Were we to disappear, your death would be assured."

Useless to argue with them, he knew it. Once more he cautioned them about the birthmark. "Never speak of it. The king knows of this mark that is peculiar to the Triggs, but you may be sure he will make no mention of it himself. Do not force his hand. Do not endanger yourselves. Do you promise?"

After they had promised, Tudor with the utmost reluctance, the earl drew them both close. He held them tightly for a moment. "For a little while it must be good-bye, my children. May God bless you and have you in His keeping." Releasing them, he went from the room.

The guard who had stolen away stepped back from the half-opened window. He was smiling to himself as he rejoined his companions. A birthmark, he thought. Indisputable proof. Sweet Anne Boleyn will be made happy with this knowledge. His eyes softened as he thought of her. He, Will Tompkins, would place this trump card within the queen's hand. But he would bide his time until she was in dire need, as he feared she might be soon. He and he alone would bring her new hope and courage. Maybe she would reward him with a smile. A smile from Anne Boleyn! To him it would be more precious than a purse of gold.

Tudor was scowling as he followed after his father. He felt like crying, but, for his father's sake, he must not break down. In any case, Madam Tudor was weeping enough for both. So many questions unresolved, he thought. So many doubts and fears. Would his father die? Dear God, let it not be so!

As she went to rejoin her father, Corianne was thinking, the king likes me, he thinks me beautiful. When he looked at me, surely it was desire I saw in his eyes. I will go to him. I will beg him on my knees for my father's life. If that will not suffice, I will offer him myself. She shuddered at the thought of that great, gross body covering her own, then her mouth hardened with resolution. But I will do it. He may do anything he pleases with me, if he will but give me my father's life in exchange. Would he give it to her? He must, he must!

Corianne saw Adam's smile as they approached him. To her, that smile was but another example of his perfidy. She looked at him coldly. "Be assured, my lord Somercombe, that I will remember this day. If I can injure you in any way, I will gladly do so."

"I am sorry to hear that." Adam took her hand. When she attempted to snatch it away, he held it firmly and pressed a kiss upon her fingers. "I will do all that I can for your father."

"I do not believe you!"

Dropping her hand, Adam turned to the hovering guard. "Bind my lord Marchmont," he snapped.

The earl stared at him unbelievingly. Then he put out a hand to restrain Tudor, who had started forward. "There is no need to bind me," the earl said wearily. "I give you my word that I shall not attempt to escape."

"I believe you, my lord," Adam spoke curtly to hide his own emotion. He could not bear the suffering in the lad's face, or the look in Madam Tudor's eyes. "It is simply that these men have been given their orders. It would go ill with them were they to disobey."

"I understand." Resigned, the earl allowed his wrists to be bound with leather thongs, then, with the aid of one of the guards, he mounted his horse, which had already been brought from the stables.

Corianne's heart swelled with grief. Would she ever see her father again? Adam had said that he would help him. Had she, with her foolishly babbling mouth, caused him to change his mind? On an impulse, she turned to Adam. "My lord Somercombe, I would speak with you for a moment."

Adam looked down into her tear-stained face. "Is there anything I may do for you? You have but to ask."

"You have said that you will help my father." She looked at him searchingly. "Can I—can I hope that you will keep your promise?" She hesitated, then, her tongue betraying her again, she added, "Can I trust you?"

The softened look left his face and the smile in his eyes vanished. "I am not such a poltroon as you believe me, Mistress Trigg,'" he said stiffly.

"I am sorry," she managed the apology with some difficulty. "I—I would be grateful if you would help my father."

Adam mounted his horse. "You are not sorry at all," he said, looking down at her. "You should guard your eyes, Mistress Trigg, they betray your hatred."

Despair in her heart, Corianne watched him lift his hand in the signal to depart. Standing beside Tudor, she watched her father ride away.

When, some time later, a fresh company of guards rode up to the house, they were still standing there. Dumbly, without resistance of any kind, surrounded by guards, they were escorted to the palace where the king awaited them. Tudor's face was expressionless. Corianne, except for the smudges of tears still on her cheeks, showed no emotion, but her thoughts were busy. Somehow I will save my father. I will!

Once or twice the guards on either side of them looked at the pair curiously. They had asked no questions, which in itself was strange. And certainly they displayed no grief for a father who, not so long since, had been escorted to the Tower under heavy guard. Was it true, the rumor that was going around, that the red-headed boy was the king's true and lawful son? The guard riding to the left studied Tudor Trigg covertly. It did seem to him that the boy, for all his height and his bright coloring, had more a look of the prisoner, my lord Marchmont, than the king. He closed his mind quickly against the thought. He must not even think it, lest in an unguarded moment, when he was high-flown with drink perhaps, he spoke the thought aloud. What the king wanted he would have, and there was no gainsaying him. For such thoughts, such indiscreet words, the highest in the land could lose their heads.

They were escorted into the presence of the king. Tudor was grave and courteous. Only when the king, the tears standing bright in his eyes, clasped him to his bosom, did Tudor show signs of breaking. "Sire," he said stiffly, "I understand nothing of this. It is said that I am not my father's son, but yours. How can this be?"

"Be seated, Tudor," Henry beamed at him lovingly. "You need not stand in my presence. I will explain all."

He waited until Tudor had seated himself, then, still smiling, he signed to Corianne to do likewise. Only then did he begin to speak. "On the day of your birth, Tudor, a very cruel trick was played upon me by this man whom you have for so long called father. Marchmont's son was born dead. And because he longed for a son, as I have ever done, he conspired with the royal physician and the midwife to cheat me of my lad. Oh, I have no doubt at all that he bribed the physician heavily to take my healthy boy and place him in the bed of his wife. The dead child was then placed in the queen's bed."

Looking into those little eyes, Tudor burned with hatred and anger. The man was mad! How dare he slander his father so. He drew a deep breath, biting back the heated retort he longed to make. "Forgive me, sire," he said huskily, "but I do not quite follow your reasoning."

Henry leaned forward and patted his hand tenderly. "I remember well," he went on, "how the physician, disregarding Court etiquette, ordered the room to be cleared of spectators. And that, if you please, included myself. He told me that the queen needed air to aid her to bear the child. Air! All the physician wanted was sufficient privacy so that he might exchange my son, when it was born, for Marchmont's dead boy."

"But the child might have been a girl, sire," Corianne put in. "How could the physician be sure that the queen would bear a boy?"

"I know not the workings of his mind," Henry said, giving her an annoyed glance. "But I do know the queen bore a male child." He pointed at Tudor. "He sits now before me."

Afraid to anger him further, lest it bring to ruin the plan she had in mind, Corianne subsided. "I beg your pardon, sire."

"Sire——" Tudor hesitated for a moment, then went on

boldly, "if such an exchange had taken place, would not the queen have been aware of it?"

"Nay. Your mother, the queen, lay in a stupor. She knew nothing. I myself was not allowed to see her until twenty-four hours had passed."

"But how was the dead child brought in, sire?" Tudor persisted. "How was the healthy one smuggled out?"

"Why, lad," Henry said tenderly, " 'Twas easily enough done. The royal midwife too was in the plot against her king. The royal midwife always carries a large covered basket in which are the things necessary to her profession. Who would dream of stopping her, of searching her basket? You, my son, were carried out of the palace in that basket."

He was mad! Tudor longed to rise and confront him with the birthmark. But he must say nothing as yet. He must remember his father's warning. "Sire," he said in a tightly controlled voice, "can this physician and the midwife be brought forth to answer for their crime against you?"

Henry could not quite suppress a note of triumph as he answered. "Nay, lad, I wish it were possible. They are long since dead and beyond earthly punishment."

The freckles stood out darkly against Tudor's face. He could not go on with this farce. He would not. "Your pardon, sire, but I am indeed the son of the earl of Marchmont."

In the silence that fell, he heard Corianne's sharp gasp of horror. Instantly he wished the words back. He waited for the king's anger, but it did not come. "Ah, lad, lad, I understand your feelings. 'Tis natural that you should protest. But we have been cruelly deceived, you and I. You are my son. Let no man tell you differently. I would have known you anywhere. You have the same stature, the same coloring. You are young Henry Tudor all over again."

"I have been told that I resemble my father, sire."

"Of course you do. Have I not just said so?"

Tudor looked at him with unhappy eyes. What could he say to this man whose self-delusion was so complete that he thought, if he willed it to be so, that his dupes must come to accept even his lightest word as the one and only truth? And even the truth, as the king knew it in his heart, must be bent to his will, the indomitable, overpowering Tudor will, or his conscience could not be easy. And no doubt the king, when it suited him, bullied God and conscience, which were after all much the same thing, into submission. So the young and be-wildered Tudor thought. He did not know then, for he was only groping to understand, that he had hit accurately on the fatal flaw in Henry Tudor's character. In his nervousness, Tudor answered with a stammer. "I—I meant the earl of M—Marchmont, sire."

Henry was not pleased with his words or with the nervous stammer. Henry Tudor's son must be bold and fearless, as he himself had ever been. He answered coldly, "Fools who have no eyes, or those who have been bribed handsomely by my lord Marchmont, might say so. One can see a resemblance in anyone or anything, if it is expedient to do so."

Again Tudor bit back his anger. To hear the king speak of his father so slightingly was almost more than he could bear. Expedient, he thought. Aye, it was expedient to you to im-prison my father and claim me for your own. Yet, save in coloring, I am no more like you than any other in your palace. But why me? Have I been chosen because, in my fa-ther's veins, there flows a trace of Tudor blood? Again he had hit on a truth, and he did not know it.

Henry stared at him with narrowed eyes. His good humor was beginning to wear thin. What did that look on the boy's face mean? What was he thinking about? If he meant to defy him, then, son or no son, he would be punished. His sandy brows drew together in a puzzled frown. He had thought that Tudor, dazzled by his good fortune, would agree eagerly to anything he might have to say, to any plans he might make for his future. It did not appear to be so, and he could scarcely believe it. His already florid complexion deepened with the hot blood of anger. He hoped that the boy was not a fool. Perhaps, he thought, it is a little too much for him at the moment. I will talk no more for the present. I will give him time to get used to his new position. If Anne does not deliver a living boy, this lad might well be the Prince of Wales, did he not understand that? But then again, if Anne did give him a healthy boy, what was he to do with Tudor Trigg? An accident could be arranged, of course. Unfortu-nate, if it happened, and he, the king, would be quite heart-broken. There were always ways. Certainly he had no need to think of them now, though. Anne's child was as yet unborn, and in the meantime he held a trump card. He looked at Tudor's almost sullen face, and the ready rage flickered within him. Sullenness, impudence, he would not endure it! He offered the boy a glittering prize, did he but have the wit to grasp it. The impulse came to him to roar aloud his displeasure, but he crushed it quickly. Tudor must love him, he must bow to his will, as all did. In time, Tudor would forget about the earl of Marchmont. Marchmont! What was he beside the glory of the king, the supreme ruler? He might allow the boy a feeling of gratitude toward Marchmont for his gentle rearing, but all other feeling must be for him, Henry Tudor. So thinking, he rose to his feet. The others, startled by his abrupt movement, rose too. "I will talk no more," the king said. "I will see to it that you are shown to suitable chambers."

Coriannne did not immediately follow her brother. She had been observing the king, the inflections in his voice, the expressions that flickered across his face, and she knew instinctively that it would do no good to plead with him for her father's life. The king, she imagined, had only two uses for women—to pleasure him, and to breed his children. Well, what must be must be. If it were the only way, then she would take it. But she must remember not to underestimate this man. He was no fool, not he! Despite his great vanity, which amounted to self-adoration, he was a cunning and clever statesman. Yet she also had an advantage, for much of her knowledge of the king's character had been gained from her father, who knew him so intimately. He was cruel, yet he could be easily moved to sentiment. One might perhaps play on that sentiment, his monstrous vanity, and his love of women, for these were his weaknesses. Nevertheless, one wrong look, one word out of place, and those little eyes would turn to a hard glare and set the astute brain to working. "You should guard your eyes, Mistress Trigg," the earl of Somercombe had said, "they betray your hatred." She would do exactly that. If the king should ever learn of her deep hatred of him, there would be no chance at all to save her father.

"Sire," Corianne curtsied again. Arising, she gave him what she hoped was a seductive smile.

The king evidently thought so. His eyes on the shadowed cleavage between her breasts, he moved closer to her. So close that she could feel the warmth of him through the padded bulk of his clothing. His eyes lifted to her face. "You smile on us sweetly," he said, reverting to the royal mode of speech, as he so often did in moments of anger or great emotion. "Why do you smile at us so? Do you fear that you will be parted from this boy you call brother?" His eyes looked deeply into hers, and the faint, fatuous smile on his lips told her that he did not believe for a moment that she was thinking of Tudor.

Corianne sighed mournfully, but the mournfulness was belied by the admiration in her eyes. Beneath those eyes, the king preened himself. But, he decided, he would play her game a little longer. She desired him, he knew it. However, he was the king, and the poor child could not be too immodest and outright of speech. "Come, sweetheart," he murmured as softly as his hearty voice would allow, "we would not be so cruel to you. You shall stay with him. We have no objection if you continue to call our prince brother."

Our prince? Tudor, Corianne knew, thought the king quite mad. But he was not mad. He was wily, and he knew what he wanted and intended to have. Modestly, Corianne looked down. What you really mean, she thought, is that you have no objection to my becoming your mistress. Had I been plain and undesirable, you would have parted us without a second's thought of the unhappiness you would be causing. You have imprisoned my father. If I could, I would kill you! Instead, I must flatter and smile and fawn upon you.

The king's finger touched her face. "Look at us, Mistress Trigg. You must never be frightened of your king."

"No, sire." Corianne smiled radiantly. "I will try not to be. But I—I fear your magnificence overwhelms me."

"Nay, sweetheart, we will not hear such words from those lovely lips. You must remember that we are but a mortal man. We endeavor always to be modest, humble, and grateful unto the Lord."

Corianne's heart was beating very fast. Now, she urged herself. Say it now. Borrowing from Anne Renshaw, she said, "You, sire, are to me more god than man."

The king's eyes grew stern, and the little, full, red mouth pursed. "We would not have you sacrilegious, mistress." His frown faded and his eyes softened as she gave a frightened cry. Instantly one arm was about her, holding her very close, soothing her. It was characteristic of Henry that, for the moment, he had forgotten that he held a girl whose father he

81

had falsely imprisoned. "Hush now! We did not mean to frighten you."

"But I—I fear I have offended you, sire. And I meant no harm."

"We know it," he said smiling. "We know it very well. Confess now, you weep more from the fear of being parted from our prince than from fear of our displeasure?"

"It would hurt of course to be parted from Tudor. But were I to be parted from—from———" She looked at him in dismay. "I—I cannot say what is in my heart, sire."

"But we would hear what is in your heart," he urged. "We command that you speak out, Mistress Trigg."

She looked at him, shrinking back a little. "Your majesty will not be angry with me?" she whispered.

"Nay. Have we not commanded you to speak?"

"Then I w—would say that although I fear parting from Tudor, were I to be parted from your majesty, it would break my heart."

Henry's eyes gleamed with pleasure. Poor frightened child, it had cost her much to make her confession. He took her face between his hands and pressed his mouth to hers. "You desire us, sweetheart? Is that what you would tell us?"

"Y—yes, sire."

"Then there shall be no parting." He kissed her again, more ardently this time. "If we come to you tonight, would you welcome us?"

Corianne longed to strike out at him. But she must do this thing she had set herself to do. But what if she should fail? No, she must not even think of failure. "Sire!" she breathed. "How can you even ask? I can imagine no greater joy."

"Then you may expect us." Henry took her hands and kissed them. "Go now, sweetheart, and leave us to our joyful anticipation."

Only after Corianne had curtsied herself from his presence, did the king remember the earl of Marchmont. His eyes narrowed in thought. Did Mistress Trigg really desire him, or was she playing a subtle game? Did she want something of him? Her father's life perhaps? She would not get it, he thought, his mouth grim with resolution. But perhaps there was more to it than that. There had been something in her eyes that had been joyful and bright when he had told her that he would come to her. It might be that she spoke truth.

MADAM TUDOR

Few women there were who could look upon Henry Tudor and not desire him. And after all, what was the loss of a father if one be rewarded with the king's love? Of course, she had spoken truth. How could he have doubted it?

Laughing exultantly, the king wandered over to his chair and sat down. Quite suddenly he felt like a young boy in love for the first time. Anne Boleyn. Jane Seymour. Beside Madam Tudor, his lovely and loving jewel, they were as nothing!

5

From his cell in the Tower, the earl of Marchmont stared out of the small square window at the rain-washed courtyard below. The sun was coming out. The small, sharp shower of rain was over. His life, too, was over. The king, unrelenting, had allowed the trial to proceed. He had been tried, judged, and condemned. Tomorrow, on the third day of this November month of 1535, he was to die.

His fingers clenched on the flaking wooden frame of the window. The king had even gone so far as to deny him the dignity of a nobleman's death. He was to be hung like a common felon. Why? he thought with a surge of bitter anger. Why must Henry carry his vindictiveness so far? He thought of his children, both of them all but prisoners at Greenwich Palace. All but? Nay, they were truly prisoners. They could not wander about the grounds without a guard following after.

He moved away from the window and sat down on a wooden bench. He had told himself that he did not fear death, but that had been a lie to comfort himself with. What man does not fear the unknown? His heart lurched uncomfortably, and he put his hand to the area, massaging the pain with his fingers. His children? What was to become of them? Adam had told him that Tudor, while not openly defying the king, was sullen and sometimes inclined to truculence. But the king, waiting in the wings, as it were, for Anne Boleyn to deliver her child, had made no hostile move against him. But if the child were a boy, what then would be Tudor's fate? And Madam Tudor, what madness had seized her that she must attempt to barter her body, believing that in this way she could secure his release from the Tower? Useless, quite useless! But his daughter, so hot-headed and loving and impulsive, but so young and unwise, had believed that she would succeed. That story, too, Adam had relayed to him. Poor Adam, who, like Madam Tudor, had worked for his release and had failed.

"I had to see the king on a matter of some importance," Adam had told him. "The hour was late. But, unless I have been specifically warned to keep away, it is not unusual for me to seek audience in his bedchamber. The king does not sleep well these days, and there are times, apart from the matters that I feel I must bring to his attention at once, when he welcomes my company for its own sake. I sought him out this night. In the short corridor that leads to his apartments, I encountered the queen, who was about to do the same."

The earl closed his eyes, picturing the scene. The king did not like formality in regard to the hours he spent in sleep, so there had been no gentlemen of the bedchamber to impede their entrance.

Anne Boleyn, pregnant with Henry's child, stopped on the threshold, the earl of Somercombe beside her. Her eyes dilated as she looked at the girl on the bed. Corianne Trigg was naked, her long, black hair unbound. Standing beside the bed, about to remove his heavy robe and join her, was the king.

Adam stepped back quickly. Madam Tudor and the king? He felt a murderous fury. Her father lay in the Tower, and she sported in the king's bed like a common strumpet! He could have killed her! He would like to kill them both! He was startled out of his fury by Anne Boleyn's high, shrill voice. "Henry! I will not endure this!"

"You have not been invited into my bedchamber, madam," the king roared. "Remove yourself at once!"

"And have we now reached that sad point when I must ask my own husband for permission to enter?"

"I remind you that I am the king, madam. Be careful, be very careful, how you address me."

Emotion was wiped from Anne's face. With that faint, scornful smile that so infuriated him, she said coldly, "You are indeed the king, sire. And, in case you had forgotten it, I am your wife."

"I would that I could forget it, madam."

Anne looked at him for a long moment. About to turn and leave the chamber, she was arrested by the look in Corianne's eyes. There was fear in those eyes, but she could swear it was not fear of herself. Now their expression had changed to one of passionate appeal.

Still hesitating, Anne thought bitterly of the irony of the situation. She, the queen, the wronged woman, was, unless she was much mistaken, being begged by this girl to rescue her. She had believed Mistress Trigg to be a young and innocent girl, and one moreover who could have no love for a king who had created such havoc in her hitherto happy family life. Then why had she done this thing? Why had she so cheapened herself? Anne frowned, trying to solve the puzzle. And then, suddenly, she knew why. The girl was selling her body, in effect, to the king. By so doing, she hoped to persuade the king to release her father from the Tower. Anne could understand her motivation. It was just the kind of mad, impulsive thing she might have done herself in a similar situation.

The king glared at Anne. He felt suddenly ridiculous, robbed of the dignity he so cherished. There was Mistress Trigg lying on his great bed and trying with shaking hands to cover herself with her long, black hair. The queen, her complexion sallow, unhealthy, dark blotches beneath her eyes, was staring at him with accusation. And Somercombe, who might have had the tact to leave the room, was unsmiling. His expression, if he could actually believe the evidence of his eyes, was austere and condemning. Yes, he felt ridiculous, and he did not like the feeling. He cursed himself for not going to Mistress Trigg's apartments, as he had first planned. It would have been better so, and he would not have been caught in this position.

"Sire," Adam's voice was as cold as his eyes, "do I have your permission to retire?"

Henry's simmering fury boiled over. "Aye, my lord, go! Go!" he shouted. "And never again come into our presence unannounced. Do you understand?"

"Perfectly, sire."

Anne touched Adam's arm. "Wait, my lord. Give Mistress Trigg your cloak. When she has covered herself decently, you will be so good as to escort her to her apartments." She heard Corianne's faint, relieved sigh, and she knew she had guessed correctly at the girl's motives. The girl did not work against the queen as many others did. She worked for her father. She was frightened now and anxious to be away. It was doubtful if she would try again. Indeed, she herself would see to it that Mistress Trigg was kept from the king's amorous intentions. She did not know how she would do it, but manage she would.

"Madam!" The king took a menacing step toward the queen. "We and we alone give the orders."

Even with the advanced bulk of her pregnancy, Anne looked magnificent in that moment. With her head held high and her eyes looking steadily into her husband's, she was every inch a queen. "Then pray give the order, sire," she said calmly. "There are things we must discuss." With a calculated movement, she put her hand to her stomach and winced.

Henry, who had never scrupled to humiliate his queen, opened his mouth to make a furious reply. Her sudden look of pain, the way she pressed her fingers against her stomach, halted him. He was alarmed now as well as angry. Anne must not be upset. Of late, she was somewhat given to hysteria. There must not be a scene, for it was his belief that violent emotion was bad for the child she carried. Swallowing, Henry said gruffly, "Aye, my lord Somercombe, do as the queen bids."

Corianne took the cloak from Adam. She found that she could not meet his eyes, but for all that she was no less aware of his contempt.

In the corridor, walking by his side, she felt like a shamed child. She tilted her chin, hoping that her shame and her humiliation was not obvious to him. She need not have troubled herself. Adam did not once look at her.

At the door that led into her apartments, Adam bowed stiffly. "I wish you a pleasant good night, Mistress Trigg." He turned away.

Corianne was trembling. She found that though she hated him, she could not bear his contempt. She cried out in a choked voice, "I had to do it! It was for my father's sake. Don't you understand? But I tell you now, my lord Somercombe, that—that n—nothing happened."

"But it would have done," he said, turning to face her once more. "It would have done, had not the queen and I interrupted."

"Yes," she said defiantly. "Yes, my lord, it would. I would do anything for my father. After all, 'tis little enough you will trouble yourself to do, I'll vow."

The coldness of his expression was replaced by fury. "You fool! You meddle with a man of whom you have no knowledge."

"I do have knowledge. My father has told me much of the king."

"Keep your voice down," he said curtly. "The king has changed. Your father does not really know him as well as he thinks."

"And you do, my lord?"

"I do. He will take his pleasure with your body, as he would with any other willing strumpet, but——"

"You dare to call me a strumpet?"

"If you behave like one, you must expect to be called so. I was about to say that whatever pleasure the king may take in your body, it will not buy your father's life."

Her face went white. "You mean that—that it is hopeless? My father will die?"

"By no means hopeless. If there is a way, be sure that I will find it."

The earl of Marchmont opened his eyes. Aye, he could picture the scene. He knew Madam Tudor so well that it was as though he had been there, looking into her mind. But Adam had been wrong in one thing. It was hopeless. It had been from the very beginning.

The door of the cell creaked open. The earl turned his head swiftly. "Adam," he cried, rising to his feet. "I had not expected to see you until morning."

The earl of Somercombe looked at him with sympathy. "I found that I could not wait. I found, too, that Madam Tudor would not wait."

"Madam Tudor? Adam! Do you—do you mean——"

"Aye, my lord. The king has granted her permission to see you this one last time."

The earl winced. "Where is she?"

"I will fetch her in a moment. The king, you see, even though I never ceased to importune him for your release, apparently trusts me to guard her." His smile was bitter. "I, perhaps I should say, and two guards. My lord, I was so certain that I could soften the king toward you. Forgive me for my failure."

"You did your best." The earl put his hand on Adam's

shoulder. "Aye, you tried, and you stood my friend. I can ask no more of any man."

"Listen to me," Adam said urgently, "you must not give up hope. A man has been known to be pardoned at the last moment."

"I shall not be, Adam. Though I am innocent of wrongdoing, I have come to think of myself as the king's example. My death will tell the people that he will punish a friend as mercilessly as an enemy." The earl frowned. "Be careful of yourself, Adam. The king's favor can change like the wind, and of late, it seems, he grows worse."

With unconscious haughtinesss, Adam said, "My life is a thing apart, and not to be ruled by the whims and vagaries of Henry Tudor."

"You think not?" the earl said wryly. "The king casts a long shadow. We must all fear him."

Adam shrugged. "Let us forget the king for the moment. Tell me how I may serve you. If there is aught I can do, you have but to say the word."

The earl looked at him. Adam, in his doublet of cream-colored velvet embroidered in golden thread and sparkling with jewels, his cream-colored hose clocked with gold, and his long fingers glittering with rings, looked like a Court dandy. But Adam was no dandy, not he. He was very much a man, and he could trust him.

Under his eyes, Adam flushed self-consciously. "I trust you will forgive the gay apparel," he murmured. "I favor a plainer style, as you know. I thought perhaps to bring you a little cheer, if such be possible. Forgive my stupidity."

"I thank you for the thought." He looked intently at Adam. "There is only one thing I want, and that is to get my children away from the king. I fear for their lives." He hesitated. "Adam, do you think you—you could get my children to France?"

"To France?" Adam frowned thoughtfully. "It will be difficult and dangerous. But if it can be managed, I will do it. I give you my word."

"Thank you. You relieve my mind. Madam Tudor, of course, because you are the king's friend, will believe you to be her enemy and mine. But I am sure you can convince her that she is wrong to regard you so."

"I will convince her," Adam said a little grimly. "And

what is more, should I think up a plan to get them away from England, I intend to be obeyed in all things."

It was hard for the earl to smile, and his eyes kept turning longingly to the door, but he continued to speak lightly. "Tell me, Adam, how goes it with the queen?"

Adam smiled "She continues to frustrate the king with her care of Madam Tudor. She protects her from the king in any way that she can."

"I am grateful to her. But I fear, if she enrages Henry too much, it could go ill with her."

"Her protection is the child she is carrying. She is in her seventh month of pregnancy, and the whole Court holds its breath. All know, like I, that upon the birth of a son does Anne Boleyn's fate depend."

"Poor lady!"

Adam nodded. "There are few who love her. Lady Rochford, her brother's wife, is a particular enemy."

"But has she no friends?"

"Myself, your daughter, and Jane Seymour."

"Jane Seymour!" the earl exclaimed. "But I had heard that the queen looks upon the lady with jealousy and suspicion."

Adam's lip curled. "As she should. But Mistress Seymour has managed to disarm her. She is a cunning baggage. I do not trust her. I have told the queen to beware, but she will have none of my warning, so completely has Jane Seymour done her work. That one will be Queen of England, if she can. The king, I know, desires her."

" 'Tis hard for me to believe that a man, having once possessed Anne Boleyn, could have desire for Jane Seymour. Tell her, if it be possible, that I hope she may be safely delivered of a healthy prince."

"It is my hope, too. There is a brittle look about Anne these days, Her fear is all too evident. In her own distress of mind, her thoughts seem to turn more and more to the sufferings of Queen Catherine."

"It is natural. Her conscience is troubled, and she fears the same fate. I never thought to say this, but a woman who links her life with Henry Tudor is greatly to be pitied."

"If she will but bear him a prince," Adam said cynically, "the king will worship her again."

"Then for her sake, I pray God that all will go her way."

Adam caught the earl's wistful glance toward the door, and

he rose immediately. "I am selfish. I will go at once and fetch Madam Tudor.

"My lord, unless a miracle happens, I will not see you again." Adam spoke the words with difficulty. He held out his hand. "Farewell, my friend. I pray that you will walk with God."

The earl gripped his hand. "I thank you, Adam, for all that you have tried to do. For all that you may do for my loved ones." He turned away abruptly. "Tell Madam Tudor to hurry. There is not much time left. And I must prepare myself for what lies ahead of me."

Adam gripped the earl's thin shoulder with fierce fingers. "Depend upon me. I will find a way." Without another word, for once more he was finding it difficult to speak, he strode over to the door and rapped sharply for the guard.

Going rapidly down the winding, stone staircase, Adam felt a sharp and bitter grief. I will keep my promise, my lord, he vowed to himself. If through any effort of mine, and if it be humanly possible, I will get your children away from this country.

At the bottom of the staircase, Corianne awaited him half in fear, half in grief—fear that her father might have been tortured, and an unbelieving grief because he was about to die. For even now she could not believe it.

Adam looked down into her white, strained face. It was streaked with tears, and her mouth was trembling. He had a sudden urge to fold her in his arms and give her what comfort he might. But the time was not yet, and he must stamp down such impulses. He said quietly, without a trace of emotion in his voice, "I will escort you to your father, Mistress Trigg."

She looked at him with hatred. "Thank you, my lord." She hesitated, then, almost whispering, so great was her fear, she added, "Has—has my father been ill-treated? Tortured?"

"Nay," Adam said gently. "That is something you need not fear."

Leading her upward, his grip on her arm was tight. She made no attempt to draw her arm away, knowing it to be a necessary precaution on his part. The stairs were worn to shallow grooves from the feet of the many who had traversed them, some in fear and hopelessness, some in screaming terror. Or, in rare cases, the joy of release.

Upstairs, Adam paused before a roughly-hung wooden door. "The guard will take you in," he said, nodding to the man who stood there. "I will wait for you downstairs."

Corianne hardly heard him. She waited for the man to select a key. When, finally, he unlocked the door and stood aside for her to enter, she was trembling so much that she feared she might fall. None too gently, the man pushed her inside. "A few minutes only, remember that, mistress. I have my orders, and I must obey them."

Corianne blinked her eyes to adjust them to the dim light in the cell. For a moment she could only stare at the gaunt man who came toward her. Her poor father! How ill he looked! She saw the smile of joy that lit his tired face. "Father, dear father!" she choked.

Then the earl was beside her, pulling her into his arms and holding her fiercely close. "My darling! My little girl! How I have prayed that I might see you once more."

"The—the k—king would not allow Tudor to v—visit you," she sobbed. "Tudor pleaded with him, but he w—was adamant."

"Then I must take my joy in you, dearest." The earl could not quite suppress a sigh. "I would have liked to see my son again. But here you are, my beautiful girl, and it is much more than I expected. I thought that I must go to my death without a glimpse of my children."

"Don't talk of death, Father, oh don't!" The tears she had beeen holding back streamed down her cheeks. "I cannot believe it. Even now I cannot believe that that monster, that liar, will send you to your death!"

"Hush!" The earl cast a worried look at the door. "You must guard your tongue, Madam Tudor. You might be overheard."

"I care nothing for that!" She clung to him frantically. "If you are to die, then it would be my wish to die with you!"

"I will not hear such talk. You must live. Your brother must live."

"Without you? How can we!"

"You think that now, but very soon your grief will become less sharp."

"Never! I—I went to the king, I tried to——"

"I have heard what you tried to do," the earl cut short her

confession. "I thank God that the queen and Somercombe arrived in time to stay you."

"My lord Somercombe again!" Corianne cried indignantly. "He is a traitor to his friends, and a bearer of tales. He—he called me a strumpet!"

"That, too, he told me. But he was very angry at the time."

"What right had he to be angry? What business is it of his?"

"He has never said so, but I think perhaps he has a little fondness for you."

"That man! If that is so, then I wish him joy of it. I can feel nothing but hatred toward him!"

"You wrong him, Madam Tudor. Adam is our friend. He will help you, if he can."

"Aye," she said bitterly, "into the Tower, as he helped you."

"That was none of his doing."

"He is the king's friend. I hope that God strikes them both dead!"

The earl held her away from him and looked into her face. "Have I not always told you that to wish ill upon another is to wish ill upon yourself?"

"How can you be so forgiving?" she cried. "It does not seem human!"

"To my shame, Madam Tudor, I must confess that in my emotions I am all too human. I do not forgive the king his crime against us. But I would wish to do so before I die. And much more than that, I would wish that you and your brother might do so."

She would not forgive, never, never! But to please him whom she would never see again, she would pretend. "I—I will try."

"And you will look to Adam for aid and support?"

The pretense grew harder. Her heart was hot with rage and hatred as she made her answer. "Aye, Father. If it be your wish."

He looked at her searchingly. "Then I am content. We live in perilous times, dearest child, and we all need friends. One other thing. I would have you and your brother cherish the love you bear each other. And I would have you curb your impetuosity. Promise me that you will be careful, darling, that you will not say or do anything to bring trouble on your-self and your brother?"

"I promise." With a little gasping cry, she clung to him tightly. How could she bear this agony? Never again to see him. Never to see the pride in his eyes when he looked at his children, the smile touching his lips, his laughter! This was no nightmare from which she would shortly awaken, this was real. Now at last she was forced to acknowledge the reality. She would never see him again! "Father! I cannot bear this, I cannot!"

"Gently, daughter," he soothed. "Try to be a brave child. I would not have the memory of your tears to take with me."

She drew a deep, quivering breath. Stepping away from him, she scrubbed the back of her hand against her face. "Then you shall not have that memory. See, I will smile for you."

Corianne did not know it, but that brave smile was even more painful to him than her tears. The pathos of it almost broke him. To hide his emotions, he drew her close again, kissing her hair. "One day we will all be together again. I would——"

The abrupt opening of the door cut off the words he would have said. The guard stepped into the room, his manner agitated. "Come," he said, grasping Corianne's arm and pulling her from the earl's embrace. "You have had more than your time."

"No!" Corianne tried to free herself from his grasp. "I want to stay with my father!"

"Just one more moment," the earl pleaded.

"Not another second." Tightening his grasp, the guard dragged Corianne forcibly to the door. "I have my orders. Already I have allowed your daughter to overstay her time. My lord Woodbury is below. Very soon he will be mounting the stairs. Should he see Mistress Trigg, he will report my conduct. She should have been gone ere this."

"Father!" Corianne screamed in wild appeal.

The earl shook his head. Useless to plead. The guard, as he had said, had his orders. To steel himself, he made his voice loud. "It must be good-bye now, my darling girl. Commend me to my son. Remember that I have ever loved you both."

Still Corianne struggled to keep the door from closing and

shutting out that beloved face and figure. "Let me go back to my father. Please! Please!"

The guard's answer was to pull her through the door. It shut behind them with a heavy slam.

The earl stared for a moment at the closed door. The grating sound of the turning key was loud in his ears. He put a hand to his shaking mouth, then he fell to his knees and bowed his head in prayer. "I pray You, Gracious Lord, to guard well my son and my daughter. Grant them the courage to face this parting, and give to me a like courage. Purge my heart of bitterness toward Henry Tudor, who has proved himself a false friend. Grant me the charity to forgive him, for I fear that charity and forgiveness are not yet in my heart."

Later, when Lord Woodbury stood before him, he found the earl calm and resigned. Standing there stiffly, Lord Woodbury said what he had come to say. The king, in his great mercy, had extended to my lord Marchmont the courtesy of his rank. He was to die by the sword, not the noose.

The earl received the news almost indifferently. Bowing his head in acknowledgment, he said, "Commend me to his majesty. Tell him that I die innocent of the charge he brought against me. To her grace the queen, I would say this, 'May God send you a fine and healthy son.'"

Looking into those calm eyes, Lord Woodbury believed in his innocence, where before he had been certain of his guilt. He took his leave of the earl, a highly discomfited man.

Corianne sat in the barge. Facing her was my lord Somercombe, and behind her, the two guards. She spoke no words. She stared straight ahead of her. The tears had dried on her face. It was white and stony.

6

Accompanying the queen and her retinue of ladies, Thomas Cranmer made his stately way across a wide sweep of frost-seared lawn. Turning left, he led the way down a short, narrow path bordered on either side by dwarf bushes. Stopping at the end of the path, Cranmer turned his pale face inquiringly to the queen. "Would you wish to return to the palace now, madam? It is a most beautiful day, but perhaps a little cold." He cleared his throat. "Nonetheless, walking, or so I have heard, is thought by many to be beneficial to ladies who are in—er—a delicate condition."

Anne's dark eyes slanted in mockery. She felt a sudden wish to shock him. "I presume you would refer to those fortunate ladies who, like myself, are with child?"

Cranmer had not expected such bluntness. His face flushed as the queen's ladies, enjoying his discomfiture, began to giggle. "Quite so, madam," he murmured.

"What can you, a man of the cloth, know of such things?" the queen teased. "For shame, sir! You should hold yourself aloof from such worldly matters as birth."

Her remark stung him. He knew she was referring indirectly to the rumor that was lately going around of his secret marriage to a woman of another country. He would neither confirm nor deny the rumor, he decided. If they wished to gossip among themselves, let them do so. But this kind of baiting was unworthy of the queen. His flush fading, Cranmer drew himself to his full height and answered her with a suggestion of rebuke. "A man of the cloth is not necessarily blind to such miracles, madam. Especially when you reflect that a child is a direct blessing from God."

Anne laughed. "You are quite right, sir. And walking, as you say, is very good for me. Pray proceed."

Cranmer bowed. Turning about again, he led them past a

small lake which glittered coldly in the pale winter sunshine. The queen followed slowly after him. Trailing her like a flock of brightly colored birds in their silks and satins and velvets, came her chattering, laughing ladies.

Anne shivered. She was warmly dressed in a gown of white velvet trimmed with dark fur. Over the gown she wore a scarlet cloak hooded and fur-lined. But she was always cold these days, no matter how warmly she dressed. Her thoughts turned to Mistress Trigg, who, only this morning, had been removed from her protection. What now? she thought. Had Henry grown tired of the reproach and hatred in the girl's eyes? She had questioned the guard. The only explanation he could give was that his majesty had commanded that Mistress Trigg and Tudor Trigg be removed to apartments more pleasing to them. More pleasing to Henry, Anne thought. What would happen to Mistress Trigg now? And what of young Tudor Trigg?

The child in her womb moved, and all other thought fled. Anne clasped her hands protectively over her stomach. Thank God the babe was alive. Of late, with the heavy weight dragging, she had begun to fear that it might be dead. Until this moment, she had not realized how frightened she had been. Her mouth quivered. What would Henry do if the child was a girl? She feared, too, that the enchantment she had once held for him was long since gone. He still came to her bed, but unwillingly. More in an attempt to placate her and keep her calm than from any desire. But the enchantment would come back if she gave him a boy, she knew it would. Holy Mother, let it be a boy!

The child moved again. With a sudden impulse to confide this small miracle to Jane Seymour, Anne half-turned. But she had forgotten that the girl did not walk with them. She was confined to her bed with one of her frequent headaches. Drawing her cloak about her, Anne hastened her footsteps. Dear Jane! How terribly she had misjudged her. But it had seemed to her that Jane cast longing eyes in the king's direction. It had turned out to be all in her imagination. Jane had been genuinely stunned when, in a gust of bitter anger, she had spoken aloud the thoughts in her mind.

"Madam!" The tears standing bright in her eyes, Jane had thrown herself at Anne's feet. "I am innocent, dear madam. I swear it. You can have no conception of how sincerely I love you."

"Get up, Mistress Seymour." Her voice had been harsh with anger.

But this was one command that Jane would not obey. "Please, madam, I pray you to look at me. I am short and slight of stature and without beauty to recommend me. But the king worships your beauty. All know it. Madam, how could you ever believe that he would look at such as I!"

Anne had found herself moved by the tears and the protestations. Looking into those pale blue eyes, she could swear that innocence shone from them. Quite suddenly she had found herself believing the girl. Since that time she had tried to make up for her unworthy suspicion. She had heaped gifts upon her. She had kept her in constant attendance. Finally, Anne had confided to her her fears that the king would cast her off should the child be another girl.

"Never, madam!" With Jane's small soft hand stroking her hair and her voice whispering, "His grace will never cast you off. You are his whole life!" Anne had pretended to believe her. If gentle Jane believed the king to be so good and virtuous and loving, why disillusion her? If she stayed long enough at Court, she would be disillusioned soon enough.

Cranmer's voice broke in on her thoughts. "Would it pleasure you to take the Flower Walk, madam?" He gave the short, dry laugh that always irritated Anne. "Though I fear that until the summer comes again the flowers must remain but a memory."

"Naturally, sir," she said in a cool voice. "It is winter."

His eyes regarded her with a pained expression. "I pray you to be careful how you walk, madam. The path winds, and it is inclined to be slippery."

"I am aware of it," Anne snapped. She saw him color, and she felt a touch of shame. "Forgive me, please," she said impulsively. "My manners are abominable."

"Your majesty is gracious," Cranmer murmured. Walking on, he felt ill-used. He had angered the queen. And the king, whom he served to the best of his ability, seemed to have forgotten his very existence. It seemed that he also forgot his friends as easily as his loyal servants. He thought of the king weeping, declaring himself to be heartbroken because he had been forced to condemn the earl of Marchmont, a man he had ever loved, to death. Yet his tears had dried easily enough. His heartbreak had not stopped him riding out each day, accompanied by a full complement of nobles. It had not stopped him drinking and feasting as hugely as ever, or his bestowing of pats and pinches on every comely maiden who happened to cross his path.

Cranmer hunched his shoulders against a gust of cold wind. The king was a clever man, he had an amazing brain, but he was also a vain, fat hypocrite. He wished that he had the courage to tell him so. But one did not, if one wanted to go on living, speak one's mind to Henry Tudor. Perhaps he should seek audience and find out if he had in some way displeased the king. He hoped, when he was finally ushered into the royal presence, that he would not find Thomas Cromwell there. He did not trust Cromwell, and it pained him that the king showed the man so much favor. He would also like to discuss with the king the matter of the earl of Marchmont's children. He caught himself up quickly. Or perhaps he should say child rather than children.

Cranmer stopped walking abruptly as a light feminine laugh sounded from around the next bend. The laughter was followed by a deep, booming voice that Cranmer instantly recognized. Hastily, he retraced his steps. "Madam," he said to the queen, "I have a fear that the long walk has tired you. I think that for the sake of your health we should return to the palace."

Anne ignored him. She too had heard the laughter and the king's voice replying. Her head held high, Anne swept past Cranmer, leaving him to hurry after her. He heard the queen's gasp, and he feared the worst. Coming closer, his nervously blinking eyes took in the scene before him.

The king was seated on a rustic bench, his arms about a small, slight girl who was perched on his knees. "Come, sweet Jane Seymour," Henry spoke tenderly. "Are you so shy that you will not even look at your king?" The plump, jeweled hand took her chin and turned her face to his. "Henry Tudor has a great wish to kiss those tempting lips."

"And it is my wish that you should, dear sire," Jane answered him in a small voice. "My love for you is boundless.

But you are already wed, and, forgive me, sire, this dalliance is not seemly."

Anne's quick forward movement and the bright flash of her red and white costume attracted the king's attention. He turned his head quickly. Just for a moment he quailed before the look in Anne's eyes, then he was himself again. Putting Jane from him, he rose to his feet. "What are you doing here, madam? It would seem to me that walking in this chill air will be bad for the child." His small, blue eyes found Cranmer, and they grew hard and menacing. "You here, too, my lord archbishop? Are you spying on me?"

It was one of the childish remarks this great monarch sometimes made, but Cranmer dared do nothing else but take it seriously. "Nay, sire, certainly not. I—I did but accompany the queen. I——"

Anne's sharp voice cut across his explanation. "I rejoice to see you in such good company, Mistress Seymour," she said acidly.

Jane Seymour fell to her knees and bowed her head meekly. "I did but seek to comfort his grace, madam. He is consumed by his anxiety on your behalf. He—he needed someone in whom he could confide."

"And he chose you? Am I to presume that your headache has left you, Mistress Seymour?"

The pale blue eyes looked vague for a moment. "Y—yes, madam, 'tis much better, thank you."

"Apparently." Anne's eyes went to the king, and the bitter scorn with which she regarded him brought a surge of hot blood to his cheeks. "And you, sire," her voice was biting, "has Mistress Seymour managed to soothe your grave anxiety?"

The jewels on his person flashed brightly as the king took a quick step toward her. "I like not your tone, madam. Now get you gone. I will not have you endangering my son's life with your careless disregard of the weather." He looked at Cranmer again. "As for you, my lord archbishop, I will have much to say to you at some future date. That I promise you."

Cranmer stared at him in horror. There was no mistaking that tone. The king knew himself to be at fault and, as was usual with him, he must have someone to blame. His choice, it seemed, had fallen on his archbishop. "I—I am innocent of f—fault, sire," the unhappy Cranmer stammered. "I beg you to believe me!"

"Seek not to hide behind this man." Anne spoke so sharply that her ladies murmured together in alarm. "The fault is yours, sire. You know it."

"You dare!" The king's eyes blazed with fury. "You dare to speak to me so, you whore!"

The color drained from Anne's face at this insult. "Whore?" her voice was high and uncontrolled. "You insult me, sire! I am the queen. I will have respect." She looked at the trembling Jane Seymour. "Dally with your sluts, if it pleases you to do so. But you will remember my rank."

Henry's heavy hands grasped her thin shoulders. "And who bestowed that rank upon you, madam? Who lifted you from obscurity and made you his queen?" He shook her. "Answer me, you barren bitch!"

Anne wrenched herself free. "I carry your child, and I have no need to prove myself. If your own seed be weak and diseased, you shall not say it is fault of mine."

The king's face was purple, his rage terrible. Lifting his hand, he lashed her across the face. "By the Rood, I'll hear no more from you, madam!"

Cranmer caught Anne as she stumbled backward. "Sire! Sire!" his voice rose hysterically. "Remember that the queen carries your child."

The king turned on him. "And do you now seek to condemn me? By God, I will not have this insubordination!"

"Forgive me, sire," Cranmer cried. "I meant no insubordination. I think only of the peril to the precious life of our unborn prince."

The king stared at him, some of his high color fading. "Aye," he said after a moment. "Aye, the prince. I had forgotten. You do well to remind me, archbishop." He turned a subdued glare on Anne. "Get you back to the warmth. And remember this. If aught happens to my son, I shall hold you responsible, madam." He looked down impatiently at the kneeling Jane. "Get up." He dug her in the side with the toe of his jeweled slipper. "Attend the queen, Mistress Seymour."

"I will not have her," Anne said coldly. With a last contemptuous look at the king, she turned and walked away. Her ladies, followed by the frightened Jane Seymour, moved off after her.

The king seemed to have forgotten his previous threats. He smiled almost warmly at Cranmer. " 'Tis the storm of a domestic life that make it interesting, eh, archbishop?"

"Yes, sire." Cranmer bowed his head meekly. Oh, Anne Boleyn, he thought. Should you not bear his grace a prince you have, with your hasty and ill-considered words, signed your own death warrant.

The king, perhaps guessing at his thoughts, settled a padded and jeweled arm about the shrinking Cranmer's shoulders. "You know, Thomas, if the child the queen carries be a boy, only God and myself know how joyfully I shall welcome him. How grateful I shall be, how generous."

Cranmer looked into the king's face. He noted its too florid hue, the lines of dissipation beneath the pouched eyes, the thin, cruel line of the lips, and he shuddered inwardly. Henry Tudor was far removed from the handsome prince he had once been, though it was clear that he still thought of himself so. Even the red hair beneath the lavishly jeweled cap was graying. "And if it is not a boy, your grace?"

"Why then, Thomas, I shall know what to do." The arm tightened about Cranmer's shoulders. "Aye, I shall know what to do."

"May I ask your grace's meaning?"

The king hesitated. The real reason for the trial of my lord Marchmont might have been kept secret from the general people in the streets, but there was no one at Court who did not know of his contention that Tudor Trigg was his own son, flesh of his flesh, born in legitimate marriage. But knowing it, and actually hearing him say it in their presence, were two very different things. And those others who knew very well his secret plans, did not dare to speak out. If Anne bore him a son, then Tudor Trigg, as he had vowed once before, would meet with a regrettable accident. If she failed him, he would claim Tudor by public proclamation. Tudor was not his son, and who should know that better than he. But there was royal Tudor blood in his veins. Aye, let Anne fail him, and Tudor was his heir. He would go further. He would find a way to rid himself of Anne Boleyn. He would take unto himself a new queen. If she bore him a son, there was still the little accident to fall back upon. The public would see him only as a sorrowing father. He would be blameless in their eyes. He glanced at Cranmer. Should he say something to him? Hint perhaps? Quickly, he put the temptation from him. Better to say nothing. He would wait and see. Cranmer was still looking at him with those pale eyes of his, waiting for him to speak. He gave a jovial laugh. "No, Thomas, you may not ask my meaning. For the truth is, I do not know myself. I was but making idle conversation."

Cranmer's heart lurched. Idle conversation? Nay, Henry Tudor was not one to make idle conversation. Was he thinking of Tudor Trigg? If Anne Boleyn bore him a daughter, would he actually dare to claim that boy? He dare not ask! It was his duty to speak, to protest, but he dare not.

The king glanced at him with narrowed eyes. There was something he could say to Cranmer. Something that would lay the groundwork for his plans in regard to Anne. Sighing, he said, "Ah, Thomas, Thomas, why did you fail me so miserably?"

"Your grace! In what way have I failed you?"

"In the most important way. I have not had the heart to rebuke you before, Thomas. But now I feel that I must speak out. Whilst planning my betrothal to Anne Boleyn, you failed to remember that I had previously had an intimate relationship with her sister, Mary."

Cranmer felt as if he had been struck a violent blow between the eyes. Cold horror filled him. What did he mean? What was he planning now? "M—M—Mary Boleyn, your grace?"

"The queen has only one sister."

A small spurt of courage came to Cranmer. Fixing his pale eyes on the king, he said, "But did not your grace remember the relationship with Mary Boleyn?"

The king regarded him for a long, frowning moment. "I see, Thomas." He reverted to formality. "We could not find it in our tender heart to rebuke you. Yet you, archbishop, do not scruple to rebuke your king."

Cranmer's courage withered. "Your grace has mistaken me. I offer no rebuke."

Tears welled into the king's eyes, those easy tears that he could summon at will. "We were in love, Thomas, and a man in love will oft shuffle aside the impediment to his happiness. That is what we did, for love, true love takes little note of details. Why did you not restrain us? Why did you not point out the error we had fallen into? 'Tis tragic indeed. We are in love. We are happily married. But now our conscience speaks out. It begins to harass us. What are we to do, Thomas?"

So that was it. If Anne Boleyn did not bear him a male child, he planned to be rid of her. He would use Mary Boleyn, his conscience, anything, but as he had done before, he would free himself from a distasteful marriage. But the blame must not be his. Never his! "Your grace," Cranmer said distractedly, "I must think."

"Think well, Thomas." Seeing that the man was opening his mouth to speak, he said quickly, "Seek not to comfort us in our tragedy, Thomas, for we cannot be comforted. We shall not punish you for your lapse of memory, though God knows we should. But, and mark us well, we ourself must be forever punished by God and our conscience."

"And if the queen should bear a prince," Cranmer said quietly, "what then, your grace?"

Henry blinked, but recovered himself quickly. "Why, Thomas, 'tis simple. It would be a sign that the good Lord had forgiven us our sin. He would be telling us that He desired us to go forward into happiness. It would be a mark of His favor to His humble and devoted servant, Henry Tudor."

Cranmer stared at him. It was his duty to reprove the king sternly. He should remind him that God did not work for Henry Tudor alone, but he could not bring himself to do it. He was not a brave man, he knew it well. He said, his voice trembling a little, "Your grace, God has ever cared for the devout of this earth."

"And the meek and the humble," the king reminded him. "For well do you know that we are most fortunately blessed with these virtues."

"It is indeed so, your grace."

The arm about Cranmer's shoulders grew heavier. "Let us stroll on, good Thomas. The wind grows cutting."

Good Thomas! Good dog! Cranmer thought bitterly. Walking silently beside the king, he was relieved to see Adam Templeton approaching. A bold, not altogether tactful young man, he had always considered him, but one who could usually be counted on to put the king in a good mood.

Seeing Adam, the king's arm dropped from Cranmer's shoulders. "So there you are, you scurvy dog," he cried in a loud, jovial voice. "And what do you here?"

Adam bowed. "I was seeking your majesty."

"You have found him." The king beamed on him fondly. "What are you after, knave, eh?"

"Some friendly conversation, sire, and your permission to absent myself from Court for a few hours."

"For what purpose?"

" 'Tis a family matter, sire. Nothing of great moment, I assure you."

Henry's beam faded slightly, and his eyes grew cold. "And no concern of your king. Is that what you would imply, my lord Somercombe?"

Adam smiled. "You have said it, sire, not I."

Cranmer trembled for the rash young man. He was relieved when Adam added lightly, "It is not a secret, sire. It is simply that my cousin, the Lady Mary Fernside, has invited me to see her newborn son."

The king's eyes darkened momentarily. "I remember the Lady Mary well. A bonny lass, and one I should like to see more often at Court. Tell her that."

"I will relay your message, sire."

"Excellent. Tell her, too, that I will send a christening gift for her son. What name has he?"

"He is not yet named."

"Henry would be a good choice. What say you to that name?"

Adam laughed. "It is a right good and noble name, sire. But what other reply could I make when the owner of that noble name stands before me?"

Cranmer studied him curiously. Somercombe was smiling, yet he had the feeling that the smile was but a surface thing. Certainly it was not reflected in his dark eyes. They looked, if anything, cold and watchful. He shot a sidelong look at the king, who, unaware of anything different in the quality of that smile, was still regarding him with affection.

"Rogue!" The king's twinkling blue eyes ran over Adam appraisingly. He was dressed for riding. He wore a short, black velvet robe with pipings of scarlet about the neck and the cuffs, and the long padded and puffed sleeves were slashed with the same color. His black cloak was lined with the vivid silk, and a flat black velvet cap adorned with a scarlet feather was set on his head at a jaunty angle. It was a combination of the gay and the sober again, the king thought. It suited Somercombe, but it was not to his own taste. "I see that once again there is not a jewel upon your person, Adam. I like it not that the people, seeing my lord Somercombe, will think that Henry Tudor keeps beggars about him."

Adam's dark brows rose quizzically as he eyed the king's costume. His gold robe with its raised silver flowers seemed literally ablaze with jewels. In the center of each flower was a large diamond, and the leaves of the flowers were composed of emeralds, pearls, sapphires, and rubies. His purple surcoat was lined and banded about the hem with ermine. His hose and his flat, diamond-embroidered cap was purple. "But then, sire," Adam answered softly, "the people, if faced with your own glory, would be entirely robbed of speech."

Cranmer expected the king's anger, but his smile was undiminished. He considered Adam's words to be a compliment to his looks and his taste in dress, and he was well pleased. "Aye, Adam, it might be so. They have a great affection for their king."

"But they do not know all of Henry Tudor, sire," Adam said smoothly.

The king's face clouded. " 'Tis true. They do not know the sad and heavy heart I carry within me." He sighed. "It would seem that others may be blessed with sons, but not I. I am again cursed with a barren wife."

Adam felt a surge of anger. Where is Madam Tudor and her brother? he thought. What have you done with them? Aloud, he said in the same lightly mocking voice with which he customarily addressed the king, "I would scarcely say barren, sire. Her grace has presented you with a beautiful princess. In the course of time, she will doubtless bear the prince of your desire."

"My lord Somercombe!" Cranmer's voice sounded almost shrill, so shocked was he at this blunt speaking. "I think you forget that you speak to the king."

The king, unoffended, cast him an impatient look. "You

106

bleat like a woman, archbishop. Have done, have done!" His eyes returned to Adam. "So you are of the opinion that England will shortly gain a prince?"

"It is not possible to look into the future, sire. But I believe it will be so."

"And I, sire," Cranmer put in eagerly. Seeing the king's faint frown, he added hastily. "Do I have your leave to retire?"

"You have it, my lord archbishop. Get you gone. Your sour face depresses me."

Cranmer, who had been smiling, felt deflated. "Yes, sire," he said meekly. Bowing, he went on his way, his robe flapping behind him.

The king stared after him. "That man and his cursed long nose," he growled, "it is forever sniffing around."

"But Cranmer's nose once sniffed to good purpose, sire. It showed you the way in which you might take Anne Boleyn to wife."

Even for Adam this was overbold, and the king's eyes took on a hard glare. "What mean you, my lord?"

"If I have offended, sire," Adam said, "I ask your forgiveness. I spoke only of that matter which all know."

"My marriage to Catherine of Aragon was no marriage, as well you know. The Lady Catherine was my brother's wife. It was mortal sin to take her in marriage and live with her, but what did I know of these things then? I was a mere lad, and vulnerable. Whilst Catherine, being so much older than I, was experienced in the ways of deception."

"Deception, sire?"

Henry glared at him. "Aye, my lord, that is what I said. Catherine's marriage with my brother was consummated. In plain words, the Lady Catherine lied to me. And now I am faced with yet another dilemma." His glare faded, and his direct look invited Adam to speak.

"If it is your wish to tell me about it, sire, I would be honored to have your confidence."

The king nodded. "I confided in you once before. Remember? I told you that I had been intimate with Mary Boleyn, Anne's sister."

"I remember, sire."

"Because of that old sin with Mary, I am sick with anxiety

lest my marriage to Anne prove to be no marriage after all. And there is another thing. Have you heard the rumors that the queen was first pledged to Henry Percy?"

"Pre-contract, you mean." Adam shrugged. "Aye, sire, I have heard the rumors. I believe them to be false. No doubt they were put about by malicious people who hope to disrupt your grace's marriage to serve their own ends."

Henry's face reddened and his eyes gleamed dangerously. "You think that, do you?"

"I do, sire. I know it must please you that I decline to believe that the mother of our future prince is guilty of these charges."

Henry was not pleased. He was suddenly furiously angry and full of malice. He loved this man well, but there were times when his smooth tongue disturbed him. There were even times when he had the monstrous suspicion that he was secretly laughing at him. On the heels of this last thought there came a wish to punish this suspected insolence. He had seen Somercombe's eyes on Mistress Trigg. If he had read their expression aright, my lord Somercombe was in love for the first time in his life. The king made up his mind quickly. He had denied it to the queen when she made inquiry, but despite this denial, he acknowledged to himself that Mistress Trigg and her brother were virtually prisoners. Tudor Trigg, because he must not be allowed to get beyond his grasp. And Mistress Trigg, because he desired her. Because he intended to have her! What a jest then to make Somercombe their jailer. Aye, Somercombe would see all too clearly that beside the glory of the king, his hopes of winning her were poor indeed. What woman would look at Somercombe when she might have the king? As their jailer, and Mistress Trigg's in particular, he would have the freedom of the apartments. He smiled inwardly. The freedom to suffer, too, when he realized that Mistress Trigg both loved and desired her king. He thought of the hatred in Mistress Trigg's eyes whenever she looked at him. Hastily he closed his mind against that particular mental picture. She would come to love him. No woman thus far had been able to resist him. By God, she had better love him, or it would be the worse for her!

"Your grace appears thoughtful."

The king started. Somercombe was looking at him curiously. "So you decline to believe the queen guilty of pre-contract with Percy," he said in a hearty voice. "And you are quite right, Adam, your belief in our queen pleases us well."

Adam noticed the lapse into formality. It showed the depths of the king's anger. "I am glad that you are pleased, sire."

"Naturally we are, naturally. You have relieved our mind to a considerable extent. But by the Rood, our queen had better bear us a prince, or else will we——" he broke off.

"I know what you would say, sire. You will have nothing in your heart but the loving wish to comfort the lady in her great disappointment. I am right, am I not? Your grace was about to say that?"

Henry's eyes narrowed. Insolence. He was almost sure of it. He would brook insolence from no man! "Of course!" he snapped. Then, gentling his tone, he added. "You know us well, Adam. We have ever been a compassionate man."

"Your grace does not need to tell me that."

There it was again, a faint but noticeable purr of insolence underlying his words. Well, he would await the return of my lord Somercombe before he acquainted him with his new duties. "You have asked leave to absent yourself from Court. Go then. You have our leave." Muttering to himself, he stumped away.

If there is no prince, Adam thought as he slowly followed, it will be off with Anne Boleyn, and onward to merry matrimony with Jane Seymour. Aye, you may cozen others, but not I. A sudden thought struck him, and his heart began a fast, angry beating. Would it be Jane Seymour or Madam Tudor?

Adam frowned. He would not think of that possibility. Not yet. But what would be the end of this coil? And should Anne Boleyn again disappoint the king, what was to become of her? Would the king sue for a divorce, this time on the grounds that Anne had first been pledged to Henry Percy?

He frowned. He had other things to think about at the moment. Things that were more important to him than Anne Boleyn's problems. For instance, where had Madam Tudor and her brother been placed? Knowing the king and the way he thought, they were unlikely to be too far away. It might even be that they were in some other part of the palace. The king would tell him in time, he was certain of that, for there was little he kept from him. But unless he guarded his mouth and trod warily, this state of affairs might not continue. He recalled the angry glitter in the king's eyes, and he cursed himself for a rash-tongued and tactless fool. But he would find them, and when he did, his first task must be to convince Madam Tudor of his sincerity and his genuine wish to help. He anticipated trouble there, so it was to be hoped that the lad would prove more reasonable than his sister. Out of respect for their sorrow, he had kept away from them as much as possible. They must, he had told himself, be given time to get over the first shock of their father's death. When he found himself in a room with them, he was polite but distant, making no attempt to engage them in conversation. But now, time became pressing. The queen's child might be born at any time. He must get them away as soon as possible. The devil of it was to think of a suitable plan.

Adam's eyes saddened as he thought of the earl of Marchmont. He had died bravely. His children might well be proud of such a father. His calm had been unshakable as he mounted the scaffold. He had said only a few words to the people who were assembled there to watch his end, and in them had been nothing of condemnation for the king. Just before he had knelt to place his head upon the block, his eyes had met Adam's. Those eyes had asked him a question, and he had nodded reassuringly by way of reply. So now it was up to him to keep his promise. After he had visited Mary and her newborn son, he would turn his mind to the problems. Still thoughtful, he came to his tethered horse. Mounting, he rode swiftly away.

Thomas Cranmer looked after the horse and rider, then he turned and made his slow way back to the palace.

From the shadow of the landing, Thomas Cromwell watched Cranmer's dignified entry. He hated the man, he thought. He would not put it past the little rat to attempt to poison the king's mind against him.

Beginning once more his interrupted descent of the stairs, Thomas Cromwell encountered the queen and her ladies. Bowing, he stood respectfully to one side.

The queen did not acknowledge his presence. She swept past him without a glance in his direction. Cromwell! She detested him! He frightened her, too. There was something so cold about him, so ruthless. She would not like to have him as her enemy.

At the top of the stairs, Anne halted, her hand gripping the carved balustrade. She felt suddenly very weak and faint. Hatred of Henry and his sordid little affairs had thus far carried her along, but now reaction had set in. Lady Rochford, who stood nearest to her, stepped forward another pace. Anne turned her head to look at her sister-in-law. "My lady Rochford," she said in a trembling voice, "pray order me a glass of wine. I am not feeling well."

"At once, your grace." Lady Rochford's lips were smiling, but her eyes were hostile.

Watching her smooth gliding walk as she rustled away, Anne shivered. Jane Rochford was her enemy, she always had been. But Jane was only one of many. She was surrounded by enemies.

"Is aught wrong, your grace?" Jane Seymour's soft voice said.

Is aught wrong? Incredible! The chit dared to ask her that. Biting back hysterical laughter, Anne answered steadily, "Nothing is wrong, Mistress Seymour."

"But your grace looks ill." Jane put out a hand as if to touch her. "Allow me to aid you."

Anne's tight control over herself was not proof against this blatant insincerity. "I advise you not to make a second attempt to hoodwink me, Mistress Seymour," she said in a freezing voice. "It would not be wise. But to answer you, no, you may not aid me. If I have my way, you will never aid me again."

Jane hung her head, looking like a rebuked child. But you will not have your way, Anne Boleyn, she thought. She followed after the queen, a small, secret smile touching her lips.

7

Seated on a brocade-covered couch in the main room of his sister's apartments, Tudor Trigg lounged at his ease. He had crossed one leg over the other in apparent casualness, but the truth was that he felt anything but casual. Yesterday, when the guard had come to remove them to these apartments in a lesser used part of the palace, he had demanded to know the meaning of the move. But for all his questioning, the guard would say only that it was his majesty's orders. His own apartments were situated in the next corridor, a little distance from his sister's. Today, for the first time in over a week, he had been allowed to pay her a private visit. They had seen each other many times, but they had not, before this, been allowed to be alone, or to hold conversation. Tudor glanced toward the door. Even now it would not surprise him to know that their every word was being noted. Worry nagged at him. "Madam Tudor," he said in a carefully lowered voice, "what do you think this move means?"

Corianne ceased her restless prowling about the room. Walking over to the couch, she seated herself beside him. "It means, Tudor, and I am sure I am not wrong, that until the queen's child is born, we are to be more closely guarded than before."

"But why?"

She should not have to tell him why, she thought impatiently. He should by now have reasoned it out for himself. She saw his look of bewilderment, and her eyes softened. "Listen to me, Tudor. I have a strong feeling that our fate depends upon the sex of the child. If it is a boy, and healthy, the king will have no further use for us."

"You mean that we shall be allowed to go free?"

Corianne stared at him for a moment. "You don't really

believe that, do you?" She waited for him to answer, but when he said nothing, she went on in a voice that shook slightly. "The king will not allow us to go free to tell our story. Even if we were not believed, he knows that there must be some doubt in the minds of the people. And Henry Tudor, being the kind of man he is, will not tolerate even the smallest shadow of doubt on his integrity. If the queen bears a male child, I have great fear that he will have us murdered, as he did our father!"

Tudor paled. "Nonsense! He would not do that. You are allowing your imagination to run away with you. Perhaps he will simply ask us for our promise to say nothing."

"The king trusts nobody."

Tudor put his arm about her quivering shoulders. "Come," he said gently, "this is not like you, Madam Tudor. Smile, please. I do not like to see you looking so frightened."

"But I am frightened!" she cried. "And you should be, too. I am certain he will have us executed."

"On what charge?"

Corianne drew away from him. "You know well that he can say anything he pleases against us," Corianne said bitterly. "Treason, perhaps, or anything else he may think up. If he can bring such a preposterous charge against our father, he will not hesitate to bring a charge of a different nature against us. The trial, like our father's, would be conducted in secrecy."

Tudor moved uneasily. "You have thought this all out very carefully, have you not?"

"Except for the company of the queen, now denied to me, I have spent much time alone. I have had little else to do but think."

Tudor nodded. "I confess, I did not think along the same lines. But many times I have thought of how we might escape."

"And?" Corianne said eagerly.

"And," Tudor said wryly, "as you might have expected from a thick-head like myself, I could not think of a plan. I must think harder. We must both think."

The flash of hope brought by Tudor's words vanished. "It is useless," she said in a dull voice, lapsing back into her former state of despair. "We are too well guarded. There are too many eyes to watch us and report our every word and movement." She fell silent. With a surge of bitterness she recalled her father's words on that last day of his life. "Adam will aid you, if he can," he had said, Her poor father, how deluded he had been. He had actually believed that my lord Somercombe would help them. Aid them! She had seen my lord Somercombe many times, and that great lord whom her father had trusted so well had scarcely deigned to glance her way. He had been stiffly aloof. It was as though, having done his treacherous work, there was no further need of a show of friendship.

"I refuse to believe there is no way out," Tudor broke in. "Have you forgotten what our father told you? He said my lord Somercombe would aid us. Perhaps, if we could speak to him, something might be accomplished."

"That man! Tudor, how can you be so stupid. Has he spoken to us beyond the normal courtesies required of him? Has he ever tried to approach us?"

"No. And yet our father was not usually wrong in his summing up of character. I cannot believe my lord Somercombe is as you believe him to be."

Corianne made an impatient movement. "In that you are like Father. He, too, was wont to believe the best of everybody."

"Perhaps. But you are too inclined to believe the worst."

"Let us not talk of my lord Somercombe," Corianne said savagely. "I hate the very sound of his name."

"He could not help bringing the warrant for father's arrest. How could he disobey the king?"

"He is the king's friend. They were in league."

Tudor gave an exasperated sigh. "You have no proof of that."

"All right!" Corianne glared at him. "Believe as you please." With a wave of her hand, she dismissed the subject of my lord Somercombe. "I think, Tudor, that we must try to soften the king's heart toward us."

"Well!" Tudor cried indignantly. "You condemn my lord Somercombe on all counts. Yet you would try to soften the heart of a man you should hate before all others."

"Oh do be quiet! You just don't understand. Of course I hate him, and always will. But we must have time. I cannot think of a way of escape, but if there is one, we will find it. But we need time."

Tudor looked at her uncertainly. "Then what must we do?"

"For a beginning, you must stop angering the king with your sullen attitude. Your manner tells him that you do not believe for a moment that you are his son. You must pretend to believe it."

"What!"

"Yes, yes, you must," Corianne cried eagerly. "The more I think of it, the more I see that it is the only way. We must lull his suspicions. Before the queen's child is born, we will have thought of a way to escape."

"You are suddenly very optimistic."

"We will think of a way because we must. You must tell the king that you believe you are his son. You must apologize for your attitude."

"I see." Tudor's voice was grim and his eyes dark with suspicion. "And you, Madam Tudor? What will you do to soften his heart?"

"I will be as he wishes me to be. Soft and warm and tender. I will play on his ridiculous vanity. I will pretend to love him, and——" She broke off with a gasp as Tudor gripped her wrist.

"You will do nothing of the sort, Madam Tudor. For I vow to you that if that man touches you, then king or no king, I will try my best to kill him."

Corianne stared at him. He was thoroughly roused, and he looked quite capable of carrying out his threat. She felt a quiver of terror as she thought of what must happen to him if he laid hands on the king's person. "Listen to me," she said soothingly. "You cannot believe that I would actually allow the king to bed me?"

"You did try that."

"But never again. Somehow I will manage to hold him off. A few kisses perhaps, but nothing more. You may trust me."

"I trust you. It is the king I do not trust."

"I will manage, I tell you. I will promise everything, but give nothing. I will appeal to his conscience. How can I let him love me when the queen is about to bear his child? But after the birth, ah, that will be a different story."

Tudor ran exasperated fingers through his bright hair.

"You women are so damned devious!" He fell silent for a moment, then he said thoughtfully, "It is said that the king's conscience must be above reproach. If that is what you mean to appeal to, then it might be done."

"You will do it?"

"I will try. But if you allow him to———"

"I will not."

Still doubtful, Tudor nodded. "All right, then."

Corianne opened her mouth to answer, then closed it again as a rapping sounded on the door. Her startled eyes met Tudor's, and the same thought was in both their minds. Had they been overheard? Before Corianne could rise, the door opened and the earl of Somercombe strolled into the room.

"You!" Corianne jumped to her feet. "What do you want?"

Adam closed the door behind him. "A very good day to you both," he said, approaching them.

"Why are you here?" Corianne cried.

"If you will lower your voice, Mistress Trigg, I will tell you." His dark eyes smiled into hers. "You see before you your new jailer."

"What!"

"I thought you would be pleased."

"My lord," Tudor rose to his feet. "What is your meaning?"

"Exactly what I have said. The king has appointed me your jailer. He did not put it quite like that, of course, but his meaning was clear." He drew a small chair up to the couch. Seating himself, he went on, "And now, if you will both be good enough to follow my example, I think we must have a little talk."

Tudor sank down on the couch. Corianne, after a moment's hesitation, sat down beside him. "And now, my lord Somercombe, what is it you want of us?" she said in a hard voice.

Adam smiled. "From you, Madam Tudor, many things, but that is in the future. For the moment all I ask of you both is strict obedience. In other words, from this moment on you will do exactly as I tell you to do. Do you understand?"

"No!" Corianne glared at him. "And do not call me Madam Tudor."

"I beg your pardon."

Tudor placed a warning hand on Corianne's knee. "My lord, if you would care to explain."

"Tudor!" Corianne said sharply. "I care not that the king has made him our jailer, you will pay no attention to this man. He is a bully and a traitor and a——"

"A king's toady," Adam supplied calmly. "You must not forget that one, Madam Tudor."

"I won't forget it. You may be sure of that."

"It is of little moment what you call me," Adam said in the same calm voice, "providing you obey me in all things."

"I will do nothing of the sort!"

"You will, Madam Tudor, I assure you. Now then, to business. I intend to get you away from here, if it can be managed."

"My lord!" Tudor cried.

"Keep your voice down, lad. Be assured that I will think of a way. It was your father's wish that I should get you to France. And, if it be possible, that is what I intend to do."

The eagerness faded from Tudor's face. "Then you have no plan."

"Not yet. But do not look so downcast, lad. When I set my mind to something, I am usually successful."

Tudor's smile returned, and with it much of the confidence that Corianne's cold statement of facts had managed to crush. His blue eyes sparkled, and he had an urge to be up and doing. "I believe you, my lord!"

"You believe easily, Tudor," Corianne said coldly. "But for my part, I do not believe one word. As for you, my lord Somercombe, I wish to hear no more."

Adam leaned forward in his chair. "I ask you not to try me too far, Madam Tudor," he said quietly. "I am, unfortunately, a man of little patience. Add to that the fault of a hasty and extremely hot temper, and you will begin to grasp my meaning."

"If you think to frighten me, my lord, you are wasting your time. I repeat, I do not believe you. I will never believe a word you say!"

"Madam Tudor, will you close your stupid mouth!" Tudor said fiercely. "Try using your brains for once. My lord Somercombe would hardly come here and say what he has

117

said if he did not mean it. He knows well we could betray him if we wished."

Adam smiled. "Quite right, lad. I have a feeling I shall be glad of your support."

"It is a trap," Corianne retorted hotly. "And if you cannot see that, then you are the stupid one."

"What kind of a trap?"

"I don't know. But I feel that it is."

"Madam Tudor, don't be such a fool!"

Adam did not seem to be listening to the low-voiced argument between them. His ears had caught a bustle in the corridor, and he guessed who came this way. "Madam Tudor," his voice cut across the argument. "Do you really intend to betray me?"

Her eyes met his, defiant and hot with anger. "I do, my lord. And will, at the first opportunity that offers. As you did to my father, so I will do to you."

Adam experienced a sudden longing to strike her. Mastering himself, he got to his feet. "In that case, you are about to be given the opportunity. Listen. They cry the coming of the king."

Corianne's face changed. "The king! He is coming here?"

Adam nodded. "I would imagine that such is his grace's intention."

Corianne's arrogance crumbled. "But—but why?" she sounded like a frightened child.

Adam hooked his thumbs in the slim, jeweled belt that decorated his dull gold tunic. "If you ask me to guess," he said, regarding her with eyes grown hard and wary, "he comes in the hope of claiming something from you which the queen's protection has hitherto denied him."

"Madam Tudor!" It was a low-voiced warning from Tudor. "Do nothing stupid."

Corianne stiffened. "I will do as I please. Remember our conversation, and follow my lead."

"I did not mean that. I urge you to say nothing about my lord Somercombe's proposal."

"As to that, I am determined, Tudor."

They stood there in silence, waiting—Tudor fuming inwardly, Corianne, as she said, determined. And Adam, still with that longing to strike her, to beat some sense into her stubborn head, feeling the building of his anger.

The voices outside rose to a high pitch of excitement, and above the voices, the booming sound of the king's laughter. The door burst open. Unannounced, resplendent in crimson silk and silver lace, his person sparkling with jewels, the king marched into the room. He regarded the bowing Adam and Tudor with a trace of annoyance. He had quite forgotten Adam's possible presence, as he had forgotten that he had given permission for the lad to visit with his sister. His sandy brows drew together in a frown. It was Anne's fault. Her constant hysterical tears and his own fears for the child tended to make his memory faulty these days. But perhaps it was as well they were here. He had wanted to see Madam Tudor alone, but it might, however, be wise to keep Anne calm until she had borne his child. Therefore he must limit his visits. He glanced at Tudor Trigg and his annoyance increased. Such a tall, well-set-up lad, but those fine features did not seem to go with his build. Marchmont features. He turned quickly from the thought. His kindling eyes rested first on Adam, then on Madam Tudor. His spurt of annoyance faded and his eyes grew soft. How lovely she was. Far lovelier than Anne had ever been. In her white silk gown with its underskirt of Tudor-green, she was like a water lily set against the rich red and gold luxury of the room. He himself went forward to raise her from her curtsey. "And shall beauty kneel before me?" he said in a hearty voice. "Nay, nay, I will not have it so."

"Your majesty. How I have longed to see you!"

The king was momentarily stunned. There was no hatred in Madam Tudor's eyes. They were soft and warm with promise. He felt a tremor of doubt, but he dismissed it instantly. Her father was dead. There could be no trickery now. Well, had he not known she would come to it? How could she stand out against Henry Tudor's desire? It had never been hatred he had seen in her eyes, but caution. He should have remembered, with her father recently dead, she could not, for appearance's sake, respond to his ardor. And all this time she had been longing for him. But her waiting was over now. Even as he thought it, he had a sudden flashing glimpse of Anne's white face. He heard once more the spiraling of her hysterical laughter. Or, he amended hastily, the waiting would be over once the child was born. It should be soon now. He, who had never liked to wait for anything, must school himself to patience. It was for the unborn child's sake. Only for his. But in the meantime there would be no harm done if he took a kiss from such lovely lips. Heedless of the other two, he drew her into his arms. "Why, sweetheart," he said in a tender voice, "why do you tremble? Does your king awe you so much?"

"Sire, your presence does awe me, as it must all. But awe alone is not the cause of my trembling." Her eyes flashed to Adam's face. "That man, he—he——," she broke off as Tudor took a quick step forward. Adam did not move. His face was impassive.

His eyes narrowing, the king looked from one to the other. "Well, Mistress Trigg?"

Corianne drew in a deep, gasping breath. She could not do it! Hate my lord Somercombe she did, but she had no stomach for betrayal. "Sire, I would make complaint. My lord Somercombe, in his zeal, is overharsh. He has ordered me to obey him in all things, and I like it not."

The king was surprised and a little disappointed. Somercombe, harsh? Had he been mistaken in his belief that Somercombe was in love with the wench? No, he was not mistaken. He was never mistaken. It was early days yet. There was time enough for him to suffer when he saw the wench fall ever deeper in love with her king. He hugged Corianne to him, his hearty laughter ringing out. "So he has been harsh with you, eh sweetheart? Worry not. Your king will rebuke him. Adam, you dog! What do you mean by it? You will not be harsh with this little wench. After all, you must look to your future. Someday this lady may be very important. You would not have her remember such a thing against you, would you?"

Adam's lips tightened. The king's meaning was clear. If Anne failed him, it would not be Jane Seymour he took to wife, but Madam Tudor. His Madam Tudor! For she was his, stubborn and maddening though she was. But he needed time to turn her heart his way. He forced his stiff lips to smile. "No indeed, sire. I would not have her remember that. I will gentle my approach."

"See that you do." The king's beam rested on Tudor, and he saw with a shock of surprise and pleasure that the lad was smiling. No more sullens, then? He was beginning to accept. He was coming his way. A fine lad, a healthy lad, such as he had always longed for. It would be a pity if he had to die to make way for the real prince. A great pity. But what must be must be.

With the king's eyes on him, Tudor flushed. Damned if he liked this plan of Madam Tudor's, but he would give it a try. It might be that a pleasant attitude would be of help to my lord Somercome, too. He made up his mind. "Sire, may I speak?"

"Of course, my son."

Tudor winced. Not his son. Never his! "When your majesty has the time to spare, might I request an audience? I have something that I must say."

The king's beam increased. Aye, he thought, and I know what you would say. You have been thinking. You have realized the grandeur of the prospect held out to you. If the time should come, you will speak out exactly as I wish. "You may have your audience in a few moments." Smiling at Madam Tudor, he pressed his lips to hers. "I will come again, sweetheart," he whispered. "I will come as soon as I may." Releasing her, he turned to Tudor. "Come, my son, we will walk in the gardens. You shall tell me all that is in your heart and mind."

Tudor's eyes met Corianne's. She smiled at him encouragingly. His heart heavy and full of hatred toward this tyrant who had murdered his father, Tudor stepped forward. "Thank you, sire."

The king's heavy arm settled about Tudor's shoulders. "Almost as tall as I," he murmured fondly, leading him to the door.

Adam did not speak until the hullabaloo that must always attend the king's progress had died away. Then he moved toward Corianne. "Why, Madam Tudor?" he said, placing his hands lightly on her shoulders. "Why did you not betray me?"

She stared into his eyes for a moment. "It was not for love of you, you may be sure," she flashed.

"Then why?"

She struck his hands away. "Because unlike you, my lord Somercombe, I am no traitor!"

"Do you really believe that of me?"

Why did he look at her like that? He was angry, she could tell that from the grim line of his jaw. Yet she could swear it was hurt that looked from his eyes. "Yes, yes, I do," she cried. "I have told you so often enough."

"So you have. For the moment, since you seem to wish it so ardently, I will relieve you of my hateful presence." He bowed and turned away.

Corianne waited until the door had closed behind him before sitting down. Oddly, she felt no sense of triumph. Instead, she felt guilty. Indignant color flushed her cheeks. That man had actually made her feel guilty! That man! That scoundrel!

There was a sound outside the door. She jumped quickly to her feet. So my lord Somercombe had decided to return, had he? He was coming back to taunt her again. Her eyes sparkled and she felt an uplifting of her heart. Let him come. She was ready and eager to do battle.

The sound died away. She listened intently. It was not he, after all. It was only the pacing of the guard she had heard. She sat down slowly. She felt deflated, disappointed. Disappointed? Nonsense! Frowning heavily, she doggedly applied herself to the task of reasoning the feeling away. There was, she told herself, always a reason for everything.

8

"The king is mad! His incessant longing for a son has driven his reason away!"

With the queen so near to her confinement, the gossip that had raged in Greenwich Palace flared up again. The Princess Elizabeth had been removed from her mother's care. If the queen failed in her duty to bear a son, was it true that Tudor Trigg was to be made heir to the throne? What claim had this boy to the throne? Some said that he was the true son of the earl of Marchmont. Others said that he was the king's bastard. But the king said, it was rumored, that the boy was his legitimate son. What was true, what false? These days, Tudor Trigg was seen everywhere with the king. But suppose he was the king's bastard, just suppose. Were they going to allow the king to foist his bastard upon the throne of England? He had wanted to place his other bastard, the duke of Richmond, in the succession. But Richmond was obviously due for an early grave. A weakling would not answer the king's purpose. But Tudor Trigg, robust with health, would. If the tales going around were true, then let the king prove the boy legitimate. Let him prove it! They thought of the Princess Mary, long ousted from her place in the succession. And what of the Princess Elizabeth? Was she too destined to follow in her half-sister's unhappy footsteps? Should the Tudor Trigg crisis really make itself felt, should he stand in the shadow of the throne, how did the king's ministers propose to deal with it?

The queen was fully aware of the danger Tudor Trigg represented to her daughter, just as she was aware of all the whispering that went on behind her back. Now, as she made her way along the corridor, she looked neither to the right or the left. Her head held high, color flaring in her pale cheeks, her cream and gold skirts rustling, she walked steadily on,

123

unaware, it seemed, of the obeisances of the ladies and gentlemen passing by. Let them go on whispering about her, she thought angrily. All the members of the Court were wondering, she knew, how she was going to take this Tudor Trigg threat to her infant daughter. And, of course, if her child was not a boy, to that child also.

Seething with anger and fear, Anne paused before the door that led to the king's apartments. The gossip had died down, but now it rose up again loud and clear. She must do something about it. She would fight for Elizabeth, and, if need be, her unborn child. Did Henry really think she would allow her children to be thrust aside for Tudor Trigg? Her anger at this prospect triumphed over fear, carrying her unannounced into the king's presence.

The king, deep in conversation with the earl of Somercombe, glared at Anne as she advanced toward him. "We did not hear you announced, madam," his voice was heavy with sarcasm.

Anne acknowledged Adam's presence with a small, tight smile. He was the only one who dared argue with the king, but even he could not go too far. He was sympathetic to her, she knew. It might be that she could enlist his aid.

Anne curtsied. "Pray forgive the intrusion, sire. I would speak with you on a matter of some importance."

Henry waved his hand impatiently. "Speak then, madam."

Anne stole another glance at Adam. "In private, sire, if it please you."

"It does not please me. There is nothing you can say that my friend and confidante may not hear."

"If your majesty will give me leave to retire," Adam said quickly, "I will return when her grace has concluded her conversation."

Henry moved his bulk in the chair. "Have done, my lord. You will stay."

Adam shrugged. "As your majesty pleases."

"Get on with it, madam," Henry ordered, his red brows meeting in a frown.

Anne looked at him with cold eyes. He was magnificently dressed in a rose satin doublet and a white velvet surcoat, the wide cuffs of which were banded with diamonds and the sleeves slashed with purple and green. His green hose were clocked with purple and his flat, white velvet cap, ablaze with diamonds, rubies, and emeralds, sported an orange plume.

"Did you come here to stare, madam, or to talk?" Henry said harshly.

"To talk, sire," she answered, "on the matter of Tudor Trigg."

Henry's face changed. "What of him?"

"You know well, sire, that he cannot be your legitimate son."

"Do I?" Henry leaned toward her, his face so close that she could see the little networks of broken veins in his puffy face. A muscle twitched at the side of his mouth. "A father knows his own son, madam," he said savagely. He sat back in the chair. "There is no more to say. You may leave us."

She ignored him. "Is it true that you intend to place this boy in the line of succession?" Her voice was high-pitched, touched with hysteria.

"It is true, madam." Henry's tight lips relaxed into a small, cruel smile. "Is aught else troubling you?"

Anne's long, pointed nails dug into the palms of her hands. "'Tis madness, Henry! What of our daughter? What of the cruel smile. "Is aught else troubling you?"

"There are some who say that your daughter, madam, bears a remarkable likeness to Sir Henry Norris. Might it not be that your next child will likewise bear the stamp of Norris's features?" he paused for a significant moment, "or mayhap Wyatt's?"

Anne swayed. Had it not been for Adam, who had sprung forward to aid her, she would have fallen. She seemed unaware of Adam's supporting arms. "How cruel you are!" she said in a shaken whisper. "I have ever been faithful to you. Elizabeth is our daughter. How can you seek to deny her, who is cast in your own mold?"

Henry's eyes narrowed to blue slits. "In my own mold? I vow, madam, I have not remarked it."

Anne drew herself gently from Adam's arms. "What of the coming child? Will you likewise deny him his rights?"

"Him?" Henry had forgotten the need to keep his queen calm. In the hatred that possessed him now, his only wish was to taunt and wound. "Him indeed! Do you truly believe you carry a prince within that skinny body of yours?"

"It might well be." Her voice quivered.

Henry laughed unpleasantly. "Thus far you have given to Henry of England one puling girl child. There was that other child, of course. But, unfortunately, it was conceived only in your imagination. What will you offer to your king this time? Another girl? A dead child?"

Tears of rage and weakness filled Anne's eyes. Thank God that Adam could be trusted! Had anyone else but he been present, how could she have endured this humiliation? She swallowed. "That is in God's hands, sire," she managed.

Henry's malicious eyes were fixed on her face. "Since God has chosen to bestow upon His good and faithful servant, Henry Tudor, yet another girl, perhaps His message is in it."

"What d—do you mean?"

"I mean, madam, that perhaps He is telling me, as with Catherine, that I have again chosen the wrong path. If you should bear me another girl, it will be His warning that I must find the right path."

Anne stared at him with horror in her dark eyes. "My lord king!" she cried out. "You would not forsake me?"

"Never, madam, if you will only give me my son!"

"And if I do, what then of Tudor Trigg?"

"I will say only this to you. Tudor is my own dear son. Yet, because I was cheated of the precious years of his growing, the child of your body would seem more of my own. There will be no trouble from Tudor. He will willingly stand aside for a healthy prince. He has not been reared to expect the crown, you see."

Anne's hands clenched at her sides. Liar! Hypocrite! Tyrant! "Thank you, sire," she said in a controlled voice. "You have answered my question."

"So I have." His mood changed. The multicolored fires of the jewels on his cap glittered in a shaft of sunlight as he leaned forward to caress her cheek. "So I have, my clever Anne. With your womanly wiles you have forced an answer from me. Give me my boy, Anne, 'tis all I ask of you. Put a son in my arms and you shall not suffer."

He kissed the top of her dark head. "Think no more of Tudor Trigg. He should not concern you."

But Tudor Trigg will be waiting, Anne thought. If I should bear a son and he prove weak and sickly, this interloper will be an ever-present menace. "I will not think of him again, Henry," she said quietly.

His arms crushed her closer. "When I hold my son in my arms, sweetheart, I will know that God has blessed our union. That it is right and good in His eyes."

Adam saw the pallor of Anne's face. Poor Anne! What would be her fate if she disappointed the king?

"Well, my love," he heard Henry say, "have I made you happy again?"

"So happy," Anne said in a dead voice. "So very happy, my lord king!"

Adam was stabbed with pity for her. It was obvious to him that she had an idea of her fate, should she fail to bear a male child. Poor Anne Boleyn! She had climbed so high that her fall, when it came, would be shattering. As for Henry, he would be embittered, but he would get over both bitterness and disappointment. He had, or thought he had, Tudor Trigg for the succession. Tudor was all eagerness to be away now. But would he stand firm? Would such a young lad be able to resist the glittering allure of all that would be offered to him? And Madam Tudor? If Henry was disappointed in love with Madam Tudor, he had yet another card to play. He had Jane Seymour. Crafty Jane, who eagerly awaited her call to the royal bed but who insisted that it must be a marriage bed. Like Anne, Jane had used her virginity to shield her from Henry's ardent pursuit. But, unlike Anne, she would maintain that virginity until the marriage service was pronounced. Jane's brothers were ambitious. If they had their way they would, through Jane, reach the heights. Adam turned and made his way to the door.

The king's sharply rebuking voice arrested him. "Where do you go, my lord? We have not yet dismissed you."

Adam turned and came back. "I had thought your grace would like some privacy." He smiled. "Was I wrong, sire?"

Henry's arms released Anne. "Look at his face, Anne. It is a sullen dog we have here, eh sweetheart? I am not deceived, you see, by his smiles or his glib words. It is plain to me that he envies his king his beautiful wife. You should pity him, Anne, the pangs of his love. For you do have a little fondness for this dog, do you not?"

Madness to speak, Anne knew, but she could not seem to

stop words from spilling from her lips. "I trust your grace will not imagine a likeness to my lord Somercombe in the features of our newborn child."

The king's small, suspicious blue eyes darted from Anne's appalled face to Adam's imperturbable one. "What is the meaning of your words, madam?" he barked. "Have you been practicing your witch's wiles on our good friend Adam?"

Anne's mouth opened and closed, but no words came. Adam said smoothly, "I believe, sire, that her grace's humor being almost comparable to your own, she was attempting to make a like jest."

Henry cleared his throat loudly. "Believe that, do you?" A smile lit his face. "Her grace has not such a ready wit as myself. Almost did I believe her to be serious."

"But I did not, sire."

"Scoundrel! I believe you would attempt to teach us the nature of our own wife."

"Nay, sire. I would not so presume."

"Aye, you would. Damn your eyes, Adam, but I like your spirit!" He turned to Anne. "What say you, sweetheart?"

Anne smiled upon Adam with relief and gratitude. " 'Tis well you have such men about you, sire. Else would your majesty have no one on whom to sharpen his wits."

" 'Tis so." Henry beamed upon her. "Now get you gone, madam. I have much to discuss with my lord Somercombe."

Anne curtsied. Henry looked at the dark fans of her lashes against the smooth ivory of her skin, the shadowed cleavage between her breasts, and his desire for her, which had been tepid of late, rose strongly. "It may be that I will be with you sooner than I thought to be, Anne sweetheart," he said in an uneven voice.

Her eyes smiled into his. "Then am I happy, dear lord."

Henry watched her glide gracefully through the door, then he turned back to Adam. "About Madam Tudor and my—my son. Have they everything they desire? Are their apartments comfortable?"

"Most comfortable, sire. Unfortunately, however, they continue to wonder why they are not allowed more freedom. They seem to consider that they are prisoners."

How like Somercombe, Henry thought angrily, to attempt

to destroy the new relationship between himself and Tudor. "That is nonsense, my lord," Henry said petulantly. "Of course they are not prisoners. I have my own reasons for confining them to their apartments, reasons that I do not intend to discuss with you. When I see fit, and only when I see fit, they will both be free to wander where they will."

Adam understood him perfectly. Tudor's head would roll if Anne bore a son. Madam Tudor played with the king at the moment. But once he came to realize that he had been deceived by sweet smiles, a few kisses, it was more than likely she would follow her brother to the block. Adam's heart lurched at the very thought. To cover his emotion, his hand went to the key that dangled from his belt. "I am still their jailer, sire. They do not love me for it."

Henry's smile was malicious. "You should thank me, my lord, for the chance it gives you to be near the wench. I had thought you had some interest in her."

So that was it, Adam thought. It was to punish him for some fault that he had been given the position of jailer. His anger rose. Believing that he cared for her did not prevent the king from taking Madam Tudor into his arms. Under his very eyes, he would kiss her. And the wench, curse her! She was all smiles and soft talk. She thought she was being so clever. But, unless she was very careful, she would find that same cleverness had led her into a trap from which she could not extricate herself. He had been appalled when Tudor had told him of Madam Tudor's scheme. There was no doing anything with her. She would have her way despite anything he might say. From time to time he believed that it was well to lull the king's suspicion. But at other times, those in particular when the king held her in his arms, he was not so sure. Crushing down his anger, he answered in a slow, careful voice, "Even had I some interest in Mistress Trigg, sire, which I assure you I do not, I could hardly expect to find favor in her eyes when I am forced to keep locked both her apartment and that of her brother."

"You will not call him her brother!"

"Your pardon, sire. I wonder if your majesty would consider leaving their doors unlocked?"

"I would not consider it for a moment, my lord," Henry

said flatly. "You have your orders. Carry them out as instructed."

"There are plenty of guards, sire. Surely such precautions are unnecessary."

Henry stiffened. "We do not care to listen to argument, my lord Somercombe." Muttering, he turned about and limped over to his chair. Seating himself, he stretched out his ulcerated leg. His pain slightly relieved by this position, he began to chuckle. "Ah, Adam, Adam, rogue that you are! Who else but you would dare to argue with the king?"

"One other, sire. I have heard that Thomas Seymour dares."

Henry nodded. "Aye, he does. Tom is just another brazen coxcomb as yourself. But however amusing it may be at the time, a man may go too far." Frowning, he rubbed his leg. "God's curse on this pain! I swear that it grows worse with every passing second."

"I am sorry to hear that, sire. In regard to Mistress Trigg, may not her door, at least, be left unlocked?"

"My lord, I have told you that a man may go too far. Be warned that my good nature is not limitless. Her door remains locked. I have plans for that maiden."

Adam started. "Might I ask the nature of those plans, sire?"

"I have no objection to telling you. There is something about the chit that stirs me strangely. Remembering that lovely face, I could almost believe myself to be falling in love for the first time."

The king looked up and saw the mocking smile on Adam's face. "And we want to hear no words from you, my lord!"

Adam waited. There was much he did not know about Henry Tudor, but he knew his vanity well. His spurt of anger would very soon be swallowed up in the need to talk about himself and the loves in his life.

"Adam, lad," Henry began emotionally, "I would that I were but an ordinary man. But from the day I was born, I was different. Not because I had been born to royalty, but because of my outstanding looks. The Golden Prince, I was called. As I grew to manhood, women were irresistably drawn to me. 'Twas not for my royalty, you understand, but for myself alone. Catherine adored me."

"I can well believe it, sire," Adam said suavely.

Henry sighed. "Yes, Catherine adored me. And I returned her love, of course, even though she was so much older than myself. How could I know that she had deceived me, she who put such a high price on her nonexistent virginity. When I was forced to recognize that our marriage was, under God's law, illegal and immoral, it broke my heart. It quite shattered me when I found that I must part with my dear lady."

"I am sure it did, sire."

"There were some who considered me overanxious to be done with my marriage, but 'twas not so. I had my duty to God, and to the nation, who had a right to expect an heir. My nature is somewhat sensitive, lad, and my conscience tender. I am not of the material for sinning."

Adam looked blandly at the king. "I pray your grace to continue."

"So, as you know, I turned for comfort to Anne Boleyn. In her arms, I found a measure of forgetfulness." Another sigh caught him. "But Anne, too, disappointed me. I tell you this in confidence, Adam, for well do you know the trust I repose in you. My Anne, she whom I worship, has turned into a nagging, screaming virago."

Adam had heard it all before, but he contrived to look sympathetic.

"I am, as you know, Adam," the king went on, "of a too gentle disposition. I cannot find it in my heart to rebuke her."

Adam marveled. Did he really believe that?

"A man must have love in his life, Adam, for without it he would perish. I bestowed a little of my starved heart on Mistress Jane Seymour. But now I find that I am indeed in love, but not with Jane."

Adam could feel anger rising. "Not with Mistress Seymour, sire?"

"Your tone is curt, my lord. Have I said aught to offend?"

"Could your majesty offend?"

"We do not care for our question to be answered with a question, my lord Somercombe."

"I pray your grace to forgive me."

Henry stared at him fixedly. "We find there is a strangeness in your manner that is not altogether pleasing."

"Again I must pray your grace to forgive me."

"Is it possible that you dare to laugh at us, my lord?"

"Never, majesty. But I know, were I to offend, that you, with your gentle and sensitive nature, would readily forgive me."

"You overstep the bounds of our good nature!" Henry barked.

"But I am bewildered, your grace. If my manner appeared insolent, it must be because I was carried away by my interest in your majesty's colorful life."

"Mayhap." Henry looked at him uncertainly. "But there are times when I find you overbold."

"I am indeed distressed that you should find me so, sire." The tone of Adam's vioce was smoothly conciliatory. "Will you not go on, sire? You were about to tell me of your love for someone other than Mistress Seymour."

Henry frowned. He was of a mind to curtly dismiss the earl from his presence, but the urge to talk about himself proved stronger. "Aye. We find ourself deeply in love with Madam Tudor."

Such fury rose in Adam then that he was forced to look away least it showed in his eyes. "Then 'tis a pity, sire, that your love can never flourish. Your majesty will not have forgotten that he is a married man?"

"Nay. And we do not need you to remind us, my lord! But we know well that Anne is not the wife for us. However, should her grace present us with an heir, then, for the sake of the prince, she will remain at our side, even though we love her not."

"And Madam Tudor, sire?"

"She will be but a fragrant memory. But mark us well. A man, even though he be a king, has a right to happiness. If I am again disappointed, it will be my right to seek happiness elsewhere."

"Does your majesty mean that you would make Madam Tudor your queen?"

Again Henry resorted to formality. "Our plans are no concern of yours, my lord. But yes, we would greatly desire to make the lady our queen."

"And has your majesty spoken of his love to the lady?"

"Nay, lad, we have merely hinted. Madam Tudor is shy.

She does not respond as we would have her do. We would not have her overwhelmed by the honor we would pay her. Therefore, we will woo her first." Henry gave him a sly look. "We know, my lord, that you would wish our wooing to prosper."

A soft knock sounded on the door, saving Adam the necessity of replying.

"Ah, Cromwell," the king said, as the man entered. "You come in good time. We have a matter of importance we would discuss."

His swarthy, pock-marked face impassive, Thomas Cromwell came to kneel before the king. "Would it be the same matter we have discussed before, sire?"

"Aye. Get up, man, get up." Henry said impatiently.

Cromwell rose obediently. He shot a swift glance at Adam before turning his eyes back to the king.

"Leave us, my lord Somercombe." Henry waved a ringed hand. "We would talk privately with our good Thomas."

Adam bowed, keenly aware that Cromwell's eyes were again upon him. Making his way to the door, he wondered if the king plotted with Cromwell to remove the queen from his life? He did not trust the man. Cromwell, he felt sure, if called upon to do so, would, if he could not find evidence against Anne Boleyn, manufacture it. If Henry desired to end his marriage, then he would be only too eager to oblige his royal master.

Shivering in the chill wind that swept the corridor and stirred the red and gold banners on the walls, Adam drew his fur-lined cloak closer about him. How far, he wondered, was the king prepared to go to rid himself of an unwanted wife?

Hearing music drifting up from the great hall, Adam leaned over the gallery rail. He saw the queen, surrounded as usual by her ladies. The daylight was fast fading, and the candles had been lit. Their light flickered across her animated face as she laughed with Tom Seymour. Seymour was leaning very close, his mouth to her ear.

"I rarely wear the pearls, Tom," Adam heard her say. "Those great ropes do not suit me, for I have such a little neck."

Such a little neck! Adam drew back and went on his way. But for some reason he was unable to define, her words had

133

disturbed him. He could hear them being repeated in his brain. "Such a little neck—such a little neck." He thought of Thomas Cromwell with his sly, dark eyes and his cruel mouth, and he had the mad impulse to return and warn Anne. To say to her, "Guard yourself, madam, against the king, your husband, and against Thomas Cromwell, who is your enemy!"

9

Corianne looked up as Adam entered the room. She regarded him for a long, cold moment, then turned her head away. The walls about her were hung with rich tapestries, but there was one in particular, a hunting scene embroidered in vivid, unreal colors, that seemed to be engaging her full attention. Refusing to look in his direction, she continued to study it with an almost fierce determination.

So much for the slight softening he had lately thought he detected in her manner, Adam thought wryly. He looked at the gown she was wearing, Vaguely, he recognized it as belonging to one of the queen's ladies. For some reason known only to the king, Madam Tudor had not been allowed to send for her own clothes. She was therefore forced to borrow where she could. The gown suited her. It was of a deep blue satin. The peaked bodice was worked with silver thread into a design of flowers. The neckline, the cuffs of the long, tight sleeves, and the hem of the wide, stiff skirt, were banded with pearls. Her black hair, held back from her face by a band of silver cloth, hung in a loose cloud about her shoulders.

Corianne fidgeted, finding his silence disconcerting. She was finally forced to turn her head and look at him. Her head rose in haughty disdain. "You are staring at me, my lord. I do not appreciate it." She looked at the key dangling from his belt. "I may be a prisoner, but I would have you know that I am not on exhibition."

Adam laughed softly. "A pity. You are beautiful enough to be on exhibition."

"Your compliments are not appreciated. Pray save them for the foolish ladies who, I am told, constantly hang around you."

Her eyes looked him over indifferently. He was looking quite disturbingly handsome, she thought indignantly, for such

135

an unprincipled scoundrel. He wore a robe of dark green velvet girdled with a jeweled chain. His stiff, upstanding collar of gold cloth was ornamented with disks of silver, and in the middle of each disk was set a small emerald. White lace edged the cuffs of his ballooning sleeves, and a short black velvet cloak held by a narrow gold chain was slung carelessly from his left shoulder.

"I will save my compliments, then," Adam said, advancing toward her. "But you really must allow me to make some comment on your exquisite gown."

She flushed. "I was forced to change my gown, my lord, in the interests of cleanliness. In case you have forgotten, my brother and I are prisoners. I am unable to obtain my own clothing."

His hand touched her chin, forcing her head up. "You need not explain to me, Mistress Trigg."

She stared into his dark eyes, feeling again that traitorous weakening of her defenses. She blurted out the first words that came to her mind. "So it is Mistress Trigg now, not Madam Tudor?"

His hand left her chin. His fingers touched her neck, stroking gently. "I will call you Madam Tudor, if you desire me to do so."

She shivered at his touch. "I do not desire it," she said, pushing his hand away. "And pray do not touch me!"

His hand dropped to his side. "As you wish."

She said sharply, "I—I never wish you to touch me!" She looked at the flashing rings upon his fingers. "I would have you know, my lord, that you are quite repulsive to me."

His right eyebrow arched mockingly. "Is it indeed so, Madam Tudor?"

"I have just said so."

"So you did." He smiled down at her. "But I can tell that you are grieved by the loss of the gown you were wearing when you first entered the palace. I will give orders that it is to be laundered and returned to you at once. His fingers touched her bodice. "I would not wish you to feel that you are compelled to wear this gown. Or, for the matter of that, any other."

"How dare you laugh at me!"

He sighed. "I accept your gratitude of my well-meant offer."

"I am not grateful!"

He looked puzzled. "You are not?"

"No, I am not!" she shouted the words. "I wish you to leave at once.'"

He bowed. "Certainly. You have but to ask."

He opened the door and was about to pass through when her voice came to him again. "Wait, please."

"Yes?" He strolled back to her side.

She saw the smile in his eyes. "My lord," she said in a cold voice, "if you think I detain you for love of your company, you are quite mistaken. It is long since I have seen my brother. I would have news of him."

"Tudor is well," he said, placing his hand upon her shoulder. "I should have told you before."

Corianne looked at the hand on her shoulder. "My lord," she said in a faint voice, "you—you are touching me again."

"Am I?"

"Yes. And I—I do not care to have you t—touch me."

There was something in her voice. Something that gave him hope. She was not as indifferent to him as she pretended to be. His arm slid downward and circled her waist, urging her to her feet. "What a cursed fellow I am for touching," he said softly. His other arm went around her and drew her close. "I should be ashamed of myself."

"Y—yes." Corianne's heart was pounding and she found speech difficult. "You sh—should be ashamed, my lord."

"I know. But I feel no shame at all. Why is that, Madam Tudor?"

"I d—don't know." His mouth was near to hers, and she half-closed her eyes. "My brother——"

"I told you. He is quite well."

"Yes, but——"

His lips touched hers. Like one in a dream, carried away be a wild, sweet feeling, Corianne unconsciously pressed yet closer to him. Her arms seemed to be possessed of a will of their own, for they reached up to circle his neck.

When he released her, she stood there silent and unmoving at first. Then, in an effort to repair her defenses, she said in a small voice, "You must never—do that again. I—I do not care for it."

He ignored her. "My name, if you can bring yourself to use it, is Adam. And Adam would like to tell you that he is in love with you. What is more, you are in love with him."

"What nonsense!" She tried to free herself, but she was forced to stand still again when his arms tightened about her. "You must be mad to say such a thing to me!" she cried. "You k—know that I detest you."

He released her so abruptly that she staggered. "Why, so you do. I had forgotten that." He drew up a chair and seated himself. "Then shall we continue to discuss your brother? I have told you he is well. His attempts to soften the king seem to be going quite well. What else would you like to know?"

"Adam!"

"The king, of course," Adam went on calmly, "is pleased with Tudor's new attitude. But as for me, I cannot say——"

"Adam!"

"Yes? You wished to say something?"

"I do not wish to discuss my brother."

"Lud! What a contrary female. The king then? He makes a very interesting topic of conversation. Shall we discuss him?"

"No!"

"There is obviously no pleasing you," Adam said, sighing. "I am doing my poor best to entertain you. You choose. Whom shall we discuss?"

"No one!" She looked at him angrily. "But there is something I would like to say to you."

"Yes?" He folded his arms and watched with some interest as bright color dyed her cheeks. "Go on. I am all attention."

"Well, I—I only wanted to say that, since I have been given the opportunity to know you better, perhaps I—I do not exactly detest you."

"Ah! You mean that now you know me better, you hate me."

"No."

"Then how would you describe your feelings toward me?"

"I don't know." She glared at him. "How can you be so exasperating!"

He smiled. "I will help you, Madam Tudor. What you really want to say to me is, 'I love you, Adam.' Is that it?"

"I don't know." She stared at him. "Don't look at me like that! I tell you I don't know. You have confused me. I am uncertain of my true feelings."

"Then we must do something about it." He held out his hand. "Come here."

She hesitated. Then, seeing him preparing to rise, she went to him quickly. "Well?"

Adam held out his hand again. "Put your hand in mine."

Like one hypnotized, she obeyed. "This is—is ridiculous."

"You would prefer me to take my leave?"

"No! What I mean is, you—you may stay, if you wish."

His fingers tightened about hers. "Say—'I love you, Adam.' "

Her hand jerked. "How can I? How can hatred turn so quickly to love?"

"It has been known to happen."

"But not to me. Besides, you are our jailer."

"Still such a child in your reactions," he said softly.

"I am not."

"You are. You must grow up just a little, Madam Tudor. But not too much. I would not have you changed beyond recognition." He smiled at her, his eyes very tender on her flushed face. "Will you say it now?"

"That I love you? It is impossible. You betrayed my father!"

His smile vanished and his brows drew together in a formidable frown. "Still harping on that old theme? You know well, you little fool, that I did nothing of the sort!"

She did not answer at once. She was seeing now the other side of Adam Templeton, the cold, austere side that seemed to present such a challenge to the ladies of the Court. Two of those ladies she had overheard discussing him. They had been standing just below her window. Adam, she gathered from their conversation, was largely indifferent to the female sex. He was cold in his manner, they said, aloof. Beyond an affair here and there, he had never been known to express an interest in any woman, no matter how beautiful she might be. It was the affair here and there, mentioned by the ladies, that Corianne found depressing. Was that what he wanted from her? An affair to pass away an idle hour or two?

"Well!" Adam spoke abruptly, causing her to start. "From

139

your silence, I assume you are making judgment on my character. What have you decided? Do you actually believe that I betrayed your father?"

She winced before the cold look in his eyes. "My father did not believe it to be so. But it seemed that way to me."

"I see." Rising, he bowed formally. "Then there is nothing more to be said."

"Adam!" The word was out before she could stop it. Now, heedless, she went on in a breathless rush, "But it might be that I was wrong."

"Might be, Mistress Trigg, is not good enough." He turned to leave.

"Wait!" She clutched at his arm. "Don't go, please."

"There is no point in staying. Unless, of course, you have something else you wish to say to me?"

Her face crimsoned. "Yes, there is something else. You were my father's friend. I know it now." She looked into his face, hoping to see his expression soften. When it did not, she felt her heart sink. "Adam, did you hear me?"

"I heard you. Are you quite sure? Or will you perhaps change your mind again?"

"I deserve that. Yes, Adam, I am quite sure."

"In that case, there is something else you have to say to me, is there not?"

"Something else? What?"

"You don't think an apology would be in order?"

"What do you mean? I have apologized."

"I heard no actual apology."

"Oh, you—you—" She glared at him. "You will have it all, won't you! What should I do, crawl before you? All right, I am sorry! I am sorry! Are you satisfied?"

"I am." He smiled at her. "I will accept your apology, Mistress Trigg."

"Do not call me Mistress Trigg!"

"Why not? It is your name."

"And so is Corianne. So is Madam Tudor. You may use either."

"You must not be too good to me, Mistress Trigg. It is liable to give me too high an opinion of myself."

"Sarcasm ill becomes you, my lord."

140

"You are quite right, Mistress Trigg. In the meantime, is there something else you would like to say to me?"

She did not pretend to misunderstand him. "Yes," she said in a low voice. "I think I have fallen in love with you, A— Adam."

"Think?"

Her eyes lifted to his face. "No, more than that. I know I love you."

He put his arms about her and held her close. "And I love you, Madam Tudor."

"Do you really, Adam?"

"I really do. Though I cannot think why." He released her. Sitting down again, he pulled her onto his lap. "And now," he said, his arms tightly about her, "we must forget love for the moment. Instead, we must discuss plans for the escape." He shrugged, adding ruefully, "The only thing is, I have not yet thought of a plan."

"But you will," she said confidently. "I know that you will."

"No doubt. But, unfortunately, time is of the essence."

Holding her close, he debated whether or not he should tell her of the king's matrimonial plans in regard to herself. He decided against it. What of Thomas Seymour? Might he not be used to help them? Tom was ambitious, ruthless, too. Above all things, he desired to see his sister Jane crowned Queen of England. Certainly he would not wish to see his sister put aside for Madam Tudor. Seymour had the king's affection and trust. He was clever, charming, quick-witted, and a great favorite with all. Might not that nimble brain and disarming manner be put to good use? To confide in Seymour, of course, did hold a certain element of danger. But for the sake of his sister and his own grandiose plans for the future, he might not be averse to aiding them. In any case, it was a chance he must take. Seymour's brain and his, working together, would surely come up with a plan.

"Adam, why are you frowning so? What are you thinking about?"

Adam put her from his knee. Standing up, he smiled at her almost vaguely. "Forgive me, Madam Tudor, but there is someone I must see. I will return later."

"In that case, you must not let me detain you."

141

Oblivious to her indignation, he kissed her quickly and then strode rapidly from the room.

Corianne's indignation at this abrupt departure gave way to serious thought. Adam had much on his mind. More than ever now, he would be concerned to get Tudor and herself away. Doubt touched her. It had all been so sudden, the feeling that had flared up between them. Or, at least, on her part it had been sudden. It had taken Adam to make her recognize that it was not hatred she felt, but love. Both of them strong emotions, and sometimes one had difficulty in knowing the one from the other. But what of Adam? Did he really love her? The thought that he might not brought with it such a wave of misery that she put the doubt firmly from her. In any case, she thought, smiling, if he thought to get away from her now, then he did not know Corianne Trigg.

She sat down. Thoughts of the king came, chilling her. Would Adam come up with a plan? He must!

10

"The king comes this way! Make way, make way, the king comes this way!" The cry echoed along the corridor. It was followed by the tramping of feet, a babble of voices, and laughter.

Corianne put aside the embroidery silks she had been sorting. It would seem that the king was about to pay her a visit.

"Nay, William," she heard the king's loud voice. "You may not come in with me. There are some things a man must do alone."

"But, sire," a light, laughing voice answered, "may we not be allowed to profit from your grace's undoubted experience in such matters?"

"No, you may not." The king did not sound displeased. "You may leave me. And pray take Seymour with you. He is a sullen looking dog today. The sight of his face curdles my stomach." A hint of impatience crept into the king's voice. "What is it, Tom? What ails you?"

" 'Tis naught, your grace." Thomas Seymour replied. "I am feeling a little indisposed."

"That had best be the reason, Tom." Corianne noted the slight edge to the king's voice. "We are much displeased with your attitude of late. Another thing, we like not your attempted interference in our plans."

"If I have seemed to interfere, sire, I pray you to forgive me. It is because I am touched by the sight of my sister's distress. Jane feels that she has displeased you in some way. Jane is simple and sweet and almost childlike in her emotions, as I believe your grace well knows. She cannot understand in what way she has offended."

"Mistress Seymour has not offended. But you may well do so, Tom. Your talk of the maiden grows wearisome, and we

143

will hear no more on the subject. Now go on your way, all of you."

Corianne jumped to her feet as the door opened and the king entered the room.

"Your majesty." She curtsied low before the king's enormous figure. He was clad in a short robe of white velvet lavishly trimmed with gold lace, and, as usual, he was ablaze with jewels.

"There is no need for formality, Madam Tudor. Raise yourself. I would talk to you."

Corianne's heart fluttered with apprehension. He looked friendly enough, but one never knew with this king. He came to stand before her. Looking into his narrow blue eyes framed with short, thick, sandy lashes, she said quickly, "I am honored by your grace's visit."

Henry smiled and nodded. Seating himself on a padded bench before the satin-draped windows, he caught at her hand and drew her down beside him. "We would honor you yet more, sweetheart." He moved closer to her, putting an arm about her rigid waist. "You like us, Madam Tudor?"

She could feel the heat of his body, her nostrils caught his rank smell. It was an effort to remember that she must be nice to this man. She must conciliate him in all possible ways. She turned a bright smile on him. "Your grace surely jests? Having once seen you, who could not like you?"

"And love, Madam Tudor, what of love?" Laughing, he caught her in his arms and pressed his lips to hers. "Could you love me, my little sweetheart?"

Corianne felt a wave of distaste. His kisses, after Adam's! How could she bear it? She said in a faint voice. "There is love in my heart for you, sire."

It had been said so unenthusiastically that she feared he must notice and be displeased. Instead, he hugged her tightly, almost crushing the breath from her. She turned her head away, trying to evade his hot, seeking mouth. There was a limit to what she could endure. "Why do you ask, sire?"

"Because you haunt my dreams," he breathed ardently. "Because, from the very first moment I set eyes on you, I was young again. I was in love. Deeply in love with you, Madam Tudor."

"Your grace pays me too much honor." She moved in his

arms. "May I ask you to release me, sire? Your arms are very strong, and I fear you are hurting me."

He loosened his arms unwillingly. "I had thought that the embrace of a lover could bring only ecstasy."

"But, sire, you are not my lover."

His little mouth lost the sullen look it had acquired. It was obvious to him now that she had no notion of what he would convey. "I know well that 'tis too much for you to comprehend as yet, sweetheart," he said eagerly. "But I long to be your lover." He smiled with indulgent tenderness, anticipating her joy. "What have you to say to that, my lovely one?"

Her heart was beating so fast that she felt sick. "Sire," she could not keep the slight tremble from her voice, "you are the king, but you are also a married man. It—it is well known that you are a devoted husband, and faithful, sire, faithful. I know well that you do but jest with me when you speak of love."

He looked at her sharply. There had been something in her voice that did not quite please him. She was smiling at him sweetly, and he told himself that he must have been mistaken. He relaxed, feeling the forming knot of his ready anger disappear. "Ah, sweetheart, think you that your king is not as other men?" Moisture sprang to his eyes, reddening them. "A king must face the world with a serene face, though often that serenity may hide an aching heart. May a king not suffer from an unhappy marriage, even as ordinary men suffer? Sweetheart, sweetheart, I yearn for love and warmth and understanding."

"I am sure, sire," Corianne said desperately, "that the queen is a lady of much warmth and understanding. I envy your grace the happiness that must be yours when your son is born."

"My son!" The king's expression darkened. "The queen, I feel sure, is barren of sons."

She was horrified that he should speak out so strongly against the queen. What could she say to him that he would not hold against her later? "Sire," she began, "no man, not even a king, may know that."

His eyes narrowed. "I do not claim to know God's will in this matter, Mistress Trigg. Nor do I care to have my words twisted into meanings they do not have." Rising to his feet, he stood before her, his hands on his hips, glaring down at her.

"Forgive me, sire. If I have twisted your words, it was unintentional."

"Was it so?" Not willing to be appeased for the moment, Henry lapsed into formality. "When we say that we believe our queen to be barren of sons, we mean just that. We will not be argued with. And we tell you in all truth that we do not want daughters. We must have sons."

He had forgotten for the moment his claim that Tudor was his son, and she had no intention of reminding him. She rose. Facing him, she smiled her most winning smile. "Never would I wish to argue with your grace." Her smile faded, and she added almost pleadingly, "But, sire, is it not possible that the queen may bear a prince?"

"We shall see, mistress." His eyes looked her over, and he felt desire rise strongly. She was clad in a plainly-cut gown of light green velvet bordered at the square neckline and the edges of the long hanging sleeves with small brilliants. She was beautiful! Queenly! Aye, fit to be his queen! With a muffled exclamation, he pulled her to him, his hands sweeping the small pearled hood from her head. He ran his fingers through her loosened hair. "I see that you have adopted the fashion of our queen," he said in a thick voice. "For our queen those hanging sleeves were designed by her to hide the deformity of her hand. But you, sweetheart, have no deformity. You are perfect in our eyes!"

She stood very still beneath his caressing fingers, enduring it when his fingers touched her breast. When his hand groped inside her bodice, her control broke. "Please, sire! I must beg your grace to desist."

His hand returned to his side for a moment. He frowned uncertainly. Then, deciding that she played the coy maiden, he thrust his hand inside her bodice again. "And why should we desist, little sweetheart?" he said, his fingers clutching and tweaking. "Are you not happy that we have honored you with our love?"

She pulled away. "I am honored, sire. But, forgive me, I would rather you did not touch me in such an intimate place."

She expected his anger, and instead was surprised by his booming laughter. "Our sweetheart is modest, eh?"

"Would you have me otherwise, sire?"

"Nay, that we would not. Yet it does seem to us that you are cold to our love."

"Never, sire!"

He saw her fear, and was inflamed by it. Unwittingly, for his original intention had been to be kind, he lapsed into anger. The bully in him uppermost, he said in a menacing voice, "If we thought you were cold to our love, if we for one moment thought you played with our heart and laughed at our sincere love, our anger would be great."

Corianne's hand grasped the back of a chair for support. "Your grace!"

"If we found that, Mistress Trigg, though it tore the heart from our breast, we would see you lodged in the Tower."

"The Tower? Surely your grace would not!"

"In our eyes, Mistress Trigg, deception is a crime that must be punished. There is little enough comfort in the Tower, we assure you. In that place are housed many instruments of torture for those who defy our will."

Her face drained of color. He would torture her? "But I have not deceived your grace!" she cried. "Why do you speak to me of the Tower? How can you be so cruel!"

He had but jested with her, he hastily excused himself. Of a certainty he had not meant to terrify her. He was about to draw her in his arms and reassure her, when her last words struck him forcibly. She had called him cruel! He, who was the kindest of men. He looked at her with eyes that were genuinely bewildered. "Cruel, Mistress Trigg? You know not what you say. Cruelty is not in our nature. We are a God-fearing son of the church. We are scrupulous in our service to both God and conscience."

Corianne stared at him. What manner of man was he that saw himself as a God-fearing Christian? While others under his domination saw him as a monster, cruel, mercilessly cruel, egotistic, determined that his way was the only way. And yet, did it not seem so farcical, she could almost believe that her words had wounded him. Was he really so blind, so self-deluded to his faults? "I—I did not mean it, sire," she stammered. Her mind chaotic, despising herself for her cowardice, she added, "Forgive me, sire. I spoke in haste."

Henry's eyes filled again, and he looked at her mournfully. "You did indeed speak in haste," he said huskily. "We are displeased. But more than that, we are grieved and sorely wounded."

Corianne moistened her dry lips. It was an effort to smile at him, for the muscles about her mouth felt stiff, but she managed it. "If you will but give me time to work a cure, sire, your wound will heal without trace. Say that you forgive me, please."

"We knew you could not mean it, sweetheart." He put his arms about her and, discarding formality, he whispered, "There is another side to Henry Tudor, one that I show only to those whom I love. If you would but meet my desire with your own, it would give me much joy to show you that other side."

"I am all anticipation, sire." She shivered as his lips touched her throat, her breasts, and his tongue flicked greedily, entering the cleavage between her breasts.

"Expect me tonight, sweetheart," Henry whispered. "I can wait no longer than that, so greatly do I desire you!"

No! She could not endure it! "Sire," her strained voice did not sound like her own, "what of the queen?"

"What of her?"

"The—the queen is to bear your child. Your grace will agree that it would not be fitting to dally with another until after her majesty's lying-in period. It would not be in accordance with your conscience or mine."

The mention of conscience gave Henry pause. It had always been the strongest force in his life. It was conscience that had made him put aside Catherine of Aragon, a woman he had loved well. And all knew how he had loved and cherished her. Conscience again when he had put aside Mary, his daughter. Though it broke his heart, as he had often tried to explain to Catherine, he could not put the bastard child of an immoral union on the throne of England. He thought briefly of Elizabeth, his other daughter, and then dismissed her. Time and his conscience would show him what he must do about Elizabeth. He looked uncertainly, half-suspiciously at Corianne. "You do not seek to fob me off with excuses?"

Even as he said it, he smiled inwardly in disbelief. She desired him fully as much as he desired her. Her hunger for him was plain in her eyes.

Corianne's hand touched his face gently. "Your grace knows better."

He sighed. "Well do I understand the torments of an uneasy conscience." His smile was regretful. "I would not wish either of us to suffer. I respect you for your honor and for your self-denial. I fear then, sweetheart, it will have to be after the lying-in period."

Corianne felt triumph. She had found the right words. She made her expression mournful as she answered. "I would that I were not so sternly governed by my conscience, sire. But so it has always been."

"Never say so! You do right to allow yourself to be thus guided." Full of sentiment, he kissed her tenderly on the forehead.

"I will pray that the queen may soon be safely delivered of a prince, sire."

"It is my earnest prayer, too." His face clouded. "But should God so honor me, it will mean that we must part."

"Sire!" she said in distress. "Why?"

He released her from his embrace. "It will be a sign of God's favor, do you see, sweetheart? Were I to work against His divine will, His wrath would be terrible. There would be no more sons for Henry Tudor."

"I understand, sire. To take another in desire would be to jeopardize future sons."

"How well you understand me," he said, looking at her sadly. "I have ever been one to do my duty, sweetheart. But mark this well. If I am not honored with a son, I will know that God finds grievous fault in my marriage." He looked at her with deep meaning. "It would then be my duty to take another wife." He stroked her hair. "A wife whom I shall raise from lowly estate to rule by my side."

Lowly estate? She had heard that he was forever prating of the lowly estate from which he had raised Anne Boleyn. "Sire! You would not divorce the queen?"

"I have lately had suspicions that it is no true marriage. But we shall see. If I find it to be so, it may well be that

God, in His goodness and His infinite mercy, has led me to you."

She? Henry Tudor's third wife! It was with difficulty that she restrained her horror and continued to smile at him.

Henry kissed her lingeringly on the mouth. "All must obey God's will. Aye, sweetheart, even your king."

She bowed her head. "I understand, sire."

"I shall visit you again, Madam Tudor, be sure of that. I am ever hungry for the sight of your lovely face." As though unable to trust himself, he strode over to the door. "I wonder, sweetheart, what miracles God has in store for you and me?"

Without waiting for her answer, he left her, closing the door behind him. Corianne could hear his loud voice ordering the guard to lock it. So for all his soft looks and his words of love, he still did not altogether trust her. Her thoughts turned to Adam, who she had not seen in two days. He too had spoken words of love to her. But had he meant them? If, as he had said, he loved her, why had he not been to see her? A man in love, no matter how busy he might be, would surely find enough time for that?

Corianne sat down. Angered by Adam's neglect, torn by painful doubts, overwrought by the strain of fending off the king, it was suddenly too much for her. She put her hands over her eyes and cried as she had not done since her father's death.

Adam looked searchingly at the queen. "Madam, you are quite sure of this?"

Anne did not reply at once. She stood up and walked over to the window. Staring out at the gardens below, she said in a hard, clear voice, "My lord Somercombe, I would not have sent for you had I not thought my information reliable."

"But information given to you by a guard?" Adam said doubtfully.

"I have known this particular guard since I was a child. He is loyal, and I know him to be devoted to me." She turned from the window. "Listen to me, my lord," she said, halting before him. "It is surely easy to prove. You have but to ask Tudor Trigg. If he is not swollen with a sense of new importance, he must wish to get away from the king."

"He does wish it, madam. And, as you say, it will be easy

to prove." He bowed. "I will go to Tudor now. In a little while he is expecting a visit from the king. But there will be time enough to prove the guard's story."

Anne stared at him. Suddenly stricken by conscience, she said in a low voice, "I wish no ill to Tudor Trigg or his sister, but I must think of my own child, and the child to be born."

"I understand."

"My lord, I have some fears on this matter. You—you do not think that the king, in his anger, will take his revenge on those two young people?"

"The king must be shown the proof in the presence of witnesses, and you, madam, have promised to be one of those witnesses."

"Yes. I will be there."

Adam smiled at her. "Then I think, madam, your fears are groundless. The king will not continue to hold them against their will, I feel sure of that." He bowed once more, and opened the door.

After he had left her, Anne stood there staring at the floor. Adam had said that he was sure that the king, in the face of such proof, would not continue to hold them. But she herself was by no means sure of that. Apparently Adam, despite his disillusionment, still had some remnants of faith in the honor of Henry Tudor. Anne put a hand to her aching head. It might be that she had signed Tudor Trigg's death warrant, perhaps his sister's too. But what else could she do? Her children came first. The guard had put a weapon in her hand, and, despite her misgivings, she had determined to use it. That was why she had sent for Adam. He was closest to the Triggs, and he had always been her friend.

Anne walked over to the door. She would go to the king. She would tell him that she had a desire to walk with him. Her lips twisted bitterly. He would not refuse her, for he would believe that a little gentle exercise would be good for the child she carried.

Tudor looked up and smiled as Adam entered his apartments. Just lately, he had felt quite hopeful that all would be well. My lord Somercombe and Thomas Seymour, who had agreed to help, would surely come up with something very soon. Seymour, of course, was in this thing for his own gain. He believed that the king, in the absence of a prince, would soon be seeking a new wife. That wife must not be Madam Tudor, but his own sister, Jane Seymour. My lord Somercombe was in it for friendship's sake, and for love of Madam Tudor. This last still amazed and amused him. Incredible to think of the great lord Somercombe being in love with Madam Tudor.

Adam came swiftly toward him. "Tudor." He looked at him with serious eyes. "There is something I must ask you."

"Of course, my lord."

"Do you bear a birthmark on your shoulder? A birthmark peculiar to all the Triggs?"

Remembering his father's words of warning, Tudor paled. He wanted to deny it, but he could not bring himself to lie to this man who had proved himself a friend. He nodded. "Yes, my lord."

"Then why the devil haven't you shown this proof of your true blood to the king?"

Tudor swallowed. "My—my father thought that it would not be wise. He advised me to wait and to see which way the wind blew. He wished Madam Tudor and me to say and do nothing that might arouse the king's anger and cause him to take vengeance upon us. He told us to wait and to watch, and to take the first opportunity to escape."

"But there is no need of that now. If the king is shown the proof that you cannot be his son, you will both go free."

"Are you sure of that?"

"I am." Adam smiled at him reassuringly. "The king has changed in many ways, lad, and sometimes I think that I have never really known him. But I know enough about him to assure you that he will not take vengeance upon you, who have become dear to him for your own sake."

For his own sake? Tudor was suddenly filled with apprehension. He could not help thinking that my lord Somercombe, usually so astute, was possessed of a lingering blind spot where the king was concerned. His thoughts turned to Thomas Seymour. Seymour, he felt sure, would see clearer, because he was not bound by a former fondness, as was this man before him.

"My lord," Tudor looked at Adam with troubled eyes, "would it not be better to continue with a plan of escape?"

Adam shook his head. "Take off your shirt and cover yourself with your cloak."

Tudor obeyed so unwillingly that Adam sought once more to reassure him. "This is the better way, Tudor. Once you have proved before witnesses that you are the earl of Marchmont's son, the king cannot continue to deceive himself. Especially when one of those witnesses will be the queen."

"My lord, how did you find out about the birthmark? Did Madam Tudor tell you?"

Adam shook his head. "No. And we will not go into that now. Speaking of Madam Tudor, I must prepare myself for a meeting with her. It will counter her rage at my neglect when I tell her the good news."

"If it is good news," Tudor said gloomily. "As for you, my lord, I cannot understand what you see to love in Madam Tudor. She has a terrible temper, and she can be cursed disagreeable when denied her own way."

"Spoken like a true brother," Adam said, smiling.

"All I can say is, you must be a very brave man."

"I have my moments," Adam agreed.

Tudor's quick ears had caught the cry of the heralds. The king would be here at any moment. He clenched his hands together, hoping that their trembling had not been noticed. "Have you thought of my sister's danger?" he said hurriedly. "I was with you, if you remember, when you told Tom Seymour that the king's affection had turned to her. Do you think he will let her go?"

"Your sister is quite another matter," Adam said grimly. "She must be got away, and the sooner the better. As you might expect, Seymour concurs with me in this. For her, I fear escape will be necessary. Now hush, lad. The moment is upon us."

Adam and Tudor bowed low as the king and queen entered the room. Following behind them were William Seton and Sir Richard Claire.

The king nodded to Adam. "My lord." His eyes turned to Tudor. "Why are you hugging that cloak about you, my son? Are you chilled?"

Before Tudor could reply, Adam was by his side, his hands removing the cloak. "Do you see this, sire?" Adam pointed to a small star-shaped mark on the boy's shoulder. "This birthmark, thus far, is borne by all the Triggs. It is unmistakable proof that Tudor is indeed the son of the earl of Marchmont."

Anne felt a wave of faintness as she saw the king's expression. He had known about the birthmark, she thought in a flash of intuition. He had known all along! And Adam had truly believed him to be unaware of it.

So it has come to light, the king thought. Had either of the Triggs come to him and spoken of the birthmark, he had known what he would do. He would have forbidden them under pain of death to mention it again to anybody. A threat to the sister, and the boy would have come his way. Curse Somercombe for an interfering swine! But he would confound him yet. He would confound them all. God's curse on the lot of them! If Somercombe thought to get the better of him, he had best think again! His face suffused with angry color, his eyes glittering, he stared at the birthmark. "What of it, my lord?" he said coldly. "I have seen many birthmarks."

"But not like this one, sire," Adam insisted.

The king looked at Adam, his fury showing in his eyes. "You are mistaken. There is nothing unusual about it. I was once shown the Trigg birthmark by my lord Marchmont. It was quite different to this mark."

"Sire!" Anne cried out desperately. "It is the same mark. I know it!"

The king turned on her like a goaded bull. "Do I hear aright, madam?" he roared. "Are you actually calling me a liar?"

"No, sire, never that. It is only that I believe you to be confused by emotion."

"I am never confused, madam."

"Sire, send for Mistress Trigg. If she bears the same mark, surely you will be convinced?"

"I have nothing more to say to you, madam." The king nodded to Tudor. "We will talk later." With Seton and Claire following, both of them trying to hide their consternation and amazement at the turn of events, he left the room.

Anne remained for a moment. "He is determined," she whispered. "God help us all!"

"Madam," Adam said gently, "it is best if you do not remain here."

"Yes," she said. "Yes, you are quite right." Her haunted eyes lingered on Tudor's face for a moment, then she turned about and fled from the room.

Tudor sat down abruptly and wiped his damp forehead with the back of his hand. "My lord, I fear the king is a man who will not see, who will not let others see. If voices should be raised against his declaration that I am his son, then punishment will follow. It is as the queen says, he is determined. Despite everything, he will have his way. But what do we do now?"

Adam did not seem to hear him. "In that one respect, I thought I knew him. I believed he still had a certain degree of honor. I have been a fool! A damned bloody fool!"

"It is done, my lord. It will not help things that you condemn yourself so bitterly."

"The king will not take this lightly, Tudor. So it would seem that we must start all over again."

Tudor looked anxiously at his unsmiling face. "But, my lord, if you should effect my escape, you yourself must then stand in considerable danger."

"Nonsense!" Adam brushed his words aside. "I will find a way to handle the king."

Tudor shook his head despairingly. Here was another man who would not see. He tried again. "But should I escape, would it not be better if you went into hiding until the king's rage cools?"

"There will be no need for me to hide. Cease cudgeling your brains on my account." His eyes went to the window. "Tudor, I want you to listen to me carefully. I have the glimmering of an idea."

Adam's expression was calm as he seated himself beside Tudor, but he was full of disquiet. The king would not easily forgive him for today's episode. He had no doubt that from now on his movements would be watched. "Listen, lad." Adam bent his dark head close to the red one.

Tudor listened attentively, his expression one of dismay. My lord Somercombe expected him to—— His thoughts broke off as he met Adam's eyes. He took a deep breath. Hoping his voice would not quiver, he said, "I will do it, my lord. I—I am not afraid."

"You are afraid. And why not? It is a great deal to ask of

you, and it requires much courage." Adam's hand touched Tudor's shoulder. "I knew I could rely upon you. I am proud of you, lad."

"Thank you, my lord."

"I hope that from now on you will call me Adam. It is only fitting between those who are about to become brothers-in-law."

Tudor grinned. "Adam it is."

"Much better." Adam rumpled his hair with a friendly hand. "A little more practise and it will come easily from your lips." Rising, he went over to the door. "Remember, Tudor," he said in a low voice, "only an unimaginative fool knows no fear, and you are certainly not a fool. Like your sister, you have a very vivid imagination. You may have a qualm or two, but that is nothing to be ashamed of."

Tudor waited until he had left the room, then he got to his feet and walked to the window. At the sight of the steep wall below, he shuddered.

11

Tudor Trigg had gone. The red-headed boy whom the king claimed to be his own son seemed to have vanished into thin air. But how had this vanishing act been accomplished? There was not an entrance or exit in the palace that was not guarded. It was a mystery to all. The king was angry, and a thrill of fear swept through the ladies and gentlemen of the Court. His anger affected the servants too, so that they scurried tense-faced about their duties. They knew that when the king was angry, his small, furious eyes were looking for trouble, and quite often finding it.

Fear is contagious. It touched Corianne. Since the disappearance of her brother, she had been questioned exhaustively both by the king and Thomas Cromwell, and later by Thomas Cranmer, who had tried in his deceptively gentle way to trap her into an admission of complicity.

The queen, fearing for her unborn child, kept to her own apartments as much as possible. She was branded by the king as sullen and intractable and unfit to be the mother of his child.

His anger steadily growing, the king gave orders that Mistress Trigg was to be lodged in smaller apartments. She was to be deprived of comforts, and guarded well. It was noticed that the king's love for Mistress Trigg seemed to have died with the disappearance of her brother. He turned for comfort to the willing arms of Jane Seymour.

Only two people were unaffected by the storm that shook the palace—Jane Seymour, whose soft voice, soothing hands, and clinging lips served to temporarily placate her royal would-be lover, and the earl of Somercombe. Just before the disappearance of Tudor Trigg, Somercombe had been granted permission to visit his sister, the Lady Margaret Fordyce.

157

The king had given him permission grudgingly. Since the earl's attempt to force from him an admission that Tudor Trigg was not his son, he was out of royal favor. Nevertheless, it seemed to the king to be a good idea to keep Somercombe from contact with Tudor Trigg for a while, and so, having granted permission, he had instructed that the earl of Somercombe's movements were to be watched. Any suspicious activity on the earl's part must be immediately reported to him.

Thomas Cromwell was called into conference by the king. As a result of this conference, Cromwell set two of his most trusted men the task of following the earl. It was unfortunate that, whilst partaking of some much needed refreshment, these trusted men managed to lose their prey.

Thomas Cromwell hardly knew how to face the king. He felt disgraced by his men's inability to carry out the task assigned to them. This disgrace was further heightened when, three days after the earl's departure from Court, Tudor Trigg abruptly disappeared. Cromwell had not been idle and he felt, or rather hoped, that he had managed to redeem himself with the king. It was he who found the length of rope. It was hidden behind the thick bushes at the bottom of the wall that was immediately below the windows of Tudor Trigg's apartments. Despite the suspicion that had leaped into his mind, Cromwell stared for a long, thoughtful moment at that wall with its outcroppings of jagged points, and he debated with himself whether anybody would be foolhardy enough to attempt to escape that way. He hesitated. Then, the fact that this particular part of the palace was left unguarded decided him to investigate further. He found a few shreds of rope clinging to the ornamental rail that decorated the window of the apartment. With this important find and a fair knowledge of how the escape had been effected, he once more sought audience with the king.

The king listened to Cromwell with disbelief written in his face. "Impossible!" he roared. "A man would have to be crazed to attempt to descend that wall. His flesh would be ripped to shreds."

"Not if he were well padded, sire, and agile into the bargain. We have observed more than once that Tudor Trigg is exceptionally nimble. Your grace himself commented upon it.

A lad such as Tudor might well have managed to use those stone points as stepping stones. As I have said, he is most agile. Someone less so could not have used his limbs in a manner to accommodate his feet." Cromwell paused, unable to hide his triumphant smile.

The king was incensed. Tudor Trigg climbing down those points which were originally meant to repel an enemy attack? Ridiculous! He had always known that Cromwell was a fool. This ridiculous story proved it. He saw Cromwell's smile, and his anger rose to dangerous heights. Rising to his feet, he brought his clenched fist down on the top of the kneeling Cromwell's head. "How dare you come before us smirking like an idiot!" he shouted. "Our son has gone, and you smirk. Who aided him in his escape? Who aided him, fool? Answer me!"

Dazed, his head throbbing with violent pain, Cromwell stammered. "I—I know not, your g—grace. Grant m—m—me permission to investigate."

"Dolt! Poltroon!" The king almost choked on his rage. "Do you need permission to investigate an outrage against us?"

Focussing his eyes with some difficulty, for the pain grew more severe with each passing moment, Cromwell managed to get to his feet. He made the king a somewhat erratic bow. "Nay, your grace, I do not need permission."

"Get out of our sight, lunatic! Get out, we say!"

"I w—will find the per—perpetrator of this crime," Cromwell muttered thickly as he made his unsteady way to the door.

"You will, unless you desire to have your limbs lengthened on the rack, or your neck stretched by a rope!"

The unhappy Cromwell sagged against the door, his trembling fingers clutching at the latch. His only desire in that moment was to retire to his bed and rest his throbbing head against a cool pillow. But although the king had shouted to him to get out, he knew that he dare not show unseemly haste. It would be like the king, he thought bitterly, to have him arrested for retiring from the royal presence without permission. The king was still glaring at him, his face reminding Cromwell of a full purple moon from which two slitted eyes blazed venomously.

"Why are you gaping at us with your mouth open?" the king roared. "Why, fool, why? We demand to know!"

Cromwell did not answer at once. In his fuddled brain, a face was taking shape, the face of a man he had always hated. "Your grace," he exclaimed. "What of my lord Somercombe?"

"What of Somercombe, imbecile? Speak up, you cringing cur, speak up!"

Cromwell released his hold on the latch and waved his hands in a placating gesture. A bolt of pain, more severe than before, pierced his temples. Gasping, he was forced to clutch at the latch again.

"Well, fool, answer us! Are you deaf?"

No fault of yours if I am not, Cromwell thought, experiencing a further surge of bitterness. He could not speak for the moment, but he managed a wan smile, the sight of which brought a further tirade against him.

"By God, Cromwell, we will not have this disrespect! We will not be served by incompetents and fools! Will you speak up, man, or must we take our fist and clout the words from your mouth?"

This threat of further violence was too much. With an incoherent cry, Cromwell stumbled forward and fell to his knees. "My lord S—Somercombe is suspect, your g—grace," he faltered, trying to see the king's face through the mist before his eyes.

"What is the meaning of these words you babble? My lord Somercombe is our very good friend." He impaled the wilting Cromwell with a venomous glance. "Aye, our good friend. Which is more than we can say for some who kneel now before us."

Pain-wracked, but badly stung by this injustice, Cromwell made a supreme effort and managed to speak out boldly. "Did not your grace himself command that he be watched and his movements r—reported? Did not your grace c—consider it the act of a traitor when my lord Somercombe attempted t—to aid the boy in his lie?"

"You dare to raise your voice in our presence!" The king raised his hand, forestalling the words of apology that trembled on Cromwell's lips. "Be silent, dolt! We wish to think. We cannot do so if you continue to gibber in our ear."

160

Grateful for this respite, Cromwell wiped his profusely sweating forehead on the sleeve of his robe. He tightened his lips to hold back a cry of pain, but a small muffled moan emerged.

"What was that you said to us?" the king rapped.

"N—nothing, your grace. Pray forgive me. I—I am feeling unwell."

The king snorted. "Interrupt us again," he said grimly, "and we promise you that you will be sick unto death."

Cromwell bowed his head meekly. The intense pain made him feel quite faint and induced in him a strong desire to weep. He reflected that he had no further need of the king's assistance. He was already sick unto death. He waited patiently, his glazed eyes fixed on the tiled floor.

"By God, Cromwell," the king exclaimed, "for once you speak sense. By the Virgin, I think we have fathomed it. 'Tis Somercombe, traitorous dog that he is, who is at the bottom of this!" He smacked a clenched fist against his leg, forgetting that it was the ailing one.

Cromwell flinched away from the roar of pain he uttered. "Your g—grace has hurt himself?" he gabbled.

"Of course we have hurt ourself, fool! Do we cry aloud in pain because we are amused? Answer us!"

"No, your grace."

"Aye, 'tis Somercombe, we know it now. He ever spoke out against our certainty that the boy was our own son. It is he who has spirited him away, we know it!"

Cromwell rose shakily to his feet. "Caution, your grace, caution. We shall require proof that my lord Somercombe was not only the instigator but an active participant in the escape."

"Prate to us not of caution," the king cried, "lest you earn yourself another buffet. We need no proof. We say that Somercombe is guilty. Mark us well, dolt. If you bungle this matter, you will seriously displease us, and it will be the worse for you. On the moment of his return, Somercombe is to be arrested. He is to be lodged in the Tower, and there he will remain until we have deliberated and pronounced upon his fate."

"I had thought m—my lord Somercombe to be a favorite of your grace," Cromwell ventured.

"Are you being insolent to us, Cromwell?"

"No indeed, your grace." Cromwell shrank back before the venomous glare.

"It is well. We do not care for insolence." The king pointed an emphatic finger. "Know this. He who is against Henry Tudor must be considered and treated as an enemy. Somercombe is to be sent to the Tower. Do you understand us?"

"Your grace, is it wise to summarily despatch him to the Tower?"

"Are you arguing with us? Are you saying that he is innocent?"

"No, your grace, not that."

"What then? Come, come, do not stand there goggling at us like a cursed fish with a hook in its gill!"

"It is advisable to first obtain proof, your grace. My lord Somercombe, as your grace knows, is not without influence."

"So Somercombe is not without influence." The king spoke so quietly that Cromwell was agreeably surprised.

"No, sire, he is not."

"Somercombe, you say!" the royal voice rose to a roar, causing Cromwell to start in terror. "What do you mean by it, eh? Are we, the king, a peasant? Are we to understand that we are without influence?"

"Sire, please! You have mistaken me."

"Have we?" Henry's eyes narrowed. "In that case, you will do as we say. Let Somercombe slip through your fingers, and by Christ, we will order that every tooth be plucked from your head. Nor, in our righteous anger, will we stop at that!"

Sighing, Cromwell bowed. "All will be as your grace desires."

"If you value that ugly head of yours, it had better be! We are tired of——" he broke off, wincing. Clutching at his stomach, he belched loudly. "Your argument has curdled a misery in our stomach," he resumed fiercely. "Go! Get out of our sight!"

"I pray you to accept my humble apologies, sire."

"Go!"

Cromwell bowed. Then, thankfully, he scuttled away.

The king sat there, rubbing his stomach, belching at intervals, thinking of his erstwhile favorite, the earl of Somer-

combe. When he finally rose to his feet and limped from the
room, the expression on his face was not pleasant.

Outside an inn in Gravesend, the earl of Somercombe took
a final farewell of Tudor Trigg. "You must bide here,
Tudor," he said, laying emphasis on the words, "until you
hear from me." He glanced at the swinging sign of the
Plough and Bull. "Your lodging is paid for," he went on,
"and you will find new clothes in that bag." He pointed to
the capacious bag beside Tudor. "Perhaps you should wear a
cap over that flaming poll of yours. The king might well order that the countryside be scoured for boys of your descrip-
tion. Keep your hair covered as much as possible."

"You may rely on me, Adam."

"Good." Adam patted the sweating neck of his horse with
an affectionate hand. "You have done well, Bess, my lass."

Tudor looked at the earl's tall, mud-spattered figure with
admiration. Adam was much older than himself, but with his
dark hair escaping from beneath his red velvet cap and curling about his face, he seemed much the same age. He looked
at the thin, ringed hand patting the mare's neck. It had a blue
tinge. "Adam," he said, "your clothes are dripping wet. Before you depart, could you not take a moment to change into
dry garments?"

Drawing his cloak closer about his shivering body, Adam
shook his head. "Thank you for the thought, lad, but I must
soon be on my way."

Tudor looked into the smiling eyes. "If you say so, my
lord."

"What happened to Adam?"

"Adam, then. I keep forgetting, for I must confess that you
awe me a little."

"In that case," Adam said, laughing, "when I am wed to
your sister, you'll not attempt to flout my authority, will
you?"

"Not until I have grown used to you. But I'll wager that
Madam Tudor is not thinking too kindly of you. She has not
seen you in many a long day. No doubt, by now, if I know
anything about her, she has consigned you to the devil."

"You comfort me, lad." Adam doubled up his fist and
touched Tudor's smiling face lightly. "In with you."

Tudor picked up the bag. "You will be careful, Adam?"

"I will. But I am in no danger. My part in the escape is not known."

"But are you sure the king won't connect your convenient absence from Court with the escape?" Tudor said, frowning.

"Why should he?" Adam spoke firmly, but he was by no means sure. With Madam Tudor still at the palace, it was a chance he would have to take.

"Do you really think you can get my sister away?"

Adam smiled. "I will get her away, never fear. But her escape, you remember, is in Tom Seymour's hands."

"Adam, you do trust Seymour?"

"No, not normally. But friend Seymour bitterly resents the love-light in the king's eyes whenever he looks at Madam Tudor. He would prefer to see it shining upon his sister. Resentment, to say nothing of ambition, will keep him working for our side."

He could rid himself of Madam Tudor in another way. By killing her, perhaps?"

"No. Tom Seymour has faults, but he is no murderer."

Tudor's frown lifted. "I am relieved to hear you say so."

Adam patted the horse again, then vaulted lightly into the saddle. "If you care to ease my mind," he said, looking down at Tudor, "you will not mention to your sister that little mishap that tipped us both into the Thames." Drawing on his gloves, he reached down his hand. "Agreed, lad?"

Grinning widely, Tudor shook his hand. "Agreed. I won't tell her what a rotten oarsman you are."

"Time enough later for her to discover my many flaws." Adam looked up at the sullen sky. "Heavy rain soon," he commented. "I hope, when I see you again, that Madam Tudor will be with me."

"I hope so too."

"Have faith, lad. Remember what I have said to you. Do not return to London on any account. If Madam Tudor arrives alone, it will mean there is a slight delay in my own plans. You are not to wait for me. You are to take Madam Tudor and board the ship for France. You know the name of the ship and the name of the captain. If the ship is not in harbor, you are to remain hidden until the captain returns. Do you understand?"

"I understand. But we will wait for you."

"You will do nothing of the sort," Adam said sharply.

"Madam Tudor may not be willing to set sail without you."

"Then knock her on the head. Do anything you must. But get her on that ship."

"But, Adam, I——"

"No more, lad." Adam's hand tightened on the reins. "You will do exactly as I have told you to do."

His eyes troubled, Tudor watched the earl gallop away. He goes back to the palace, Tudor thought, and yet he has no notion of what has happened in his absence. He walks deliberately into danger. What fools love can make of men. Shaking his head, he turned and made his way into the inn.

A short, apple-cheeked woman with plentiful white hair skewered into a tight knot on top of her head bustled forward to greet him. "Come along, young gentleman," she said, smiling at him, "your room is ready." She led him toward a steep staircase. "It's the room facing you, at the top of the stairs." She pointed with a plump finger. "And when will the handsome gentleman be returning?"

"Soon, I trust."

"He's the earl of Somercombe, isn't he?"

Tudor had begun to ascend the stairs. He turned about so sharply that the woman was startled. "How did you know that?" he demanded.

The woman smiled. "As to that, I was just teasing. I know him because he is my own little Adam. I was his nurse, you see. He knew you'd be safe with me."

"Then you know my reason for being here?"

She nodded. "Aye, his lordship confided in me and my man. Never you fear, lad. We'll keep you from harm's way."

12

In his apartment in Greenwich Palace, the earl of Somercombe divested himself of his muddy garments. With the help of Ganford, his valet, he bathed quickly. Then he changed into clean linen and a short robe of amber velvet embroidered with gold thread. Kneeling at his feet, Ganford drew on his hose and fastened them securely, then he fitted on the square-toed shoes with their ornate ruby buckles.

The earl, watching him, thought that he seemed ill at ease. "What ails you, Ganford?" he questioned. "Are you ill?"

The man raised a pale face. "My lord," he said in a shaking voice, "the truth is that I am ill with fear." Tears gathered in his blue eyes. "I have been warned to say nothing to you. I am not a courageous man, but you have been good to me. I feel that I must speak, must warn you. My lord, you are suspect in the disappearance of Tudor Trigg!"

The earl stared at him for a long moment, then he laughed lightly. "By the Virgin, were that not so absurd it would be amusing! There, don't worry, man. And get up. I am not the king that you must kneel before me."

Ganford twitched a buckle on the earl's left shoe to bring it in line with the right, then he got weakly to his feet.

Adam rose, too. Turning away, he studied his reflection in the round mirror of polished silver. A frown appeared between his brows. "Do you know, Ganford, I am inclined to think that the slashings of scarlet and silver in these sleeves are a little too garish. What say you?"

Ganford was biting his lower lip in agitation. "M'lord!" he burst out, "the king awaits you. I am greatly feared for your safety!"

"And his majesty does not like to be kept waiting. Yes, Ganford, I know." He motioned to him to place his fur-lined

166

amber velvet cloak about his shoulders. Ganford hastened to obey, his fingers trembling as he fastened the gold chain at each shoulder. Then, bowing, he opened the door. "I pray you to have a care, my lord," he said breathlessly. "May God be with you!"

The earl's eyes met his. "You are a good fellow, Robert," he said gently. He patted the man's thin, stooped shoulder reassuringly. "Thank you for your good wishes. But have no fear for me."

At this mention of his seldom used first name, the man's eyes filled again. "M'lord, if—if the worst should happen, be sure that I will accompany you to the Tower."

"Aye, Robert, I know you would. But I could not allow it."

Walking toward the king's apartments, Adam noticed that the gentlemen, while bowing to him as he passed, avoided his eyes. The ladies appeared flushed and uneasy.

Tapping on the door of the room where the king awaited him and receiving permission to enter, he felt decidedly uneasy.

"Your grace," Adam bowed before the king. " 'Tis good to see you again."

The king said nothing. He was sprawled in his chair, a vast figure in purple velvet sewn with pearls and diamonds. His cap, of the same color, contrasted unfavorably with his florid complexion.

The king tapped his heavily ringed fingers on the arm of his chair. "So you have returned, traitor?"

"Traitor? I trust your majesty speaks in jest?"

Ignoring him, the king turned his head toward an inner door. "Cromwell," he bellowed. "Get in here!"

The door opened immediately, and Thomas Cromwell entered. As usual, he was dressed in black. His black hat, pulled low, emphasized his sallow complexion. Without looking at the earl, he bowed before the king. "I am here, your grace."

"I can see that!" the king spoke testily. "My eyesight is not yet failing. Cromwell, look well upon this knave who stands before me. Tell me what you see?"

"A traitor and a liar, sire," Cromwell answered.

The king leaned forward in his chair. "I have not said he is a liar. Wait until you have questioned him, fool! Then, if he denies the charge, you may call him a liar."

"As your grace commands."

Without waiting for permission to speak, Adam turned smiling eyes on the king. "Of what am I accused, your grace?"

The mildness of his tone, the smile in his eyes, ignited the king's wrath. "You conspired to spirit our son away!" he shouted.

"Nay, your grace. I did not know he was missing. I know nothing of the matter."

Henry pointed at Cromwell with a stubby finger. "You heard him! You may now call him a liar."

Cromwell flushed faintly. "You are a liar, my lord," he said in a strained voice.

Adam swept the embarrassed man an ironical bow. "Thank you," he murmured.

Henry fixed him with angry blue eyes. "You dare to say you had no part in our son's escape?"

"Since your grace has no son, how could I have had a part in it?" As soon as the words had left his lips, Adam cursed himself for a bold-tongued fool.

Cromwell gave one startled look at the king's congested face. "Sire! I bet you to be calm!"

The king pointed a shaking finger at the earl. "You will regret those words! The boy was my son, you aided him to escape. I will send for Mistress Trigg. Let me hear you deny it before her. For each time you do, my lord, I will increase the punishment I have in mind for the lady. Go, Cromwell, fetch in Mistress Trigg."

"Mistress Trigg knows nothing," Adam said hoarsely.

"But you do, my lord."

Adam turned his head as Cromwell returned, pushing Corianne before him. A furious anger filled him. Corianne's red gown was stained with damp and torn at the hem. Her hair fell untidily over her face. As she raised her head, he could see a livid bruise extending from her eye to her chin.

"Adam!" Joy flushed Corianne's haggard face. "I prayed you would come!"

Adam swung around on the king. "What have you done to

her?" He advanced upon him, his eyes dangerous. "By God, I'll kill you for this!"

"Guards!" the king shouted. "Seize this man!" he commanded, as six men filed into the room.

Two of them sprang forward. The earl's arms were grasped and twisted painfully.

The king smiled with satisfaction. "Now then, my lord Somercombe, did you or did you not aid my son to escape? Answer me truthfully, and you have my word that Mistress Trigg will not suffer."

"Your word!" Adam said contemptuously. "I fear that the word of Henry Tudor is not greatly to be relied upon."

"Adam!" Corianne's voice was anguished. "For God's sake be silent!"

"You may well call on God, Mistress Trigg," Henry snarled. "'Tis the rogue's only hope." He turned back to Adam. "Well, my lord, will you answer?"

"And if I give you the answer you require, what of Mistress Trigg?"

Corianne sprang forward. "You must not think of me, Adam!" she cried out desperately. She struggled against the guards who sought to restrain her. "Say nothing, my darling!"

The king's eyes were hot as they rested upon her. "You speak as though you are in love with this traitorous swine, Mistress Trigg. Yes 'tis not long since that you professed to be enamored of your king."

Her head jerked up. "How could you believe that I could be enamored of my father's murderer?"

"Madam Tudor!" Adam's urgent voice was loud. "Hold your tongue, you little fool!"

Cromwell stepped forward. "You are hardly in a position to bid the wench be silent, my lord," he said, his lip curling, "when only a moment ago you threatened our sovereign lord, the king."

A vein in Henry's temple began to throb. He made use of Cromwell, but he had never liked him. Often he referred to him as "that tradesman's son!" and sometimes as "that damned butcher's cur!" But even with rage boiling through his veins, he could not altogether forget his affection for my lord Somercombe. The truth was, affronted and furious though he might be, he could not help feeling a sneaking admiration for the earl who, even though his life trembled on the word of his king, had not hesitated to threaten him. Henry admired courage before all else. But even so, not even Somercombe could threaten his king. He must be made to pay for the insult to his royal dignity. Furious at the position in which he found himself, longing to forgive Somercombe but unable to bring himself to do so, Henry shouted at Cromwell, "Shut your mouth, idiot! We do not recall giving you permission to speak." His glare turned on Adam. "Well, my lord?"

"I will tell you what you wish to know," Adam answered with a calm he was far from feeling, "if you will allow Mistress Trigg to go free. Have I your word, sire?"

"Our word, according to yourself, my lord, will be of little use to you."

Adam shrugged. "I must believe that your grace has some honor."

Henry's hand clenched. He would not take this much from any other man. Again he felt that stir of admiration. By God's precious soul! Why did the fool not beg for his life? Why did he not give Henry Tudor the chance he was even now seeking to show mercy? His little eyes flickered. "The maiden will be comfortable enough," he grunted.

"Then I will admit that I aided Tudor Trigg to escape."

Henry let out his pent-up breath. "Where is the lad?"

"I have no idea."

"Where is he?"

"I repeat, your grace, I have no idea."

Henry rose from his chair. "Take Mistress Trigg," he ordered. "She is to be locked in her apartment until such time as I decide what shall be done with her."

"So that is Henry Tudor's word?" Adam cried, as Corianne was dragged from the room.

"Aye, that is the extent of our word, my lord, until such time as you see fit to tell us where our son may be found."

"Your grace has no son!"

Henry sat down again. "We will see how you like a sojourn in the Tower, my lord. There are instruments there that will cajole the stubbornest man into giving tongue. No doubt you have heard of them?"

Adam's face paled, but he answered as though indifferently, "I have heard of them, sire, and seen them."

"Then you know what to expect," Henry said grimly. "You will not be so bravely silent when you are stretched on the rack and your limbs jerked from their sockets, I'll wager." Surrendering to a sudden weakness for the handsome rogue before him, Henry said gruffly, "Come, Adam lad, don't be a fool. I do not intend to hurt the boy. Rather do I wish to honor him. What harm is there in telling me where he may be found?"

Adam shook his head. "I do not know his whereabouts, your grace. But I can tell you that Tudor Trigg would be harmed if he has glory thrust upon him which he does not desire. He is not your son. Were you to proclaim him so to the people, he would be living a lie. And even worse, your grace, you yourself would be lying to your people."

Henry's moment of weakness vanished. "Take him!" he shouted. "For three days, on every hour, he is to be asked the whereabouts of my son. At the end of the third day, if he continues stubborn, he is to be racked." He turned his head irritably as the door opened to admit Thomas Seymour. "What is it, Tom? What do you here?"

Thomas Seymour removed his cap and made a graceful bow. His bright blue eyes twinkled as he answered, "Your grace sent for me."

Henry frowned. "Aye, so I did. You may remain, then, but do not interrupt."

"I would not dream of doing so, your grace."

Henry grunted. "What was I saying?"

Cromwell said smoothly, "Your grace was saying that my lord Somercombe is to be racked."

"At the end of three days, I said! Art deaf, fool?"

"No, your grace."

"Then hold your tongue! You have heard me, Somercombe. If the rack fails to break you, then mayhap the sight of Mistress Trigg suffering a like fate will serve to loosen your tongue."

Adam was about to reply when he met Thomas Seymour's eyes. They conveyed an unmistakable warning. "Your plans are made then, your grace?" Adam's words were addressed to the king, but they were meant for Seymour. From the corner of his eye, he watched him. Would he understand? He saw

171

Seymour nod very slightly and he was conscious of relief. Seymour would aid Madam Tudor. He could trust him.

"My plans, as you say, my lord," the king answered, "are made. They cannot be altered, save by yourself."

Still watching Seymour covertly, Adam said, "Think you they will be successful, your grace?"

Again he caught Seymour's nod. "The rack, my lord, is invariably successful," Henry said grimly. He waved his hand. "Take him away."

Seymour was thoughtful as the earl was taken from the king's presence. Mistress Trigg seemed to have fallen from favor, for the king had returned to Jane's arms. If Anne Boleyn miscarried or was brought to bed with another girl, Jane, from the knowledge he had gleaned from incautious remarks the king had dropped, was certain to be Queen of England. If that were so, why take the unnecessary risk of aiding Mistress Trigg? He turned upon the king his most charming smile. I could not very well stop my ears, your grace, therefore I could not help overhearing your remarks concerning Mistress Trigg. I would regret greatly if such a charming creature were racked. I will confess to your grace that the lady more than interests me."

Henry scowled. "The threat to rack the maiden was made in jest," he said curtly. "And if you value your head, Tom, your interest in Mistress Trigg had best die a speedy death. I am in love with the wench."

"In love!" Seymour exclaimed, dismayed. "I had thought my sister claimed your grace's affections. Of late, you have shown her much favor."

Henry's eyes shifted. "Jane is well enough. She is a soothing companion, but perhaps not the most exciting. Mistress Trigg is different. She denies her love for me, but she does not mean it. I find her exciting. Full of fire and spirit." He chuckled. "Her object in denying her love for me is to turn me from Jane, whom she mistakenly believes possesses my heart."

The blind fool! Seymour thought. He possessed Mistress Trigg's hatred, not her love. Could he not see it? But no. He saw only what he wanted to see. He had ever been that way.

Seymour moistened his lips. He must make quite sure. "If

your grace will forgive me for saying so, Mistress Trigg's treatment of late has not been of the best."

Henry shrugged. "I had need to know my son's whereabouts. But I forbade the use of actual brutality. Mayhap there were times when she went a little hungry, or, owing to her cursed stubbornness, was somewhat bruised, but I have Somercombe now, and Mistress Trigg can rest easy." He smiled. "Think you I would allow harm to come to the lady who holds my heart?"

"Then you are satisfied that she did not conspire in her brother's escape?"

"In my son's escape, you mean," Henry corrected him coldly. "Nay, I am satisfied that she knows nothing." He looked at Seymour with narrowed eyes. "You seem upset, Tom," he said softly. "Can it be because the ambition of the Seymours has been thwarted?"

"The Seymours have no ambition save to serve your grace."

Henry's eyes softened. As always, Seymour was looking elegant. He was clad in a doublet of blue trimmed with gold. There was lace at his throat and wrists, and silver and green spiders clocked his blue hose. A black cloak, slung carelessly about his broad shoulders, showed a lining of silver-gray fur. He was a handsome knave, the king mused, with his thick, curling, chestnut hair, and his brilliant blue eyes. He was of much the same kidney as Somercombe. But where Seymour's manner was warm and charming, Somercombe, if you did not know him well, tended to anger you with the haughtiness of his bearing and the cold look his dark eyes could assume.

Looking at the king, Seymour wondered of what the overfed and egotistical fool was thinking? He corrected himself quickly. It did not do to underrate Henry Tudor. He was no fool, save where his self-blindness and his overpowering vanity were concerned. Perhaps he was seeing Mistress Trigg smiling up at him from his vast bed. Nay, it must be Jane! The Seymours could not be balked now! "Your grace," Seymour's voice broke the silence, "have I your leave to depart?"

Henry nodded. "I have forgotten why I sent for you. Aye, go. I would be alone for a while."

Smiling, Seymour placed his feathered cap over his heart

and swept a deep bow. "God give your majesty a serene heart and sweet repose this night."

Henry laughed. "You are in a hurry to be gone, Tom. Have you an assignation with a maiden?"

"Aye. With Elizabeth Jennet, sire. I doubt my bed will grow cold this night."

"She who was recently wed to Sir Thomas Lacey?"

"The very same, sire. And a sweeter armful it would be hard to find."

Henry's smile disappeared. His mouth pursed primly. "We do not approve of immorality in our Court, sir. The lady is married." He drummed his fingers on the arm of his chair. "The lady is not for you. We forbid you to make a mockery of a marriage which has our full approval."

Seymour lowered his lids to hide his laughing eyes. Damn, but here was a hypocrite! He to prate of morality! By God's sacred thumbs, but that was a rare jest. "I understand, sire. Your grace has my assurance that I will not again approach the lady."

Henry eyes him sternly for a moment, then, on an impulse, he held out his hand. " 'Tis forgotten, scoundrel."

"Your grace relieves my mind." Seymour's lips brushed the king's fingers lightly. Releasing the hand, he bowed again, and made his way from the chamber.

Walking briskly along the draughty corridor, Thomas Seymour told himself he must keep in mind three things: the queen, who would shortly give birth, and if she bore a boy his hopes would be in ruins; Mistress Trigg, that danger to his plans, who must be removed as speedily as possible; and his sister Jane, who must try once more, harder this time, to ingratiate herself with the king. Henry needed but gentle persuasion to turn to her once more. With Jane Queen of England, the future of the Seymours was assured. As for Mistress Trigg, his plans for her escape were all but perfected. He would be forced now to carry them through.

Seymour turned a corner, scowling as the wind tore at his hair and his small pointed beard. His mind worried over the problem of how to remove Mistress Trigg from under the very noses of her guards.

13

The earl of Somercombe stared down into the gray water of the Thames. It lapped against the worn stones that bordered the way to Traitors' Gate. Piles of rotting debris bobbed about the slow-moving barge, giving off a strong and offensive odor. A water rat dived briskly beneath the water, and Adam watched the tiny upheaval it made. The head of the rat emerged again, its eyes darting, suspicious, then it once more submerged. Glad of something with which to occupy his mind, Adam continued to watch the bubbles of the rat's progress. He wondered if the "sweating sickness" that periodically attacked London might not be the result of the rubbish and the animal and human excrement that was daily thrown into the water.

The guard positioned near to the prisoner stared at the calm profile with hostile eyes. He told himself that he did not like my lord Somercombe's haughty bearing and his seeming lack of fear. The guard spat over the side of the barge. My lord Somercombe had not once spoken to him, had not asked any questions about his possible fate, as was usual with most prisoners. Perhaps, the guard thought, my lord thought himself to be far above honest, hard-working men. That attitude wouldn't do him any good, not once he was lodged in the Tower. Aye, he wouldn't look so good once he'd been broken on the rack. His superiority would vanish quickly enough then. My lord was a traitor, and he was to be detained at the king's pleasure. It was quite likely that he would be racked to death. Making up his mind, the guard jostled the earl with his elbow. "Here, you!"

"Yes." Adam turned to face him. "You wish to speak with me, fellow?"

Beneath that cool, appraising glance, the guard flushed

crimson. He sought for something to say that would be bit-ingly sarcastic. He could think of nothing. Chagrined, he heard his tongue forming words of apology. "Your pardon, my lord. We—we are almost at Traitors' Gate."

"Thank you." Adam turned his head away. The shadow of the Tower loomed above him. The water blurred before his eyes and he was conscious of a coldness all through him. Did all men feel this way upon entering this accursed place? Did they, like himself, wonder if they had the courage to stand fast while their bodies were stretched upon the rack? Did they scream out a confession as joints were jerked from sock-ets, flesh torn by hot pincers, their bodies impaled upon spikes? Adam felt a wave of nausea. It would be so easy to give the king the information he required, the thought whis-pered in his mind, tempting him. So very easy. The king, or so he had said, did not seek to harm the boy, instead he thought to honor him.

Adam's fingers gripped the rail before him. No, he could not do it. There was more to it than that. If the queen bore a male child, Tudor would lose his life. There was Madam Tudor's future to think of, and his own, if he had any. At this moment, Madam Tudor was as much the king's prey as he was himself. Adam relaxed his grip on the rail. Nothing remained for him to do but to place himself in God's hands. Maybe he would be given the courage to remain silent.

The barge bumped against the landing. The guard stole a quick, malicious look at the prisoner. He was annoyed to find that the earl of Somercombe's face was quite expressionless.

The barge was tied up at the landing. As Adam alighted, he saw the grave-faced Sir William Kingston, Constable of the Tower, come forward to greet him.

Greetings, Adam thought. Welcome to your prison. What irony! He could do very well without that particular greeting. Facing Sir William Kingston, he was once more in command of himself. "Good day to you, Sir William," he said calmly. "I regret that we meet again under such circumstances."

"I also," Sir William answered. "I regret it deeply." His eyes turned to the small company of stiffly drawn up guards. "My lord, these men will escort you to your lodging. Pray go with them."

Adam nodded. "Lodging? That is a tactful way of putting it." He turned away.

"Wait!" the single word was urgent in tone. Lowering his voice, Sir William spoke rapidly. "Your quarters are as comfortable as it was within my power to make them, but at best they are miserable. My lord, I beg you not to continue stubborn. If you do, your life will become a hell on earth. Believe me, I know!" He looked pleadingly at Adam. "Tell the king what he wants to know. Do not let the torturers use their instruments upon you. You cannot conceive of the agony such instruments can inflict upon the human body. I have seen sights that would turn the stomach of the strongest man. My lord, heed me!"

The governor's eyes were brown and mournful in his deeply lined face, and his usually firm mouth was unsteady. "You are not the man for this job, Sir William," Adam said gently. "You are too compassionate. Why do you stay?"

Sir William flushed. "I am not deserving of the compliment. There are times when I am exceedingly harsh. I have to be. It is true that I have no belly for this job, but the king himself appointed me to the post. Since I cannot leave it of my own free will, I have no choice but to regard my appointment as an honor."

Adam placed the tips of his fingers for a brief moment on the governor's arm. Bowing, he strode toward the waiting guards.

Despite all his will power, Adam could not prevent the slight faltering of his footsteps as the dank chill of the Tower closed about him. Nobody seemed to remark the hesitation. Nobody spoke. He walked on, the clanking of armor in his ears.

He was thrust into a small, dark room. One of the men stepped forward and unbound his wrists. He thanked the man. The door slammed shut before the last word was out of his mouth. A key grated in the lock, the clanking of armor receded into the distance. He was alone.

Adam sat down on a rough wooden bench that was set beneath a slitlike window. He shivered as a blast of cold air blew in upon him. He listened to the shrill cries of the circling birds, and, in the distance, a child's raised, laughing voice. It was strange, he thought, to hear the voice of a child in this place of horror. Strange, and somehow obscene. But he knew that many of the guards lived at the Tower, and their children with them. Also, it was not uncommon for children to be brought to the Tower and held there as prisoners. He was reminded uncomfortably of the fate of the two little princes. The royal children had been lodged in the Tower at the command of their uncle, who later became King Richard III. The present king's mother had been the sister of the two ill-fated boys. While in the Tower, the boys had abruptly and mysteriously disappeared. They were never seen or heard of again. There were many speculations as to their possible fate, and all of them chilling.

Adam rose and began to pace restlessly. Stale rushes crackled beneath his feet, adding their stench to the all-pervading miasma that rose from the Thames. He thought of Madam Tudor. Where was she? What had been done to her? Adam's mouth softened. Madam Tudor! Until he had met her, he had believed himself to be incapable of falling in love. She had changed all that. He was vulnerable now. It was not only her beauty he admired, though it delighted his eyes, but her courage and her fighting spirit. He loved her. She was everything he had ever hoped to find in a woman.

He stopped pacing. What of his own courage? When a demand was made upon that courage, would he fail to meet it?

He walked slowly over to the window and pressed his face against the bars. He must not fail. Somehow he would endure, if he knew that Madam Tudor was safe. "Help her, Seymour," he said aloud. "Honor your promise to me. If you default, and if I should survive this place and walk into freedom, I will find you and I will kill you!"

With the waning of the daylight, a guard entered the earl's cell. He placed a guttering candle in a pewter holder on the planks that did duty as a table. Stealing a quick look at the prisoner, he found that he was smiling. His manner, when he thanked him for the light, was calm and pleasant.

Returning to his companions, the guard remarked, "If you was to ask me, I'd say that m'lord Somercombe's a rare plucky one. He's sitting in his cell as bobbish as you please. He don't show no fear at all." He shrugged. "All the same, I'd sooner it was him than me."

"Me too," another man put in. He grinned, and then,

178

stretching his arms above his head, he yawned loudly. "He won't be so bobbish once he's had a taste of the rack. I'll bet he opens his mouth at the first twist. He'll tell 'em what they want to know, you mark my words."

The first guard considered this. "I don't think so," he said, shaking his head. "He's got a look about him, this one has. Aye, I'll have a bet with you, Stanson. I don't think he's going to tell 'em nothing."

"Save your money. You'd lose."

"Not me. I'll double the bet, if you like. M'lord Somercombe reminds me of Stephen Philmore. Remember him? They nearly tore Philmore apart. But nothing they could do to him would make him speak."

The other man rubbed thoughtfully at his chin. "Right," he said at last. "If you want to throw your hard-earned money away, I don't mind picking it up."

14

The queen heard the sound of approaching footsteps. They were muffled as yet, but they seemed to be drawing steadily nearer to her apartments. With that presentiment of danger that was always with her now, she began to tremble. Beneath the stiff casing of her green satin bodice, her breasts rose and fell with the agitation of her breathing. She folded the little coat she had been embroidering and laid it to one side. Then she sat up straighter in her chair, her attitude one of waiting.

The queen's ladies, unaware of anything amiss, went quietly on with their work, their subdued chatter making a pleasant and soothing background. Margaret Vane, the youngest of the ladies, glanced at the queen at that moment. She was immediately aware of her tension. Poor lady! Margaret thought. Who would be the wife of Henry VIII, if it meant that one must ever walk with fear? She felt a rush of pity for the queen. The people of the streets said, "She is a whore! She has broken good Queen Catherine's heart. The Princess Mary is thrust to one side to make way for Elizabeth, her bastard!"

Margaret felt sincere compassion for the unhappy Catherine and her daughter, but she could not help feeling that Anne Boleyn had paid in terror for usurping her position. Remembering the touch of the king's caressing hand on her own flesh, Margaret shuddered. I would not stand in Anne Boleyn's shoes, she thought, if I were offered all the riches of the universe!

The footsteps had stopped outside the door. Anne rose unsteadily to her feet, one hand in her familiar gesture, stroking her slender white throat. She could hear voices outside, as though whoever stood there were debating among themselves.

180

Then, without the courtesy of a preliminary knock, the door was flung open.

Anne stared at the four men who stood on her threshold, noting that they appeared to be as agitated as she herself felt. She singled out one of them. "What means this intrusion, Sir William?" she said coldly. "How dare you enter my apartments in so boorish a fashion?"

Sir William Wychwood, who had long resented "the concubine," as the Spanish ambassador had dubbed her, said, "I crave your pardon, madam. We bring grave news."

Anne's hand clenched. "What news is this?"

Wychwood glanced at the startled faces of the ladies, then he looked once more at the queen, "The king, madam, has been injured whilst hunting. 'Tis feared that his gracious majesty is dead."

"Dead!" The room seemed to tilt before Anne's eyes. "He cannot be dead!"

The men standing behind Wychwood looked red-faced and uncomfortable. "We must pray that 'tis only a rumor, madam," Wychwood said in a clear cold voice. "But I greatly fear it is true."

Anne's stiffly held shoulders sagged. "I must go to him," she said in a dull voice.

One of the men, Adrian Peterson, casting an angry look at Wychwood, stepped forward. "It would be better to wait, madam," he said gently. "The king is being carried here." He looked at Wychwood again. "I, for one, am by no means certain his grace is dead."

Anne caught at the back of the chair, gripping it tightly with both hands. "Then I will wait, gentlemen. But for now, I pray you to leave me."

The men bowed and went hurriedly from the room. Anne looked so stricken, so white, that her ladies stared at her in alarm.

"Madam!" Margaret Vane went to her side. "Remember that it has not been established that his grace is dead." She touched Anne's rigid arm. "Let us kneel in prayer. Mayhap it will aid you."

Anne stared at her with burning eyes, then she gave a burst of hysterical laughter. "Yes, pray!" she shrieked. "Down on your knees, all of you. Pray for the soul of Henry Tudor!"

Terrified of the distraught queen, the ladies fell to their knees and bowed their heads. Anne turned to Margaret, who was still standing. "Listen to them," she said in a low voice. "It will take a world of prayer to save the soul of the king."

Margaret was shocked, but she endeavored not to show it. In a low, soothing voice, she said, "Dear, madam, you are distraught. You know not what you say."

All of Anne's carefully built up reserve, her armor against those who held her in enmity, dropped from her. She spoke not as queen to subject but as woman to woman. "I hate him, Margaret. I have done so for a long time. He is a monster!"

Alarmed, Margaret glanced at the kneeling ladies. "Madam, you must be careful. I pray you to say no more."

"What does it matter? The king is dead."

"He may not be. Madam, I believe you know that I would never betray you. But there are others who would not scruple to do so."

Anne stared into her eyes. "I believe you, Margaret." She put her hands to her stomach. "Oh, Margaret, who will pray for Anne Boleyn? Who will pray for the little bastard yet to be delivered?"

Margaret drew in her breath sharply. "Bastard? I do not understand you, madam."

Again Anne burst into uncontrolled laughter. " 'Tis what they will call him. And my Elizabeth, what will her future be? My children will be spoken of as the bastards of Anne Boleyn, the king's whore!" She covered her face with her hands, her shoulders shaking.

The prayers had ceased. The ladies peered between their fingers, wondering what to do next. At a sign from Margaret, they rose to their feet and flocked about the queen. Unresisting, she allowed them to lead her to her bed. She lay there like one already dead, her wide-open eyes fixed unblinkingly on the purple and gold canopy above her head. The ladies stood silently, looking helplessly at each other. The duchess of Ardeth was the first to move. She reached for the white fur cover folded at the foot of the bed and drew it over the queen. "You must try not to worry, your grace. It will be bad for the child."

Anne's head turned slowly. "It may be that the king is dead, Elizabeth. How can I help worrying?"

"And it may be that he is not. Your grace must think first of the child."

Anne's eyes sought those of Lady Rochford, her sister-in-law. "I have a feeling this child will not live, Jane," she said clearly. "If it should be so, I am sure it will please you to know that I am fallen into such calamity."

It will, Jane Rochford thought, with that bitter hatred she had always borne her husband's sister. It will please me, and may you be damned as a black-hearted witch! She said calmly, "Your grace is most certainly overwrought, else would you know that I have ever wished you well." She folded her long pale hands before her. "I believe the king lives, madam. I believe, too, that the child will live."

Anne's fingers plucked at the fur coverlet. "But if the king is dead, Jane, will you uphold and support me? Will you shield me from those who, in their hatred, will turn and rend me?"

Jane Rochford's eyes were as hard as stones. She looked about her at the ladies, who were staring at her speculatively. "Your grace must know the answer to that," she said at last.

"Aye, Jane, I fear I do."

"Surely, madam, my loyalty is not in question?"

Anne's smile was bitter. "Nay. No more than it has ever been. Where is Mistress Seymour?"

"I am here, your grace." Jane Seymour, her face pale, her blue eyes wide with distress, pressed forward.

"What, Mistress Seymour, not yet fled to your lover? Not yet clasping his dead body in your arms and mourning the downfall of your great hopes?"

Jane could not look away from the queen's drawn face beneath the small, pearled hood of white velvet. There was both misery and mockery in Anne's eyes. "M—M—Madam," Jane stammered. "With all respect, I must protest!"

"Alas, poor Mistress Seymour, you will never now be Queen of England."

"Madam, it is not true! Never did I cherish such an ambition."

"So small and delicate a maiden, and yet so treacherous," Anne's softly mocking voice went on. She looked at Jane's pale blue gown. "I do not approve of your mourning robes, Mistress Seymour. They show a lack of proper respect for his grace."

A sob broke from Jane Seymour. She curtsied; then, her face flaming with humiliation, she stepped back.

Anne did not notice in the sudden pain that struck her body. She moaned aloud. "God have mercy! The child comes before his time!"

"I believe your grace to be mistaken," Margaret Vane said in a sharp, firm voice. "I pray you to lie still. You must compose yourself. For it is yet to be proved that the king is dead."

Anne started up on the bed. "Why are you all standing here?" she cried wildly. "Get you gone! As soon as word comes, bring it to me. I must know. I cannot too much longer endure this suspense!"

The ladies fled from the room, all save Margaret Vane. Anne lay back against the pillows and closed her eyes. Henry, she thought, I lie here mourning, but not in grief for you, who have killed all feeling within me. Nay, I mourn for the future of my children. What will become of Elizabeth, of this other child, should he live? After a while, worn out with doubt and fear, Anne Boleyn slept.

Confusion reigned throughout the palace. It had been said that the king was dead. But he was not dead, for here he was striding among them, looking huge and healthy in his mud-stained doublet of green velvet.

He looked at their faces, and his laughter echoed through the great hall. "Why," he bellowed, "I vow you believed that Henry Tudor lay dead. Aye, and you were all for burying him, I'll wager. It would take more than a fall from a horse to kill me. I am bruised, but otherwise unhurt. Come, good people, let there be no more long faces about me. Wine for everybody! You must drink to the good health of your king."

A babble of voices broke out. For once the king did not rebuke them. It was a sign of their love and loyalty, he thought. Hands reached out to touch him, as though to be assured that he was really there. Laughter echoed through the hall as they toasted the king, and each gentleman strove to outdo the other with flowery compliments.

The king, his bruised leg propped upon a stool, beamed at them all. "You are wonderful, my people. I thank God that he spared me to reign over you!"

Henry's face, already flushed, grew redder from the effects of the wine and the heat from the great log fires blazing at both ends of the hall. Some of the eyes that watched the king were blank with disappointment. Henry did not notice. He continued to laugh, to thump shoulders in hearty good fellowship, and to rejoice in what he believed was universal jubilation.

Lady Margaret Vane came into the hall. Her pearled skirts swaying, she made her way through the crowd until she stood before the king. She curtsied. "Sire," she said, a little frightened catch in her voice, "the queen is in premature labor."

Those nearest to the king heard the words, and they saw the color drain from his face, leaving it pasty, his heavy jowls quivering. When he rose to his feet to follow after Lady Margaret, they made way for him hastily.

"The queen is in premature labor!" the words were tossed through the gathering. There were only a few there who pitied Anne Boleyn, or thought of what this could mean to her.

Thomas Seymour did not pity her, rather was he delighted with the turn of events. Smiling, he flicked an imaginary speck of dust from his wide, russet-red sleeve. *I thank you, Anne Boleyn. A premature child seldom lives, so, in your graciousness, you will be clearing the way for Jane. Also, while all thoughts are with you in this critical time, it will be much easier for me to smuggle Mistress Trigg from the palace.*

Later that afternoon, the palace guards saw Thomas Seymour approaching. He walked with leisurely steps, and clinging to his arm was a woman. She was wearing a red hooded cloak. Her face could not be seen, for her hood was drawn well forward and her head was snuggled affectionately against Seymour's shoulder. The guards exchanged uncertain looks. When the woman spoke in a shrill, laughing voice, "Don' make me laugh no more, Tom Seymour. Be the death o' me, you will!" their uncertainty turned to indulgence.

Such behavior, they told themselves, was not unexpected in

185

a frisky gentleman like Thomas Seymour. He was not only a favorite of the king's, but a law unto himself. His behavior, of course, showed little concern for the queen, who, they had heard, was still in labor and fighting for her life, and the life of the child. But Seymour was Seymour. It was not seemly to smuggle a common woman of the streets into the palace, a whore probably, if one went by her general behavior. Still, as long as the king didn't find out, they were prepared to close their eyes. Grins were exchanged. How had he managed to get the wench into the palace without being observed? Leave it to Seymour to find a way. He'd probably hoisted her through a window. The king, no matter his own morals, had always held that his Court must be rigidly moral. It was just like Seymour to take full advantage of the turmoil at present prevailing.

Seymour gave the guards a friendly, man-to-man wink. "Not a word, lads," he said softly, "if you place any value on my neck."

Still maintaining his stiffly upright position, one of them, a hint of laughter in his voice, answered, "Depend upon us. We have seen nothing."

"You're good lads, and you'll not be sorry." He drew the woman past them. "Come now, sweetheart," he said in a coaxing voice, "dally not. You must away to your lodgings, and to more of your amorous work."

The woman gave a shriek of laughter. "There's them as wouldn't turn Moll out so early. Still, it was worth me time. You're a pretty gentleman, an' you pays well. You come'n see me again, an' I won't charge you nothin'. Tha's just to show how much I likes you."

"You are as generous as you are beautiful," Seymour said smoothly, continuing to urge her along. "Why wait for some-time? I was ever one to accept a generous offer. I myself will escort you home."

They vanished from sight, borne along on the waves of the woman's shrill laughter.

Thomas Seymour did not speak as he conducted the woman to the waiting carriage. His lips were set and his eyes flickered nervously as he handed her in.

The carriage bowled over several miles of rutted, muddy roads, stopping finally before a dark, narrow house in one of

London's meanest districts. Seymour heaved a deep sigh. Taking the woman's hand in his, he raised it to his lips. "My felicitations, Mistress Trigg, on a truly admirable performance."

Corianne drew her hand away. "Thank you," she said, pushing the red hood back. "I found it easy, after all, and I had feared it would be extremely hard. I trembled lest my voice be recognized."

"Hardly," Seymour drawled. "The cursed shrillness of your tone set my ears to wincing." He grinned. " 'Tis the guards who absented themselves from their post outside your door who had best tremble, and one of them so far gone with wine that it was child's play to filch his key. Poor devils! I'd not like to be in their shoes. We have Anne Boleyn to thank for that piece of luck. Between toasting the unborn child and enjoying the unaccustomed relaxation, 'twas easy. And as my reputation with ladies of all classes is well known, the guards will not connect the hussy in the red cloak with Mistress Trigg."

Corianne considered him, a faint frown between her brows. She was grateful for his help, but she felt she knew exactly why he had troubled himself on her behalf. She said severely, "I pray that her grace may be safely delivered of a prince." She hesitated. "I feel sure you must wish for the same?"

Seymour smiled. "Why no, sweetheart. 'Twould upset my plans, you see."

Looking into his laughing eyes, she thought, he is quite shameless. Yet it is impossible not to like him. Adam sprang into her mind and she forgot Seymour. Adam, Adam! What is happening to you? The king had threatened torture. Thomas Cromwell, that hateful smile on his thin lips, had come to her and told her. If Adam would not speak, he was to be broken on the rack. He might be dying, for all she knew! How could she go to Gravesend and join Tudor as though nothing had happened? She looked at Seymour. "What of my lord Somercombe?"

Her eyes looked haunted as she asked the question, and her mouth was trembling. He found himself moved. Despite his plotting and his ruthless, driving ambition, he was tenderhearted. He took her hand in his and held it lightly. "You are in love with him?"

"Yes," Corianne said simply. "I thought you knew. I will not go to Gravesend unless it is with my lord Somercombe!"

Her voice was so determined that Seymour fell into a brooding silence. The wench might yet ruin everything. He said slowly and carefully, " 'Tis best to be prepared, Mistress Trigg. Should Somercombe preserve his silence, and if I know him, he will, he may well die. Or if he does not die, he may wish himself dead."

"No!" She wrenched her hand from his. "I will go to the king and humble myself before him. I will tell him where he may find Tudor!"

Seymour shot an uneasy look at the coachman's broad back. "Gently, gently," he warned. "Millington is loyal to me, yet 'tis best to be careful." He lowered his voice to a whisper. "If you go back, you will be forced to submit to the king."

"I know it. Yet, if it means my lord will live, I will do it."

Seymour was annoyed. A plague on the chit! "Even if Somercombe were pardoned, you could still lose him. He is not the man to take your submission to the king lightly. He can be hard and unyielding. Believe me, I know."

"But he will live! I will not be the king's mistress, I will be his wife. He has offered me marriage."

Seymour's face changed. "It would make no difference to Somercombe. In any case," he added harshly, "the king is already married."

"Aye. And he was married when you made your plan to place your sister on the throne of England."

For a moment Seymour's eyes were hard and menacing, then he smiled faintly. "*Touché*, Mistress Trigg. I admire your spirit. However, I must insist you leave London."

Corianne shook her head. "Unless you think of some plan to aid my lord Somercombe, I will return to the king." She touched his knee. "You are clever. You will think of something. You can do it, if you will."

Seymour sighed. "You are adamant?"

"I am. Can you help him?"

"Aye, confound you! I think I can, but it will be difficult and damned fatiguing, to say nothing of the risks involved." He shrugged. "Fortunately, I have friends in many places."

"Even in the Tower?"

"Even there."

MADAM TUDOR

Her eyes were shining, and she looked so beautiful that he was tempted to pull her into his arms and kiss her. "How can I ever thank you?"

"Save your thanks," Seymour said irritably. " 'Tis not yet done. Plans, I have, and loyal friends. But both may fail me, for all I know." His eyes sharpened. "If I do this, my life will be in your hands. How do I know you won't betray me?"

"I give you my word."

"A woman's word!"

"Listen to me," Corianne pleaded. "If I were to betray you, my lord Somercombe would be lost to me. Is that not enough for you?"

"But afterward, when Somercombe is well away?"

"Do you think me so treacherous and ungrateful?" she cried. "I pray you to take my word!"

Seymour stroked his small, pointed beard. "Ambition may stir, Mistress Trigg. You may see yourself as the next Queen of England."

She looked at him impatiently. "How can you be so foolish! The man revolts me. I could only endure him if it meant that by doing so, Adam would go free. In any case, sir, 'tis the reflection of your own ambition for your sister you see, not mine."

"Mayhap. Mayhap."

"Then you will help me?"

He shrugged. "It may be that I will try."

Corianne's eyes hardened. "If you do not, I will doubtless find ambition stirring after all."

"I could have killed you. I could very easily make such arrangements."

Her hand touched his knee again. "But you will not employ such desperate measures, will you? Say instead that you will aid my lord Somercombe to escape."

He capitulated suddenly. "I will do my best. I promise you." He looked down at her hand. "And the price will be one kiss."

"Take your kiss, if you desire it. You are an attractive man, and 'tis an easy price to pay."

"You are not easily discomfited, are you, minx?" he said, drawing her into his arms. His lips hovered over hers, his

189

warm breath fanned her face. "How do you know I will keep my word?"

"Thomas Seymour, so I have heard, has a proud boast. He always keeps his word."

He smiled wryly. "And I have given my word, have I?"

"You have. You cannot deny it!"

"I won't attempt to deny it." He thrust her from him. "Keep your kiss. Tom Seymour was never one to kiss unwilling lips." He touched her hair with gentle fingers. "I envy Somercombe."

For the first time, Corianne leaned forward and looked at the house. It looked dark and forbidding. "I am to stay in that place?" she asked in dismay.

"You are to hide there," he corrected. " 'Tis a dingy place, I know, but 'tis safe. Peg Barnes, who lives here, is a good friend of mine. I saved her man from hanging. He is long since dead, but she had never forgotten. You may depend upon her to keep you safe."

At his nod, Corianne rose to her feet. "You are a rogue, Thomas Seymour, but a likable rogue. I shall never forget you."

Springing down, he assisted her to alight. The road was muddy and strewn with garbage of all descriptions. His bright blue eyes laughed into hers. "I am gratified, Mistress Trigg." He swung her around and prodded her toward the door. "In with you. Peg has curious neighbors, and we have already given them a feast for the eyes."

He lifted the large, round knocker, rapping it impatiently.

" 'Ere, then," a querulous voice sounded above the creaking of the slowly opening door. "Who in the name o' the bloody fiends is it?"

The door was flung wide. The woman who stood in the doorway was so tiny of stature that she was almost a dwarf. She wore a white, lace-bordered cap upon a mop of graying hair, and her shriveled figure was lost beneath an overlarge gown of black cotton. At the sight of Seymour, her wrinkled face broke into a radiant smile. "Well, if it ain't me own boyo! What the 'ell kept you? I been expecting you these past few days." She stood back from the door. "Come on in, me lovie." Her small brown eyes twinkled at him. She looked quickly at Corianne. "Your pretty one is welcome, too."

With Corianne following him, Seymour strode into the dark hall. Gathering the woman in his arms, he kissed her cheek. "And how is my dainty Peg, my one true love?"

"Fiends seize you!" Peg cried, pretending to struggle. "Keep your 'ands to yourself. I'm a decent woman, I'd 'ave you know."

Releasing her, Seymour gave her a playful slap on the behind. "You're a trollop, and you know it." Turning to Corianne, he drew her forward. "This is Mistress Corianne Trigg. She will be staying with you for a while."

Peg's sharp eyes surveyed the girl. "Right," she said briefly. "Come this way."

They followed her along the short, musty-smelling passage, into a large, cluttered room. Two lean, white dogs were sprawled at their ease before a blazing log fire. They bounded swiftly to their feet, their yellowish-brown eyes suspicious.

"Down Ruff, down Muff," the woman said absently. "Sit you down, Master Tom, and you, mistress. Don't stan' around cluttering up me room." She seated herself. "Tell me 'bout it, Master Tom."

They talked for a long time. Peg looked thoughtful when Seymour had finished. At last, she said abruptly, "You going to 'elp this poor child get 'er sweetheart out o' the Tower?"

He nodded. "Aye. As soon as it is expedient."

"That's me boy! And when will you be comin' for the wench?"

"In a few days' time, I think." Seymour snapped his fingers at the dogs. They came to him at once, their tails waving. For all their fierce appearance, they wriggled in ecstasy as his hands caressed them.

"Look at them 'ounds!" Peg cried in outrage. "Supposed to protect me, they are. For all the use they are, I could be murdered in me bed. I'll go'n get you some o' me wine."

The door slammed shut behind her. Seymour smiled at Corianne. "Don't be put off by her manner. Her bark has ever been worse than her bite."

"And yours," Corianne said softly. "I knew you'd help me."

"The deed is not yet done," he warned. "I may fail."

"I don't think you'll fail," Corianne answered him calmly. "Were you to do so, it would sadly disturb your plans."

"More threats?"

"Aye. 'Tis the only weapon I have to fight with."

"Minx!"

"Exactly, Sir Rogue," Corianne said.

Seymour sprawled at his ease in the chair, his lazy eyes taking her in. She was too beautiful, he thought, for his peace of mind. Firelight flickered over her, highlighting the rich black of her hair and casting a golden glow over her face. "Should you tire of Somercombe, Mistress Trigg," he murmured, "you will find me ready and waiting."

Corianne looked at him with amused blue eyes. "Since I will never tire, the question does not arise."

Seymour nodded. "A great pity. You know not what you are missing, and I cannot but marvel at your folly."

Corianne smiled. "I, sir, am quite content to remain in ignorance."

15

The king paced the small anteroom that led directly into the queen's suite. His afflicted leg, owing to his fall, was more painful than usual, but he scarcely noticed it. Anne's cries of agony as she struggled to bring forth the child made little impression on his mind. All his thoughts were concentrated upon his son. For surely, this time, it would be a son? God must heed his prayers. He must not cheat him again!

He stopped his pacing. With his ear pressed to the door, he listened intently. A curse on the fools! What were they doing in there? Was the child born, and if so, were they actually daring to keep him waiting?

He limped wearily to a padded bench. Sitting down, he covered his face with his hands. Without warning, he found his thoughts turning to Catherine, his first and unlawful wife. Catherine had died at Kimbolton Castle, at two o'clock in the afternoon, on the seventh of January. Today, January the twenty-ninth, she was to be buried. Death! Why must he think of death when a new life was about to enter the world? He remembered his words when the news of Catherine's death had been brought to him. "Thank God!" he had exclaimed. "She is dead at last!"

Wincing, he began to massage his leg with a trembling hand. Had he been too brutal? Had God recorded his words? But God knew that Henry Tudor was His loving servant in all things. In casting Catherine from him, he had but obeyed God's will. He began to think of Catherine, as she had been when he first married her. Emotion seized him. Poor stupid, obstinate Kate. Why in plague had she fought him for so many years. She had known full well that their marriage was no marriage. Had she but consented to recognize this fact, he

193

would have provided her with every luxury she might have desired. But Kate would have none of it. To the very end she had proclaimed herself Queen of England and his true and lawful wife.

He thought of the last letter she had sent him. That cursed letter! It breathed Catherine in every line. He put his hand in his pocket and drew out a sheet of folded parchment. Why did he carry it with him still? He should have burned it. The words it contained haunted him. It was as though she reproached him from the very edge of the grave. Unwillingly, yet with a certain horrified fascination, he smoothed out the parchment and began to read.

"My most dear lord, king, and husband," the letter began. "The hour of my death is fast approaching. The tender love I owe you forceth me, my case being such, to commend myself unto you. I remind you of the health and safeguard of your soul, which you ought to prefer before all worldly matters, and before the care and pampering of your body, for the which you have cast me into many miseries and yourself into many troubles. For my part I pardon you all, and I wish and pray God that He will pardon you also. For the rest, I commend unto you our daughter Mary, beseeching you to be a good father unto her, as I have heretofore desired. I entreat you also, on behalf of my maids, to give them marriage portions, which is not much, they being but three. For all my other servants I ask the wages due them, and a year more, lest they be unprovided for. Lastly I make this vow, that mine eyes desire you above all things. Farewell."

Blinking tears from his eyes, the king crumpled the parchment in his hands. Words from the letter raced through his mind. "Lastly I make this vow, that mine eyes desire you above all things. Farewell."

"Oh, Kate," he said aloud. "You know well that I did but do my duty by God and my people! Why did you force me to act against you?" He thrust the letter back into his pocket, and as he did so, a comforting thought came to him. Catherine had said, "Mine eyes desire you above all things." It meant that, at the very end, she had recognized that his actions were right and just. And that she, in her obstinacy, had killed herself in the chastisement of herself and the lacking of her body of those comforts which he would willingly have provided.

His head swung around as the door leading to the queen's suite opened. He stood up, trying to control his trembling, and stared at the white-faced Margaret Vane. "Well?" he demanded. "What of the child?"

"Sire," Margaret's voice shook. "H—Her grace is r—resting well."

"Yes, yes! What of the child?"

"It was a boy, sire. But he, most unfortunately, was born dead."

Henry thought he heard a woman laugh. Was it Catherine? Had she come back to mock him? His hands clenched, and the veins in his temples stood out prominently. "By Christ!" he roared. "The Boleyn bitch has killed my son!"

"Sire!" Margaret stared at him in horror.

He did not hear her. Pushing her to one side, he strode into the bedchamber. With an imperious gesture, he dismissed the doctor and the ladies who stood about the bed.

Anne lay flat on her back. Her face was drained of all color. There were purple shadows beneath her eyes, and her hair was still damp from the strain she had undergone. Her weary eyes lifted and looked straight into his furious face. Her lips trembled. "My lord king, you have heard?"

He loomed above her. She saw with horror that his hand was raised to strike. "You bitch!" His hand cracked hard against her cheek. "You tawdry whore! I have given you a son, and in your carelessness, you have killed him!"

Oh, God help me! Anne struggled to raise herself, but fell back helplessly. "It—it was the shock, sire," she babbled. "I had heard you had suffered an accident and died of your wounds. It—it brought on a premature birth."

In his rage-contorted face, his eyes were terrible in their mercilessness. "Christ's wounds! You have killed my son!"

She cried out in her terror, "Do not look at me like that, I pray you! I will do better next time. I will be more careful!"

He gripped her by the shoulders, lifting her so that her face was level with his own. She could smell his sour breath as he spat words into her face. "There will be no next time for you, madam! I'll give you no more sons of mine to murder!" He flung her from him. "No, madam, never again!"

She heard the door crash shut behind him. She put a clenched fist against her shaking mouth. She was doomed! What was to become of her? "Holy Father," she whispered, "In your charity and mercy, please help me!"

The king limped along the corridor. His eyes were so blinded by tears that he did not notice Cromwell approaching him.

"Sire," Cromwell bowed. "I fear that I bring you ill news. The lady, Mistress Trigg, has escaped."

Henry's throat worked as he struggled to bring out words. "My son!" he said at last. "My son is dead!"

Appalled, Cromwell stared at him. "Forgive me, sire. I did not know."

Henry gripped him fiercely by the shoulder. "Tudor, my son. He must come to me. I care not that Mistress Trigg has fled, it is a matter I can deal with later. But Tudor must be found, I need him!"

"My lord Somercombe is the only one who knows his whereabouts," Cromwell reminded him.

Henry's eyes glared. "Torture him! Tear his body apart, I care not. But make him tell."

"He has been tortured, sire, but to no avail."

"Has he been racked?"

"Your grace will remember that you later gave orders that we were to try other tortures first."

"Rack him!"

"It shall be done, sire."

Henry moved away from him. Unconsciously, he whispered words. "Oh, my son, mine eyes desire you above all things!" Again he thought he heard Catherine laugh. "Go away, Kate. Get back to your grave and leave me to mourn my son in peace!"

He did not notice the furtive glances of the ladies and gentlemen who passed by, or their hastily executed obeisances, so tightly was he locked in his agony. "How have I failed you, God? Have mercy upon Your heartbroken son. Give me another chance, I pray You!" He thought of Jane Seymour with her soft voice and her tender touch. Jane would understand. She would comfort him.

Blindly, he entered his apartments. The gentlemen gathered

there to attend him took one look at his face. Bowing, they filed silently from the room. The king had not been aware of their presence, nor of their going. He sat down on a chair. It seemed to him that his middle years rested upon him like an intolerable weight. He was getting old, and still he had no son. Again, without willing it, his thoughts turned to Catherine. He remembered the last time he had seen her face. She had been sallow of complexion, her lips a tight line, those deep, dark Spanish eyes of hers tormented. Was the death of his son Catherine's revenge? Had she, forsaken by him and dying alone, denied even the comfort of her daughter's presence, cursed his unborn child? No, Kate, no! I loved you until I found that you had deceived me! His conscience, for once unrestrained, reminded him, "You did not wish to believe in Catherine's innocence. You did not really believe that her marriage with Arthur, your brother, had been consummated. You wanted to believe it. You were on fire for Anne Boleyn. You had to have her. Anne, with her dark eyes, her white skin, and her sensuous body. Anne Boleyn, who drove you crazy with desire!"

Henry moaned aloud as he fought with and finally restrained his conscience. "Anne Boleyn is a witch, I know it," he muttered. "Only by witchcraft could she have held me so long enthralled." His eyes narrowed to glittering blue slits. "I am blameless, for what man can fight against witchcraft? I will cast her from me even as I cast Catherine!" He closed his eyes and rested his head against the back of the chair. Cromwell would advise him. His clever brain could be relied upon to think of a way out of this unholy marriage. God would approve. He would once more shine the light of His countenance on him once more. His next marriage would be fruitful.

What of Tudor Trigg? Let his people call the boy a bastard, he cared not. Let them clamor for Mary, herself a bastard. Let them howl for Elizabeth, daughter of a witch and a whore. But if he was not blessed with a legitimate son, Tudor should mount the throne of England. He opened his eyes, and for the first time he smiled. He was suddenly convinced that God had shown him the way.

Henry sat forward in his chair, his hands gripping his knees. As God was his judge, he had no real desire to hurt Adam. He loved him like a son. But he must be made to tell.

If he would speak, he would show him mercy. The injuries he suffered from the torture would be tenderly cared for. He should go forth from the Tower with a full and free pardon, secure in the knowledge of Henry Tudor's friendship. Aye, Adam should live to sing his king's praises. For had he not ever been a just and merciful king?

And Anne Boleyn? His eyes, which had softened momentarily, hardened again. He must free himself from her. But free himself for whom? Would it be for Mistress Trigg, or Jane Seymour? He frowned, remembering that Mistress Trigg had fled. But she would come back on her knees, suing for his pardon. Deny it though she may, she loved him well. In the meantime, there was faithful, patient Jane. As for Anne Boleyn, it would be necessary to proceed with great delicacy. It was true that she was unpopular with the people, but who knew but what they might not reverse themselves and rally to her cause?

He rose abruptly to his feet and strode over to the door. He would send for Cromwell and reiterate his desire concerning my lord Somercombe. He would also put to him the question of the witch, Anne Boleyn.

16

Adam's swollen lids lifted slowly. He moved his limbs cautiously, and the movement stirred a nauseating odor from the filthy straw beneath him. Somewhere near to him, he could hear somebody moaning. It was a broken, whimpering sound, like that of an animal in pain. With an icy sense of shock, he realized that the sounds came from himself. He tightened his bruised and bitten lips. The simile was apt, he thought bitterly, for was he not an animal caught in Thomas Cromwell's trap?

He shuddered violently, remembering the horrors of the torture chamber. The stench of blood and fear, the agonized cries of the broken and dying. He put his hand to his forehead, his trembling fingers feeling for the deep groove that had been made by a rope. The rope, expertly wielded, had bitten deeply into his flesh. Just before unconsciousness claimed him, he had believed that his head was about to burst asunder. He thought of Morehead, the wielder of the rope, with hatred. And Thomas Cromwell with his soft, almost whispering persistent voice. His goading, his bullying, his lying promises of mercy. All he had to do was to open his mouth and give them the information desired. He had not spoken yet. And if he had the strength to maintain his resolution, he never would. If opportunity came his way, he would kill Cromwell and his torturer, Morehead!

A laugh escaped his dry throat. But they need not fear. Their instruments would kill him instead. Why didn't he speak? he asked himself now. Why didn't he save himself? He was not of the stuff of which martyrs are made, so what sealed his lips? Was it obstinacy, pride, a love of his country, that refused to allow him to see an impostor mount the throne of England, no matter how reluctant and free from intrigue that impostor might be? Or was it the tragedy of three lives destroyed, if he should give them the information? Corianne's would be destroyed, because she would never then be able to escape the king. Tudor's, because he wished to live a free life, and his own, because he could not visualize life without Corianne. But he was a fool! There must be a way out, if only his tired brain could think of it.

The shudder shook him again as he remembered the sights he had seen. Thomas Cromwell, as though conducting an honored guest on a tour, had shown him the torture chambers of the Tower of London. He had seen men stretched on the rack, their tortured limbs straining, their eyes almost bolting from faces that were drawn into masks of agony and terror. He had seen other men, their bodies pierced with thick iron spikes. He had seen fingernails and toenails brutally torn out, white-hot irons applied to the soles of feet or searing into the scalp. With the smell of blood in his nostrils, the pungent scent of burning hair and flesh, the shrieks and the begging for mercy sounding in his ears, Cromwell had led him to yet another chamber. Here he had seen a man with both his feet cramped into iron boots. As he watched, the bolts at the side of the boots were screwed tighter and tighter until, finally, the man's bones were splintered, crushed to powder. And could he ever forget the mad screaming of those victims who were thrust into a tiny chamber where they could neither stand nor sit? After a long, agonizing while, their screams had stopped as hordes of gray and hungry rats gnawed them to death.

Cromwell had said to him, "Look well upon these sights, my lord Somercombe. Do you hear the screaming, the begging? It is what you yourself will come to, if you do not give me the information I seek."

Adam put an arm across his eyes. He had not come to it as yet, but he greatly feared that he would, should the torture be increased. He had undergone the torture of the rope. His feet had been seared with hot irons, but never quite enough to cripple him. In this he suspected the hand of the king, who, because of some lingering spark of affection, had doubtless commanded that the torture be not too severe. But what did the king know of the suffocating terror of one who is trapped within an iron figure whose inside is bristling with knives, knowing that when the two halves of the figure were closed, one would be impaled. Did the king know of the madness bred by water eternally dripping slow drop by drop onto the top of the head? The rope pulled tighter and tighter about the forehead. The fear, the sickness, the bursting brain. The spiked gloves, flesh shredding, the great gouts of blood. The rat chamber!

Adam tried to subdue the trembling of his body. What had Thomas Cromwell planned for him today? Would it be the rack? He could hear Cromwell's voice sounding in his ears. "Stretched on the rack, my lord Somercombe, speech will burst from you. One little twist is enough to break the most courageous. You will be a fool if you allow yourself to suffer this most exquisite of agonies."

Adam's heart pounded as a rattle of keys outside announced the arrival of Kilkirk, his warder. The moment was here, then? He was to be taken from here to that underground room that contained the rack. The door creaked slowly open. He did not turn his head. He waited, tense and still.

Kilkirk came into the cell and stood over the earl of Somercombe. He remembered him when he had first entered the Tower. He had been upright, handsome. But he was not handsome now with his drained face, his swollen eyes, and his bleeding lips. The dark, curling hair, plastered with perspiration, was flat and lifeless. He had the look of a dead man already, Kilkirk thought, and he had not yet undergone half the torture suffered by some. The warder knew a moment's regret that he must forego the pleasure of seeing my lord Somercombe tortured beyond his endurance. But he was a poor man, and he had had his orders from Thomas Seymour. Gold in his pocket was what he craved, and Seymour had promised a plentiful supply. He couldn't, in any case, refuse to help Seymour, who knew enough of his disreputable life to have him sent to the gallows. Like it or not, he must play his part in the planned rescue. My lord Somercombe would go to the rack, it was true, but he would scarce be on before he was off. Still, there would be Seymour's gold at the end. It was a consoling thought.

Kilkirk stirred the recumbent man with his foot. "Up wi' you. 'Tis time, me lord."

"I regret," Adam answered, "but I am unable to rise without assistance. Be so good as to lend me a hand."

Kilkirk fumed. The careless ease of that voice, the arrogant tone of the swell. Kilkirk had always hated the swells. He crouched down beside the prisoner. "I'll lend you a 'and, if I got to," he said in a sullen voice. "But I got something to say to you first."

Arrogance in the face of terror. It was Adam's only defense. He said in that light, almost drawling voice, "Then pray proceed, good fellow."

"I'm not your good fellow, me lord, and don't you never think it. But I got me orders from that swell friend o' yours, Thomas Seymour."

"Tom?" Adam's heart began to beat in thick strokes. "I don't understand."

Kilkirk's lip curled. "Why, your fine friend's going to 'ave a try at rescuing you."

Rescue? Nay, it could not be! He was asleep, dreaming.

"He says to tell you he's not got 'is plan worked out perfect yet," Kilkirk's sullen and reluctant voice went on, "but you'll be 'earing from 'im again." He paused, then added in a tone of deepest gloom, "I'm to 'elp."

With the warmth of hope stirring, Adam said gently, "You dislike me. Why should you help?"

"I'm not doing it out o' no love for you. I'm doing it for me own good, see. This 'ere swell Seymour, he knows too much 'bout me."

"I see." Adam forced his painful mouth to smile. "How—how is the rescue to be accomplished?"

"Ain't I just got through telling you that 'e's not got it worked out perfect?"

"My apologies. Go on, please."

"When you go to the rack, Seymour says, you ain't to talk before they gives the first twist. When they does, you're to stop the racking by giving 'em the name o' the place where you got this Tudor Trigg 'id. It ain't got to be the right place, he says, save that it's far off and difficult to get to." Kilkirk scowled down at him. "It's to give 'im time, do you see? Then he says 'e'll 'ave you out o' 'ere before they discovers they been tricked. Understand?"

Certainly he understood, Adam thought. But it was foolhardy and almost bound to fail. True, he could stay the torturer's hand for a while, but after that, what? He had heard of many who had tried to escape from the Tower. From the very first their efforts had been doomed to failure. How, then, could Tom hope to succeed?

Kilkirk was watching him, his brown eyes malicious. He seemed to know the thoughts passing through the prisoner's head. More from fear of Seymour than from any intention of reassuring, he said quickly, "I don't see no cause for you to fret. Seymour ain't like other men. Whatever he sets 'is 'and to gets done. And 'e's got 'is fingers in more pies than I c'n count. If anyone can get you out, it's 'im. And it's no use you asking me 'ow it's to be done, because I don't know yet."

Adam did not know it then, but he was not to be condemned to the rack for some time. Cromwell desired to administer the racking himself, and he would not delegate the task to another. So, as the matter of Anne Boleyn came first, it was postponed. The postponement had the king's full approval. His desire to find Tudor Trigg was as fervent as ever, but his uneasy conscience was a little relieved. He told himself that Adam should taste the mercy of the king. After his respite from bodily torture, he had the feeling that he would be only too willing to speak. And as Cromwell had said, the planning of his freedom from Anne Boleyn was, for the moment, of primary importance.

Thomas Seymour, seeing in which direction the wind blew, laid aside his half-formed plan for Adam's rescue. Anne Boleyn's star had set, he knew the signs. He continued to watch and wait, sure in his mind that a better plan for the rescue of Somercombe would suggest itself.

17

"Adultery!" The king swallowed his rage with some difficulty, and the effort left his lips pinched and white. "Do I actually understand that you are charging the queen with adultery?"

From beneath his sparse lashes, Thomas Cromwell studied the king warily. He knew exactly how the king's mind worked. He would rather have heard any other charge than the one just uttered. Adultery! It struck at his pride and his overweening vanity. But if he were to rid the king of Anne Boleyn, this was the best way. He must swallow the pill, bitter though it was.

"It is with deep regret, sire," Cromwell said, "that I am forced to bring this matter to your attention. I would have died rather!" His voice was slow and husky with the fear his sovereign lord inspired in him. With Henry Tudor, one never knew. He dreaded that the king, rather than suffer this affront, rather than face his people as a cuckolded husband, might yet dismiss all charges and refuse to listen further. And Cromwell knew that if that happened, his head would no longer be safe on his shoulders.

The king's vanity was indeed suffering. He would have given much to roar out a protest, to kick the sly fool from his presence. But greater at the moment than his vanity was his desire to be free of Anne. He leaned forward, his eyes fixed on Cromwell's face. "The man?" he said in a difficult voice. "Give me the name of the man!"

Cromwell's heart fluttered with relief, and he felt the taste of triumph. He sighed heavily. "Not one man, sire. Men."

"What! You dare to smear the queen's grace!"

It was a formal protest, Cromwell knew, no more. He said boldly, "I have proof, sire."

The king regarded him with hard, glittering eyes. He was

204

forced to respect the man's devious brain, but he could never like him. "Go on," he commanded.

"I will, sire. It is a great grief to me, but——"

"Have done with your prating!" the king shouted. "Get on with it. Give me names, *man*, names!"

Cromwell licked his dry lips. What if he should say more than the king could reasonably digest? "Henry Norris is one, sire."

"Norris!" The king's face purpled. "You are telling me that Norris, whom I ever loved, ever trusted, is a traitor?" The glittering eyes pinned him again. "I want the names of the others!"

Cromwell's mouth twitched nervously. "Sir Francis Weston, sire, William Brereton, and Mark Smeaton."

"Smeaton!" the king said in an awful voice. "He is naught but the queen's musician. Surely you jest?"

"Nay, sire."

"Do you tell me that the queen would so demean herself?"

Cromwell hastened to defend himself. "I could not believe it at first, sire. The boy is of humble parentage and far below the queen's notice, or so I thought. But I found that it is all too true, sire. Hearing rumors, I invited Smeaton to my home on the pretext of giving him dinner, and there I questioned him. He was finely dressed, and on his finger he wore a great jewel. It was given to him by the queen, this he freely admitted. But of other intimacies he was reluctant to speak. Much against my will, I was forced to coerce him." He stopped for breath, omitting to add that it had been a little more than coercion. That he had, in fact, with the help of two trusted servants, tortured the boy. Failing to extract a confession, he had then had Smeaton conveyed to the Tower. With the help of more refined torture, Smeaton had at last gasped out the words he wanted to hear.

"Smeaton!" The king was still unwilling to believe.

"The boy is handsome enough," Cromwell said. Seeing the expression on the king's face, he went on hastily, "But he is most uncouth of manner. He is charged not only with lewd and unbecoming behavior, but with attempting to take back his confession."

"What did he say?"

Despite his fear, Cromwell was beginning to enjoy himself. "Smeaton said, sire, that his confession was all lies. There was nothing between the queen's grace and himself, nor ever had been. He said he would not be forced to blacken the name of a gentle lady who had never been other to him than kind, gentle, and good." Cromwell rubbed his hands together, making a dry, rustling sound that irritated the king. " 'Tis a different story, now, though. Faced with more torture, Smeaton said that his former story was true. He had but tried to defend the queen's good name."

Henry took in a deep breath. "By God's holy body, she should not be suffered to live!"

Nor shall she live, Cromwell thought. He hated Anne Boleyn. He had always hated her for her contemptuous indifference to himself.

"Go now," the king said abruptly. "Our queen has broken our heart. We would be alone with our grief."

But Cromwell had not yet finished. "There is one more name, if it please you, sire."

"Say it quickly, then."

"It is George Boleyn, sire. My lord Rochford."

The king seemed about to choke. "Her own brother! You go too far, knave!"

" 'Tis true, sire. My lady Rochford herself cries out in condemnation against them."

"Dear God!" The king covered his face with his hands, his shoulders suddenly shaken by sobbing. "We have given her our whole heart, and this is our reward!"

Cromwell's lip curled as he stared at the blubbering figure in white velvet heavily encrusted with jewels. He wanted to laugh aloud in derision. The king knew well that the charges against Anne Boleyn were not true. For all his vanity and self-blindness, he was shrewd and clever. But for his own sake, and for the sake of crafty, simpering Jane Seymour, or mayhap Mistress Trigg, he was prepared to appear as a betrayed and heartbroken man. It was simpler that way, and his conscience did not carry too heavy a burden.

"Go!" the king spoke in a muffled voice. "We know well that you have done your duty to us. But for the moment we would have you out of our sight."

"But the queen, sire. Surely you would wish to issue a warrant for her arrest?"

The king looked up sharply. "We will discuss it later. Get you gone. It sickens us to look upon your face!"

The king was working himself into a rage; in another moment he would be blaming him for the whole affair. The blue eyes, tear-misted though they were, held a warning flame of anger. Cromwell, bowing low, took his silent departure.

Walking along the corridor, Cromwell laughed silently. He told himself that he should know his royal master by now. The king must ever have someone to blame. He himself had forced this issue, but he must not be made to feel guilty. He must always be good Henry. Saintly and blameless Henry! Cromwell smiled grimly. "As for Anne Boleyn, she would very soon know the extent of the power wielded by the king's minister. When she looked at him, there would be no more indifference in those dark eyes. No more small and contemptuous smiles. She would die! Your time has run, your grace. You will be soon enough forgotten when you are disgraced and headless. Cromwell heaved a contented sigh. Death by the ax! Aye, he was determined upon it. It would take only gentle persuasion to turn the king's thoughts in that direction.

Anne Boleyn ran swiftly along the corridor. She was heedless of the startled glances that followed after her. A moment's carelessness on the part of those men set to guard her and she was temporarily free. Her one thought was to get to the king. Names pounded in her throbbing brain. Weston! Brereton! Norris! Smeaton! They had all been arrested on a charge of adultery with the queen. Then there was that other, so very dear to her, her brother George. Christ have mercy! They are innocent. I am innocent. Help me to say the words that will prove it. Oh, George, my brother, that you should be brought to this, to be accused of incest! Who has put this malicious story about? But it shall not be. I will not let it be!

There was a stabbing pain in her side as she arrived, panting, at the door that led into the king's apartments. She leaned her head against the door, praying for strength to convince, for resolution in the face of terror. She felt so weak! It had been four months since the premature birth of her child, but how could she be expected to regain her health when those months had been filled with such crushing anxiety? She stood up straight and laid her hand upon the latch. She must not be apprehended now that she had come this far. God save that the king be not absent. Her hand shaking, she pushed open the door and entered the room.

The king turned, amazement and consternation in his face. Had she come to rebuke him? Even in her guilt, it would be like her. And who had set her free to run to him? For the moment he was bereft of words, and he continued to stare at her. This woman standing before him did not resemble his beautiful Anne. With her pallid face, her colorless lips, the dark smudges beneath her eyes, she had the appearance of a wraith. Always slender, she was thin to the point of emaciation. Wisps of dark hair had escaped from beneath her small, pointed hood, and her skin was shiny with perspiration. For a moment he knew regret. He had loved her once. Was it possible that he still loved the wanton and incestuous harlot? He pushed the thought from him. Nay, it was Jane he loved. Jane, or the lovely Corianne. He could not seem to make a choice between them.

"Sire!" Anne's voice, breathless, pleading.

In his heart he knew Anne to be innocent, and guilt put a hard edge to his voice. "Go away, madam, I would be left in peace. Have you not done enough to me? You have broken my heart! And now, by your presence here, you do but add to my grief."

Anne's eyes went past him to the gentlemen at the other end of the room. They had fallen silent upon her entry. Faces carefully blank, they avoided looking at her. "Grant me the boon of a word alone with you, sire," Anne pleaded. "Please! For the sake of what was once between us."

Henry hesitated. He looked at her with eyes that were cold blue slits beneath sandy, frowning brows. It would do no harm to accede to her request, though he had no mind to be alone with her. Whatever the bitch had to say, it would profit her nothing. He waved his hand toward his retinue. "Leave us!"

They made a hasty departure. The door clicked softly shut behind them. "Well, madam?" Henry said in a surly voice. "You can have nothing to say to me that I would wish to hear. But speak, if you must."

Anne stared at the tall, portly figure clad so splendidly in red and silver. His face was implacable, his eyes so hard that she knew despair. He was determined not to listen to her! Proud Anne Boleyn sank to her knees before him. "My lord king, I am your wife, and once was beloved of you. For the sake of what has been, judge me not guilty before ever I am tried. Judge not my brother, or those gentlemen accused with him. They are innocent, even as I."

He saw the tears gather in her eyes and spill down her cheeks. Even now she was beautiful. Those dark eyes, lustrous with tears, were still capable of bewitching him. His face flushing, he glared at her. "Think not to move me, madam!" he flung the words at her savagely. "Do you dare to tell me you are innocent, trollop?"

Anne's fingers clutched at his leg. "Before God, sire, I swear it!"

He lifted his foot and thrust her from him. "Get you gone! Do not goad me too far, lest I not be responsible for my actions."

She lay there, her rose-red satin skirts ballooning about her, and still she pleaded. "Sire, do what you will with me, for I see well that you are determined to cast me off. But do not accuse my poor brother of so monstrous a crime. Let him and those other innocent gentlemen go free."

All feeling left him, he could feel for her nothing but distaste. "It was not I who accused your brother, but his own wife, my lady Rochford."

Anne gasped. "That liar. That witless fool! Sire, hear me. She is driven by jealousy. She does not understand the strength of the affection betweeen George and me, and she has ever resented it. But that she should tell so wicked a lie! I pray she may burn in hell!"

Henry's lips curled into a sneer. "She is not like to do so, madam. But have a care for yourself, for I greatly fear that you will suffer that fate."

She stared up at him, and something in her eyes made him feel uncomfortable. "You will not heed me then, sire?"

"Nay," he shouted. "You are a liar and a wanton. Not all your words, not all your pleading can move my heart!"

"I see." Anne got stiffly to her feet. "You are determined to find me guilty."

His eyes flashed fury. "I would give my life to know you innocent. I love you. Aye, I love you still. But I cannot condone your filthy conduct!"

She smiled bitterly. "I was a loyal and faithful wife to you, sire. But you! Did you not take to your bed many a wench who thought to replace Anne Boleyn? Would you not take to your bed, if you could, that sly, white mouse, Jane Seymour?"

She was accusing him! He could scarcely believe it. By God and all His saints, he'd not endure her insolence! His rough hand thrust her hood back, his fingers seized her hair and twisted cruelly. "You harlot!" He pushed her toward the door. "Get out! The sight of you makes me want to vomit!"

She pulled her hair free. How could she have thought this vain and selfish hypocrite would listen to truth! It was lies he wanted, the more lies the better to build his case against her. Anger stiffened her. "I will go, sire," she said coldly. Her eyes looked directly into his. "I trust you may sleep easy. Had I your conscience, I would not."

"My conscience is clear, madam. What of your own?" He thrust his face close to hers. "In four days' time you will be summoned before the Council to answer for yourself. Look not for mercy, for you will find none. They are all good men and true, and loyal to their king."

Four days! She stood very still. On the second day of May she would be called to answer the charges against her. And she would be proved guilty, because that was the verdict the king wished to hear. She looked at him scornfully. "I know well that I will find no mercy. Who in that Council would dare to stand out against the wishes of Henry Tudor? We are already condemned. Even poor, foolish Mark Smeaton, whose only crime was that he loved me too well. I did not respond to that love, nor to any man's, save yours." She shrugged. "But I have done with pleading and protestations of innocence."

"Poor, foolish Mark Smeaton," Henry sneered. "Why, madam, 'tis poor, foolish Mark Smeaton who has condemned you."

Her eyes flew wide with shock. "But how could he condemn me? I am innocent!"

"Yet he did, madam."

She turned blindly to the door. "May God have mercy upon his soul!" She looked at him again. "My hope and my prayer is that the next world will not contain you, sire!"

Long after she had gone, Henry sat in his chair, stunned. That she could say such a thing to him! If ever a man deserved a place beside God's golden throne, that man was surely Henry Tudor. Jane Seymour's clear, small voice came to him. "The people hate Anne Boleyn. She is a witch! She has taken your love, dear majesty, and spat upon it!"

Sitting there, Henry laid his head upon his arms and wept. The golden, wonderful days when he had loved Anne were gone, never to return. But there would never be another quite like her. "Oh, God, listen to Thy servant. You know that I do but follow Your will. Take this love I still feel for the witch, Anne Boleyn, from my heart. Take it, and I will be grateful all the days of my life!" So Henry pleaded for the mercy he had denied Anne.

Anne hardly noticed the alarmed guards, who were waiting outside the king's apartments. She made no protest when her arms were grasped roughly and she was hustled back to her own apartments. Locked in her room, with only one woman to attend her, Anne lay on her bed and wept her own tears. What was to become of her, and of George? Her fists clenched. Oh, God! I wish I had never set eyes on this monster king!

Yet she was not entirely blameless. She had had her own ambitions. She would be Queen of England, nothing less. She had not cared for Catherine's tragedy, so who now would care for hers? She began to laugh, high-pitched, hysterical laughter. Elizabeth, my daughter! They will tell you that your mother was a witch, an adulteress. Believe not their lies, my darling! I love you, I will go on loving you after death. Believe them not, my little daughter!

Her anguish subsided after a while, and she lay there very quietly. It would be death for her, Cromwell would see to that. Death? In all her laughing, careless, gay life, she had never given a thought to death. When her time came, would she face it with courage? Would she die bravely, with dignity?

18

My lord Somercombe was to be allowed the privilege of visitors. Thomas Seymour, through his contacts in the Tower, heard the news. He was elated, but utterly astonished.

Pacing his room restlessly, Seymour asked himself what this most unusual concession could mean. It was unusual indeed for a man kept in close confinement to be treated so leniently. What new trick did Thomas Cromwell practice now? The king was sly, but Cromwell more so. Perhaps, advised by Cromwell, he had decided to make a show of mercy. It might be that in giving Somercombe a taste of the outside world, he hoped to induce him to confess the whereabouts of Tudor Trigg. Seymour pinched his lip thoughtfully. It might work, too. Somercombe had been alone in his dark cell for four months now, and loneliness did strange things to men. He must hurry his plans for Somercombe's escape. But in the meantime, he must be given hope. And who best to supply that hope but himself and Mistress Trigg.

He sat down on a chair. The escape would be best if it coincided with Anne Boleyn's entry into the Tower, or better yet, with her beheading. He had no doubt in his own mind that the queen was to suffer this fate.

He thought of the three guards who would aid him. Each were bound to him in various ways—Kilkirk, through fear, Thompson, through gratitude for favors received, and Belmore, whose family held a long record of service to the Seymours, through devotion. A smile curled Seymour's lips as an idea suggested itself to him. He would visit Somercombe, and he would take with him Mistress Trigg, disguised as a boy. He himself, because the king must not hear he had been visiting Somercombe, would wear the clothes of a man of humble estate. Discovery, of course, could mean that he would be the next guest lodged in the Tower. But it was necessary to speak to Somercombe, so it was a risk he was determined to take.

Seymour's thoughts turned to Corianne. He had visited her occasionally at Peg Barnes's home. If he could not get Somercombe free, he had meant to carry her to Gravesend, by force, if necessary, and with a promise to continue with his plans for the escape. But the swift moving turn of events at Court, and his interest in the fate of Anne Boleyn, had intervened. Mistress Trigg's abrupt disappearance from the palace still remained a mystery. The negligent guards had been imprisoned. And Cromwell, in that disturbingly smooth way of his, had questioned all those who might have had a hand in her disappearance. Seymour chuckled. Cromwell, who was suspicious of everybody, had not left Tom Seymour out of his calculations. But he had not been allowed to question one who might, one day, be the king's brother-in-law.

Lying on the narrow bed in his small, damp cell, Adam was aware of acute depression. It attacked him more and more as the slow, dragging days passed. He was so weary of the unbearable loneliness and the lack of news from the outside world. But there had been one piece of news. Kilkirk had brought it to him only this morning. Anne Boleyn had fallen from grace and the king was prepared to bring about her death.

Kilkirk had smiled his sneering smile. "Going to chop off her 'ead, they are, you mark me words. And a bleedin' good job, too. Anne Boleyn ain't nothing but a painted-up whore what the king fancied. If you was to ask my opinion, she ain't no better'n she should be."

"Since I am unlikely to ask your opinion," Adam's freezing tone rebuked the man, "the question does not arise. It would please me greatly if you would remove yourself."

"What, before I've given you the grand news?"

"What news?" Adam snapped.

"You're to be allowed visitors, me fine m'lord."

Adam had ignored him. He believed that it was simply a desire on Kilkirk's part to add to his sufferings. His torture had been suspended these past four months. But he was still held in close confinement and not allowed visitors.

He moved his position on the bed. He moved with ease now, where once it had beeen agony. He glanced across at the scratches he had made on the wall. Four months! What was happening? Was he doomed to spend the rest of his life rotting in this place? He was certain now that no matter what he might do, he would never gain his release. He had no faith in Henry's promise to let him go free, and certainly he had lost all faith in Seymour. Since that one time when Kilkirk had repeated to him Seymour's words, he had heard nothing. He had only his wits to rely upon, and they were becoming dulled. He felt pain as Corianne entered his thoughts. Never to see her again! That was the real torture. Had Seymour kept his promise to help her escape? Surely he had, believing as he did in Jane Seymour's future, and incidentally his own? He remembered how he had instructed Tudor to take ship for France on the moment of his sister's arrival. They were not to wait for him. He would join them later. If Tudor had obeyed, then they were both safe.

Adam frowned as a disturbing thought occurred to him. What if Madam Tudor had refused to board the ship? It would be like her to refuse to go without him. Where she loved, she was impetuous and not given overmuch to thought.

The grating of the key in the lock brought him swiftly to his feet. If it was Kilkirk again, it would give him much pleasure to ram his fist in the man's face. Why not? He'd nothing to lose.

"What is it?" he snapped, as Kilkirk entered the room. He took a menacing step toward him. "What do you want with me now?"

Kilkirk backed away. "Don't you touch me, or you'll be worse off'n what you are now. I could 'ave you put in irons, I could. I come to tell you that you got two visitors. Best enjoy 'em while you can. You ain't likely to get no more. 'Ere's the first of 'em."

Kilkirk stepped to one side to allow the lad behind him to enter the cell. Then, with another insolent grin, he took his departure.

Adam stared at the slight figure. The boy stood there, not moving, his head downbent and his face shadowed by a broad hat brim. "And who might you be?" he demanded.

"Adam!" The boy's head lifted. He saw dark blue eyes brilliant with tears. The long imprisonment must have turned his brain, Adam thought wildly. It could not possibly be

Madam Tudor standing before him! Afraid to move or speak, he could only stare.

Corianne's eyes took in the gauntness of him, the dullness of his once brilliant, dark eyes, the deep lines about his mouth and beneath his eyes, and the sprinkling of white in his hair, and she was anguished. "Adam!" She ran toward him, her arms outstretched. "Adam, my darling!"

He felt her against him, warm, living, he saw her eyes full of love. She was no figment of a disordered imagination. She was actually here! His arms lifted and closed tightly about her. "M—Madam Tudor! I can't believe it. H—how can this be?"

Hearing his slight stammer, feeling him trembling against her, he who had always been so calm and sure of himself, the pain she felt for him stabbed deeper. "I am here, my darling," she said huskily. "It is all that matters for the moment."

His arms tightened. He bent his head and touched her lips with his. "It is a miracle!" he said after a long moment. "I had thought to die without ever seeing you again."

"Let there be no talk of dying!" She kissed him again passionately. Her voice dropped to a whisper. "There is a plan for your escape. I will tell you about it in a moment."

Sanity returned with a rush. There was danger for her here. Kilkirk? He did not trust the man. He was probably standing outside, his ear pressed to the door. His dark brows drew together in a frown. "You little fool!" it was the old imperious Adam who spoke. "How dare you come here and prate so foolishly of escape? Why are you not in France?"

She could not help smiling. So the torturers had not managed to kill his spirit. How like him, she thought tenderly, to upbraid her in the midst of their reunion.

He saw the smile, and his fear for her grew. He thrust her from him. "I demand to know why you are not in France!" His frown grew more formidable. "This is the fault of Seymour, I'll vow. He did not keep his promise to get you away. But you! You should have had more sense than to come here in this ridiculous garb." His fingers plucked at the thin silk of her black jacket. " 'Tis a paltry disguise. A child could see through it."

"But you did not see through it, my lord." She covered his mouth with a gentle pressure of her hand. "Hear me out, please. Seymour is not at fault. He was all eagerness to have me gone." She smiled. "I need not tell you why. You must know that he kept his promise, or how else could I be standing here? It was I who refused to leave London."

He pulled her hand away from his mouth. "You refused? My orders, in case anything happened to me, were that you should go straight to Gravesend, where you would join Tudor. After that you were both to take ship to France. It was all arranged. Yet you stand here and tell me you refused to leave London!" His mouth tightened grimly. "It would give me great pleasure to beat some sense into you. Why have you disobeyed?"

She knew that his rough tone was to cover the fear he felt for her, but she was nonetheless indignant. "Do I really have to speak the reason aloud?" she answered with spirit. "While you are in this place, while there is the slightest hope of getting you out, I will not leave London. I love you, Adam, can you not understand?"

"I take no reckoning of love, yours or mine. Your safety is the only thing that concerns me. That! Nothing more."

Her arms crept up and twined about his neck. "But for all my stupidity and disobedience, you love me? Say that you do, Adam."

He felt suddenly very weary. She was defeating his anger, even his fear for her, by her nearnesss. "You have the brains of a bird," he said thickly, "yet I love you well. Too well!"

Her fingers felt the bunched and twisted muscles of his shoulder beneath his thin shirt. "Adam!" she cried out. "What have they done to you?"

"Hush! It is nothing to what they might do. If you are discovered, it will mean that everything I have suffered has been in vain. The king will never let you go again. And if you do not soon arrive in Gravesend, Tudor will come seeking you."

"I'll not be discovered, dear m'lord. And I am not the empty-headed fool you think me. We have a plan, Seymour and I. A plan you will do well to listen to."

"Seymour? Is he the other visitor?"

"Aye." She laughed softly. "If you did not recognize me, you most certainly will not recognize Tom."

He shook his head. "Your folly grows." Releasing her, he went over to the bed and sat down. "I once thought that Seymour's self-interest would see you safe. But now I know not what to think."

"He is still serving his own interest." She sat down beside him. "He knows I won't leave until you are away from here. Seymour had a plan—you knew of that one—to help you out of here, but it did not seem to him to be the right time. But now the right time has come. Anne Boleyn takes barge for the Tower today, and on her do our fates hinge. But I will let Seymour tell you for himself."

Adam's hand restrained her as she made to rise. "It is true, then, the news Kilkirk brought me of Anne Boleyn? Of what is she accused?"

"Of adultery."

His fingers gripped her arm. "Adultery with whom?"

"What does it matter?"

"I would like to know," he insisted.

Quickly she told him. When she brought out my lord Rochford's name, she saw his face change. "Nay, Adam," she added, " 'tis not merely gossip. Seymour himself told me."

"May God protect her, poor lady! Adultery with her own brother? By God, I believe not a word of such an imfamous charge! What was the king about to allow her to be so defamed? Who accused her?"

"Thomas Cromwell."

"I might have known it. In order to climb high, that man will touch any filth!"

"The king has allowed her to be slandered. He wishes to be rid of her."

He looked at her with sorrowful eyes. "I had heard of her stillborn child. Seymour must be well pleased with the course of events."

"We are pressed for time, my love," Corianne said. She rose and made her way to the door. She tapped softly.

She stepped back as the door opened again and Seymour entered. With his broad-brimmed linen hat pulled low over his eyes, his rough, brown breeches, and his plaited straw shoes, Seymour was quite unrecognizable. He looked like a poor farmer. But it was more than his clothes, it was his attitude. He walked forward, shoulders hunched, his manner servile. He said in a deep, rough voice, "I come to pay me respec's to you, me lord. An' I come to offer me services, if so be you'd be kind enough to accept 'em."

Looking into those laughing, blue, daredevil eyes, Adam could not help smiling. In answer, he made a slight bow. "Good day to you, farmer. How fares your crops?"

"Rare well, me lord." Grinning, Seymuor seated himself.

"Tom," Adam said at once, "I feel sure there can be no escape from the Tower. But I will listen to what you have to say."

"You are gracious, my lord," Seymour said dryly.

"If I have offended you," Adam said impatiently, "I apologize."

Seymour's eyes twinkled. "Is this haughty Somercombe apologizing? Wonders will never cease!"

"Get on with it, Tom." Adam held out his hand to Corianne, and she took it eagerly in hers.

"Mistress Trigg has doubtless told you that the queen comes here today? The date of her confinement was a closely guarded secret. But I, as you know, have my ways of finding out the things I wish to know."

"I know it well. What has the queen's imprisonment got to do with anything?"

"I'm coming to that. I have planned the escape to coincide with the day of her death."

"So she really is to die!"

Seymour shrugged. "Aye, 'tis inevitable. She has yet to face her accusers at her trial. But adultery will be proved against her."

"Even if it be proved, a divorce may be obtained. Or, if the king show mercy, she could be allowed to enter a convent."

"He wants her death, and that right speedily. I know well they are resolved upon their verdict before ever the trial takes place." Seeing the look in Adam's eyes, Seymour paused. "No one can prevent her death, if it's what the king desires."

"I am sure of that."

"We must push ahead, Somercombe. Listen to what I have to say. On the day the queen dies, attention will all be on her. A man will come to you. Not Kilkirk, though you can trust him, for he'd not dare betray me. This man will hand you a friar's robe and cowl. Put it on and follow after him. He will lead you by devious ways to where the friars are gathered to witness the queen's death. You will mix with them. Afterward, when the queen's body has been gathered up, you will follow the friars through the gates and so to freedom. A simple plan, but I doubt not it will prove effective."

"Too simple, perhaps. So I am to witness the queen's death? I like it not."

"My lord, what is to be will be. You cannot prevent it."

Adam looked at Corianne, and he saw the pleading in her eyes. "I am not the hero you think me, Madam Tudor," he said softly. "I have no intention of refusing. With you in the world, I have no wish to die."

She squeezed his hand tightly. "We will be together very soon."

Seymour rose to his feet. "We must go now. 'Tis best not to linger. Oh, by the way, Somercombe, my little plan, simple though it is, will succeed. I have greased the way with gold. Did I tell you that three extra passengers will be sailing with you for France? Kilkirk is to be one of them. Think of it, you will be able to enjoy his charming company."

"What the devil are you up to now, Tom?"

"'Tis simple. When I chose my accomplices, I chose those without family ties of any kind and with no particular love of England. The poor devils could not very well stay here, could they? Not when they had been careless enough to leave your cell door unlocked." He smiled. "I had to guarantee them a goodly amount of gold, as well as safe passage to France. After you land, they will lose themselves. And you will be rid of your delightful companions. When Tom Seymour does a thing, he does it well." He strolled over to the door. "Hurry, lass."

Corianne clung tightly to Adam. "I know I must go, love. But before I do, let me hear you say that you love me."

The tenderness in his eyes answered her. "I love you! Go now, Madam Tudor. Hurry!"

19

Sir William Kingston's face was grim and unsmiling as he helped Anne Boleyn from the barge. He felt anguished by the trembling of her hand in his. The queen to be imprisoned! Hastily he reminded himself that queens had been imprisoned before. As Constable of the Tower, he should be hard and detached. Yet for all that, his heart was wrung with pity. There was nothing he could do about it. Sighing, he looked at the frowning walls of the Tower. Somercombe was right. He was not the man for this job. If I feel like this now, he asked himself, what will my feelings be when this sweet lady is condemned to the block? For she will be, I am certain of it!

The queen tucked her hand in his arm. Kingston, obeying an impulse, tightened his grip in an effort to convey his sympathy. How small she was, how defenseless and lost looking. In her plain black gown, the delicate ruff at the neck resembling a drift of foam, she looked very fragile. Beneath the black, gable-shaped bonnet, her face was almost as white as the ruff and her lips were trembling.

Again Sir William's pity conquered discretion. "Madam," he said huskily, "I beg you not to fear me, nor yet this place where you must temporarily lodge. You will be judged innocent. As for me, I remain your devoted servant. I am yours to command."

Struggling to hold in her hysterical laughter, Anne looked at him with blank, dark eyes. "You are m—mine to command?" The hysteria, stronger now than her will, caught her. Tears streamed from her eyes as her body was shaken with high-pitched laughter. "Then—then my first c—command shall be that you r—release me," she gasped. "I am innocent. Before God, I am innocent! I must be allowed to go free!"

Sir William bit down hard on his lower lip. She reminded

him of a terrified animal caught in a trap. A trap that the king and Thomas Cromwell had contrived between them. "Madam, if I could set you free, I would. But such is not within my power."

She placed her other hand on his arm, her knuckles whitening with her fierce grip. "Do you believe me innocent?"

He hesitated. He should not answer such a question. But her eyes were pleading with him, begging for reassurance, some small show of friendship. "Aye," he said. "I do believe you innocent, madam." It was not a lie. He did believe it.

The laughter shook her again, and she put her hand over her mouth to stifle the sound. After a while, she said in a muffled voice, "God bless you for that!"

Sir William looked at the guards assembled a little distance from them. "I fear, dear madam, I have forfeited the right to God's blessing. I look constantly upon suffering, but I dare not stay it. I must look with blind eyes."

Oddly, pathetically, it was she who now tried to comfort. "It is no fault of yours, Sir William. You are trapped, even as I." Her mind turned back to her own troubles. "Did you know that the duke of Norfolk, my own uncle, has refused to listen to my plea of innocence? My own uncle! I fear that I am already condemned and my fate decided upon!"

"Madam, I beg you to be calm."

"You ask me to be calm, when you know well that I am brought hither to die?"

She was trembling so violently that he feared she might fall. "Nay, madam, you must not say that. You have not yet been tried."

She put her hand to her neck, her fingers digging into the flesh. "Did I not tell you that I am already condemned? What manner of death shall I suffer? The king has said that he believes me to be a witch. Perhaps, then, it will be the burning! Or mayhap, if the king shows mercy, my head will be severed from my body!"

Kingston could not repress a shudder. In his imagination, he saw that reed-slim, graceful body bound to a stake. He saw the faggots crackling about her feet, the flames leaping higher and higher. The smell of burning flesh! Her face, the face of Anne, Queen of England, obscured by the choking pall of smoke! With an effort of will, he collected himself. "I beg of you, madam," he muttered, "do not dwell upon such things. You must call upon your courage to uphold you."

Anne stiffened at his words. She looked at him, trying to smile. "I have courage," she said in a low voice, "though it is not much in evidence at this moment. I will try harder. I promise you." She took a step forward, hesitated, then turned those haunted eyes on him again. "Shall I be lodged in a dungeon, Sir William?"

He heard the catch in her breathing and he hastened to reply. "Nay, madam, never think it. You are to have that same lodging where you prepared yourself for your coronation."

She stared at him. "The same?" she whispered. She closed her eyes for a moment against the welling of fresh tears. "Oh God!" she cried out in bitter sarcasm, "I swear it is much too good for me!"

"Madam!"

Without warning, her legs gave way. It was his arm that upheld her and forced her to stay on her feet. "I must beg that God, in His divine mercy, will show unto all men that I am guiltless," she said in a broken voice. "I am the king's true and loving wife! How can he thus condemn me!" With the sobs shaking her, it seemed to Anne that someone else was speaking. It was Catherine of Aragon's voice! Poor, deserted Catherine! "I was the king's true and loving wife. Not you. Never you! Your turn to suffer now, Anne Boleyn. Your turn!" To drown out that accusing voice, she cried aloud, "Catherine, my lady queen, forgive me!"

The guards had not moved, but Kingston knew they were listening intently to that raised and anguished voice. "Madam, please! There are ears that listen. There are eyes that watch your every action."

She shook her head helplessly. "Sir William, you must tell me! Where is my dear brother? What have they done to him?"

"He—he is well, madam."

She would get no more from him. She knew it. She bowed her head and let him lead her away.

At the door of her prison, she said in a voice devoid of emotion. "I have been accused of adultery with five men, one of them my own brother. Lies. All lies. But how shall I prove this to my accusers?"

He looked at her helplessly. "Madam, I know not. We must pray that God's truth will prevail."

"Yes," she said. "Yes. I know that Mark Smeaton has accused me. Have the others? If so, shall I die without justice?"

"You must know that the poorest subject of the king is granted justice," Kingston said uneasily.

"The poorest subject of the king? Aye, perhaps. But I shall not have justice. I know it!"

He had no words to answer her. Giving her into the custody of those ladies appointed to watch her and to attend to her needs, he was not prepared for Anne Boleyn's look of horror. "This is the end!" she cried, pointing a finger at the ladies. "If Thomas Cromwell has seen fit to put about me these women whom I have ever despised and distrusted, then indeed my doom is sealed!" She whirled around to face Kingston. "These women are Cromwell's creatures. They have been put here to spy upon me. They will report to him my every word and action. I will not have them! Take them away!"

Kingston's face reddened. "I regret, madam, but I cannot. I could not have them removed from your presence without orders to that effect."

"I see there is no way out," Anne said in a quieter voice. "Let be, then. Since I am forced to it, I will try to endure their company."

Standing there before him, with her hands clasped loosely, she seemed to Kingston to assume a new dignity. She looked like a queen. He was startled by the next question she put to him. "Before you go, sir, pray tell me of my lord Somercombe. How does he prosper in this dreary place?"

For her own sake, she must not ask such questions. His voice purposely abrupt, he said, "Madam, it is forbidden to discuss the prisoners."

She laughed, and he heard again the note of threatening hysteria. "You must not discuss my lord Somercombe? Yet, sir, I know well that he was imprisoned because he dared to look with love upon Mistress Trigg, the king's chosen. And, adding to his sin, he made away with Mistress Trigg's brother, Tudor Trigg, the king's stolen but legal heir. Or so his grace would have us believe. Tell me, has my lord Somercombe confessed where he has the boy hid?"

Hoping she would understand and keep her silence, he

flashed her a warning look. "I do not understand you, madam."

Either she did not understand, or she chose to ignore the warning. Had she forgotten the avidly listening ears of the women grouped behind her? Kingston wondered. "Let us talk of the new queen that is to come after me." Anne's light, almost gay voice deceived everyone but Kingston. "The king has two choices, you know," she went on. "Will he make Mistress Trigg his bride, a lass who despises him and would make a most unwilling wife? Or will his choice fall on Jane Seymour, who, for these many months, has been all agog to step into my shoes?" Her voice changed again. "God's teeth! I wish the smug hypocrite joy of them!"

"Madam!" Kingston said hoarsely. "I beg you to say no more."

Anne laughed, her eyes flashing toward the women. "Come closer," she invited them. "Since you are paid to spy, it behooves you to listen well to the indiscretions of the queen."

The women looked at each other, but they did not move. "Ah well," Anne said contemptuously. "I imagine you have heard and inwardly recorded every word. Those who work for Cromwell dare not do less than earn their money."

Kingston took a quick step forward. "You do your cause no good by this, madam."

"My cause! It is already lost. You know it, sir."

"No, madam. There is justice in this land. I must and will believe that!"

Seized with a sudden fit of shivering, Anne drew her black cloak closely about her. "I have already told you, sir, there will be no justice for Anne Boleyn. I'll warrant that justice will be drowned by the strength of the king's new desire."

Kingston would listen to no more. If he stayed longer, he feared that she would go from one indiscretion to another. With a cold look at the hovering women, he bowed to the queen. Once outside, he walked with heavy tread to his quarters.

Entering his comfortably furnished rooms, he sat down. What would the outcome be? he wondered. If Anne Boleyn should be condemned to death, what of the little Princess Elizabeth? Would she too suffer the Princess Mary's fate? Would she be cast aside, bastardized, in favor of the children the new queen might bear? What was to become of England, straddled by a king who would lie and cheat to gain his own ends? A king who could apparently convince himself that whatever infamy he chose to commit was at the dictates of God and his own tender conscience?

Unaware that his wife had entered the room, Kingston closed his eyes. But what was he thinking of? It was not for him to judge the king. The king's private life, the shifts he might make to mold that life nearer to his heart's desire, was nothing to do with him. King Henry was a good and a strong king. The people might mutter against him, but the country prospered. Kingston sighed. He might pity the tragic Queen Catherine, who, save for one friend, had died alone at Kimbolton. He might and did pity Anne Boleyn, but he must not take it upon himself to criticize his sovereign lord. That way lay disaster. He must force himself to be harder, sterner, less inclined to sentiment. If he did not, who knew but what his own neck might not be safe from the ax? As for Anne Boleyn, he would make her as comfortable as possible. But in the future he would turn a deaf ear to anything she might have to say.

Lady Kingston looked up from her embroidery. She studied her husband's profile with worried eyes. Why must he agonize so over the prisoners? Last night, when he had spoken to her of Anne Boleyn, his hands had trembled and his face had looked drawn. Later, as she lay in her bed, she had heard him vomiting. If only he would not take things so hard!

Deprived of Kingston's supporting presence, Anne found that she still could not keep her tongue from babbling. She must talk, even if only to these women whom she heartily despised. "I am guiltless of the sins of which I am accused," she told them.

"Yes, your grace," a soft voice encouraged her.

Anne tucked a straying wisp of hair beneath her bonnet. "As for Henry Norris," she went on, "often did I chide him because he was not married. Was it my fault if he looked upon me with the eyes of desire? I said to him, 'If aught should happen to my lord king, do not look to possess me. 'Tis impossible.'"

Meaningful looks were exchanged. One of the women,

leaning forward, said, "I understand, your grace. Pray to continue."

Anne stared ahead. She could not look at them. She knew, who better, that she should curb her tongue, but she could not. Her private demon drove her on to further speech. "Weston was at fault," she continued. "He did not render to his wife that love which she deserved. He told me that he loved me better than his wife."

"Indeed, your grace?"

"Yes." Sitting down, Anne clasped her trembling hands on her lap. "Oh!" she cried out piteously, "is there no one to speak in my defense? Even my uncle Norfolk has judged me guilty."

"Surely your grace is mistaken. The duke of Norfolk loves you well."

"Love has nothing to do with it. My uncle, you see, seeks to preserve his influence with the king."

One woman, a fleeting pity softening her eyes, put a question to the queen. "What of your father, your grace? What of Archbishop Cranmer? He has ever declared himself to be your friend."

Anne's mouth trembled. "Off and on he has been my friend. Perhaps more off than on. As for this matter of which I am unjustly accused, I know nothing of the archbishop's thoughts. My father, too, has turned his face from me." Anne's shoulders sagged. "I could not turn my face from Elizabeth, no matter the consequences to myself. How could he do this! How could he be so cruel!"

A shocked murmuring came from the women. Anne turned her head and saw their unguarded eyes upon her. Only then did she remember that she was the queen. In babbling on like a brook in full spate, she had shown less than dignity. They would report her words, of course. They were paid to do so. She rose quickly to her feet. "I am hungry," she said in a haughty voice. "I pray you to do what you must to obtain food and wine."

Later, paying a reluctant visit to his royal prisoner, Kingston scarcely knew her for the same woman. Febrile color stained her cheeks. She was gay, sparkling bright with laughter.

"Your grace," Kingston said, bowing before her, "I rejoice to see you in good spirits."

Anne smiled into his solemn face. "But your face tells a different story," she cried. "Would you lower my spirits with your mournful expression?"

"N—no, madam," Kingston stammered. " 'Tis the last thing I would wish to do."

Anne picked up a piece of chicken from the platter before her. "You see, Sir William," she said, waving it in his direction, "I cannot yet complain of ill-usage. Come, sir, smile for me, or you will have me in tears."

"Yes, madam. I will do my best."

Anne nodded. Her small white teeth tore the meat from the bone. She chewed for a while in silence, then she turned her full attention to him once more. "I do believe I have recovered my faith in my lord king," she said slowly. "He loves me well, as he has done from the moment of our first meeting. Soon, I know it, he will remember that love. He will arise in wrath and crush my accusers."

There was an uncomfortable lump in Kingston's throat. He swallowed hard. Forgetting his resolution not to be moved, he said gently, "His majesty will very soon discover that he cannot bear to have you far from his side."

The color drained from her cheeks, leaving her skin a yellowish white. Her eyes slanted in delicate mockery, as if at some jest against herself. "Do you truly believe that, Sir William?"

He stared at her, unconsciously crushing his feathered cap between his big hands. It would seem that her moods changed like the wind. What was he to say to her now? "Aye, your grace. I—I do believe it."

"Liar!" Anne summoned a bright smile. "But I vow and declare that I love you for the lie."

"Not for too long will you be held a prisoner, your grace," Kingston blundered on. "You will see."

The tears, which were so near to the surface, swam in her eyes. "You are right, Sir William. Not for too long will I be held prisoner. I shall be dead, and my troubles with me." She put a hand to her neck, stroking it with nervous fingers. "I have done evil to some, but to others I have done much good. I have tried to be a good queen, and most certainly I have been a faithful wife to my lord. Now men accuse me unjustly. They blacken my name. How shall I fight them?

How shall my daughter, and the generations that come after her, know that Anne Boleyn went blameless to her death?"

"The truth will prevail, madam."

"But of what use is truth, if men regard it not?"

He stared at her. There she sat, the woman for love of whom King Henry had set mighty Rome at naught. The woman whom many of the people still called "Harlot! Sly whore! That accursed Anne Boleyn!" His eyes took in the whiteness of her skin, the midnight black of her hair and eyes, the sensuous curve of her mouth, and the reedlike slenderness of her body. Her eyes met his, and he was held by that strange fascination that had enthralled the king for so many years. Forgetful of the watching women, he went down on his knees before her. "I beg you, madam, to think of me not as your jailer, but as your friend and confidant."

She looked into his earnest face. "I would that I could believe you, Sir William. But where once I trusted, I find that I can trust no more." Her black gown rustling, she leaned toward him and placed her mouth on a level with his ear. "Are you not afraid that my fair companions will report your words to Thomas Cromwell, their master?" she whispered. "I would not have it said, Sir William, that Anne Boleyn had likewise committed adultery with the Constable of the Tower."

He looked at her in shocked horror. He saw something in her eyes that gave the lie to her mocking words, and his pity overcame him. Rising to his feet, he took her hand in his and carried it to his lips. "May God forgive me, your grace, if word or action of mine further imperil your position!"

Dropping her hand gently, he turned to face the silent women. "Look well to the queen," he bade them. "If harm come to her through your chattering tongues, be sure that I will see you suffer for it." Cold-faced, he bowed to them. "I bid you good day, ladies."

Anne sensed that this was a courageous speech for this beset man. He was, she guessed, as much a prisoner as any other in the Tower, for he was the victim of a too tender heart. As he turned to leave, she said softly, "It would be a boon, sir, if you would supply me with writing materials."

"It shall be done, madam."

Far into the night, heedless of swiftly passing time, Anne

sat at the table composing a letter to the king. He had once loved her well. Surely he would not ignore her plea.

She started as one of the women spoke. " 'Tis past three in the morning, madam. Will you not rest?"

"Later," Anne answered curtly. "You need have no concern for me."

Turning away from the woman's inquisitive eyes, Anne stared at the guttering candle flame. She blew on her hands to warm them. Then, clutching the quill tightly, she began to write. "To the king," she began afresh. "From the lady in the Tower. I scarcely know what to write, for your grace's anger with me and my imprisonment are things strange to me. I am altogether ignorant of what to excuse in mine conduct—" She hesitated, then resumed writing, her hand shielding the parchment from prying eyes. Her quill scratched busily. "Let not your grace imagine that your wife will be brought to acknowledge a fault where not so much as a thought preceeded. To speak a truth, never did a prince have a wife more loyal in duty, and in all true affection than you have found in Anne Boleyn. You have chosen me from low estate to be your queen and companion, far beyond my dessert or desire. If then you found me worthy of such honor, your grace, let not the counsel of mine enemies withdraw your princely favor from me; neither let the unworthy stain of a disloyal heart toward your grace ever cast foul blot on your dutiful wife, and the princess, your daughter Elizabeth. Try me, but let me have a lawful trial; let not my sworn enemies sit before me as mine accusers and my judges. Let me receive open trial, for my truth shall feel no shame. But if you have determined that not only my death, but an infamous slander must bring you the enjoyment of your desired happiness, then I desire God that He will pardon your great sin and call you not to a strict accounting of your unprincely and cruel usage of me. We are both required to face God, and whatsoever the world may think of me, mine innocence shall be known. My last request shall be that myself alone bear the burden of your grace's displeasure, and that it may not touch the innocent souls of those poor gentlemen who, I understand, are likewise in imprisonment for my sake.

"If ever I have found favor in your sight, if ever the name of Anne Boleyn hath been pleasing to your ears, then let me obtain this request; and so I will leave you to trouble your grace no more; with mine most earnest prayers to the Trinity, to have your grace in His good keeping, and to direct you wisely in all your actions.

"From my doleful prison in the Tower, the sixth of May. —Anne Boleyn."

Anne laid down the quill and straightened her aching back. She could feel the vigilant eyes of Cromwell's spies upon her, but she did not glance their way. She sanded the letter, then folded it carefully.

Lying sleepless in her bed, she contemplated the future left to her. Henry, she felt sure, could no longer be moved by words of hers. Her only hope was that perhaps, for the sake of a love that was once so sweet to him, he would be good to their infant daughter. Her lips began to move in silent prayer. She was still praying when she fell asleep. Her dreams brought her a vision of her brother's face. "George!" she cried out in agony. "Oh, my sweet brother, forgive me if my stupidity and my sisterly love have brought you to this sad pass!" The vision passed. She turned over on her side, mumbling unintelligible words.

Two of the women, unable to sleep, looked at each other. "Even in her sleep she pines for her brother and her lover," one said.

"Aye," the other answered with satisfaction. "I vow that it will make pretty telling."

"How she suffers, proud Anne Boleyn!"

"Why, Bess, you sound almost sorry for her."

"Nay, not I. I am glad her day is run. For in all truth, to see a trollop on the throne of England was more than I could stomach."

"As soon as Anne Boleyn is dead, your stomach may take its ease." Smiling, the woman lay down and composed herself for sleep.

20
❦

The earl of Somercombe was surprised and more than a little perturbed when the door of his cell was thrown open and Sir William Kingston entered. Since his imprisonment, they had met on precisely three occasions. The first time, greeting him at the landing, Sir William, obviously sympathetic, had seemed concerned for his fate. On the two occasions since that time, he had been courteous, but his manner had been cold and distant, as befitted the Constable of the Tower toward a prisoner held under the king's grave displeasure. Certainly he did not make a practice of visiting prisoners kept in close confinement unless he had news of a grave nature to impart. Adam could not but wonder if Seymour's madly daring plan to free him had come to the ears of authority. Had Kilkirk and the other two decided that the lure of plentiful gold and a chance at a new life in another country were not worth the risk?

Annoyed with the sudden trembling of his limbs, Adam rose and made a slight bow. "Sir William," he said in an admirably controlled voice, " 'tis an unlooked for and unexpected pleasure to see you."

Kingston looked as though he had not been sleeping well. He looked at Adam with heavy, brooding eyes. "How do you fare, my lord Somercombe?" he said after a moment.

"Well enough," Adam answered cautiously, "for one in my most unenviable position." He looked at the other man closely. There were beads of perspiration on the constable's forehead, his mouth had a drawn look, and his hands were trembling. "Are you unwell, Sir William?" he added.

Kingston sat down heavily on the bench beneath the window and motioned to Adam to be seated. "My health is of little concern to me at this moment," he answered. "But I imagine you must be wondering why I am here?"

Seating himself, another terrible possibility came to Adam. "Aye," he said, trying to speak calmly. "But mayhap you have come to tell me that the torture is to be resumed?" His heart began to beat suffocatingly fast as he waited for Kingston's answer.

"Nay, lad, rest easy. 'Tis just that I felt the need to talk to someone."

Adam's brows rose. "To a prisoner?"

"Aye, if the prisoner knows the king and the workings of his mind well. I believe that you do."

Adam looked at him with puzzled eyes. After a moment, Sir William began to talk, almost mumbling the words. "What manner of man reigns over us, that he can condone this cruelty, this humiliation of a woman?"

"The queen?"

"Aye, the queen. I remember you telling me, my lord, that I was not the man for this job. You were right. Ever since the queen was brought to the Tower, I have been unable to sleep, so sick with anxiety am I on her behalf. I believe you to be a man of great discernment, of much sensitivity. I am sure you will understand how I feel. She is so small, so alone, so beset on all sides by her enemies!"

Adam looked at Sir William's hands nervously twisting his cap out of shape, and he said gently, "Should you confide in me? The king would not be best pleased if he came to hear of it. Nor would he wish to know that the constable of his Tower felt so strongly for his disgraced queen."

Sir William's eyes met his. "Will he know, my lord?"

"Not from me. But your actions are noted. This place, I am sure you are aware, is not without its spies."

"I know that. I am no fool, my lord. I have learned to take my own precautions. I have spoken to no one else on this matter, nor will I. But I felt that I had to voice my disgust at the handling of the queen, and my hatred of the monster who has made her suffer this pain and humiliation!"

Adam's eyes went swiftly to the door. "Have a care," he warned.

"You need feel no alarm for me. There is no one near. I made sure of that. My mission, as far as the warders are concerned, is to persuade you into giving me your confession." He smiled grimly. "They know that I would not wish to be disturbed, and they dare not disobey me. I have my own spies, you see. Any disobedience to an order would be immediately reported to me. I may be too soft for this job. But with my warders, I assure you, I have made myself felt."

"I said you were a compassionate man, Sir William. I did not suggest that you were soft. But you have much on your mind. Pray tell me, if you think the telling will bring relief."

Kingston sat forward, his eyes feverishly bright. He began to talk, and it was as if he too suffered the humiliation of the abandoned and disgraced queen.

Adam listened intently. Kingston had a gift with words. Adam saw clearly the way Anne Boleyn had stood before the judges at her trial. He felt her desperation as she fought for her honor and her life, and for the honor of those men accused with her.

Anne Boleyn was garbed all in black, save for the white ruff about her neck. Beneath a small, black hood ruffled about the underbrim with a narrow edging of lace, her face was pale and drawn. Her hands shook with nerves as she faced the men who were to say whether she lived or died. Three of her judges were the duke of Norfolk, her uncle, Thomas Boleyn, her father, and Henry Percy, who at one time had professed an undying love for her. Anne did not know it then, but earlier that same day, her brother George had been tried. He had pleaded innocent. But for all that, he had been found guilty and condemned to death. Nor did she know that Weston, Norris, Brereton, and Mark Smeaton had, just a few days after her own arrest, been tried at Westminster. Of these four men, only Mark Smeaton, in a futile attempt to save his life, had pleaded guilty. They were all under sentence of death. But Anne believed that her words this day would go far to establish their innocence.

The first sonorous and accusing words came. "Anne, Queen of England, you have been the wife of our beloved sovereign Henry, by the grace of God, the eighth of this realm, for more than three years?"

"Yes," Anne answered. "Yes."

"In those three years you have, with your lust, your wicked and depraved tastes, worked much evil against our sovereign lord. What say you to this charge?"

As if for support, Anne's hands clenched on the rail before her. The slight color that had touched her cheeks at her first sight of Henry Percy drained away, leaving her face bloodless. All life seemed to be centered in her huge, dark eyes. She answered the charge in a clear, carrying voice. "My lords, gentlemen, I do heartily deny this charge. I have been faithful and true unto my lord, the king. Never by word or action of mine have I sought to work him evil.'"

Norfolk leaned forward, his glittering eyes fixed on her face. "Did you not kiss, touch, and incite the king's erstwhile loyal servants to invasions of your body? The body that should be sacred unto his majesty, the king?"

Anne looked at him scornfully. "No, Uncle, I did not."

"Do not call me uncle!" Norfolk said sharply. "This is a formal hearing."

"If your grace has forgotten your relationship to me," Anne said quietly, "then I must endeavor to do likewise." Her eyes turned to her father's set face. "Just as I must forget a yet closer relationship."

Norfolk's lips tightened. "You will not make saucy quips. You stand before us on trial for your life."

Anne's eyes left her father's slowly flushing face and sought that of Henry Percy. He was unable to look at her. He sat rigidly in his seat, his eyes staring straight ahead of him. He looked gaunt and wasted of frame, and a fine film of perspiration glazed his face. Clearly, Anne thought, he was a very sick man with little time left to spend upon this earth. Once she had loved him deeply, but now she could feel nothing for him. She turned a politely attentive face to Norfolk, who had begun to speak again.

"Do you deny," Norfolk said in his decisive voice, "that you had intercourse at various times with four of the accused men, one of them your own brother? And likewise with a fifth man, Mark Smeaton, your musician?"

"I do deny it!"

"Let us return to the matter of your brother, my lord Rochford. The charge is that you did incite the said natural brother to violate your body."

Anne's nails dug deeply into her palms. This must not be! Oh God, let not this vileness, this filth, be recorded against my brother's name or mine! With a desperate inner weeping, she saw her brother's face clearly in her tortured mind. Oh, George, we played our innocent childhood games and we loved each other deeply, truly, in the most natural way in the world! How could we know then that we would be brought to this—this degradation! Still gripping the bar, her haunted eyes went from face to face, and found in them nothing of understanding or mercy.

"Answer, if you please, madam!" Norfolk barked.

"It is a lie!" Anne cried out in a trembling voice. She took a moment to collect herself. "My lords, gentlemen, do what you will with me. Take my life! But do not, I beg of you, heap this disgusting infamy upon me, or upon him who is beloved of me!"

She might never have spoken. Norfolk's remorseless voice went on and on. "That you cajoled the said George Boleyn, my lord of Rochford, with your tongue in his mouth. And that he, in his lust, did insert his tongue into your mouth. And thus, with the twining of tongues, was this unholy lust born between you. My lord Rochford, entering deeply into your body, did derive much carnal pleasure from this act. And he, urged on by your kissing and your touching and the sensuous licking of his body with your tongue, did spill into you his unnatural seed."

Anne was like one turned to stone. She scarcely seemed to breathe, so still she was, so stricken. When admonished to speak, she lifted her eyes slowly to the duke of Norfolk's face. What he saw in those eyes caused him to visibly flinch and to hurriedly avert his face.

"You know it is a lie," Anne whispered.

"Speak up! The Commission desires to hear."

"It is a lie! A lie!"

"Then you plead innocent?"

"I do. I have said it."

"At his trial, my lord Rochford likewise pleaded innocent to knowledge of your body."

"His trial!"

The papers in the duke of Norfolk's hand rustled. Anne had not moved, yet it seemed to him in that moment that she had already begun to die. In a gentler voice, he said, "My lord Rochford was found guilty. He has been sentenced to death."

"No! Oh, George, no!"

After that, it seemed to those who watched her that she had lost all interest in the preservation of herself.

"Anne, Queen of England, you have been heard to say openly to your lovers that you never loved the king. That you could not love him, since his person was disgusting and repellent to you. Clearly then, since you sought to deny your body to your true lord, you were in a frenzy to indulge your lust with others. So much so that you promised to give yourself in marriage to him who would free you from the king. To contrive the king's death was your dearest wish. To this end did you and your fellow conspirators work. Did you not promise to give your hand and your heart to the perpetrator of this foul act?"

Anne stared at the questioner vaguely. Her lips moved silently. Perhaps she spoke to God, or to some other person visible only to herself. When the question was put to her again and again, she began first to shake her head, and then to nod it. She seemed to be no longer sure of who she was or what she was about.

"Answer!"

With a tremendous effort of will, she shook herself free from the shock and horror that bound her. Once more her voice was heard, clear, cold, ringing. "My lords, gentlemen, I am innocent. My brother and those other gentlemen accused with me are likewise innocent."

Once more Anne's eyes rested on her father's face. He was like one hypnotized, for he could not look away from her. When Anne spoke again, she seemed to be addressing her words solely to her father. "As God is my judge, I say this to you in all truth. Save only for the body of the king, I am unviolated. Even these the last words I should ever speak on this earth, I would say the same. I have been a good wife to my lord, a loyal and true wife. On this truth I present unto you now, must I stand or fall."

The trial went on and on. At last, after an interminable time, each of the judges gave his verdict secretly. Whether it be life or death for Anne Boleyn was contained in those scribbled-over pieces of paper handed to the duke of Norfolk. Anne waited, her manner calm. It was noticed that her eyes kept turning to the door, as if she could not wait to have done with the sordid business. When Norfolk stood up to read the verdict, her expression was no more than politely attentive.

Norfolk's voice shook slightly as he pronounced sentence. "Madam, you have been found by us, all here agreeing, to be guilty of the charges against you. You shall be taken from here by the constable and returned to your prison in the Tower. There you shall wait until the king commands that you be brought from there to Tower Green. There shall you be burned or beheaded, as shall please our most sovereign lord. Have you anything you wish to say?"

Anne nodded. "Your verdict does not surprise me, though God knows I have never earned the infamous reputation that prompts it. I am prepared to die. But I say to you that I am stricken to the heart that innocent gentlemen, the king's true and loyal subjects, should be called upon to share my sorry fate. I go from here in innocence, serene and secure in the comforting knowledge that God knows the truth in which I am armored."

She fell silent. The duke of Norfolk put out his hand as though he would touch her. Drawing his hand back hastily, he said, "M—Madam, have you m—more to say?" his speech was thick, his tongue stumbling over the words. "If you w—wish to add more, I hereby grant you p—permission."

"You are very kind." There was a slight edge to Anne's voice. "I would wish to request that I be allowed sufficient time to prepare my soul for death."

"Anne!" Thomas Boleyn, his complexion resembling wet, gray clay, cried out to his daughter. "Anne! Anne!"

She smiled at him fleetingly. "I pity you more than myself, Father," she said in a soft voice. "George and I will be dead and past all pain, but you must go on living with your conscience."

"Anne, forgive me! Forgive!"

"I forgive you freely, Father. For the sake of your immortal soul, I pray that God will do likewise."

On the arm of the constable, Anne Boleyn left the court. Thomas Boleyn stared after her a moment, then he put his hands to his face, his body shaken by his violent shuddering.

After Sir William Kingston's voice had faded into silence, Adam could not at first find words. Finally, he said, "And now?"

"And now she waits to die, poor lady!" Kingston said bitterly.

"When?"

"In three days' time, Anne Boleyn will be no more. It has been conveyed to her that she is no longer a queen. The king, through his ministers, has said that she was never his legal wife, because he, previous to the ceremony, had had carnal knowledge of her sister, Mary Boleyn. And likewise because of pre-contract between Anne Boleyn and Henry Percy. God, and the king's conscience, have told him that his union with Anne Boleyn is not acknowledged in our good Lord's eyes, and is therefore no true marriage. Neither wife nor queen now, Anne goes to her grave disgraced. And with the added and bitter knowledge that Elizabeth, her beloved daughter, is now declared bastard."

Adam's hands gripped the edge of his rough bed. "What manner of death will the queen suffer?" he asked in a stifled voice. "She—she is not to be burned?"

Because he had used the word "queen," Kingston, who had been so strongly brushed by Anne Boleyn's own particular magic, looked at him almost gratefully. "No, thank God, not by the fire," he answered. "The queen is to die by the sword. It would seem that the king has called upon a special executioner to behead her. When she heard about it, what do you think she said?"

Adam turned his eyes away from that too revealing face. "She laughed, my lord," Kingston went on in a labored voice. "She said, 'It should prove an easy job for my executioner. I hear that he is very good at his work. I am glad he is skilled, for I have such a little neck.'"

Adam's startled eyes met Kingston's. His mind went reeling back to that day when, leaning over the gallery rail, he had heard Anne say in a laughing voice to Tom Seymour, "I rarely wear the pearls, Tom. Those great ropes do not suit me, for I have such a little neck." For some reason, those words of hers had always haunted him. He wondered now if when he had heard Anne Boleyn make that remark to Seymour, he had been given a flashing glimpse into the future. He remembered how urgently he had wanted to tell her to guard herself. Such a little neck! And now it was to be severed!

Kingston was watching him, waiting for him to speak. "I believe, Sir William, that were I Anne Boleyn, I would be glad to die."

"She is glad. From the moment she was returned to her prison, she has taken much pleasure in the thought of death. And in her pitiful position, who would not? There is only one thing I have been able to do for her, and that was to prevail upon the king to allow her to have those ladies about her whom she both loves and trusts."

When Kingston rose to take his leave, Adam's thoughts were in a turmoil. He felt grief for the queen, and yet, if the escape plan proved successful, the day of her death would see him free of this place. He would be with Madam Tudor. A new life would begin for them.

Adam wandered over to the window. His hands gripping the bars, he stared at the gulls circling the Thames. A new life for him, but death for Anne Boleyn! He leaned his head against the bars. "Forgive me my joy," he whispered. "If I could save you, madam, I would. Aye, with all my heart, I would! Since I cannot, I hope that some part of you will live on, and that that part that lives will know and be glad that your death has set another free."

Finding little comfort in his own words, Adam turned away from the window. And still he could not help believing that Anne Boleyn would know and approve.

21

The ladies and gentlemen of the Court stood about in small groups, conversing together in low tones. Now and again eyes would turn to steal a look at the king. He sat in his chair, his hands clenched on the arms, so still and silent that none dared approach him.

Even Thomas Seymour was subdued as he covertly studied the huge, motionless figure. The king was clad in pale blue velvet. Unlike his usual flamboyant attire, the costume was almost plain, and he wore fewer jewels than usual. Beneath his flat, pale blue cap, his heavy, red face was brooding, the small mouth pursed. Now and again his chest rose and fell in a heavy sigh. What was he thinking of? Seymour wondered. Most certainly he did not look like the happy bridegroom he was to become. Perhaps he had regrets. Perhaps he was thinking that Jane Seymour, his bride-to-be, was small compensation for the loss of Mistress Trigg. Seymour frowned. The hunt was still on for Mistress Trigg and her brother. The king would never give up. Seymour smiled to himself. If I have my way, he thought, you never will find her. Nor will you be able to rack Somercombe for the information you desire. Not, that is, if my plan proves successful.

The king was thinking of Anne Boleyn. On May nineteenth, three days from now, Anne would go to her death. This year of 1536 would see him freed forever from her spell. It would also see him the contented husband and lover of Jane Seymour. He was resolved to wed Jane on the thirtieth, early in the morning. Anne would not have been twenty-four hours in her grave before he became betrothed. He tried hard to conjure up the faces of Jane and of Madam Tudor, but both dissolved into Anne's face. Anne! Anne! Nay, he deluded himself, he would never be free of her. But she had cheated him. He had loved Anne with passion and fire. And what had she given to him in return? More often than not she had shown a cold displeasure in his company. He! The king! She had shown him contempt, too. It had been veiled, but nonetheless apparent. And all she had managed to produce was a carroty-haired daughter and a stillborn son. His thoughts went to Jane Seymour. Did he love Jane? He supposed that he did, in a placid sort of way. But she was not exciting, as Anne had been. She was not the challenge that, he felt sure, Madam Tudor would have been.

Scowling, he moved for the first time in several minutes. Christ's body! He was a robust and full-blooded man, and he had never been one for a milk-and-water miss! A vast discontent filled him. Jane would not be a flame in his arms, as Anne had once been. But perhaps, he thought, trying to suppress the discontent, if Jane bore him sons, he could endure the occasional boredom he felt in her presence. He felt the burden of discontent lighten a little, and he relaxed in his chair. If Jane prove not fruitful, it would simply be another sign from God that she was not the one for him. God had shown His displeasure with Catherine, and, later, with Anne Boleyn. He had always been guided by God and his conscience, and he always would be. After all, was he not a good and simple man, a clean-living and moral man? And for his observance of all God's laws, he asked only the reward of healthy sons to secure the succession and to comfort him when old age came upon him. Sons! Other men begat them easily enough. Men not so pious as he. So he would prepare himself to await God's sign. There were plenty of women for a man as strong and healthy and lusty as he. He had sons a-plenty in his loins, could he but plant his seed in fertile ground. There was, for instance, Madam Tudor. Soon, if Cromwell's agents did not fail him, he would have Madam Tudor back at his side. He would never let her go again! By Christ, Cromwell had better not fail, or he would have his head! If he had no legal sons, there was always Tudor Trigg. And now he came to think of it, how went the hunt for the lad? Cromwell was pretty long-winded about the whole thing. Perhaps the man was getting lazy about duties. Tomorrow he would call him into his presence, and he would question him at length.

Henry frowned. At one time, whilst waiting for news of

Madam Tudor, he had hoped to put off marriage with Jane Seymour. But he was an honorable man, and how could he break little Jane's heart? Of course he must marry her. After he and Jane were safely married, he would instruct that fool, Cromwell, to resume the questioning of my lord Somercombe. Aye, just questioning at first, for he could not help his lingering fondness for the handsome rogue. But if he would not respond to questioning, he would order that he be racked until he gave the information about Tudor Trigg's whereabouts. In the end, he would have them both. Madam Tudor, and young Tudor. With God on his side, as He had always been, they would not for too long remain hidden from him. Perhaps he would punish them a little. Just a little. It was only fitting that they learn the folly of flouting Henry Tudor. The king smiled at this last thought, his plump, jeweled fingers playing idly with the emerald-set chain about his neck.

Thomas Cranmer, standing by the door, saw the king's smile. The sight of it made him want to weep. What fresh cruelty was he thinking up? Had it not been cruelty when the king had appointed him the queen's confessor, for thus in his mind Cranmer still thought of Anne Boleyn. He could wish that any other than he had been chosen to hear her confessions. It troubled him heart and soul to be with her. She was aloof and dignified at one moment, but, at the next, she would be swept with wild hysteria. But calm or hysterical, always the same words issued from her lips. "I swear on my eternal soul that I have never in thought, word, or deed, been unfaithful to his grace, the king!"

Cranmer rubbed his fingers across his aching eyes. His trouble was that he believed her. He could not absolve himself, as he would like to have done, by saying, "This woman, Anne Boleyn, is guilty. She has deceived our sovereign lord. She deserves to die!"

Cranmer felt an inner trembling as he faced the full and bitter knowledge that he, a man of God, had become naught but the king's tool! And what of Jane Seymour? Would he again be called upon to extricate the king from a marriage grown distasteful? He considered the peril to his immortal soul. When he stood before the Heavenly Throne, could he say to God, "Lord, forgive me. I helped free the king from his unwanted wives, not because I believed it to be right and just, but because I was a coward, a coward too ambitious to disobey." He shuddered at the thought of the retribution that might well be meted out to him. His quivering fingers touched the cross that dangled from a chain about his neck. "Lord," he prayed silently, "if I should be called upon to die a violent death, such as many men of ambition are brought to, give me the courage to die bravely!"

Cranmer's hand dropped. A violent death! On the seventeenth of this May month, the men accused with Anne Boleyn were to die. And Anne, from her window, would see them die. What thoughts would be hers as she watched her beloved brother lay his head upon the block? The king had commanded that she watch. It was too cruel! Knowing that he could no longer control his emotion or the tears that kept trying to fill his eyes, Cranmer turned away. He hesitated. What if the king should notice his emotion and demand an explanation? But he could not stay in the king's presence a moment longer. He could not! Furtively, he wiped his damp cheeks. He was a man with a heavy burden on his conscience. He needed to be alone for a little while. Keeping his eyes carefully lowered, he edged his way through the door.

The king saw Cranmer go. The man looked upset. Now he came to think of it, Cranmer had worn a long face these many days. What the devil was the matter with the whining, sanctimonious prater? For a moment he considered sending somebody after the man. He would demand to know how he dared to leave the royal presence without permission. The king frowned thoughtfully, then, abruptly, he changed his mind. Let him go. Cranmer and Cromwell between them had done excellent work in the matter of Anne, and he was not ungrateful. The work they had done had been God's work, of course, he reminded himself hastily, and so he might consider himself indebted to them. Cromwell, it was true, was lagging in the search for Tudor and the maiden, but after he had shown Cromwell his grave displeasure, he had not the slightest doubt that he would hasten in his search.

Sighing, the king carefully moved his sore leg to an easier position. He would think no more of Anne Boleyn. It was the future that counted. He would crush down the memory of her dark eyes, her supple, yielding body, and her scarlet mouth. He was done with her. The chapter in his life that had contained Anne Boleyn, his love! his torment! was finished with. Now a new chapter was about to open up. Life stretched golden and glorious before him. He could plainly see the fruitful and fulfilled years. And he, the faithful, loving, and generous husband, with Jane beside him. Or, if God did not smile upon the match, it would be Madam Tudor. Aye, perhaps it would be her sons that romped before his delighted eyes. Anne? Bah! What did he need with that thorn in the flesh, that goad to his male pride? He was free! It was over!

Filled with good will to all, the king struck his hand against the arm of his chair. "Wine!" he shouted, beaming upon the company. "You must all drink to the new happiness that is coming to your king!"

They crowded about him with cries and exclamations and excited laughter, each striving to outdo the other in an effort to be the first to offer their good wishes. Only Thomas Seymour hung back. He saw the king place a padded arm about the slender waist of Lady Mary Crawford; then, knowing that he would not be noticed, he followed Cranmer's example and slipped through the door. If the king should miss him and ask for an explanation, he would say that he had felt unwell and he had not wished to disturb the king's pleasure.

Making his way from the palace, Seymour gave the same explanation to those who inquired where he might be going. "I fear I am taken with nausea," he told them, smiling a charming but wan smile. "I must have air." When, after completing the explanation, he clapped a hand across his mouth, each questioner hurriedly stepped aside to let him pass.

Seymour smiled to himself at the success of his artistic performance, but he quickly sobered. He must see Somercombe. There were final arrangements to be made. He shivered, feeling suddenly cold as he thought of the danger in which he placed himself. But he had given his word to Mistress Trigg. In all his life he had never broken his word. It was perhaps his only virtue. And, too, he must see the deed through to see Jane safely enthroned.

22

❈

The friar's head was bowed in prayer. His tightly clasped hands, hidden beneath his wide, hanging sleeves, felt very cold. He let his lips move as the other friars were doing, hoping that their praying would successfully cover his own mouthed silence. Behind him, somebody stumbled, causing his elbow to prod the lady standing directly before him. "Your pardon, madam," he said in a low voice.

Lady Riverdale, one of the few women allowed to witness the execution of the queen, turned her head to bestow a forgiving smile on the clumsy friar. In the shadow cast by his cowl, she caught a flashing glimpse of deep, dark eyes, unruly, black hair that curled over a broad forehead, strong features, and a deeply clefted chin. A remarkably handsome face, she thought. It did not occur to Lady Riverdale until long after the incident had faded into the past that it was strange indeed to see such thickly curling hair on a friar of the St. Charles Order. Later, when she recalled the moment, she was puzzled. She had always thought that the friars of that order shaved their heads. But at this present time, the lady, who was of a naturally flirtatious disposition, merely thought that it was a great shame and a cruel waste for such a handsome man to have taken to a secluded religious life. The thought came to her that it might be that even a man of religion could be tempted to stray. Just a little, of course. Enough to make such an affair, forbidden as it was, very exciting.

Her cheeks pink, Lady Riverdale turned her head to smile at the friar. She hoped to hold those dark eyes with her own and convey to him a bold invitation. She was disappointed to find that the friar's head was lowered and he apparently absorbed in prayer. If he heard the little fidgeting movements she made, designed to attract his attention, he gave no sign.

Sighing, Lady Riverdale sternly collected herself. It was really too wicked of her that here, in this place where the unfortunate queen must shortly come forth to die, she had actually been hoping to bring about a love affair with a man of God. She shivered. She must indeed be an evil and heartless woman. Tomorrow, as was only fitting in view of her lascivious thoughts, she would make her confession. Perhaps, in doing so, she could feel herself to be absolved from sin. The very thought made her feel virtuous again. She would not look at him again. From this moment on, she would keep her eyes fixed ahead of her.

Adam cursed his carelessness. When he had followed the man along those innumerable winding corridors that seemed to be in the very bowels of the Tower, he had known that the band that held his hair back had worked loose. But between the pitiful calling out of the prisoners, who, seeing them pass, hoped for a word of comfort from the good friar, and his own driving anxiety to be on his way, he had not stopped to remedy it. When he had accidentally jostled the woman with his elbow, he should not have looked up. Tom Seymour had impressed upon him that he must remember to keep his head lowered. "It will not seem at all unusual," Seymour had said in a laughing voice. "When they are abroad and about their duties, I do not recall ever having looked directly into the face of a friar of the St. Charles Order. One wonders that the muscles in their necks do not atrophy, so zealously do they keep their cursed heads lowered."

Adam's teeth nibbled at his lower lip. Had the woman noticed his hair? Was she thinking that the man who stood behind her, clad in his sober, brown robe with his cowl pulled well forward to hide his face, was an impostor? If so, would she shortly raise the alarm? He heard her voice in light conversation with the gray-haired man beside her, and he felt a wave of relief. She did not seem to be suspicious. Christ's mercy, if he got away with it this time, he must remember to control his instinctive reactions!

Without moving his head, he raised his eyes in an effort to see where Kilkirk might be standing. Not seeing him, he lowered them again. In any case, he asked himself, how could he hope to recognize him? Kilkirk and the other two warders were likewise dressed in friars' robes. To his eyes, they all looked alike. He wondered if they felt the same dread as he, believing that they must be discovered at any moment? His thoughts dwelled particularly on Kilkirk. To the very last the man had been sullen and ungracious. But when the time for the escape was actually upon him, he had changed. He had done his part, if not eagerly, at least efficiently. As had Thompson, who had smuggled in the robes. It was Thompson's key that had unlocked that first door. Belmore, the third warder in the plot, had shown no signs of agitation when he had opened up that final door that would lead, if they were lucky, to freedom. After that, it had been a matter of hiding until the signal was given that the friars had assembled. Then had come a truly nerve-wracking part, the slow walk toward the brown-clad holy men. He had expected at any moment to be challenged. And would the friars notice that four more had been added to their number? But there had been no muttering among the friars, no sidelong, puzzled glances. He still could not believe he was actually standing here, to all intents and purposes one of their gathering. It had been too easy. Something was bound to go wrong. Perhaps the friars would wait until after the execution before demanding an explanation.

Despising himself, Adam wondered why he should have less confidence than Seymour. Or, for the matter of that, Kilkirk and his two companions. Was it the torture and the long, lonely time in the dark cell that had weakened him? It would not do! He had been called many things in his life, but never a coward. A plague on it! He must pull himself together, he must be as cool and calm as ever Seymour could wish. Doubt whispered again. All very well to make such a resolve, but when he thought of what must come first before he could walk with the others from this place of misery and death, he could feel the trembling beginning to afflict his hands. Would Anne Boleyn cry out in terror as she mounted the three steps to where the masked executioner awaited her? When she knelt upon the straw, her poor little neck bared for the stroke, would she plead for mercy and for life? If she did, could he bear to witness her anguish without making some impetuous move that would betray them all? He tightened the clasp of his hands, feeling them tingle with the increased pressure. He could not help Anne. He could only bring disaster down on their heads. Let him remember that! Let him think only of Madam Tudor!

Anne Boleyn knelt in prayer. She tried hard to concentrate on the words, but, with a welling of fresh despair, she found that she could not. Oh, Lord, have mercy! The moment was almost upon her. Would she die at once, or would the executioner have difficulty in severing her head? Would the sword be sharp enough? Dear God, let the blade be keen! But if it were dull and her head only half-severed, would there be terrible and unbearable pain?

Anne's thoughts turned to her brother. Had he suffered? Had the others? She prayed fervently that they had not. They had gone to their deaths almost cheerfully, those brave and gallant gentlemen. They had even attempted to make small jokes—she had heard them. Whatever their feelings might have been when they laid their heads upon the block, they had not allowed them to show. When the fatal stroke had been delivered, she had closed her eyes. She could not watch that final extinguishing of life. She thought of Mark Smeaton. Of the five defamed gentlemen, only Mark, still frantically trying to save his life, had pleaded guilty. In the end, his suffering had been worse. He had not died from the stroke of the executioner's blade. Instead, he had been hung, cut down while he yet lived, and disemboweled. Poor Mark! Yes, she could still pity him, if only for the stain he had put upon his soul.

Anne's hands clenched as she fought against terror. What was it like to die? What awaited one in that great beyond? Were all the fears that beset one in life, the trembling lest one offend God, the eternal strife, the blood that had been shed in the name of religion, was it all for nothing? Was there really a God and an eternal life, or was it only a myth put about by men to soothe grief at the loss of a loved one, and to help one through the darkness and strife of life?

Anne wiped away the sudden tears that blinded her eyes. There was a God, and she would enter into eternal life. She must and would believe that. It might even be that her brother George would be there to greet her. If she concentrated hard, she could almost see him strolling toward her with his hands outstretched in welcome. Perhaps his dark eyes would be smiling. Perhaps he would say, as he had so often said in life when she had been late in meeting him, "At last, Anne. You've been a plaguey long time arriving."

Her heart plunged and then began a furious fluttering.

Would her brother be headless? Or had God, in His great mercy, already restored him to his familiar and beloved form? She shook her head, sighing for her hopes and fears. Tears dropped cold upon her clasped hands, surprising her. She had forgotten that she was crying. Tears cold upon her cheeks! As cold as the doubt she could not quite suppress, as cold as her fear of the unknown! She began to pray then, silently, fervently. "Do not let me fear, Lord! Give me courage to face what I must!"

"Madam." Anne started as a hand was laid upon her shoulder. "You will take a chill kneeling there in only your shift."

Anne turned her head and looked up into Lady Margaret Sampson's concerned face. "A chill, Margaret? Does it matter?"

Margaret bit her lip. "Forgive me, madam, please. It was a foolish thing to say."

"One must say something, Margaret, I suppose." Anne got to her feet and surveyed her attendants—her friends, all three of them. Margaret's face was red and puffy from her incessant weeping, and so were the faces of Dorothy Vinely and Elizabeth Bletchford. Anne forced her lips into a wavering smile. "I should ask forgiveness from you," she said gently, "for this misery you must suffer with me, for my sake."

Elizabeth ran to her. "Do not say that, madam. Where else should we be but at your side?"

Anne looked at Dorothy Vinely. The girl was trembling, but for all that she appeared to be the calmest of the three. "Is Sir William Kingston without?" Anne asked her.

"Yes, madam," Dorothy answered in a tear-husky voice. Her eyes slid away from Anne's face. "He—he awaits your call."

Ann laughed, a hard and bitter sound. "Had the execution not been postponed, I should have now been past my pain."

"Forgive me, madam," Dorothy said quickly, "the postponement was no fault of Sir William's."

"I know that, Dorothy. But had everything gone as planned, he would not now be waiting to lead me to my executioner."

"Madam, please!"

The girl's face wore such a stricken look that Anne felt a

faint contrition. "I am sorry, Dorothy," she said. "I know that I do but make it worse when I put it into bald words."

"Why should you not put it into words, madam?" Elizabeth said quietly. "We are here to share your burden, if it be possible. It is for us to think of your feelings, not for you to spare ours."

Anne touched Elizabeth's arm briefly, then she turned her eyes to Dorothy again. "I pray you, Dorothy, to inform Sir William that I should like to see his lady. Impress upon him that it is most important that I do so. Say to him that I have something to say which is for Lady Kingston's ear alone." She hesitated. "Say, too, that if he will allow me a short time for my robing, I will be obliged to him if he will then bring his wife to me."

Dorothy hastened to obey. In the silence that had fallen upon them all, they could hear the low rumble of Kingston's voice, and then his footsteps receding.

Dorothy returned to the queen, her face devoid of color. "Madam, Sir William has agreed to bring Lady Kingston to you. But he—he asked me to remind you that there is not much t—time."

Anne flushed hotly, then paled. "I know," she managed to say. "Come then, help me to dress."

They assisted her into her crimson petticoat with its froth of white and silver lace about the hem. Over it they placed her gray gown. It was banded with dark fur about the low, square neckline and the edges of the long hanging sleeves— the sleeves that Anne Boleyn had made so fashionably popular.

Margaret brushed out the queen's long, black hair. She coiled it high upon her head, secured it, and then placed over it a snood of silver thread to keep the hair firmly in place. "Oh, M—Madam," she said, breaking down again, "you look so—so beautiful. One would think that y—you——" she broke off, wiping her eyes with a small kerchief.

Anne stood very still as her gray velvet, pearl-embroidered headdress was put on. "Death is gloomy enough, Margaret," she said. "I would not wish, in my dress, to add to that gloom. Oh, Margaret," she rushed on impulsively, "if ever I have been considered beautiful, I would wish to be more so today. I would like to be remembered that way!"

Shy Elizabeth Bletchford said, "You have your wish, dear

madam. You have always been beautiful, but today you are radiant!"

Anne did not believe her for a moment, but she respected the girl's wish to comfort her. "You are kind, Elizabeth." She turned to Dorothy Vinely. "My cloak, please."

Placing the crimson cloak about the queen's shoulders, Dorothy's cold, trembling hands touched her neck. At the feel of those fingers against her skin, hysteria rose strongly in Anne. The force of it shook her slender body. Oh God help me! She had a sudden urge to weep, to scream, to throw herself to the floor and beg for mercy. She was afraid! So terribly afraid! They were all looking at her. She could see her own terror mirrored in their eyes. With an effort so tremendous that it seemed to sap all her remaining strength, she forced herself to be calm. Her head rose. "You may tell Sir William that I am ready. I wish to see Lady Kingston alone. You will wait without, please."

As Lady Kingston entered the room, they left reluctantly. Lady Kingston was a tall, slender woman. She was normally pale of complexion, but as she faced Anne, she looked haggard. "You wished to see me, your grace?"

Anne nodded. "But you need not address me thus, my lady. I am no longer the queen."

"You will always be the queen to me, madam," Lady Kingston answered in a muffled voice.

There was pity in the blue eyes regarding her, and Anne knew that it was pity that had prompted Lady Kingston's words. To her, Catherine was the true queen, and at one time she had been openly condemning of Anne Boleyn. Before answering, Anne looked down and stared fixedly at her small, crimson slippers. She was uncertain how to proceed. Finally, looking up, she said in a clear, calm voice, "I pray you to be seated, my lady."

"But you are standing, madam. It is not fitting that I be seated."

"This is scarcely the time for ceremony, my lady." She indicated a chair. "Please!"

What now? Lady Kingston thought uneasily, as she seated herself obediently.

"My lady," Anne began breathlessly, "I have much sin upon my soul. In my ambition to be Queen of England, I did not regard the feelings of Queen Catherine, or her daughter,

251

the Princess Mary." She paused, and then went on in a slower voice. "There was a time when I wished to befriend Mary, but she would not have it so. To my shame, I hardened my heart against her. I spoke against her to the king. And those words were responsible for much of her misery."

I know! Lady Kingston thought. I know! She felt a flare of antagonism, but she crushed it down. Very soon now, Anne Boleyn would go forth from this room to her death. She would not wish to have it on her conscience that she had let her go with the sound of hard, condemning words in her ears. "Your grace," she said quietly, "I do not understand why you should confide this to me."

Anne looked at her with pleading eyes. "When I am dead, I want you to go to Mary. Tell her that——"

"Your grace! I cannot!" Lady Kingston tried to rise. She fell back in shock as Anne dropped to her knees before her. "Your grace, please! Do not humble yourself before me."

"Yet I do humble myself, my lady Kingston. It is not for myself I plead, but for my daughter. I pray you to go to Mary. Tell her that with all my heart I ask her pardon. If she cannot forgive me the misery I have caused, ask her instead to endeavor to look with love upon her half-sister, my innocent daughter. Beg her on your knees, as I do now to you, to support and uphold my Elizabeth. Ask her not to hold the sins of the mother against the child. Hate Anne Boleyn, if she will, but try to love Elizabeth. To please try!"

Lady Kingston looked at the kneeling queen. The large, dark eyes, brilliant with unshed tears, made her feel uncomfortably conscious of a pang at her heart. It was too much! She must end this scene, for she simply could not bear it! She rose abruptly to her feet. "Rise, madam, I pray you." She purposely made her voice harsh. "It is not fitting that you kneel to me."

She had lost, lost! Anne got slowly to her feet. Mary would never know of her sincere repentance. She would never hear her last plea that she be kind to the little daughter of Anne Boleyn. "If you will not, you will not, my lady," she said in a dull voice. "I had hoped that you would not refuse my last request."

Lady Kingston was anxious only for the harrowing scene to be over. For a long time she had disliked and resented Anne Boleyn, and she could not change all at once. But because she was fundamentally a kind-hearted woman, she pitied her. She felt that she could do no less than deliver the message. "Your grace has mistaken me," she said quickly before she could change her mind. "If it will give you ease, I will go to the princess. I will go down on my knees, as you bade me do. I will deliver your words as faithfully as it is in my power to remember them." She stopped short, confused by the glow that transformed Anne's face. "You may be easy in your heart, madam," she added gently. "You may trust me."

"In this time of crisis, my lady, you have made me very happy. I thank you for that. Thoughts of my child have been much on my mind, for I love her as I never thought to love any being on this earth! Thanks to you and your goodness, I can go to my death with a quiet heart." She held out her hand.

Moved, Lady Kingston took her hand in hers. On an impulse, she pressed a kiss on Anne's fingers. "May God give you peace, your grace!"

After the door had closed behind her, Anne stood there motionless and waited for the others to enter. Sir William Kingston was the first in the room. With a little shock of surprise, Anne saw the tears on his face. "Do not weep for me, Sir William," she said in a gentle voice. "Very soon I shall be past all pain."

Sir William nodded. He scrubbed at his face with his sleeve. Then he dug in his pocket and produced a leather bag. "Here is twenty pounds in gold, your grace," he said, handing her the bag.

Anne weighed the bag on her palm. "Twenty pounds?" she said in a wondering voice. "But what is it for?"

"It is to distribute as alms, your grace," he answered in a gruff voice. "It is the usual procedure." He placed his hand on her arm. "If your grace pleases, it is t—time to go."

Hot color stung her cheeks. The eyes she turned on him were full of terror. Kingston trembled. Vomit rose in his throat, and he swallowed hard against the sour, bitter taste. He could not bear this! Not for her, not for himself! Even less could he bear the thought of her breaking down now. His fingers squeezed her arm in a painful grip. "Anne Boleyn will die bravely," he whispered. "I know it, madam!"

"You will be there, Sir William? You will not leave me alone?"

"I will be there to the very end."

She struggled against terror and conquered it temporarily. "Then let us go," she said. "I will show them how to die. I will put on a fine show for them!"

"Madam! Dearest madam!"

She turned and looked at him fully. Taking her kerchief from her sleeve, she dabbed gently at the fresh tears on his cheeks. Then she kissed him softly on the mouth. "There," she said, smiling at him, "that is the last kiss Anne Boleyn will ever give on this earth. I pray you to remember me always, and to know that I die innocent."

"With all my heart, I believe you. And I will never forget you!" Kingston took her arm again and led her forward.

Anne's friends and attendants were waiting outside the door. She paused briefly. "When it is over," she told them, "I wish you to divide my possessions among you. It is not much I have to leave, I fear. There is my prayer book and my lace kerchief, my chain and pomander, my necklace, and, if it be not too much soiled with blood, my headdress."

Only weeping answered her. But Anne, walking with Kingston at her side and her ladies following behind, was dry-eyed. For the moment, she had the victory over terror. She prayed that it would not return when she knelt in the straw and laid her head on the block.

Adam heard the slow, muffled beat of the black-draped drums. The queen was coming. He raised his head just sufficiently to see her.

To the beat of the drums, she walked with slow grace, without any visible faltering of her footsteps. The sun, pale for May, shone on the brave crimson cloak, gave a luminous shimmer to the pearls decorating her headdress, and brought flashing sparks of light from the jewels in her necklace. In her left hand she held a lace kerchief, in her right, a small book of prayers bound in white leather. As she walked, she glanced continually at the book, as though hoping to draw comfort from the remembered words it contained.

She hesitated by the steps that led to the scaffold, and Adam sucked in his breath sharply. He need not have feared for her. Anne paused only long enough to give her prayer book and her kerchief into the keeping of one of her ladies. Then, a hand either side of her gray skirt, she lifted it slightly so that she might not stumble over it and mounted the three steps. Adam saw the flash of her crimson petticoat and the froth of white and silver lace that bound the hem.

The drums faded into silence. It was noticed by all present that the queen did not once look at the executioner. The man stood well back, his masked face turned away from her, his sword hidden behind his back.

Briefly, Anne's eyes lingered on Thomas Cromwell's face, on Suffolk's and the young Duke of Richmond's, the king's bastard by Bessie Blount, then her eyes returned to Sir William Kingston's face. Seeing his nod of encouragement, she suddenly remembered the purse she had placed in her pocket. She drew out the purse. Opening it, she distributed the alms as he had instructed. This task finished, she asked for permission to speak.

Again Adam felt alarm. For God's sake, Anne, he thought, do not accuse the king of sinning against you! Do not let fall one word of blame or resentment. If you do, you will be taken back to your prison, and there you will stay until the time comes for you to be led forth again. Only this time, to the stake. I know, I have seen it happen to others. It will happen to you, too. Say nothing against him. You cannot save yourself, and the sword is more merciful than the burning!

"Good Christian people," Anne's voice was clear and carrying. "I am come hither to die, according to the law, and by the law I am judged to die, and therefore I will speak nothing against it. I am come hither to accuse no man, nor to speak anything of that whereof I am accused. I pray God to save the king, and send him long to reign over you, for a gentler or more merciful prince was there never." Adam heard the edge of irony in her voice as she added, "To me he was ever a good and sovereign lord." She paused again, and for the first time her voice was unsteady. "If there be any among you whom I have not treated well, or whom I have wittingly or unwittingly harmed, then with all my heart do I beg your charity and forgiveness! Likewise, if any person will meddle in my cause, I require him to judge the best. And thus I take my leave of the world and of you. I heartily desire you all to pray for me. And unto God do I commend my soul!"

Adam closed his eyes for a moment. When he opened

them again, he looked at the scene through blurred vision. He would have liked to look away from Anne, but he felt that he owed it to her to remember these moments. Later, perhaps, when the first shock and horror had faded, he would take it upon himself to record her dignity and calm in the face of terror.

Anne removed her necklace and the chain and pomander about her waist. She handed them to one of her sobbing ladies. Then she took off her cloak and handed that over, too. Her hands lifted to her headdress. She hesitated for a moment, then quickly removed it and gave it into the hands of a slight, blonde girl. "I had intended to wear it, Dorothy," she said, "but I fear it will become much bloodied. I wish you to have this memento to remember me by. It is best if it be unsoiled."

After the girl had retreated, Anne stood there for a moment, the silver snood shining on her coiled-up hair. In her low-necked gown, her neck looked very white and small and vulnerable. She seemed uncertain of what to do next. Adam saw her look at Kingston inquiringly. When he again nodded, she gave a long sigh. Sinking down, she knelt upon the straw and arranged her skirts about her. The drums began. A muffled beat—a pause—another beat. Death serenade for a queen!

Anne's heart was behaving oddly. It was as though a bird were imprisoned inside her body and fighting frantically to free itself. She could not breathe. She was suffocating with terror! Let it be quick and clean. Let the executioner be skilled. Do not let me scream out or beg for my life. Help me! God, in your mercy, help me!

Someone came up behind her. She did not turn, as every instinct bade her do. Only the slight quiver of her shoulders betrayed her fear. She heard the sound of quick, distressed breathing. A man's voice said, "Forgive me, madam. It is my duty to cover your eyes."

She did not trust herself to speak. She nodded. Light was blotted out as a linen cloth was bound about her eyes. She heard the sobbing of her ladies. She heard the released, almost concerted breath of the crowd, and it sounded to her ears as if a giant sighed. Now she found her voice, a small and unsteady voice. "If one of you gentlemen would be so good as to guide my head to the block, I will be much indebted."

She let herself go limp as gentle hands touched her. She felt the smooth coolness of wood against her neck and the little rush of blood to her head as it dangled forward. I am afraid, Lord! I am so afraid! She tensed at the rustle of movement by her side! Then suddenly, miraculously, her fear left her. She was calm. It was almost as if a soothing hand had been laid on her head. In that trembling moment between life and death, it seemed to her that a presence stood near to her. A vast, loving, yet awe-inspiring presence. Just before the executioner's sword descended on her neck, she spoke for the last time. "I do not fear. I am ready to follow after you. Oh, Christ, receive my soul!"

It was all over! Anne Boleyn's severed head lay in the straw. Adam could not seem to tear his eyes away from the grisly sight. He heard the praying of the friars rising in volume, he saw Lady Margaret Sampson approach the body of the queen. Blinded by tears, she had to fumble to find the head. Lifting it up, she swathed it in a clean cloth. Then, her steps dragging, she bore the head carefully to the chapel.

An indignant murmuring broke out among the friars when it was discovered that there was no proper coffin to receive Anne Boleyn's body. One of the friars, his voice rising slightly, said, "Come with me, my brothers. I know where are piled some chests that originally contained arrows. Better an arrow chest than nothing at all."

Adam felt that he moved through a feverish dream as he followed after them. When they returned, bearing the chest, he was the first to reach Anne's sprawled body. He touched her very lightly. "God blesss you, Anne," he whispered. "May you forever walk with God!"

The young duke of Richmond could not make out the friar's voice, so low it was. The duke saw a tear fall upon Anne's gray bodice, and he looked at the brown-robed holy man with some surprise. It had always been his impression that men who served God were normally too occupied with their prayers, too intent upon saving their own souls to have time for a human emotion. Watching, his own eyes filled with responsive tears, and he felt anger toward his royal father. He had liked Anne. She had been kind to him. She had never been too busy for a word or a smile. When he was on one of his visits to Greenwich Palace and he was taken with a sickness, as so often happened, Anne would come and sit by his bed. She did not stand there scowling at him as the king, his father, did. His father was always so angry with him when he was sick. But Anne was never angry. She had a fund of amusing stories, and always a new one to make him laugh. When he had one of his coughing fits, Anne would raise him in the bed so that he could breathe easier. He was afraid of the blood that came bubbling to his lips after such a spell. But Anne made nothing of it. With her smile, her stroking of his hair back from his damp forehead, the gentle way she wiped the blood from his lips, she took much of the fear away. And now, because of his father, he would never see her again!

The young duke crouched down beside the friar. "I share your grief, Father," he said in a low voice. "I liked her well!" He put out a hesitant hand and laid it on Anne's stiffening fingers. "Aye," he repeated on a note of defiance, "I liked her well, And I care not who hears me say so!" A sudden fit of coughing strangled any further indiscretion he might have uttered.

Adam, who had frozen at the sound of the duke's voice, was relieved when one of the gentlemen of his household came to lead the wheezing, spluttering boy away. Poor Richmond! he thought, thinking of the blood-stained kerchief pressed against his lips. How long had Richmond been spitting blood? Did the king know about it?

The questions in his mind broke off as the friars gently lifted Anne's body. From beneath the concealing cowl, he watched them as they carefully placed her body in the arrow chest. He walked with them as they carried the chest into the little chapel of St. Peter ad Vincula.

The chest was laid down. Light from the stained glass windows made a rainbow dazzle of light across Anne's gray-clad body.

Adam noticed with a jerk of emotion that one of her gay little crimson slippers had fallen from her left foot. He picked it up from the floor, held it for a moment, then placed it carefully in the makeshift coffin. Lady Margaret Sampson came forward from the shadows where she had been standing with the other two attendants. She stooped down and put the swathed head in the coffin. For a moment she stood still staring at Anne's mortal remains, then, with a little gasping cry, she fled from the chapel. After a hesitation, the other two girls crossed themselves, then followed after her.

Adam stood with bowed head, praying as the others did for the soul of Anne Boleyn. Their prayers were intoned in Latin, and, since he had never been able to grasp that language, he did not understand what they were saying. Letting his lips move as before, he inwardly prayed his own prayer for her peace and the repose of her soul.

The Tower guns boomed out, announcing the death of the queen, their thunder shaking the little building. They waited for the firing to cease, but when it went on and on, the prayers were finally abandoned.

One of the friars knelt down beside the chest and traced the sign of the cross over Anne's body. Rising to his feet again, he said in a grave voice, "This place is sanctified, my brothers, but I fear it is surrounded by much death and evil. There is nothing further we may do for this poor, martyred lady, and I find myself oppressed by evil. Let us go from here. We will retire to our peace and seclusion, and all this night we will offer up our prayers to God that Queen Anne may know eternal peace and happiness."

As one man, they turned and made for the door. Adam guessed that the man who had spoken must be the head of the Order, so unquestioningly did they obey him.

Walking slowly toward the gates, Adam could feel the beads of perspiration gathering thickly on his forehead. He felt the wet trickles sliding down his face and his neck. Did Kilkirk, Belmore, and Thompson feel this same dread? Or was he the only coward among them? His lip curled in bitter self-contempt. If he should escape, what manner of man would Madam Tudor be getting?

Adam peered from beneath his cowl. Where were the other three men? Which of these anonymous figures were theirs? They all looked so alike with their shuffling gait, dust-powdered toes exposed in sandals, downbent heads, one hand touching the chain at their side from which dangled a large silver cross. To further divert his mind from anxiety, he began to ponder on where Seymour had gotten the robes and the accoutrements that went with them. That Seymour was a man of many connections and talents, he had long known. So perhaps, after all, it had not been too difficult for him.

The gates loomed up before them. Adam swallowed against the tight knot of fear that constricted his throat. Almost through! Just beyond these gates lay freedom! But would they be stopped? Would a command ring out at any moment—"Halt!"

They were through! He could not believe it! Without thinking, he hastened his steps, then, remembering, he dropped back to the shuffling gait. Haste would not serve him now. A stone had worked its way into his sandal. He felt the small, stinging pain almost with pleasure. With agonizing slowness, they proceeded along the walk. Now they were turning left and going toward the right bank, where their barge was moored. Adam sniffed the foul aroma rising from the Thames, feeling that same curious pleasure. He was dizzy with a sense of freedom, and the aroma was to him like a delicate perfume. He could see gulls bobbing on the water, some of them circling above it. Flowers were growing near the edge of the far bank, a blur of purple and pink and white.

At last it was Adam's turn to take his place in the barge. Now, having got so far, he waited with mounting impatience for the clumsy vessel to start on its short journey. "Go!" he wanted to shout. "Hurry! Hurry!"

The barge slid away from the bank. The bobbing gulls rose from the rubbish-strewn water in heavy flight. Their shrill, indignant cries had a loudly triumphant sound in Adam's ears.

Beside him, a voice said quietly, "Put your anxieties to rest, my son. All is well now."

Adam's fingers gripped the rail tightly. He could not speak. He could not move! But he must move. He must face this new calamity, this destruction of all his hopes. Slowly, jerkily, like a puppet pulled by a string, his head turned. It was the tall friar who stood beside him. The one who had knelt down beside Anne Boleyn's pitiful coffin and traced the sign of the cross over her body. "You knew, Father?" His own voice, harsh and unsteady, sounded strange in Adam's ears. "You knew all the time!"

"Yes, my son, I knew. We all knew. We had been told to expect an addition of four to our number."

"What!" Adam stared at the downbent head. "I don't think I—I understand."

"You will. All will be explained to you."

Adam would not yet admit the relief that was clamoring to make itself felt. "But the friars all look alike. How did you know me?"

The friar raised his head. He had dark blue, twinkling eyes in a round pleasant face, a thin, sharply pointed nose, and full smiling lips. A face of contradictions. "My son," his low, pleasant voice answered, "do you think I do not know the form of every one of my brothers? They look alike, you say, but to me they are characterized by small but familiar things. In any case, I am the tallest member of our Order. And you, my son, have a yet greater height."

"But if you knew, why did you not——"

"Betray you?" the friar interrupted calmly. "In any event, I would not have done so. But the thing is, I had given my word to help."

"Your word?" Adam put a hand to his head. He must be dreaming this, for it made no sense at all. Would a holy man do such a thing, even for a charming rogue like Tom Seymour? "You g—gave your word to Seymour?"

"I did. Thomas came to us for help. And right willingly did we promise to aid him."

"To aid Tom Seymour? You!"

The friar smiled. "I know what you are thinking, but Thomas is a good boy at heart. He has done much for our Order. It is true that he is worldly, ambitious, and in many and distressing ways, quite unscrupulous. Yet he has many virtues, too. Virtues which he is at great pains to hide. He has given us much, and he has asked nothing in return. So when, for the first time, he asked for something, how could we refuse him?" The friar sat down on a green-padded bench and patted the place beside him. "Come, sit down."

Adam sank down beside him, glad of the excuse to rest his suddenly weakened limbs. "But were you aware of the terrible risk you were taking, Father? Had you been discovered in aiding fugitives to escape from the Tower, you and your brothers would have been hanged. Or, if not hanged, you would have been disgraced, driven forth from your sanctuary."

"I knew. But the risk was not so great as you imagine. Because the queen was to meet her death, there was a greater laxity. Thomas knew this and, being Thomas, he took full advantage of the situation. Another thing. A friendly drink was

261

offered to those guards who patroled near that part where you were imprisoned. The drink, of course, was drugged. It was given to them by the guards who escaped with you."

"Drugged?" Adam looked at him in amazement. "You speak of it so calmly, Father. Surely you could not have approved?"

The friar smiled. "There are many things of which I do not approve. But neither do I set myself up as a judge. When a true friend asks my aid, I do not stop to preach to him of right or wrong." He touched the silver cross at his side with loving fingers. "God is wise and good and all-seeing. He is the one and only judge. I think, under the particular circumstances, that He will forgive my sin." He looked almost shyly at Adam. "If you would care to know, I am called Brother William."

Adam held out his hand. "Adam Templeton, Earl of Somercombe. "I thank you from my heart, Brother William!"

"I knew your name," the friar said, taking his hand and shaking it briefly. "Thomas tells me that you are a good man who has suffered much injustice and cruelty."

Adam laughed. "Seymour told you that? He must be wandering in his wits!"

"Why?" The dark blue eyes turned on him inquiringly. "Are you saying that you are an evil man?"

"Well, no, not evil," Adam answered in some confusion. "But I have never considered myself to be a particularly good man."

"Yet you shielded a young boy from our tyrant king. Even when they tortured you, you would not disclose his whereabouts. That, to me, is a good man."

Adam flushed. "I had selfish motives, too. But I imagine you know everything?"

"Everything. But I do not as yet know you. I should like to."

Adam hesitated. Then he began to talk, the words pouring from him. He told of his doubts and fears, his feelings when he was walking toward the gates, the suspicion that had lately come to him that he must be a coward.

When his voice ceased, Brother William said mildly, "I understand but you may absolve yourself from the charge of cowardice, my son. Your fears were but natural and human. Do you think, despite our supreme faith in God, that I and my brothers did not fear? Another thing, a coward would not have kept silent under the torture, I assure you. Nay, you have no reason to scourge yourself."

Listening to that quiet voice, Adam believed him. He felt a great sense of relief. "Thank you," he said. "Your words bring me comfort!"

"I only told you what you should have known for yourself. Not only was your body weakened by torture and long imprisonment, but, to add to the burden already on your mind, a queen died today."

"Aye, and she died proudly, bravely, as one would expect of a queen." He hesitated. "You know, of course, that the king plans marriage with Jane Seymour?"

"Thomas told me. I know, too, that he has been much concerned in the king's plans. But I told you, my son, it is not for me to judge."

Despite his words, the friar plainly showed his distress, and Adam hastened to change the subject. "Where are the three guards who aided me?" he asked.

"Over there," Brother William said, pointing. "Do you wish to speak to them?"

"Later, perhaps. For now, I want you to know that I'll not trouble you for long. As soon as it is full dark, I'll be on my way."

Brother William shook his head. "The escape will have been discovered. The roads will be watched. Thomas wants you to stay with us until such time as he deems it safe for you to travel. And even then, you will go in disguise."

"As a friar, you mean?"

"No. Thomas has other plans for you."

Suspicion clouded Adam's eyes. "What tomfoolery is he up to now?"

"He has not confided in me. But whatever his planned disguise may be, I am sure you will play your part in the masquerade."

Adam heard the faint quiver in his voice. "Brother William! Are you laughing?"

"Aye, I am. But why do you look so astounded? I did not leave humor behind me when I joined the Order. I must admit that I find Thomas vastly entertaining. He has brought much laughter into my life."

"Glad as I am to hear that, Brother William, I have no intention of allowing Seymour to make me look foolish."

"Thomas would not do that. And you must admit, my lord, that his ideas are daring and original."

"I agree," Adam said with a trace of gloom. "It might be that his ideas are a little too original for my taste."

Brother William rose. "We are almost at our destination," he announced. There was laughter in his eyes as he regarded Adam. "Look not so cast down," he said. "All will be well. There is a secret room in the place we call home. We have named it 'The Sanctuary.' You may be sure that Thomas seized avidly on this knowledge. With typical Seymour lavishness, it has been prepared for you and your companions."

23

The king heard the booming of the Tower guns. It was the signal he had been waiting to hear. His hands tightened on the reins of his restive horse, causing the animal to snort and toss its head angrily.

Without warning, tears filled the king's eyes and ran down his cheeks. It was really over! Anne Boleyn was dead! And yet it did not seem possible, his vibrant, lovely Anne! His thoughts turned to Thomas Cromwell, and his small mouth pursed to a tight button. Dear Christ! What had the evil knave made him do? If ever he should find the evidence brought against Anne to be untrue, the accursed man should pay with his head!

He patted the horse absently. He had loved Anne. Not for the world would he have put her from him. Nay, it was the fault of Thomas Cromwell. The whole affair was his fault! How dare he bring this tragedy into his king's life? He himself was blameless, for God knows he had not wanted to listen to scandal against his darling. But the man had forced him to listen. What else could he do but listen, when such damaging evidence against Anne was laid before him? He had not wanted to sign the warrant for her arrest. It had broken his loyal and loving heart to have her imprisoned in the Tower. Nor had he wanted to sign the death warrant. It had been Cromwell again, spitting and purring in his ear, that had driven him to sign. God's curses on the man! With Cromwell reminding him again and again of Anne lying with her brother, with Smeaton, with Norris, with any other man that took her fancy, he had had no choice. Cromwell! By God's sacred bones, he liked the man not! The king's blue eyes glittered. I will make him pay for Anne, and for this anguish of spirit he has caused me. Aye, one day he will pay, and dearly!

Sir Richard Valentine's eyes dwelled with some amusement on the king, who was seated astride his horse, magnificently garbed in purple and gold, the sun bringing a blaze from the rings that loaded his fingers. "Behold the bridegroom!" Sir Richard said to his friend. "Do you see the tears on his fat face? I'll warrant he is trying to fix the blame for Anne Boleyn's death on Cromwell, on Cranmer, on anyone but his own hypocritical self."

"Be quiet," Benjamin Carter snapped.

The irrepressible Valentine winked. "He cries now for Anne Boleyn, but his tears will soon dry. Already, if I mistake not, his heart has flown ahead to Jane Seymour."

Benjamin Carter frowned. "Richard, you fool! Your words could be heard and reported."

"I vow, Ben, you are too cautious."

"And you are an imbecile! If you have so little concern for your own life, I would remind you that I have a great fondness for mine. Mount your horse. His grace is making ready to depart."

"And now begins the sweet journey to romance and the fair Jane," Valentine said, swinging himself into his embroidered saddle. "I wonder, when Jane's day is done, if it will be Mistress Trigg who joins our merry monarch on the throne of England?"

His lips tight, Benjamin Carter ignored him. It was safer so, he told himself. Richard was like young Suffolk, a rash fool with a wagging tongue, who gave no thought to danger or self-preservation. Richard was his friend, and yet it might be prudent to drop him.

The king rode at the head of his glittering cavalcade, his huge person the brightest of all. Through small towns and villages they went, the king responding with bluff good humor and beaming smiles to the people who rushed to cheer him. "Long life and happiness to your grace!" came the ringing shout.

Some of the people hung back and watched his triumphant progress with sullen eyes. But they were few and his well-wishers many, and the king's feelings were not harrowed by the lowering faces of those who deplored his conduct.

On went the cavalcade, passing through woods whose trees were clothed in young green leaves, along lanes whose hedgerows were bright and scented with the wild blossoms of May.

The king no longer thought of Anne Boleyn. In the joy that possessed him now, he tucked her uneasy ghost away to be examined another time. Even the thought of Madam Tudor he put from him. He had not lost her. His time of joy with her was still to come. But for now, Jane awaited him. Dear little Jane, who loved him well! His heart swelled with emotion. Jane thought him a god among men. He would be so kind to her. He would so love and cherish her that she would know the joy of having a slavishly adoring husband. What woman could ask for more? Without willing it, Madam Tudor's face rose before him. Corianne! So beautiful, so alluring! She is more to your taste than Jane. She is as spirited as Anne, and even more beautiful.

The king scowled heavily. Yet did he want a bold display of spirit? Did he want a saucy tongue? Madam Tudor, in a way, was just such another as the Boleyn witch. She might even be scornful of him, as Anne had been. Did he want that?

The king rode on, trying to make his mind a blank, but the question kept repeating itself. At last, anxious only to be at peace with himself, he convinced himself that it was Jane he wanted. Only her! She was to be his bride, his love! Aye, and in a few days she would be his bride in very truth, and England would have a new queen. A good and virtuous queen, not a harlot like Anne Boleyn! Anne! Anne! Always it came back to Anne. Would he ever forget her? He must, he would!

To distract himself, he looked down at the large diamond nestled in a wide band of gold that adorned his middle finger. Jane admired the stone. She all but went into ecstasies over it. And so she should, for it was worth a fortune. But she should have it. He would not begrudge it to her. He would have the diamond set into a pendant. He would enjoy seeing her wear it. It would set off her fragile beauty. There were some, he knew, who thought Jane to be dull and plain, but in his eyes she was beautiful. In a sudden burst of poetic fancy, he thought, she is like a daffodil. A delicate, golden daffodil! They were fools who did not appreciate her subtle charm. But they would appreciate it when she was his queen. There would be many then to sing her praises. Oh, Jane, I will be so good to you! If you will give me sons, there is nothing you may not ask of me!

Sons? The king's sandy eyebrows drew together in a frown, and his mouth pursed uneasily. Jane's hips were narrow, her constitution inclined to be delicate. Sometimes, when he had strode with her about the palace grounds, his long legs taking no thought for her shorter stride, she would become quite breathless. Her little, pointed face would be robbed of all color. She tired easily, too.

He thought of this for a moment, then his frown lifted and a tender smile touched his lips. Ah, but he would consider and respect her delicacy. No, no, he would not make a brood mare of the little lass. If she would give him at least four healthy sons, he'd not press her too hard for more. After all, had he not vowed to be a kind and considerate husband? Aye, if they be healthy, four sons would satisfy him. And perhaps, if her heart was set on it, he'd not say no to a little wench. It was not good for boisterous lads to have all their own way. They needed a gentle sister to look up to. What was his Jane doing now? he wondered. Was she eagerly anticipating her betrothal?

The king's horse, a high-spirited animal, shied slightly as a piece of paper blew acrosss the lane in front of it. Instantly subdued by the king's skillful hands, the animal trotted on placidly enough, the bells on its harness making a merry jingle, the diamond-sewn backcloth glinting in the sun.

The heat seemed to be affecting him more than usual, the king thought. In his bulky, jeweled clothes, he felt hot and uncomfortable. Even worse, he was beginning to imagine that he heard voices. His hands clenched convulsively on the reins. Yes, there was Catherine's voice, low, mournful, saying aloud the words she had penned in her letter, "Lastly I made this vow, that mine eyes desire you above all things."

No! His violent inner protest brought fresh beads of perspiration to his forehead. Go away, Kate! Leave me in peace!

Her voice was louder now. "I love you, Henry. No one will ever love you as much as your devoted Catherine!"

"No, Kate, no!" he muttered. "I want no ghosts at my betrothal."

The duke of Malmbury, catching the mutter, trotted his horse forward. "You spoke, sire?"

The king turned a fierce glare on him. "Nay. Get back in your place."

The duke bowed his head. "Your pardon, sire."

Catherine had gone. Now Anne Boleyn's voice sounded in the king's flinching ears. "Sire, I cannot be your wife. I am come from humble estate, and you, my lord king, are already married. I must repeat, as I have ever done, your mistress I cannot and will not be!"

So she would haunt him now? The king ground his teeth together in rage. Bitch! Whore! He was glad she was dead!

Anne's voice again, broken, trembling, trying to excuse her failure to give him a living son. "Do not look at me like that, Henry, I pray you. I will do better next time! I will be more careful!"

More careful? Damn the barren slut, she had ever deceived him! He shook his head from side to side, hoping to clear it. He must be ill, he thought in alarm. Her voice sounding in his ears had been bad enough, so why must he now start recalling her letter? The words seemed to dance before his eyes, writing themselves on the very air. "I am altogether ignorant of what to excuse in mine conduct. . . . To speak a truth, never did a prince have a wife more loyal in duty, and in all true affection than you have found in Anne Boleyn. . . ."

He shut his eyes tightly, then opened them quickly. The words were still forming. "Let not the counsel of mine enemies withdraw your princely favor from me. . . . If ever I have found favor in your sight, if ever the name of Anne Boleyn hath been pleasing in your ears. . . . From my doleful prison in the Tower—in the Tower—in the Tower—the Tower——"

"Sire, are you ill?" Malmbury's voice again, loud and irritating.

"Nay!" the king roared. "Leave me in peace!"

Dropping back into his place, the duke had a strong conviction that the king's words had been addressed to someone other than himself. What could have happened to the king, he wondered, to drain the ruddy color from his face? He was pasty-white, trembling. He looked like a haunted man.

Could he have read the duke's thoughts, the king would have laughed bitterly. Of course he was haunted. Haunted by the ghost of Spanish Kate and that cursed black-eyed strumpet, Anne Boleyn! But he was done with the voices now, done with reproachful letters. He would have no more of it. Soon he would be with Jane, bless her sweet, pure heart! In her soothing and gentle company, ghosts could not linger. He stirred uneasily. But what of the long night hours? What when Jane was sleeping peacefully beside him? Who would chase away the ghosts then? "No!" he said in a loud voice. "I will not endure it! By God's sacred body, I will not!"

The duke of Malmbury exchanged a startled glance with the other gentlemen who had heard the king's outburst. Malmbury did not move from his position, for he knew he would not be thanked should he interfere again. He could see the perspiration beading the king's white, quivering face, the way the plump hands were tightly clenched on the reins. He shrugged indifferently. It was for the king to live with his uneasy conscience, so let him get on with it. The duke smiled grimly. He had been a secret admirer of Anne Boleyn's, and Henry Tudor had murdered her! A plague on him! Let his conscience hound him to death!

Jane Seymour heard the clatter the horses made in the courtyard below. Her pale face flushed with bright color. The king was here! She did not love the gross man who would make her his queen, but what did that matter? She had pleased the men of her household, and even more important, she had pleased herself.

Jane smiled a small, secret smile. Her brothers thought of her as meek and pliable. But they did not know that she would not have set one foot before the other if it had only been to please them. It was her own ambition to be queen that she was serving.

Jane thought of Anne Boleyn, and again the smile curled her lips. Anne, who had been so superior, so condescending to Jane Seymour! "Little white mouse," Anne had called her. And now Anne Boleyn, that brazen whore, was dead, and the little white mouse was about to become Queen of England. How do you like that, Anne Boleyn?

She turned abruptly from the window. Why think of Anne Boleyn? Thoughts of her could spoil this wonderful day. She was dead, as she deserved to be. But had there ever been a more shameless strumpet? Imagine making love with your own brother!

270

What was addling Mistress Jane now? Polly Howard thought impatiently. Just now, with the rose-color flushing her cheeks, she had looked almost pretty. Now the color had receded, and she was plain again.

Grimacing, Polly Howard picked up an enamel-backed brush, stared at it for a moment, and then replaced it. It was not easy, she thought, to be a serving woman to Mistress Jane Seymour. She was not the sweet creature that most people thought her. She had a nasty temper, and she could be malicious and spiteful. Today, eleven days after the death of Anne Boleyn, she would become Queen of England, but Her Majesty would not be taking Polly Howard with her. Nay, not she! Polly Howard was good enough to wait upon Mistress Jane Seymour, but certainly not good enough to wait on her grace, the queen!

Jane's voice broke in on Polly's angry thoughts. "Don't stand there gaping, Howard. Arrange my train. Tell me, do you really like me in this gown?"

Polly stooped to arrange the train, then, straightening again, she inspected her mistress. The ivory gown she wore was sewn at the bodice, the hem, the wide hanging cuffs, with alternating bands of pearls and diamonds. It hugged tightly Jane's slight breasts and slim waist. The huge, spreading skirt was flounced and ruffled like the petals of a flower. The gleaming satin, the bright glint of jewels, gave majesty to her rather meager figure. Her blonde hair shone beneath an ivory lace cap sewn with diamonds, and her ivory satin slippers had high diamond-studded heels, which gave her the extra height she needed. It was a fitting wedding gown for a queen, Polly thought.

Jane fidgeted beneath the maidservant's prolonged stare. "Well?" she snapped.

Polly curtsied before her. "Your majesty is quite beautiful."

"I want no insolence from you, Howard!"

"Insolence? But I had thought your majesty asked for my opinion," Polly said in an injured voice.

Jane's hard glare softened a little. "Well, if that be your true opinion, it might be that I have misjudged you."

Polly noted with inner amusement that Mistress Jane had made no attempt to correct the gratuitous title she had bestowed upon her. Already, it would seem, she thought of herself as the queen. "Your majesty thinks too little of herself," Polly murmured.

Jane laughed, that slightly coarse laugh that was so strangely at variance with her delicate appearance. "You are mistaken, Howard, I assure you. I think very highly of myself. I know that I shall give the king many sons. That is how highly I think of myself. What have you to say to that?"

A noise from without caused Polly to flush with sudden excitement. "Someone is coming for you," she said in a breathless voice.

Obviously, Jane thought, the girl was awed by the historical moments they were about to live through. She nodded, "Open the door, Howard."

Polly flew to obey. Flinging the door wide, she curtsied to Edward Seymour, Jane's older brother, who stood on the threshold. Edward Seymour acknowledged the maidservant with a brief nod. Stepping into the room, he went to his sister's side and took both her hands in his. "Why, Jane," he said, "you look beautiful!"

Jane stiffened indignantly. Edward had paid her the compliment as though surprised she merited it. She was about to say something cutting, then she relaxed, smiling up into his hard, knowing eyes. What need had she now of Edward's compliments, sincere or otherwise? He and Thomas had always domineered her, for both her brothers were hard and ambitious men, and they expected to reap many advantages from this marriage. Let them, if they could. She would not stand in their way. At the same time, they had best not stand in hers. A word from her, a tear or two shining on her face, and Henry, who was so madly in love with her, would have them both thrown into the Tower. She would be the queen! It would be as well if Edward and Thomas realized that fact and changed their attitude toward her accordingly.

Something of her thoughts must have showed in her eyes, for Edward, looking a little startled, dropped her hands. "What is it, Jane? Why do you look at me that way?"

"What way?" Jane's smile was very sweet. "I do not understand you, dear brother. Oh, I am so happy, Edward! This is a glorious day for Jane Seymour, is it not?"

Edward's lips tightened. He did not like that look in her eyes. It filled him with a vague uneasiness. What was she thinking about? For a moment he wondered if he had ever really known this little sister of his. The moment passed. In the cold voice he was wont to employ with her, he said, "It is a glorious day for you. But I hope you will not think only of yourself, sister. It is a great day for all the Seymours, I trust?"

She did not answer the question in his voice. Instead, she lowered her eyes demurely. "I cannot see into the future, can I?" Looking up again, she placed the tips of her fingers on his blue-velvet-clad arm. "Shall we go, Edward? His grace will become impatient of the delay."

The king could not take his eyes from Jane as she came gliding down the broad, uncarpeted stairs, her little hand clinging to her brother's arm. She was to be his, this fragile girl. She would drive the ghosts from his life. She would give him strong and healthy sons. Dear Jane! His face worked with the force of his emotion.

"Jane!" he said huskily, as she reached the bottom of the stairs. "My dearest Jane!" He strode forward, intending to take her in his arms. Before he could do so, Jane dropped to her knees before him.

"Do not kneel to me, Jane," Henry said tenderly. "This day will see us equal. United together as man and wife."

Jane kept her head bowed. Equal? she thought. Henry Tudor saw no man as his equal, and certainly no woman. But when she had presented him with a son, it would be a different matter. She would rule him through his need of more and more male issue. She looked up at him, tears shining in her pale blue eyes. "Do not forbid me to kneel to you, dear sire. Our marriage hour approaches swiftly, and I am overcome with the honor you pay me!" She sighed. "I am so small and insignificant, and you are so great and glorious!"

Henry beamed his delight. How different from Catherine was this shy and worshipping child. How different from Anne! Overcome, he reached down and gently pulled her to her feet. "Nay, my love, you shall not say so!" he said, folding her into his arms and crushing her tightly against his chest. "You are to be my queen, my dearest delight! You are everything I have ever desired!" Completely carried away, transported, he believed what he was saying. There were actual tears on his cheeks, those tears he so easily shed when he was emotionally moved. For the moment he had forgotten Anne, he had even forgotten Madam Tudor, whom he still desired, and later intended to have, if not as wife, then as mistress. Strongly ruled by sentiment and emotion, he lived for this moment only. Likewise, he had forgotten that Jane often bored him. His own words rang in his ears with the sound of truth, and he was deliriously happy.

With her face hidden against his chest, the diamonds on his tunic pressing painfully into her cheek, Jane smiled to herself a small, secretive smile. The king had said that she was everything he desired. She intended to be. She would endeavor to please him in all things. And somehow she would contrive it so that she would not be put aside for another of the king's fancies. She would be as unlike Catherine as it was possible to be. And certainly she would never allow herself to go the way of Anne Boleyn. That way led to disgrace, the Tower, and death. She would confound her enemies, and enemies she would have, that much was certain. She would be so pure. And, where men other than her husband were concerned, so aloof and virginal. Not a whisper of scandal would she ever allow to touch her. So, in her blissful ignorance of the true nature of the man she was to marry, did Jane Seymour plan. Obviously, she told herself now, Anne Boleyn had been guilty. Such vile accusations as had beeen hurled at Anne, could never touch or bring down an innocent woman.

A faintly cynical smile touched Edward Seymour's lips as he looked on. He wished that Tom could have been here to see the pretty and appealing picture Jane had made as she knelt before the flushed and heavily-breathing king. How Tom would have laughed. A sudden thought struck Edward, and his blue eyes narrowed. Jane's impetuous move had been one well calculated to touch the king's vanity, to say nothing of that accommodating organ, his heart. He had the feeling that his sister had known exactly what she was doing. It might be that she was not so brainless as he and Tom had assumed. And that being so, she would bear watching.

At this evidence of mellow good humor in their royal master, smiles were exchanged among the king's gentlemen. Thoughts went to the favors he might well be induced to grant, should he continue in this particular mood. After the wedding would perhaps be the best time to strike.

The duke of Malmbury thought only of Anne Boleyn. Lovely Anne. It pained him when he thought that he would never see her again. Anne, with the smile in her dark eyes, the humorous curl of her soft, red lips. Instead, Jane Seymour, that pallid and insipid upstart, would be Queen of England. He looked at the king, his hatred showing clearly in his eyes. The king was certainly not haunted now. His heavy, florid face was radiant with smiles, his paunch jerking with laughter. There was a glaze to his eyes, too, a looseness to his lips that told all present that he was thinking of the delights of the marriage bed. The duke of Malmbury frowned. For the first time, he found himself feeling sorry for Jane Seymour.

Sir Richard Valentine leaned toward his friend. "See how the great bear beams and prattles," he whispered, nodding toward the king. "Why, I vow he capers like a schoolboy who is in love with love." He smiled, mischief dancing in his brown eyes. "If the little Seymour should have the good fortune to present the bear with a son, then it might well be that she will be able to lead him around by the nose."

Benjamin Carter, beyond a frown, made no reply to Richard. He stared down at the floor. He was thinking that he must give up this dangerous friendship. He liked Richard well. But he would have no share in his folly.

It was time for the wedding party to be on their way. The king took Jane by the hand and led her over to the door. His one thought now was to get the marriage over with. This time he would know everlasting happiness with Jane, his third queen. The one and only love of his life! As he passed through the door, he had a sudden fevered fancy that Catherine and Anne walked with him. He opened his mouth and roared out defiant words to those persistent ghosts. "I am happy! By God, I am happy!"

Jane smiled up at him. The king squeezed her fingers. It only needed Thomas Cromwell to find the runaways, and all would be perfect in his world. There would be Madam Tudor to bring fresh delight to his sexual appetite. There would be the lad standing by, in case Jane should fail to give him his heir.

Unaware of the king's confused and contradictory thoughts, Jane Seymour walked on like one in a dream. Queen Jane! Queen Jane! The words sang in her mind. Tonight, when she wore the gown of golden velvet trimmed with emeralds, she would look like a queen. She was Henry's love. His dearest delight. He had said so. She would live and die his queen. She would never allow him to put her aside for another!

24

The sun was setting when the solitary rider came into view. He came on fast at first, then, gradually decreasing speed until the horse was slowed to a walk. Reining in, he sat motionless in the clumsy saddle that appeared to be more fitted for a plough horse than for the sleekly elegant lines of the animal beneath him. Looking out to sea, he saw the waves curling dark green and crested with crisp white foam. Small boats rode at anchor on the restless waves, their white sails furled for the night. Above the bobbing boats the screeching, ever-present gulls circled and swooped. The man wondered if the birds ever nested for the night. If they ever ceased pursuit of the scraps of food, dead fish, and other garbage thrown up by the sea. The horse snorted, and the man's hand moved to caress the sweating chestnut coat. Bathed in the orange-red splendor of the setting sun, man and beast stood out like black silhouettes against the flauntingly extravagant background supplied by nature.

The salt-laden breeze blew stronger now, presaging bad weather to come. It stirred the mane of the animal and blew a strand of the rider's dark blond hair across his face. Smiling, Adam Templeton tucked the strand behind his ear and dismounted. Why, he wondered, had he ever allowed Seymour to persuade him into adopting this ridiculous disguise? And why, once having been persuaded, had he not removed it once he was well out of London?

Adam walked slowly toward the edge of the sea. He stopped by one of the rocks that here and there edged the shoreline and examined the spongelike plant with its small, pink blossom that sprouted from a crevice. He wondered, as he had always done, what the name of the plant might be. It grew out of various nooks and crannies, seemingly, flowering in all seasons and without need of the earth's sustenance.

Gravesend seeemed to be its native home, for as far as he knew, this particular plant was to be seen in no other part of the country.

Straightening up, Adam stared at the increasing turbulence of the water. If he were to be honest, he knew why he had not removed the disguise. He had wanted to see Madam Tudor's reaction, or lack of reaction, when she set eyes on him.

Thomas Seymour, having planned the disguise, had worked hard for dramatic effect. Tom's enthusiasm could be irritating at times, but he had done a very good job. Seymour, having acted in a good many plays at Court, was skilled in the art of make-up. Adam grinned. Thanks to him, he now bore not the slightest resemblance to Adam Templeton. His height, owing to the slight artistic hump on his back, was diminished by the stooping posture he was forced to assume. His arched eyebrows were covered by false dark-blond eyebrows, and his own hair was hidden beneath a raggedly cut wig of the same shade as the eyebrows. In addition, he wore a thick, bushy mustache and a full beard.

Adam's nose wrinkled in distaste. The hair had a stale and unpleasant odor, and he did not like to dwell on where it might have been procured. As a further touch, Tom had triumphantly produced a round pot of a gummy substance. This, molded to his nose and skillfully worked, had given it a slight bump on the bridge and a pointed tip. Once the stuff had dried, Adam had to admit that the effect was quite realistic. Only his eyes remained the same. Tom, to his annoyance, had been unable to do anything about them. When he had suggested a saffron paste for dyeing the black lashes the same color as the wig, Adam had hastily and firmly refused. Despite this, in his rough, brown homespun clothes, with a pack of goods strapped to his back, he looked as Tom had intended him to look—a traveling tinker of distinctly unsavory appearance.

The unexpected sound of Adam's laughter startled the gull who had ventured across the silver sand to regard him from hopeful, fast-blinking, beady eyes. Adam watched the bird as it took off in heavy flight. Tom Seymour was a rogue, he thought. He admitted as much himself. But there was something about him. Charm, perhaps? Whatever it might be, one could not help liking him. As he worked at the disguise, he had been as enthusiastic as a young boy, his lips smiling, his brilliant blue eyes sparkling with laughter. He had a great zest for living, and this was apparent in his every action. Brother William, accompanied by six of his brethren, had entered the secret room to watch the transformation. With their cowls thrown back, their shaven heads gleaming in the light of the candles, they had sat there entranced, looking on with wide-eyed and innocent curiosity.

"I got this false hair from my barber," Seymour had explained to them in his lazy, drawling voice. "He has such an abundance of false hair, in all colors, that I have no doubt he shaves it from the heads of corpses. The fellow was curious as to what I wanted with it. I told him that I was playing the part of a vagabond in a play the king had interested himself in. I had far rather have pushed his cursed inquisitive red snout into a tub of his lather. But there are times when one must satisfy curiosity, I suppose."

"Now, Thomas!" The gentle reproof came from Brother William. But in the brother's eyes, Adam noticed, there was a glint of that laughter Thomas Seymour could always inspire.

The unrepentant Seymour grinned at him. "Well you know how it is, Brother William. You cannot expect me to turn into a saint overnight."

"Not overnight, Thomas, or ever. I know you too well. There are times when I fear for you."

Seymour laughed. "Dismiss your fears. I will die roaring drunk, with an arm about a cuddlesome wench, I promise you. And I'll be as happy as a lark at nesting time."

"You will have much to answer for, my son."

"Not I. I will entertain the good Lord with bawdy stories. He will invite me to sit down and have a drink with Him, and relate to Him from beginning to end the whole of my scandalous life, in all its lurid details."

Kilkirk and his two companions, seated in a corner of the room, guffawed their appreciation. But Brother William, looking seriously offended, rose to his feet. "Thomas! I will not tolerate such sacrilege!"

Instantly Seymour changed. He was a man who could play many parts, and each one adapted to the particular situation. Since he had a genuine affection for Brother William, the effect of his repentance was the more sincere. "Forgive me, Brother," he said. He placed his hand on the friar's stiff shoulder and smiled his charming, slightly crooked smile. "You know well that I meant it not."

"But that is just the trouble, Thomas," Brother William's voice was sternly accusing. "You did mean it. I am fond of you, as you know, and your attitude makes me tremble with fear. What is to become of you?"

"Nay, nay, I tell you that I meant it not. Come! Will you not forgive me?"

The friar hesitated. Seymour said softly, "God willingly forgives a sinner, if his repentance be true. Will you do less than He?"

Sighing, Brother William seated himself again. "Nay, Thomas, you know well that I can do no less. But I have my doubts of your sincerity."

"Brother!" Seymour said in a shocked voice. "Is that a charitable thing to say?"

"Bah! You are naught but a rogue."

"Very true," Seymour agreed amiably. "And I have created another," he went on, pointing at Adam. "Behold this ugly fellow. Does he not look villainous? What a pity I cannot add a squint to his eyes. It would complete a devilish pretty picture."

Brother William got to his feet again. He stared at Adam, his round, rosy face split by a grin. "My son," he said, "I hope I am a man of charity. Yet I do believe I would hesitate to buy goods from you." He turned to the other friars. "He has the look of one who would think nothing of murdering us in our beds, has he not?"

Adam bore their scrutiny patiently. Then he said in mild complaint, "You need not regret the lack of a squint, Tom. Because of this cursed large nose you have concocted, my eyes slide inward of their own accord."

Seymour shook his head reprovingly. "You were ever a cursed sour and ungrateful fellow, Somercombe. The devil if I can see what Mistress Trigg finds in you to love."

"Nor I. But when she sees me thus, she will find nothing at all to love." Adam smiled. His teeth were white and perfect, but their effect in that strangely altered face was grotesque.

"Damn!" Seymour exclaimed. "Must you show your fangs? Flashing them so suddenly upon one's vision is liable to overset the nerves." He studied Adam thoughtfully. "I have it! I will black out your two front teeth. I know of a mixture that will——"

"Aye," Adam interrupted hastily, "I dare say you do, Tom. But if it is all the same to you, I'll have none of it. You have done quite enough."

Seymour hid a smile. "It might be wise if I journey to Gravesend with you, Somercombe. Mistress Trigg, having seen you, will fly to my willing arms for protection."

Adam laughed. "She will, if she cares naught for the sting of my hand on her backside." Meeting Brother William's eyes, he said quickly, "Your pardon, Brother. I did not mean to offend."

"I know." Brother William smiled at him. "Thomas never means it either. I am of the opinion that I shelter a couple of hardened rogues."

Adam nodded his appreciation of this shaft. "May I remove the disguise now, Tom? If I am not to leave here for ten days, I see no reason to wear it now."

"You are pining for that pretty face of yours, eh? Aye, I'll strip you of it in a moment."

A sudden clamor of bells filled the little room. Wincing, Brother William put his hands over his ears. "What is happening?" he asked in a raised voice. "The bells seem to be ringing from all parts of London."

Seymour looked discomfited at the question, and an unusual flush stained his cheeks. "I have been expecting to hear them," he shouted above the noise. "The king commanded that they be rung at this hour. The bells are telling us that the king is wed. Long live Queen Jane!"

Shocked, Brother William stared at him. "Anne Boleyn only eleven days in her coffin, and the king has already wed your sister? It is beyond belief!"

Seymour looked challengingly at the friars. "Well, Somercombe," he said, his eyes turning to Adam. "Shall we now hear what you have to say?"

Adam shrugged. "It is done. No words of mine can undo it. I imagine that the king will find it strange that you were not there to see him wed."

The bells stopped as suddenly as they had begun, and a throbbing silence descended upon the room. Now it was Seymour's voice that sounded unusually loud as he answered. "I had sound enough excuses. They satisfied the king."

"I see."

Again Seymour's eyes met Adam's. He looked away quickly, feeling the whole of the tragedy like a sudden crushing weight between them. He cursed his overactive imagination for showing him pictures he had hoped to avoid. He saw Anne Boleyn mount the three broad steps to where her executioner awaited. He saw her kneel in the straw, the flashing glitter of the upraised sword, and the smashing descent. Anne's head, that proud head, separated from the body like a flower from a stalk. The dull thud as the head dropped. Blood spouting! Blood everywhere! Shuddering, he said in a hoarse, unsteady voice, "Why are you all looking at me? I did not send Anne Boleyn to her death. I had no part in it! And certainly I did not ask the king to pursue my sister."

"No, Thomas, you did not ask it," Brother William said quietly. "But when you noted the king's interest in her, you did your best to encourage it."

The flush in Seymour's cheeks deepened. "I did. What of it? I saw my chance at a glittering prize, and I grabbed for it. What man would not? Like it or not, my sister is now queen. As for me, you have always known that I am ambitious. Through Jane, I intend to climb to great heights."

Brother William folded his hands before him and looked at him with sad eyes. "Take care that you do not stumble and fall, my son. It will be a long and hard way down."

Seymour's laughter had a hard edge. "I'll not fall. I know how to take care of myself, and I always know exactly what I am doing and where I am going."

"For your sake, Thomas, I hope so."

"Discussion is useless," Adam put in. "We must accept the fact that we have a new queen on the throne."

"It sounds very well when you put it that way," Seymour answered harshly. "But to Henry Tudor, a wife has only two functions. One is to pleasure him in the bed. The other to breed him sons at intervals, with the regularity of a farrowing sow. While he awaits her first litter, her second, and her third, Jane will have his ear. And that, my friends, is what I have worked for."

"And when she no longer pleases the king, Thomas, what then?"

Seymour shrugged. "Why then, Brother William, she must look out for herself."

"Nay, Thomas, you cannot make me believe you are so cold-blooded."

"It may be that you are right. By God, yes! When I reflect upon it, I could almost be sorry for the lass."

"Only almost?"

"Very well, Brother, if you insist that I put it into words. Aye, I feel damned sorry for her! But for all that, I'll not pretend to any regrets that the wedding has occurred."

Brother William made no answer to this. Seymour hesitated for a moment, as though he had more to say. Changing his mind, he turned about and walked over to the concealed panel in the wall. Opening it, he paused there and said in an uneven voice, "I will relieve you of my unwelcome company." He looked at Adam. "Once you have rid yourself of the disguise, you are not to stir from this room. I have no doubt that a search will be made, but the king's guard will never find this room. In exactly two days' time, if I do not return before, I will make you ready for your departure."

"God go with you, my son." Brother William said.

"Thank you." Seymour smiled his old charming smile.

That two days had seemed like a lifetime, Adam reflected, his eyes on the sliding waves. It was as well there had been the secret room to shelter him and the three warders, for Seymour had been right. The quiet of the friar's retreat had been invaded by the king's guard. The place had been thoroughly searched.

Adam, with his ear pressed against the false partition, had listened intently. Over the sounds of the noisy, ruthless searching, rough, aggressive voices came to him. Furniture was overturned, pottery shattered. He could hear Brother William's indignant voice. In that moment he had known that if Brother William and the others were taken, he would have no choice but to give himself up. He could not let them be hung, as they probably would be if they were in any way suspect, while he rode away to safety. If it should turn out that way, he would think of something to say that would absolve the friars of complicity.

Kilkirk and the other two men seemed to know what was passing through Adam's mind. They stared at him with malignant eyes.

Adam heard their whispered conversation, but he paid no attention to it at the time. When he turned around, he saw their terror, their profusely sweating faces, and the hatred in their eyes. Looking at them, he wondered why he had ever believed them to be calm and unmoved at the time of the escape. He wanted to say something reassuring to them, but he could think of nothing. It might be that they could get away. For their sakes, he hoped so.

It seemed hours before the king's guard took their departure. And yet more hours before Brother William came to them. One look at his smiling face told them that all was well. Weak with relief, Adam was tempted to ask the friar what lies he had been compelled to tell in order to keep them safe. He said nothing, however, for there was a look in Brother William's usually serene eyes that told him that those lies, whatever their nature, weighed heavily upon his conscience.

His concern must have showed in his face, for Brother William, going toward the panel, paused to smile at him. "Do not fear for me, my son," he said. "Because of the nature of the emergency and the dangers involved, I am sure that God will understand and forgive His erring son."

When the friar had departed, Adam sat down abruptly. "Well," he said, looking at the other men, "it would seem that all is well. We can relax now."

There was an ugly look in Kilkirk's eyes. "Bloody lucky an' all for you, it is!" he snarled. "You was itching to go an' play the 'ero, wasn't you? But you wouldn't never 'ave got out o' this room. Me an' me mates would 'ave murdered you afore we'd 'ave let you go squeaking on us to the guard!"

Adam shrugged. It was useless to tell them that his idea had been to give himself up, and, if possible, to avoid disclosing the secret room and involving them. They would not have believed him. One look at Kilkirk's face told him that the man's threat had been sincere. Before he could have taken a step from the room, they would have murdered him.

Now he was here at Gravesend. And, unless something unforeseen occurred, the danger was behind him. In a short while, God willing, he would be with Madam Tudor. She, knowing the date of the queen's execution but without knowledge of just when it would be safe for him to travel, would no doubt be on the lookout every day.

284

Thinking of the difficulty Seymour had had in persuading her to travel to the safety of Gravesend and await him there, Adam smiled to himself. She gave no thought to safety, she told Seymour. She flatly refused to leave London. It was only when Seymour threatened to withdraw his help that she had finally given in. According to Seymour, she had breathed threats of vengeance upon him should he fail her. Then, still threatening, she had taken her reluctant departure. That Madam Tudor was impetuous, he knew all too well. He would not put anything past her. For all he knew, she might be preparing to journey back to London, intent on finding out for herself what was afoot. She never paused to think, she acted. She was inclined to look on the black side, and, quite possibly, sure in her own mind that something had gone wrong, her immediate idea would be to go to the king and beg for his life.

Adam's eyes softened. He knew her so well that it was as if she were a part of his own body, but for all that, the strength of her love, her capability of self-sacrifice in the name of that love, could still move and amaze him. Well, he would be with her soon. Would she know him in his disguise? He laughed aloud. He had heard it said that love was able to penetrate any disguise. If that were so, then his present dilapidated appearance might be said to be another test of her love.

His smile disappeared as his mind turned to Kilkirk and his companions. Had the three men arrived at the Plough and Bull Inn yet? Disguised by Seymour's cunning hand, and delighted with the results, they had felt themselves to be safe from detection. So he had not been displeased when they had elected to ride without him. He had had more than enough of their surly attitudes and the hostility and dark suspicion with which they persisted in regarding him.

Adam turned away and walked toward his patient mount. Enjoying his first real sense of freedom, he had lingered longer than he had intended. It was almost full dark now. A sliver of moon showed itself briefly against the smoked sky before once more disappearing behind the rapidly gathering clouds. Vaulting into the saddle, Adam patted the drooping neck of the horse. "Home soon, old lad. Then you can rest and fill your belly."

Riding off, he shivered in the chill rising wind that plucked at his brown cloak and sent it sailing out behind him. With memories of many summers and winters spent in Gravesend, he decided that it would likely be blowing gale-force by midnight. There was rain in the air, too. Unless he missed his guess, a devil of a storm was brewing. He only hoped that the weather might not delay their sailing. Seymour had relayed a message to Tudor that their ship, the *Anna Lee*, was due in. Had the lad contrived a sailing date yet?

Trotting the horse along the rutted road that led to the Plough and Bull Inn, Adam pondered on the mysterious way Tom Seymour seemed to know most things. How, for instance, had he known of the *Anna Lee* or the fact that the ship was due in? How many men did he rely on to aid him in his various enterprises, and in how many different parts of the country? He seemed to extract loyalty from most men by that easy charm of his. Or, when charm failed, there was always something he could find out from the past to be held over their heads. A little delicate blackmail caused him no concern one way or the other. It was an amiable case, on his part, of "If I go down, you go down, my friend." In his manipulation of men, he ran terrible risks. But obviously he felt himself to be reasonably safe for, in the long run, he was really only out for the good of Thomas Seymour. Adam liked Tom, and he knew the liking was mutual, but he had no illusions about the man. Tom would not have lifted a finger to help him had his rescue not meant some gain to himself.

By the time Adam reached his destination, he was already soaked from the heavy rain that had begun to fall some minutes ago. His wet cloak alternately clung dismally to his shoulders, and then, its weight overborne by the howling wind, flapped wildly behind him. The long, ragged-looking blond hair beneath his wide-brimmed, brown hat with its broken white feather sent icy trickles of water down his neck. He was relieved when the rain-blurred light of the inn loomed out of the darkness.

Mistress Morgan, her cheeks as rosy and her white hair as tightly skewered as the last time Adam had seen her, came bustling forward as he entered the candlelit warmth of the inn. There was disapproval in every line of her plump, black-gowned, and white-aproned figure, her blue eyes filled with suspicion of the tall, villainous looking stranger. She looked first at the pools of water forming about his feet on the stone-flagged floor. Then her eyes went over his person very carefully, and finally came to rest on the pack dangling by a strap from his right arm. She sniffed. "What do you want here?" she said in a sharp, no-nonsense voice. "This is a decent house. We don't take in just any riff-raff. And besides, my prices are too high for the likes of you."

She looked at the pack again. "You'll be wanting to sell me something, I suppose? Well, I'll tell you straight out that I'll not be buying any of the rubbish you have to offer. Now get along with you, or I'll be setting the dogs on you!"

The peddler's shoulders hunched, his expression becoming woebegone. Mistress Morgan faltered in mid-tirade. She was a kind-hearted woman, and her sharpness of tone was assumed. "Well, there, now," she said in a softer voice, "it is a dirty night." She shrugged. "I confess that 'tis not in me to be too hard on you. Take yourself around to the back entrance. I'll serve you a meal in the kitchen." She drew herself up to her full five feet two inches. "But after you've eaten, my man, I'll thank you to be on your way."

"Thank you, ma'am." Adam said in a low, husky voice.

"None of your tricks now, or I'll——" Meeting his eyes, she broke off, staring.

"Is something wrong, ma'am?"

"No. It was just that——"

"Just what?"

"Just that your eyes reminded me of someone. Now then, around to the back door with you!"

Adam looked swiftly about him. There was no sign of Madam Tudor or young Tudor. Except for one lone gentleman, whose shoulders were hunched beneath a wet cloak and his elbows propped upon the table as he stared moodily into his tankard of ale, the inn parlor was deserted. "It is a wet and muddy way to your back door, Bessie Morgan," he said in a low voice. "Shame on you!"

Mistress Morgan turned pale. "Master Adam!" she whispered. "Oh, Master Adam!"

He put a warning finger to his lips. He was dismayed when he saw the tears filling her eyes. "No, Bessie, for God's sake don't cry!" he whispered hastily. "All is well."

She put a trembling hand on his arm as if to reassure herself that he was really there. "The young lady told me all. I've been so afraid for you!"

"She is still here?" he said in sudden sharp concern.

"Aye, she's here right enough. And as jumpy as a cat before birthing time." She rubbed a hand across her wet eyes. "I didn't know you in that get-up, Master Adam, and that's a fact."

"That was the idea." He smiled at her. "Take me to the kitchen. We can talk there."

She touched his arm again, nodded, and then set off briskly in the direction of the kitchen. Following her closely, Adam glanced briefly at the lone gentleman. The man looked up as they passed and then returned his disinterested eyes to his tankard of ale.

In the kitchen, Mistress Morgan dismissed the two women working there. "Take yourselves a little rest," she bade them. "I'll call when I have need of you."

One of the women, who had been busily stirring a large pan of savory-smelling stew, withdrew it from the fire and set it to one side. With inquisitive eyes on the stranger, both women bobbed curtseys and hastily withdrew.

"They'll likely be thinking to find me murdered in my own kitchen," Mistress Morgan said in a voice that was distinctly unsteady. "Oh, my dear lad!" She flung her arms about his waist and hugged him tightly. "You'll never know what a torment you've put your old nurse through."

"I do know, Bessie." Adam patted her head gently. "But I'm here now. Everything is all right."

Releasing him reluctantly, she looked at him with a growing expression of severity. "You're half-drowned!" She stretched out her hand. "Here, give me that cloak at once. You sit yourself down by the fire, for I'll not have you taking a chill. The next thing you know, you'll be getting one of your coughs. And I doubt not it'll be settling on your chest, the way it always did."

Adam handed her the cloak. Seating himself, he stretched out his long legs to catch the heat of the blazing logs. "I'm not your nursling now, Bessie," he said, looking at her with some amusement. "You may find this hard to believe, but I am well able to take care of myself."

"Tush!" she retorted. "To me, you are still my babe. And as for taking care of yourself, Master Adam, a fine job you made of it, I must say! Getting yourself flung in the Tower, and those wicked men torturing you! I never heard the like." Tears filled her eyes and run down her seamed cheeks. "They might have killed you, Master Adam!"

He sighed. "So they might," he agreed. "But the point is that they did not. If you would stop that infernal crying, Bessie, I would be grateful for something to eat. I'm starved."

"Of course, loon that I am! Wait just a moment."

Seated at the well-scrubbed kitchen table, Mistress Morgan looking on happily as Adam did full justice to a large plate of stew. She knew that sooner or later he would tell her all that had happened to him since the day he had left Tudor Trigg in her care. But for the moment, she was content just to look at him and to wait.

Complimenting her on the stew, and refusing a second helping, Adam pushed his plate to one side. Seeing her air of expectancy, he abandoned his intention of going in search of Madam Tudor. He was silent for a moment, wondering just how much he should tell her. When he did begin to talk, Mistress Morgan, listening intently to his low voice, punctuated his story with cries of indignation and horror. But the only comment she made at the conclusion was, "And now you and the young lady will have to be leaving England, Master Adam." Her mouth trembled. "I know it has to be, but 'tis likely that I'll not be seeing you again."

Adam felt a responsive pang. The thought of leaving England behind hurt far more than he would have believed possible. But what must be, must be. How many years must pass before he and Madam Tudor could return and take up their lives again? How many years before Henry Tudor died? He said gently, "It is not quite as bad as that, Bessie. After all, you did not know me in this disguise, did you?"

She shook her head. "No. But what has that to do with anything?"

"It means that I can return to England from time to time. Not looking like myself, it is true. But I will return."

"I'd not have you taking any risks for my sake, Master Adam. But if it could be managed, I'd like well to see you."

"France is not so very far away, Bessie. Perhaps you could visit me?"

"Me?" She stared at him as if he had taken leave of his senses. "Me go visiting in a foreign country! Why I've never set foot out of England, and never thought to do so."

"But you could," he persisted. "Why not?"

Mistress Morgan was silent. Adam watched her, waiting for the idea to take root. "Why, so I could, Master Adam!" she burst out at last. "And why not, I should like to know?"

"Exactly. We'll work something out, never fear."

Her manner almost gay, Mistress Morgan rose from the table. "I'll take you upstairs now, and you can get yourself out of that garb. For I don't know what Mistress Trigg would think, should she see you looking this way."

Adam smiled. "Aye, I wonder what she would think. It might be interesting to find out."

"What! Never tell me you'll be greeting her thus, and you looking such a fearsome rogue?"

"Why not? I have a fancy to find out if the eyes of love can penetrate any disguise."

" 'Tis a schoolboy's trick," Mistress Morgan said, looking at him with scandalized eyes. "I never would have thought it of you, Master Adam. And that poor girl breaking her heart for you these many days. Oh, we've had a time with her, indeed we have! There seemed to be just no holding her. Bound and determined, she was, for posting off to London. Wanted to mingle with the crowd on the day that poor lass, Anne Boleyn, lost her head. Wanted to find out for herself, she said."

"It sounds just like her."

"I understand her feelings. She loves you, Master Adam."

"I know. Perhaps more than I deserve. But for all that, you'll not deny she's a feather-top?"

"Is that a way for a man in love to talk?" Mistress Morgan cried indignantly. She met his smiling eyes. "Oh, aye," she added reluctantly, "mayhap she doesn't always stop to think. But for all that, your're lucky to be getting such a fine lass."

Adam got up from the table. "I know it well," he said, putting an arm about her waist. "You may smooth down your ruffled feathers."

25

Corianne swept into the firelit parlor, with Tudor following close behind. Her color was high and her eyes looked heavy, as though she had done much crying. She stood still for a moment, looking at the dozen or more people assembled there, then she sat down at the table. Meeting her brother's eyes, she said in a low, furious voice, "I see from your expression that you intend to take up the conversation where we left off. I will not have it, Tudor! You must stop badgering me. If I wish to ride to London, I will do so. You have nothing to say about it!"

"I think I have," Tudor answered, seating himself beside her. His eyes rested briefly on the blond man with the large nose who was seated near to them. Offended by the man's intent stare, he regarded him haughtily. "Keep your voice down," he went on, looking at her again. "Do you want everyone to know our business? Listen to me, Madam Tudor, passage is booked on the *Anna Lee*, and Adam should be here at any time. Yes, yes, no need to look at me like that, he will come. Have you forgotten that Seymour said that you were to stay here? On no account were you to return to London." Tudor put his hand over hers. "And stay you will, even if I have to tie you to the cursed bed!"

She snatched her hand away. "You have no heart or feelings! 'Tis what I might expect from you. Don't you understand? Adam m—might be dead, or dying. But if he is s—still alive, I must somehow contrive to see him for one l—last time!"

At the break in her voice, Tudor's eyes softened. "Come," he said gently, "as usual you are letting your imagination gallop away with you. Dead? Dying? Nay, not Adam. He's just a little late arriving, that's all."

"But the men who helped him are already here. Oh, Tudor, I just know that something has gone wrong! I cannot stay here and do nothing. Surely you would not expect that of me?"

"I do expect it," Tudor said firmly. "Even were you to go to London, what could you do? What if you were seen? Aye, we know that the king has married Jane Seymour, and we also know he is vengeful. What if you were taken?"

"It would matter little to me," she said in a weary voice. "If Adam is dead, I care for nothing! The king may take my life, if it please him to do so. I would thank him for it."

"I would care very much!" Tudor said gruffly. "Pest though you ofttimes are, I happen to care for you."

"Tudor, please! I——"

"No, you listen to me for once. We know that Adam is not dead. Kilkirk told you that the escape was successful."

" 'Tis well enough for that man," she said bitterly. "But have you thought that Adam might have been recaptured?"

"Never think it," Tudor said, forcing heartiness into his voice. It would not do to let her know that he himself was beginning to be plagued by doubts. In an attempt to distract her, he went on quickly, "Look at that man over there. By God, how he stares! I've a mind to go over and tweak his long nose for him. I'm surprised that Mistress Morgan would take in such a person."

Corianne glanced at the man with the roughly-cut blond hair with indifferent eyes. "He has the look of a fine rogue," she agreed in a toneless voice. "But I care not if Mistress Morgan fills her inn from cellar to attic with rogues, it is all one to me. I can think only of Adam." She rose to her feet.

"Where are you going?" Tudor said sharply.

Corianne pulled her red cloak about her and drew the hood over her head. "I'm going for a walk."

"In this storm? Have you completely lost your wits!"

"It might be that I have. I'm going to walk along by the sea. The weather, at least, is in keeping with my mood."

"You'll be drowned."

She shrugged. "You must stop worrying about me. I'll keep well back from the edge."

Tudor rose. "I'll come with you."

"Tudor, no!" She looked at him with pleading eyes. "I

must be alone for a while. If you care for me at all, you will stay here."

He stared at her for a moment. Then, reluctantly, he resumed his seat. "All right. But if you do anything foolish, I shall break your infernal neck!"

"Never fear, I won't attempt to drown myself." The smile she gave him was forced. "Nor will I ride off without telling you. I promise." She turned away. Her hand on the door-latch, she called to him, "If he should come, Tudor, tell him to come after me. He is not to wait for a moment."

Tudor looked away, not wanting her to see the pity in his eyes. "Aye," he answered. "I will be sure to tell him."

Tudor watched moodily as the blond man, having finished his beer, rose to his feet and clapped on his hat. The hat had a broken feather, Tudor noticed. He was surprised when the blond man paused at the door, gave him a smiling nod, and then walked out into the storm. One would think he knew me, Tudor thought, trying to work up a mood of indignation that would cover the misery he was beginning to feel. And how he stared! Some people had no manners at all.

The wind battered at Corianne as she made her way along the sea front. Lightning flashed, dazzling her, and the thunder crashed loudly in her ears. Rain sheeted down, and the wind howled like a million demons in torment. Shivering beneath her sodden cloak, she found herself gasping for breath. She walked on doggedly, glancing now and again at the great, heaving waves. Adam! Adam, where are you? Oh God, what can have happened? She blinked her eyes, trying to clear them of rain. Perhaps, while she was walking, Adam was even now arriving at the inn. She allowed the hope to warm her. Why was she wasting her time battling the elements? She would go back, and she would find him there awaiting her. He must be there! Please God, let him be there! Adam! Adam! Nothing is any use without you!

She turned quickly. Lightning forked the sky. In its glare she saw the tall, stooped figure of the man from the inn. Her heart raced with sudden fear as she saw him advancing quickly toward her. His rain-soaked cloak flapped in the strong wind and gave him the appearance of having giant, dark wings. An unreasoning panic seized her. Had he a reason for walking in this weather, or had he purposely followed her? Perhaps he intended to rob her, even to rape her! At this last thought, she whirled about again and began to run. Glancing over her shoulder, she saw that the man was running, too, his long legs covering the ground rapidly. He would be on her soon. Adam, Adam, help me! He was shouting something at her, but she could not hear the words above the scream of the wind.

Gasping for breath, a pain stabbing in her side, she stumbled over a rock and fell heavily. In a vain attempt to save herself, she flung out her hands. Her body, gaining momentum, sent her rolling over and over to the water's edge. She gave a wild despairing scream as a wave washed over her. It lifted her up, carried her a little way, and then retreated. She was going to drown! Adam would come, but too late! She screamed again as hands grasped her and dragged her up to a safer level. The man had found her! What was he going to do? Was he intending to murder her?

He was a huge, dark shadow looming over her. Then, gasping, he fell on top of her, his heavy body pinioning her to the wet sand. "Don't!" She tried to claw at his dimly seen face. "Don't! Let me go!"

Laughing, he caught her flailing hands in his and held them fast. "No!" he shouted. "I'll never let you go. You said that I was to come after you. You said that I was not to waste a moment."

She was mad! Dreaming! Adam's voice? Lightning flashed again, and she saw his eyes. His eyes! Adam's eyes! "Adam!" she shrieked above the howling wind. "Is it really you?"

"Aye," he shouted back. "It is really me."

"Adam! Adam, my darling!" Her arms reached out to clutch at him. Tears of joy mingled with the rain, blinding her for a moment. She blinked rapidly, remembering the grotesque face of the man at the inn. "It was you all the time! Why did you not say something? Oh, how dare you put me through such torment!"

In the wind, his laughter was a thin, echoing sound. "You should have known me. Love is supposed to penetrate any disguise."

"Oh, just you wait! I'll make you pay for——" His salt-wet lips closed firmly over hers, silencing her.

Locked in a close embrace, they were indifferent to the

soaking rain, the buffeting of the wind, and the hard lash of the spray. It was only when a wave raced inland, curled over them, and broke, showering them with icy sea water, that they at last rose to their feet.

ABOUT THE AUTHOR

Constance Gluyas was born in London, where she served in the Women's Royal Air Force during World War II. She started her writing career in 1972 and since then has had published a number of novels of historical fiction, including *Savage Eden*, *Rogue's Mistress*, *Woman of Fury*, *Flame of the South*, and *The House on Twyford Street*, available in Signet editions.